Scorpion

Brian Willis
& Chris Poote

razor blade Press

Brian Willis & Chris Poote

This book was first published in November 2002 by RazorBlade Press,108 Habershon St, Splottt,Cardiff, CF24 2LD.

Scorpion is a work of fiction.
The characters and events described are imaginary and any resemblance to people living or dead is purely coincidental.

Designed and typeset by RazorBlade Press

Printed and bound in the UK

British Library in Publications Data.

A catalogue record for this book is available from the British Library.
www.razorbladepress.com

ISBN 0 9542267 12

Scorpion

I sent my soul through the Invisible,
Some letter of that Afterlife to spell:
And by and by my Soul returned to me,
And answered "I Myself am Heav'n and Hell".

-The *Rubaiyat* of Omar Khayyam

FOREWORD

The authors asked me to act as technical advisor throughout the writing of this book. They also asked me to point out that the persons and events described herein are fictitious, which is to say they are products of the genii of the authors. Any resemblances to historical persons or events are therefore purely products of the genius of the reader. However, should the reader detect any ideas or suggestions not obviously originating from the genii of the authors, the text contains clues. Where names have been dropped, you can pick them up.

One more thing. While the rituals and practices described in the text never actually happened, any responsibility for the consequences of attempting to reproduce them rests solely with the person(s) making the attempt. For the sake of authenticity, I have tested many of them myself, and in the words of Aleister Crowley, 'by doing certain things, certain results follow.' Be cautious before being bold.

Farewell.

The Kite.

Prologue;

Banishing

He is being watched in this dark upper room, although he is alone.

He is being watched from five squares of canvas which stand beyond each of the points of the pentagram he earlier chalked about himself, each illuminated by a single candle, each boiling in his imagination with half-formed shapes emerging from the paintings and falling short of recognition and back into the void. Each waiting. For him.

His paints and brush stand beneath the newest of the group. There is something untamed about this one. It alone has no signature; the artist's initial wrought as the sign of Scorpio. Like a cave mouth, it suggests that among the whorls of reddish-brown pigment something crouches, ready at his call to come forth and be recognised.

Or to pounce.

He steps out of his dressing gown, tossing it into a far corner. Naked, he calls on the Archangel whom he made present in this painting, and paints the sign of Scorpio onto his chest.

Khamael. The Severity of God. Be with me now.

The words he chants leave his mouth as though he is expelling rather than speaking them. Words heavy with power, a power that would blister his tongue if restrained from utterance. They burst forth from him, they churn the air, thickening it around him, and swirl amongst the points of the pentagram, filling, engorging the space.

The candlelight stirs uneasily around him.

In another room, a young man stirred. His dreams had been heavy with the sense of foreboding, the source of the unease hidden from him in images better left half-forgotten. There was a tightening in his gut, and a cold sheen of sweat on his body, that seemed to forewarn of fever, but he knew it was no physical malady that troubled him.

His arm reached over to the other side of the bed, and he found what he had already half-expected to find: nothing. They had experienced the ecstasy of two becoming one flesh. And as had happened four times in as many weeks, his lover had murmured in ancient languages as he approached the orgasm of orgasms, and afterward had slipped away while the young man, exhausted, slept. Tonight they had been together like Spartans before battle.

The unease ratcheted up another notch.

He rose, wrapping a borrowed dressing gown about himself, and opened the door. The passageway outside was silent, but the odour of incense – not overpowering, just unmistakeable – told him where his lover would be. Barefoot, he padded along the wooden floor to the stairway to the upper room.

As a boy, I was a rogue, an adventurer.

As a student, I was a Hell-fire rebel.

As a man, I became a soldier, and ah, came my undoing.

Death.

I used to court Death as an intriguing partner in this great game of living. But I grew appalled at His rudeness, blundering into the lives of myself and my comrades-in-arms. I saw Him toss them into the air and drop them broken and twisted. I heard Him tear their flesh and leave them gasping their breath away.

As he gazes into the canvas, scrying, the visual puzzle is beginning to solve itself. Colour swirls downward and backward into the distance, only to curve back on itself and rise again, rushing forward to culminate once more in the forefront of the image. It is returning, moreover, with its power enhanced, a power that finds its ultimate expression in ... what?

It is the most solid feature in the picture, crimson as blood, shocking in its distinctiveness, a downward-stabbing triangle, a spike with a vicious tip.

The coalescence of this figure signals a further transformation in the thick atmosphere around him, the living energies falling into an unnatural stillness as when songbirds fall silent at the approach of the hawk. The flow of words falters and stops. All of his terrors, that he thought bound or banished, have broken loose.

I would not die. Face pressed into the mud, with the iron taste of blood in my mouth and the weight on my back of my comrades, my friends, my lover, all gone before me, blasted and shredded into the unknown. In blood-soaked mud I myself wrestled Death as Jacob wrestled the angel, coming away, like Jacob, with a permanent reminder in my gait.

But I would. Not. Die.

Something emerges from the cave mouth. Demonic in aspect, with the fury of a charging beast. Rushing, roaring, an irresistible locomotive with him as its destination. Thrashing and tearing its way towards him, maddened by an unshakable desire, a desire for *union* with him who courted Death.

No escape.

The smell of incense was stronger now, as was an altogether different ... he struggled to recall the word ... *aura*, that clung at the young man as he ascended. He had never liked this section of the house, and had been told enough times never to come up to the studio unbidden, but his fears overrode his submission. Cautiously, he tapped on the door.

"Nicholas? Are you all right?"

Suddenly the air seemed unseasonally hot and dry, as though the door would open upon a desert wasteland. He was now very afraid for his lover.

"Nicholas, answer me!" he called, voice breaking. "Nic-"

A scream answered him from within.

He tried the door, but it was of course locked. He banged on the door, shaking it in its frame, by now shouting for his friend in a voice just this side of hysteria. Nicholas had ensured that this room, his sanctuary, was virtually impregnable.

From the outside, at least.

The young man rushed back to the bedroom, taking the narrow stairs three at a time, and returned with the heavy black iron poker from the bedroom fireplace. It took just moments of frenzied battering to smash the lock and splinter the frame enough for him to shoulder the door open and stumble into the studio.

Breathless, he took in the paintings, the candles, the five-pointed star chalked on the floorboards, but his eyes were drawn down to the figure lying in the middle of it all, naked and pale, a paintbrush in one hand. As he moved forward, his eyes met those of the figure, which were open and still.

"Nicholas ..." he whispered.

There was no reply. Nor did he expect one.

Looking around in bewilderment he noticed the nearby trunk, draped with red silk, furnished like a table with plate and silver cup, wand and dagger. Oh God. What terror had been conjured here? The young man gingerly, tenderly, checked over his dead lover but found no clue to whatever horror had befallen him, and the paintings on their easels remained silent witnesses. The young man, kneeling, sobbed with grief.

Panic arose in him, intruding on his pain. What was he to do? Nicholas was dead, naked in this attic garret with the trappings of conjuration and a homosexual lover. Questions would be asked. Questions asked by a press intoxicated with the shameful details of the death of the industrialist's prodigal son. Questions backed by the force of a law which punished the sin of Sodom. Questions linking that sin of Sodom to the sin of Cain, which that same law would punish with hanging.

Chest tight with fear, he rose and rushed from the room without looking back, dressed, stuffed his few belongings into his suitcase, and made for the door. However, pulling his coat on, he halted on the threshold, unable to simply abandon his lover to the dark empty house.

He picked up the telephone earpiece, dialled the operator and informed her (without mentioning his own name, of course) that a doctor was required at that address at once. Then he slammed the door of the house and hauled his suitcase into the rain, which had just started to torrent from the midnight sky.

He got away from the house as fast as he could with his suitcase, his face turned to the ground, although at that time of night there were no passers-by on the street to see his tears of grief and shame or to wonder what drama was being played out here. And the scream in his heart – his lover's last sound – he likewise kept to himself.

I

Lesser Invocation

There was a pyramid in the centre of the room, a pyramid of dazzling white. For one millisecond when he'd first seen it, Robert Pierce had been impressed, despite himself; it caught the light coming through the glass roof directly above it very effectively, and the sheer size of the thing – almost twenty feet from base to apex – commanded the attention anyway.

But then his critical faculties kicked in and reminded him that the pyramid was constructed entirely of toilet rolls.

The 'artist' responsible for this edifice was, at that moment, engaged deep in conversation with a gaggle (as appropriate a collective noun as Robert could come up with) of cronies and hangers-on, most of whom were critics from this newspaper or that magazine, with a minor rock musician or two and the current editor of *Loaded* thrown in for good measure.

The 'artist' was called Justin Maxwell, and he was, by general consensus, a prick. Robert, however, was in a minority amongst the art *cognoscenti* in considering him to be a *talentless* prick. But then, the gallery didn't employ Robert for his opinions, it employed him as one who understood the vagaries and vicissitudes of the art world and could accordingly buy in those items or collections that might have, to use his employers quaint terminology, 'legs', or marketability. Most of the time he was able to put his own tastes (or prejudices, as some called them) aside and be the quintessential 'team player', but not today. Not for that prick.

Chardonnay in hand, Robert ambled closer to Maxwell and his entourage, curious to hear what timeless *bon mots* were issuing from the mouth of the Young Turk of BritArt. He was getting very passionate in his praise of somebody, that much was obvious, a passion assisted by the copious amounts of expensive Mexican lager he was downing and which stained his khaki t-shirt. His great hairless head, pink-tinged and oddly spherical, swivelled from side to side as he sought, and received, approval from the onlookers.

The object of his eulogy was Arsenal's latest midfield acquisition. The *Guardian* correspondent nodded sagely.

One member of Maxwell's audience, who had until that moment been obscured from Robert's view by the Great Man himself, detached from the rest and strolled toward him. Charlotte (Charlie) Keating was one of his fellow buyers, and the only one of his colleagues in whose presence he could remain for more than a few minutes without wanting to do them serious harm. It helped, of course, that she was intelligent, attractive and shared some – but not all – of his opinions on the value of the stuff that passed through the gallery portals.

"Not joining us then?" she said mischievously, when she was close enough to be out of earshot to the others. "Justin's views on the outcome of this season's Premier League are enthralling. It might broaden your horizons."

"My horizons would be broad enough, thanks, if there weren't a fucking pyramid of bog rolls in the way. I mean, where did this man study art? The Royal Academy, or Sainsbury's?"

"Don't be elitist, Bobby."

"I'm not elitist. Just discerning. And stop calling me Bobby."

"Sorry, Bobby. Come on, we need another drink."

Arm in arm, they strolled out of the Pyramid Room and into the adjoining section of the gallery, where more examples of Maxwell's work were being displayed. They passed (without comment) a crushed lager can entombed in perspex, a large reproduction of Michelangelo's 'Last Supper' in which the faces of Christ and all the disciples had been replaced with Polaroid snapshots of Maxwell, and a TV set smothered in bubble-wrap which appeared (it was difficult to tell for sure) to be continually showing episodes of *Bagpuss*, all in order to reach the drinks table.

"So where's this girlfriend of yours these days?" said Charlie, probably in order to divert Robert's mind from his immediate surroundings. "I've only met her the once, and I'm starting to wonder if that was a set-up job. After all, you can afford escort agencies ..."

"Very funny. Truth is, we don't get to see that much of each other at the moment. There's a chance she could be in for a partnership at that PR firm she works for, and she's putting in some hours to make sure she doesn't get passed over."

"You've got some time on your hands then."

"Too much. Leaves me lots of space in which to brood on how shit my life is right now." He gave a humourless smile, and glanced around the room to add emphasis.

"All right," said Charlie, "so get painting again."

Robert winced.

"I've told you before, Bobby, there's no point in rubbishing people like Maxwell – deserving of it as they are – if someone like you isn't prepared to walk the talk. For Christ's sake, it's not as if you don't have the talent ... I've *seen* some of your stuff, remember?"

They wandered over to one of Maxwell's more controversial older pieces, a semen-stained centrefold from Penthouse, the model's face and breasts obscured by a series of knife-slashes.

"Take a look at that, Charlie," said Robert. "*That's* what 'the punters' want. Event. Controversy. The Seven Wonders of the World re-created in toiletry form. Not vision, not a mainline into the heart of Mystery, not the whisper of the Eternal ... not even simple fucking talent, by the looks of it. Just something that'll get Maxwell, or those like him, in media line of sight for their own little fifteen minutes, as the grandaddy of the lot of them said, God rot him. They'd do just as well to go on Jerry Springer and fling their shit around."

"That's not the whole story, though, is it?" said Charlie, having given him a few moments to get his composure back, and look around to check that his outburst hadn't attracted any untoward attention.

Robert shrugged, and ran a hand through his mop of straight, dark hair. "I don't think I'm up to the task, Charlie. The stuff of mine that you've seen ... technically, I've got it, no doubts on that score. But 'the vision thing'? Different matter. Talent without anything greater to back it up ... that would leave me not much better off than these bastards. Blake, Van Gogh, Bosch ... they all had access to the 'inner eye', everything they painted was an attempt, however imperfect, to capture what they saw with that eye. Me? I just seem to have a bad case of Inner Eye Blindness."

"You should have said. I have friends who can get hold of some stuff that'll get those doors of perception cleansed for you while you wait."

"I knew I could depend on you to understand," said Robert, tartly.

"You really want my advice?" Charlie asked, suddenly serious. "All right then, here it is. Don't just stand around wallowing in self-pity, get back to work, and *paint.* If you're that serious about finding this 'vision thing' then the only way to find it is to give it some sort of avenue for expression. And I don't think that's going to happen with you just whinging about the prevalence of *scheissmeisters* like Justin Maxwell. I mean it, Bobby ... I don't want to be having this same conversation with you again in six months."

"OK, OK, deal. I'll get back to work tonight, that satisfy you? Exhausted and heartsick and in need of a shag as I am, I shall drag myself to my easel this very evening and churn out a couple of masterpieces before dawn. Any preferences as to subject matter?"

"Not really," said Charlie with a smile. "Just let your Inner Eye be your guide."

"Thank you, Jiminy Cricket." He parted her fringe of blond hair and kissed her forehead.

"Sorry to interrupt the mood of cameradie that you two appear to have going on here," said an unctuous voice from beside them, "but aren't there punters you could be schmoozing with? Given that we're here to sell art to them, after all."

The speaker was a stick-thin slash of paleness called

Tim van Lier, one of their colleagues and, since day one at the gallery, the principal object of Robert's contempt (the feeling was mutual). Robert was on the verge of replying with something Anglo-Saxon and uncomplimentary, when Charlie butted in.

"I thought most of this stuff was already sold," she said.

"Justin's stuff, yes. We're just giving the public a last chance to see it all in one place before it goes off to its various new homes."

"Oh, yes?" said Robert. "And which particular McDonalds outlets are they going to be displayed in? Just so I know which ones to avoid."

There was a pause while van Lier's gaze swung around to fix Robert with a stare of pure, Arctic loathing. "You *really* shouldn't be drinking so much of that stuff while you're working, Robert."

"This?" He held up his now-empty glass. "Oh, I've hardly had any. Wait until I *really* get into my cups, Tim, I'll tell you what I *really* think."

Charlie cleared her throat. "Well, maybe you're right, Tim. I'll catch you later, Bobby ... and remember what you promised, OK?"

With Charlie gone, Robert was turning away also, when van Lier's limpid hand on his shoulder stopped him. "Oh, I nearly forgot. Gregory's been looking for you."

Gregory Webster was the gallery manager, a strange, inscrutable little man who was quite prepared to let his staff 'have their head', so to speak, so long as nothing interfered with what he apparently saw as the main purpose of the gallery, i.e., giving him enough money to disappear for large chunks of the year to his home in Antibes. He was the younger brother of the gallery owner, Raymond Webster, who bought the gallery as a kick in the teeth to those who said that, as one of the country's foremost advertising gurus, he was without culture.

In the eyes of at least one of his employees, the charge was still valid.

"What does he want me for?" asked Robert, not particularly interested.

"Sorry, Robert, I wasn't made privy to that. Perhaps he needs someone to go and get his laundry for him."

Robert turned away again, conscious of the almost involuntary clenching of his fist.

"Oh, and I'd have a mint before you see him, too, if I were you," van Lier sneered at his back.

"It should be OK, Tim," replied Robert without turning around. "He spends so much of his time in your company, I'm sure he's used to bad smells."

The silence sounded like someone trying to find a riposte to that, and failing. Robert ostentatiously put his glass down on the top of the perspex cube containing the beer can – adding, he thought wryly, an extra three grand to its value – and set off in search of Webster.

Gregory Webster's office, on the top floor of the gallery, overlooked one of the city's main thoroughfares, with a view of the city skyline denied to those who scurried below him. This seemed to be singularly in keeping with Gregory's view of himself, as one who, although positioned at the privileged heart of society, managed to maintain a cool and detached relationship with it.

If he was honest with himself, Robert had so far failed to get any sort of handle on his 'boss'. Their lack of any real contact was, of course, the main reason for this, and there was also the manner in which he delegated so much of the gallery's day-to-day administration to arseholes like Tim van Lier (which wasn't particularly endearing). However, on the rare occasions when they *had* occasion to deal directly, he'd found the man curiously amiable. 'A likeable idiot' was how Charlie referred to him.

"How's it going today, Robert?" he asked, leaning back in his chair. He seemed to have his attention split between his employee and the TV set in the corner, which was mutely displaying an old black-and-white movie starring Robert Mitchum. For a moment, it wasn't too clear which Robert he was addressing.

"Oh, you know ..." replied Robert (Pierce), vaguely. "It seems to be going well enough."

"Good. Good." The reply obviously didn't satisfy Gregory, but he wasn't in the mood to pursue it. "I'll probably pop down there afterwards, have a nose around."

His expression took on a comical air of concern. "And is Justin, er ..."

"As a newt, yes."

"Well, that's all right, then. Keep the talent happy, eh?"

Robert said nothing.

"Actually, Robert, there's something quite particular I wanted to talk to you about. I suppose you think I'm completely out of touch with what goes on 'on the shop floor', so to speak?"

Robert carefully considered his options here. His limited experience of Gregory's management style couldn't rule out the possibility that he was being tested, and that his entire future with the gallery depended on his answer. Perhaps van Lier had been whispering stuff into the boss's ear about his commitment to the gallery's aims, whatever they were.

What the hell. The truth.

"I don't think we see enough of you down there, no. To be honest, I think you put too much faith in ... *certain people,* to do your legwork for you."

"Yes, I know who you mean," said Gregory. "And I know he's an arse-kisser, but he's a highly efficient arse-kisser. Gets things done. But that's beside the point. What I'm trying to say is that, despite what you may think, a lot of intelligence does, in fact, reach my ears. And not just via Tim, either."

"Ah-ha," said Robert.

"I know, for instance, that you have some rather definite opinions about the stuff we exhibit."

"Hm," said Robert, "well ..."

"You've made several suggestions to the effect that we should broaden the gallery's remit, start giving some exposure to artists you think have been unjustly neglected." He picked up a piece of paper from the desk. "You even supplied some names."

By now, Robert couldn't even think of a suitably incoherent monosyllable with which to express his nonplussedness.

"A little personal history, Robert. Don't worry, I'll be brief. My big brother put me in charge of this gallery to give me something to do. I was hanging around after I left university, living off my inheritance, doing nothing but enjoying myself. This irked Raymond considerably. When the money ran out ... as it has a disturbing tendency to do ... he found me at his mercy.

"Now, it's long been a dream of his to own a place like this, ever since he went to art school briefly in the sixties and found out he had no artistic talent whatsoever. Making money, he has a genius for, however. So if it helps, look on this place as my brother's revenge on the art world. Selling the muses into slavery to Mammon, if you don't mind me mixing theologies. Thing is, I think the public ... sorry, *punters* ... are getting a bit tired of this Situationist crap that Justin Maxwell and his ilk are allowed to foist upon us. His stuff just doesn't have the 'legs' that it used to. The tide's turning, Robert, and it's turning in our favour."

Our favour?

"Of course, I won't pretend that I know too much about art, Robert; I'm here as an administrator, not a critic. But I know what I don't like, and as a general rule of thumb I don't like what my brother likes. If you can prove to me that these artists you're championing are worthy of digging up and exhibiting, then I'll back you all the way. It's about time I took some hands-on control of this place, and stopped leaving it to the likes of Tim van Lier."

"All right," said Robert, "where do you want me to start?"

"I know the very place. One of the names on this list ... Nicholas Mosley?"

"Molesey," Robert corrected, gently.

"Yeah. Sorry. What do you know about him?"

"Not much, on a personal level. He was pretty much a lone wolf, couldn't easily be classified in any one of the 'camps' extant at the time. Surrealist, Primitivist, Vorticist ... didn't fit in anywhere on those axes. His early stuff, pre-1914, had this amazing sense of line, and colour, coupled with a bit of post-Beardsley decadence ..."

He saw Gregory's blank, if somewhat amused, expression. "I'm talking like a thesis again, aren't I? Anyway, after the war ... he was wounded in the trenches, in France, I think, 1917 ... he seemed to abandon all attempts at representational art in favour of something ..." He groped to find the right word, failed. "No-one seems to know what he was up to in those last few years of his life, what he was trying to achieve. Most of his completed work from that time has disappeared. He died in 1929, in circumstances which haven't been explained properly."

Gregory nodded, thoughtfully.

"Er ..." Robert prompted him, "what about Molesey?"

His boss reached into a drawer and pulled out a small flyer. "This sort of thing lands on my desk all the time. But the name struck a chord, and I remembered where I'd seen it before."

He pushed it across the desk to Robert. It was illustrated with a picture well-known to him, a self-portrait of Nicholas Molesey, circa 1905, showing the artist framed in a large gilt-edged mirror, his face taut and pensive, but still handsome. His hair, like Robert's, was dark, and it tumbled in waves off to one side from a jagged parting on the right. A wisp of moustache lurked beneath the nose. The eyes were blue and intense, positioned at the exact epicentre of the portrait, looking out at the viewer like a challenge.

Above the picture, the artist's name, in large bold type. And above that, in Celtic script, two words: *Guiding Spirit.*

"Apparently," said Gregory, saving Robert the chore of reading the blurb at the bottom, "those pictures you were speaking about have re-appeared. Molesey's estate turned them up in a clear-out of the old family home, which is being renovated. So they've teamed up with this New Age bookshop run by someone they know to set up this viewing-cum-valuation.

"So, your mission, Robert – should you choose to accept it – is to go to this viewing, see if these paintings are something we can find a buyer for, and if they are, snap them up. Fair enough?"

"Fair enough. Yeah. No problem." As ever, Robert's attempts to appear cool made him seem – to his own ears, at least – a complete imbecile.

"You've got a couple of days to brush up on your Molesey studies. In the meantime – painful as it is – go back downstairs and spread a little happiness."

"It could do with a little happiness," said Robert, rising and extending his hand.

Grasping it, Gregory said, "Ain't that the truth. I don't know if you noticed, but somebody's left a pile of toilet rolls in one part of the gallery ..."

Helena McCallum was looking in the mirror again, and still not liking what she saw.

It wasn't that it was by any means a *bad* reflection. Alright, the nose was a little too long, skin was a little too blotchy, and hair was a bit on the greasy side – oh, and there was, of course, the perennial problem of her weight, which numerous diet regimes had thus far failed to address – but, all things considered, she was doing OK. Not great, but OK.

The problem was what that reflection represented to Helena. It was the face of a twenty-seven year old woman who, for all the events and dramas that constituted her biography, appeared to have virtually come back to where she started, as if she'd hit a run of snakes and had yet to find a ladder.

Also, she had a headache. The previous evening had been spent in yet another unwise and wine-soused attempt to sort out the tortuous love life of her housemate, Debbie. The Boyfriend (or The Bastard, as he'd been re-christened last night) had apparently been seen in the company of another woman, not for the first time either. If she'd taken Helena's advice in the first place, and not gotten involved with this particular Bastard, then a lot of tears and heartaches (and headaches) could have been avoided.

The snores percolating through the thin bedroom wall told Helena that Debbie was still asleep, and she recalled being told that this was her day off from the hospital. Good for her, she thought. Some of us not only have to work at other people's problems, but we have day-jobs to go to as well.

And that was when she saw the clock, realised how long she'd been sitting there in front of the dressing-table mirror, and that she was going to be late for work. Again.

"Sorry, Sheelagh," Helena called to the woman standing beside the counter, re-organising a display of Feng Shui cd-roms.

"Third time this week," was the reply, with only the most cursory glance over her shoulder. "Buses again?"

"No, for once." She was tired of blaming her tardiness on the public transport system, particularly since it wasn't always true. "I'll explain later. Tea?"

"Please. I was worried you'd forgotten about today. We can't be doing without you today, Hel, there's too much to sort out."

Helena stopped on her way to the back of the shop, squinting at Sheelagh in puzzlement. "What's so special ...?"

Sheelagh stood up straight and looked at her with exasperation over the top of her half-moon spectacles.

"Oh, shit. The art show. I remember now." Another, more annoying, recollection came back to her. "And I've got to work late tonight."

"This is *important*, Helena. The first time we've managed to host anything this important. It could mean a whole new lease of life for the shop, and I need all hands on deck for it. You *do* understand, don't you?"

Helena sighed, unable (as ever) to stay annoyed for very long in the face of Sheelagh's plaintive appeals to her better nature. "Yeah, sure. I understand. Have the pictures arrived?"

"Not yet, and I must admit I'm concerned that they're cutting it a bit fine. I don't want to get anything else sorted out in that upstairs room before I know how much space the paintings are going to occupy."

Helena frowned. "You mean you haven't even seen them yet?"

"No. No-one has, outside of the Molesey family. That's why this has been arranged, so they can get some experts in to tell them if they're worth anything." Sheelagh smiled. "Maggie Turnbull ... well, Maggie *Molesey*, these days ... she and I go way back. We were at school together. We kept in touch a fair bit, and she knew about the shop, so when these paintings turned up in her attic, she contacted me for advice."

"This Molesey ... he was some sort of magician, wasn't he?"

"So I'm told. That's why Maggie contacted me rather than a mainstream art dealer ... seems his connection with all that stuff made him a bit of a *persona non grata* in the art world. She seemed to think our clientele would be a bit more appreciative." She noticed Helena give a slight shudder. "What's the matter?"

"Never liked this sort of thing. Just looking at a picture of that Aleister Crowley is enough to bring me out in a cold sweat." She looked out of the shop window at the street outside, at the rain and bustle and colour, as if trying to fix her mind on something mundane.

"That surprises me. I thought you were a Wiccan."

"That's different. Wicca's all about connection, about being a part of nature. Most of this stuff is about *control.* It makes me uncomfortable. Besides, I'm not as involved in all of that as I used to be."

"Well, you're the only one on the staff who knows anything substantial about the subject. I certainly don't, not my field at all." Sheelagh was more inclined towards Celtic mysticism than anything else, and that was where the shop's original orientation had centered, but in the twelve years since *Guiding Spirit* had first opened its doors it had diversified, along with its somewhat fickle customer base. There were four full-time members of staff now, as well as three part-timers, and each one of them had his or her own area of expertise, ranging from aromatherapy to meditation to channelling the spirits of Atlantean High Priests (this last one was the particular thing of the only male member of staff, Ken, and even by *Guiding Spirit* standards this was considered pretty weird. Especially when he started speaking in Dolphin).

"So," said Helena, shrugging off her unease, "no bunking off early tonight then?"

"I don't think so. Now, what happened to that tea?"

The morning passed as mornings in the shop generally did. The usual steady flow of browsers who came in out of the rain to stand steaming gently over the display of the current bestsellers (this week- *The Tao of Thomas the Tank Engine* and *The Jain Cookbook*), interspersed with the occasional, far-too-rare, purchaser of said bestsellers. Helena busied herself with re-arranging displays, phoning distributors, and sending back to one of these distributors the dozen or so unsold copies of last month's bestselling title *First There Is A Mountain; Healing Your Irritable Bowel The Zen Way.*

The paintings arrived at lunchtime in a small white rental van driven by a young man who didn't look old enough to have passed his driving test. Sheelagh was, by this time, almost vibrating with anxiety, and all the herbal tea in the shop couldn't placate her. She had tried phoning the Molesey house on three separate occasions, and had received no reply; the driver of the rental van informed her, after she had given the unfortunate lad an earbashing about this, that the renovations at the house meant the phone was temporarily disconnected.

Ken and the driver took the paintings, still wrapped in tarpaulins, straight up to the exhibition room, and despite herself, Helena was disappointed. She'd hoped to be able to see the pictures before anyone else had the chance. She stopped and looked at the picture of the artist on the flyer blu-tacked to the front of the counter; he'd painted himself from his reflection in a mirror, and Helena had always felt uneasy about this method of self-portrait. It made her feel as if *she* was the artist, as though he'd somehow managed to insinuate himself into her head. As though the mere act of looking into the eyes of Nicholas Molesey was acquiescence to violation.

A customer came to the cash desk, and she was very glad that she couldn't see that face from the other side of the counter.

Five-thirty came, and the shop began to fill up with people; many of who, in their varied ways, looked rather uncomfortable and out-of-place in the environs of a New Age bookshop. Helena could virtually pick out the individual types; the curious art lover (middle-aged, conservative of dress), intrigued by this show of work by somebody they'd never heard of, and along to see whether his obscurity was deserved or not; the magical tourist (younger, dressed predominantly in black, with either masses of hair or none at all), here to get some perspective on a name they may have come across in some text or other; and the friends of Sheelagh, clustered together in one corner, here only to show support for her latest endeavour. They milled about, talking in low tones, looking at the stock on the shelves with either outright bafflement or amused disdain (depending on whether you were here for the art or the magic), until Sheelagh announced that the show had commenced, and ushered everybody up the stairs.

All the other members of staff immediately disappeared with them, the smell of wine and vegetarian vol-au-vents in their nostrils, leaving Helena to finish with the last customer of the day (a heavily pregnant woman looking for books on Tantric Sex, obviously with a view to delaying her partner's next orgasm for as long as possible), and shut up shop.

It was ten minutes into the show before Helena managed to get upstairs. She emerged at the top of the spiral staircase into a room heaving and oppressive with the presence of too many people. The paintings were arranged in a semi-circle at the far end of the room, and were for now completely obscured. She looked for Sheelagh, and thought she could make her out amongst the crowd in the far right hand corner. It looked as if she was deep in conversation with a tall young man with dark, longish hair that she'd noticed earlier, someone who looked as if he belonged to none of the aforementioned 'tribes'. Quite a good-looking man, too.

Before she could plunge into the throng in her direction, however, Ken materialised at her side. "Oh, Hel, you're here. Do us a favour, will you? Circulate with these for a minute while I nip off to the little boy's room."

And he thrust a half-full tray of drinks into her hand, before jogging off towards the staff toilet.

"Bladder still playing up, Ken?" she asked with a smile as he disappeared. Ken had problems with his 'water' totally unbefitting an Atlantean High Priest. He didn't hear her.

Most of the guests were already sorted for drinks – some of them were beginning, in fact, to look as if they'd been fairly well sorted before they arrived – so Helena was largely ignored. Her circulations gave her the chance to single out some other people who looked, if not out of place, then certainly conspicuous. Some of them she now recognised as local art or antique dealers, keen to pick up on a new 'trend' that had hitherto passed them by. One or two of them she'd had dealings with, and the epithet 'bandit' was not inappropriate to them.

The old man sitting at the side of the room, looking at the paintings through a gap in the crowd, was, like the young man at the front (on whom she still had a most careful eye) unfamiliar. As she approached, she took in details about him; reasonably vigorous looking, and probably considerably older than he appeared; well dressed, but not ostentatiously so; dignified bearing. The hands clasped on the walking stick in front of him were gnarled with arthritis, and appeared to be trembling slightly.

"Excuse me, sir?" she said softly, reluctant to disturb his reverie. "Can I offer you a drink?"

He turned his head slowly to look at her, and behind his glasses she was surprised to see what looked like tears in his eyes. These he blinked away before giving her a delightful smile and holding up one of his tremulous hands.

"No, thank you, my dear. I'm afraid my doctor would be most disapproving if I availed myself, much as I'd like to. She has a hard enough time with me as it is, poor thing."

"Is there anything else I can get you?"

"Not at the moment." She realised she was still wearing her name badge as he peered at her left breast, "Helena. Thank you again."

For some reason, she was unwilling to simply walk away and leave him. There was a sadness about this charming old ... and here the word was, for once, completely appropriate ... gentleman that brought out what had been described variously as her 'nurturing' or 'mother hen' tendencies.

"Are you enjoying the show?" she said, wishing immediately that she could have come up with something a little more inspired.

The old man's smile became wistful, and he glanced at the paintings again. "I wouldn't say *enjoy* would be quite the right word ... but I'm glad I came, nevertheless."

There was nothing more to say. With mutual courtesies, they parted. But she had the strangest feeling this would not be their last encounter.

Her trail, despite her best efforts, seemed to be taking her further and further away from the paintings, about which her curiosity was growing by the minute. Every so often, she would be detained in conversation by one of the guests, usually someone she knew (asking her for more details about the artist, which she was, at that moment, unable to provide; the biographical flyer which had been circulated earlier was obviously deficient in most respects), but occasionally someone would stop her with the 'wouldn't usually catch me dead in this sort of place' or the 'you don't actually believe in all this stuff, do you?' gambit. Her response to both might have been different, more ready with the dialectical, had she not had a steadily depleting tray of drinks in her hand, and a mind that was preoccupied with other things; so instead she just smiled and moved on without reply.

Just as she thought she might actually be close enough to see what all the fuss was about, the reaction, based on Helena's eavesdropping, seemed to be fairly evenly divided between those who had no idea what the paintings were about and didn't like them, and those who had no idea what the paintings were about and did. If strength of reaction was the deciding factor, however, the former seemed to be winning. A tap on the shoulder made her turn. Sheelagh was standing there, apparently quite tipsy already, judging from the lack of focus in her gaze. The tall, good-looking young man with the dark hair was beside her.

"Oh, Helena. I'd like you to meet Mr Pierce. He's come all the way from the Webster Gallery to be here today. Have you heard of the Webster Gallery?"

She had turned around before she asked the latter question, and found herself addressing it to Pierce. "Oh, of course *you* do, I was asking Helena." She turned her bleary eyes on Helena again. "Have you? Heard of it?"

"Er ... I think so."

"Oh, good! I hadn't. You two have something to be

talking about then." And she weaved away into the crowd, towards where her friends were standing.

After a pause which would become legendary in the annals of awkwardness, Pierce said, "I'm sorry, but ... did I just get dumped on you?"

"Oh, don't worry about Sheelagh," Helena said with a laugh. "I don't think it was personal. It's just that when she has a drink, all etiquette goes out of the window."

"Common problem," he said. "The name's *Robert*, by the way. None of this 'Mr Pierce' crap. You're Helena, right? Name-badges and sloshed middle-aged women seldom lie."

"Right. Helena." Pause. "Helena McCallum." They shook hands, a difficult manoeuvre with a tray of drinks between them. "And I'm your waitress for the evening."

"Also one of the few people here who knows anything about these paintings, or so Sheelagh tells me." He caught the flicker of annoyance on her face. "You don't know anything about these paintings, do you?"

"How could I? I haven't even seen them yet." Memo to self; have a good long talk with Sheelagh when she sobers up. "You're probably in a better position than I am to judge whether they're good paintings or not. Are they?"

Pierce didn't seem willing to commit. "Well, they're ... interesting. I mean, I know Molesey's earlier stuff, and I've always been keen to see these pictures from his 'lost' period, but now that I have ..."

"Disappointed?"

"Hard to say. It's as though ... as though I don't know how to *read* them. As if there's some sort of key, a Rosetta stone that I need to find first. You follow?"

She nodded, although she didn't really understand. To Helena, pictures weren't for *reading*, they were for experiencing. It sounded to her as if Robert really needed to turn off his left brain once in a while.

The subject of art seemed exhausted. "So, Helena, what do you do here? Apart from sell books, that is?"

"Oh, this and that," she said. "I run a couple of workshops here every now and again."

"Really? What in?"

Here goes. Deep breath. "Tarot, usually. I do readings for people as well. Sometimes I'll give a few sort of 'Wiccan for Beginners' lectures. Nothing too complicated, just a sort of 'idiot's guide', really."

"Wiccan?" Pierce had a sort of impish smile on his face that Helena might have found attractive if she didn't know what was coming next. "You mean you're a witch? Spells, and stuff like that?"

"Well, I suppose I'm more of a lapsed Wiccan," (she emphasised the word) "these days, but yeah, I used to do spells."

Pause again. Pierce nodded, the smile still present, as he seemed to consider what to say next.

"It's not all Harry Potter, you know."

"Oh, no, I ..."

"We don't have broomsticks. And we don't all have cats."

"Well ..."

"My landlord won't let me have one. He's allergic to them."

"Broomsticks?"

"Cats."

"Oh."

It was Pierce who broke the next awkward silence by clearing his throat, rather too ostentatiously.

"Anyway," said Helena, brightly, "must be going. These drinks don't serve themselves, and all that."

"Yes, of course. Well, it's been nice meeting you, Helena. Hope the ... er – cards turn up OK for you."

"Thanks. If you're interested in a reading, just contact the shop, we'll work something out." Yeah, right. As if.

"No worries. I'll do that."

She turned to walk away, but halted, bothered by a feeling that crept upon her for the second time that evening. "You know, Mr – Robert, sorry – I really think that you *will* be in touch. Maybe not for a reading, but for something else. Something much more important."

She gave him a wan smile, and turned away before he could think of a reply. What the hell was going on with her today? Strange intuitions were not her *forte*, as a rule; all right, people had often pointed out that she could get the measure of a person from a few words on the first meeting (Debbie was currently regretting that she hadn't put more faith in this talent of Helena's) but precognition? That was a new one.

And yet it was as strong an impression as any she'd received in her life. There was also a more vague feeling she was picking up, a feeling that all three of them – herself, Pierce, the old man whose name she hadn't ascertained – were in some way mutually circling something else. Something that was also in the room with them. Something that didn't want its presence known just yet.

Shrugging off these fancies, she noticed, with some annoyance, that Ken had returned to the room and was, glass in hand, currently in conversation with a group of people she recognised as some of the 'pirates' she'd disdained earlier. She resolved, as soon as she'd cleared this particular tray (and empty glasses were by now outnumbering full ones), to pop back there and get Ken back on serving duty; after all, everybody had so far had time to socialise except for her. Not fair.

It was with some surprise, therefore, that she found she was now at the front of the room, close to the Molesey paintings, about which she had been so curious. Since nobody for the moment was too bothered about 'topping up', she took the opportunity to begin her study of the pictures.

Only now she realised just how limited was her experience of, and vocabulary in the world of modern art. They weren't pictures *of* anything, just abstracts, and Helena, with her own predilection for art that actually bore some resemblance to the things of everyday experience, felt as disappointed as Pierce must have felt a few minutes earlier. The self-portrait reproduced on the flyer was, in this respect, rather misleading; it promised images of strange power, powerful as the visage of the artist himself.

But these? At first glance, they seemed to be little more than swirls of colour; to be sure, a different colour was prevalent in each one – green in the one closest to her, for example, black in another – but the over-riding feature of each appeared to be that there were no straight lines in any of them. No lines, no divisions, just whorls of pigmentation that melded from one colour to another with the smoothness and organic flow of hallucination. The varnish over each of them added an extra dimension to the pictures, reflecting back the room's strip-light glow and creating a further barrier between the artist and the viewer.

In all save one, that is. At the end of the line stood a painting that even Helena's untrained eye could tell was incomplete. It had all of the vortice-like quality of the others, but two things distinguished it from the rest. For one, it was unvarnished, and swallowed, rather than reflecting, the light. And for another, it had in the upper middle of the picture the only sharply delineated figure in all five: an inverted triangle, the colour of fresh blood, its sides bowing inwards.

Helena's gaze fell into the whorls of colour – predominantly red and reddish-brown – like a ship caught in a whirlpool. For a few seconds she was unable even to blink as it led her attention back into a distance that seemed to be sculpting, before her eyes, a landscape that had no right to exist, its perspectives twisted and mocking, a landscape alien and hostile ...

... from which something was emerging, something which she saw now as merely the fully-realised form of an entity which she saw as present in each brushstroke of the picture, a sleeping dragon which she had awoken, now rushing toward her with a roar that was both the triumphant cry of the predator, and the laughter of the lover, rushing to be re-united with the one without whom it is not complete ...

Helena was only dimly aware of someone screaming, less so that it was herself. Her legs gave way beneath her, and she fell in a rain of tinkling glass, wine, and shocked hush.

The sound of breaking glass was, it had to be said, something of a relief for Robert. He was in the midst of that most pernicious of social nightmares, Entrapment by Complete Bore. There was this man standing between him and the rest of the civilised world, and there was, despite all attempts at dislocation (by means of 'oh my God is that the time' or 'I'm really sorry but

I've just seen somebody that I must go and speak to rather urgently'), no shifting the bugger. On the lower side of middle age, the Bore was clad in the perennial Bore uniform of blazer, beige slacks and cravat. Robert could almost make out the phantom copy of the *Daily Mail* protruding from his pocket, like an excised limb.

"Sack the juggler!" cried the Bore, as Bores do, at the sound of the crash. Robert turned to see a frontal wave of assistance moving, in complete silence, to the side of someone who had fallen to the floor. He craned his neck to try and see who it was, and was surprised to discover (he couldn't see the face, but recognised the long purple dress through the legs of the crowd) that it was Helena, the girl he'd been speaking to only a few minutes before. He recalled seeing her, too, just a matter of moments ago, out of the corner of his eye, standing in front of one of the Molesey paintings as though entranced.

Strange girl.

"Looks like some woman's had a funny turn," said the Bore, redundantly. "Still, that's what women do, isn't it? Must be her time of the month, or something. Anyway, as I was saying ..."

Robert realised that he didn't have the faintest idea what the Bore had been saying, either at the time of the distraction or, for that matter, since he'd started talking.

"Art, it's a big investment opportunity these days, isn't it? Well, you'd know all about that, working in a gallery, and all. Did you see that article in the FT last week? Fascinating stuff. Wish I'd seen it earlier. Would have given me some ammunition to use against the Missus when she insisted that we sell off the paintings ..."

"Sorry," said Robert, who was by now feeling that the whole day was slipping out of his grasp, "what paintings?"

"Well, those ones, of course." He gestured in the general direction of the Molesey paintings, which now were unobscured thanks to Helena's 'turn' and the subsequent shift in public attention. "I thought you knew? Good God, where are my manners? Must have forgotten to introduce myself properly. The name's Molesey, Derek Molesey. Those daubs over there were produced by my mad old Uncle Nick."

Robert found his hand clutched and pumped, clammily.

"Ah. I see. Well, it seems, Mr Molesey," and it pained him greatly to say what he now said, "that you're the person I came here to see anyway." He explained as briefly as possible about the Webster's interest in the Molesey pictures.

"Wish you'd spoken to me earlier, old man," said Molesey. "I had a very, *very* good offer for them right at the beginning of the evening. Quoted me a figure that was way over what we'd dreamed of for the things. Chap even gave me a deposit on them, just to make sure no-one else gazumped him."

He fished a folded cheque out of the inner pocket of his blazer, flattened it out, and held it out for Robert's inspection. There were an awful lot of noughts in the figure scrawled on it, far more than was at Robert's disposal from the gallery.

"And this is just a deposit, you say?"

"Oh, yes. Fifty per cent, up front, the rest on delivery."

"Just out of interest, who was the buyer?"

"Oh, that old codger over there ..." He pointed in the direction of the far wall. "Looks like he's gone. Never mind. What was his name, again?" He peered at the cheque. "Burgess. Mr P Burgess. That's as much as I know."

Robert's shoulders slumped. "That's a great shame, Mr Molesey. I was hoping that your uncle's work could get more of a public airing ..."

"Ah, well, first come, first served, eh?" said Molesey smugly, pocketing the cheque again and bringing on a sudden urge on Robert's part to hit him square between the eyes. "No hard feelings, I trust. Of course, when we've sorted out the rest of his stuff, you're more than welcome to put in a bid for that, though I don't know whether anything there would be of interest to you."

"The *rest* of his stuff?" Christ, he wished this old fart would stop letting out his information in instalments. "This isn't all of it?"

"Oh, Lord, no," said Molesey. "Nothing like this, of course ... just a trunkful of notes, diaries, the odd sketch. Can't make head nor tail of it myself, but it might be of some use to someone such as yourself."

Robert forced his face into a smile. "Well, you know, Mr Molesey ... Derek? I'd be more than happy to come over and sort through it myself with you, give it a bit of an expert eye, that sort of thing. The Webster Gallery would, naturally, like first refusal on anything of merit that's in there."

"Oh, goes without saying." Molesey was putting on a great show of giving the proposal hard consideration, but Robert could almost see the pound signs already ticking over in the man's piggy little eyes. However much this Burgess bloke had promised him, it was never enough for someone like this.

"All right, agreed." More soggy handshaking. "Can you make it over tomorrow? It's not that far away from here." He handed over a rather crumpled business card. "Shall we say ten o'clock? Be prepared to spend most of the day there, there's quite a bit of it."

"Perfect. See you then."

With an avaricious smile pasted on his face, Molesey trotted away. It was more than likely, thought Robert, that the real gems of his uncle's 'lost' work were in that trunk, and greed had simply forced the family to put the more obviously 'marketable' items up for sale first. Without inflating his hopes too far, Robert was feeling more optimistic than he had in some time.

And who knows? That trunk might contain the 'Rosetta stone' to those paintings that he'd intuited might exist.

Since there was now no further reason to stay, he headed for the exit. As he did so, Robert noticed a knot of people clustered around a chair to one side of the room. They were fussing over a young woman in a long purple dress whose face was as pale as the wall behind her. As he passed, her eyes lifted and met his, and her words came back to him - "You *will* be in touch." They were almost an order.

Uncomfortable again, he turned and walked away.

It was coming for her again, and this time it had a form.

There was something familiar about that form. It seemed composed of all the faces of all the monsters that had scared her as a child ... Big Bad Wolves were in there, and

Trolls, and Rumpelstiltskin, and just a hint of Dalek as well for good measure. But more than that; as it got closer she saw that all these faces were melting away too, revealing behind them the faces of people, people she knew from life, her family, her old schoolfriends, all of them with distended features and the jaws of some terrible predatory beast, ready to tear at her flesh.

Then they became one face; that of the man Pierce, the man at the shop. There wasn't any expression on this face, just the altogether more terrifying emptiness of a soul in torment who knows that he is confronting the most terrible trial of his life.

This also vanished, just as the face took up all of Helena's vision, to be replaced by that of one just as empty, just as tormented. She woke, to see, for a few brief moments, that face superimposed on the ceiling above her. It was the same one she saw in the mirror each morning.

How long it took her to turn her head and look at the clock, she couldn't tell; it seemed as though empires and oceans could have risen and fallen in the time it took to complete that simple action. And it still would have been only 5:06 a.m.

She rose and (avoiding the harsh gaze of the mirror) left the bedroom and headed downstairs. There was the sound of a radio coming from the kitchen; Debbie was already up, preparing for the early shift at the hospital. She looked at Helena curiously from the kitchen table as she shuffled barefoot to the kettle and filled it at the sink.

"Morning," said Debbie at last. "Notice I didn't say 'good' morning."

"Do I really look that bad?"

"For once, I'd say you look as bad as you think you do. What happened at that art show thingy last night? You came in looking like death, didn't even stop to say hello, just straight up to your room and into bed."

"That's just it," said Helena, filling up a mug with hot water, adding a camomile tea bag and pummeling it with a spoon. "I don't know what happened last night. I just, sort of... came over all strange."

"Look at the start you've got."

Ignoring the attempt at levity, Helena launched into an

account of the previous evening's events. When it was over, Debbie gazed into the middle distance over the top of her coffee mug before looking back at Helena, eyes narrowed in suspicion.

"You're not *on* anything, are you?"

"Come off it, Deb. You know me, a couple of glasses of wine and I'm all over the place. Drugs are a no-no for me, always have been."

"Medication, then? Taking anything new on prescription?"

"*No*," said Helena firmly. Apart from a brief spell on Prozac a couple of years ago, after she got back from the States, she hadn't even seen a doctor about anything.

"Well, what do *you* think it was then?" Debbie asked with a helpless shrug.

Helena shook her head, unable to reply, and they both returned to their contemplation of empty space above the table. It was Debbie who at long last broke the silence.

"I think your problem, Hel, is you spend more time worrying about other people's problems and don't pay enough attention to your own."

"What's that got to do with anything?" snapped Helena. "And what 'problems', exactly?"

"Oh, like you've had just a rosy life since you and wossisface, Adam, split up. How long were you together out there?"

"Two years." They'd met during Helena's 'time-out' year from University, a time-out that became permanent when she married and joined him in California (he came from Sacramento, but they lived in Los Angeles). It hadn't worked out, a messy failure. Divorces are difficult enough, transatlantic ones more so.

"Right. And you think you're over it? You're good at keeping it under wraps, but I know the wounds are still hurting. There's been nobody since then, has there? Well, has there?"

"What is this, the third degree? You know there hasn't. I'm not ready for it yet."

"But in the meantime, you spend all your time trying to sort out everybody else's problems ... like mine, and don't get me wrong, I'm grateful, but you've got to see that it's a kind of denial thing you're going through. You're on edge. You don't want to look at your own situation; you'd rather shift your attention elsewhere. But you've repressed it for too long, Hel."

"That's it, then? Your considered opinion? I'm loopy. Those psychology night classes are really paying off, aren't they?"

"Don't be facetious. All I'm saying is, you need to talk to someone about this. Someone qualified. I've been worried about you for a while now, Hel. You're my best friend. I don't want to see anything bad happen to you." She reached out and took Helena's hand. "And this thing that happened to you last night? Sounds bad to me."

Is that it – thought Helena? Am I having some sort of delayed nervous breakdown?

Even as the thought passed through her, she knew that it was not the answer. There was something about that painting she had seen, something *external* to her. True, she had the feeling that it was feeding on something in her, that it had found some sort of chink in the armour which she had, with varying success, managed to construct around herself in the time since she had returned to Britain. But it most definitely did not have its origins with her. To suggest otherwise would be, in effect, blaming the victim.

And we're back to violation again ...

However, she saw the concern in Debbie's face, and kept her own counsel on this for the time being. "All right. I'll go and see my doctor; maybe I can get a referral to someone. I don't know what they can do with a complete Loopazoid like me, but I'll tell them to send the bills to you."

"Go, girlfriend," said Debbie with a reassuring grin. She glanced down at the watch hanging from the breast of her uniform. "Christ, time I was going. I'll talk to you again tonight, OK? My turn to get the drinks in."

With Debbie gone, Helena considered going back to bed, but decided against it, preferring the quiet melancholy of the early morning to the prospect of jumping back into that dream again (and she knew that she would). A replenished mug in hand, she wandered into the living room, drawing comfort from its shabby homeliness, its clutter of magazines and haphazardly arranged, cigarette-scarred furniture. The television tempted her for a moment, but she knew that the early morning schedule of news and cartoons would just deepen her depression.

Well, at least I don't have to go in to work today. They'd impressed that upon her very forcefully, with Sheelagh falling over herself (and, in her inebriated state, everyone else) to be understanding.

There was a mirror above the fireplace. She forced herself to look in it, just to find out if Debbie's estimation of her physical state was accurate. To her dismay, it was; her henna'd hair bore an even closer resemblance to rats' tails than usual, and there was a pallor to her complexion at which even she, in the depths of her most Pre-Raphaelite phase a few years before, would have balked.

The mirror was embossed with a design of flowers and vines, giving it a kind of kitschy, William Morris-esque feel. Her face was framed in reflection by a swirl of greenery that, even as she watched, seemed to be changing colour from emerald to ruby, merging with her face to create something else, some new form of life that she didn't recognise, didn't *want* to recognise.

She blinked hard, and it was once more just a rather over-ornate mirror, showing a reflection of a rather nervous, pale young woman. A woman breathing heavily, listening to the sound of her own heart performing an improv-jazz drum solo. A woman who suddenly didn't feel safe anywhere, even in her own home.

I might as well go into work, she reasoned. At least there they might understand.

A few hours later, Helena was having serious doubts about that particular bit of reasoning.

It wasn't that they were unsympathetic. If anything, they were overflowing with care and concern to the point where Helena had to consciously bring a lighter tone into her voice, and the odd smile to her expression, simply to get rid of any doleful faces, which, at that moment, happened to be opposite her. The 'troops' (both of them) rallied round to ensure that she wasn't on her own for more than a few minutes at a time; well-intentioned, but rather annoying when she went to the toilet, or to keep her workload to a minimum.

The price for all of this concern? She had to listen to her workmates individual – and most definitely unique – attempts to explain what happened to her on the previous evening. So far, Sheelagh and Ken had suggested that her chakras were out of alignment, that the paintings had been arranged in such a way as to focus the negative energy of all the people in that room (containing so many representatives of the press in it simply *had* to be tilted toward the negative) on to the precise spot where she was standing. Furthermore it was more than a possibility that she had at some point in her life been abducted by extraterrestrials. From the Pleiades.

Her afternoon tea break (not that there was much distinction for Helena, that day, between rest periods and any other) was taken with Ken. He sat opposite her in the small office that doubled, on days such as today, as a stockroom, and frowned at her from beneath his greying dreadlocks.

"I was really worried about you last night, you know, Hel. We all were. But me even more so ..."

"Why?"

"Well, if I hadn't asked you to circulate with the drinks ..." He shrugged, unable to put anything closer to a logical spin on his guilt.

"Don't be daft, Ken. Wasn't your fault."

He leaned in closer, almost conspiratorial. "I asked Unnas about you. I hope you don't mind."

For a moment, Helena simply stared blankly at Ken, torn between bafflement and the urge to giggle at his earnestness. Then it came to her.

"Oh, *Unnas.*" Unnas was Ken's Atlantean pen pal, currently residing out in some mystical dimension of light where peace and harmony reigned, and where the dolphins didn't have to worry about tuna nets. " No, no, of course not. What did he say?"

"He seemed concerned, naturally. You have a lot of friends *out there*, you know, Hel, even if you're not actually aware of it."

Nice to know. Helena had the feeling she was going to need all the friends she could get.

"I described to him what happened, and he said that it looked like your energies were out of sync with the planet. It's quite common, apparently. Unnas said that he saw quite a lot of it back in the old times, particularly in the days just before – well, you know what ..." He made a point of resisting any sort of explicit detail about the fate of Atlantis, just in case any of the 'Great Ones' happened to be eavesdropping and got upset.

"So ... how do I get them back in sync?"

"Well, fasting always helps. Prayer too, but only if you're using the right kind of crystals to focus the energies into yourself. I can help with that ... or rather, Unnas can. If you like, I can set you up a channelling this week ..."

"Ken," Helena was aware that she sounded slightly impatient, but she had to ask. "Do you honestly think it's *me*? You said that 'I'm out of sync' but you really think that all of this – whatever 'this' is – is just something that's inside me? Inside my head?"

"Not your head as such, no. Your whole harmonic vibration is off-key, and that's your whole body ..."

"But you still think that my turn last night – shit, I'm running out of ways of talking about it – you think that it was brought on by something that's wrong with me?"

It was Ken's turn to look at her blankly. "Well ... yes. What else could it be?"

Before she could frame any sort of response to that, Ken made his excuses and headed for the toilet, though whether his inability to provide her with assistance was the reason for the awakening of his bladder, Helena couldn't say. She was left staring around the room; a room piled high with books, frequented by some of the kindest, most caring people she had ever had the good fortune to meet, and none of them, books or booksellers, had the slightest fucking clue how to help her.

So here I am, she thought. Two separate cups of tea, hours apart, with people who, for all their good intentions, both think that what happened last night was a brainstorm caused by (a) lack of connection with Mother Gaia, or (b) good old fashioned neuroses. Either way, they were both saying, it's down to me to sort it out by getting my own shit together.

But I know that's not it. There was something else out there, something that inhabited those paintings.

Something ... evil?

She had to find someone else to ask about this, someone who might be able to give her some answers about the nature of this thing. And she had no idea where to start.

Patience, Robert, patience. Plenty of time.

The mantra rolled over and over again in Robert's mind, interspersed with an annoying radio ad jingle that had lodged in his brain a couple of days before, returning to him every time he tried to still his mind. He wasn't even too sure what it had been selling; double-glazing, possibly, or perhaps a haemorrhoid treatment. He stared listlessly out at the world over the steering wheel of his BMW, counting (for the eleventh time) the line of immobile cars stretching away to the horizon, a high proportion with roof racks loaded with luggage, bicycles, surfboards and other accoutrements of the British holiday-maker headed for the seaside. The rain had dispersed, the sun was shining, and it was a Saturday morning.

Cue the gridlock.

He reached into the breast pocket of his shirt and produced the business card given to him by Derek Molesey the previous evening. *Not that far away, my arse.* Maybe not for you, Derek, old man, borne on the wings of your own superciliousness, but for us mortals who use the internal combustion engine on a holiday weekend, trying to get out of the city, it might as well be on fucking Mars.

Just about then, the traffic deigned to move slightly, and Robert dutifully nuzzled the car up against the bumper of the Volvo estate in front. He fell to wondering – *apropos* of nothing in particular – what Derek's 'mad old Uncle Nick' would have made of all this. Robert had the impression that Molesey, like so many other artists, writers and poets of his time, was motivated to do what he did by the things he had seen happening in Europe in the so-called 'Great War'. Molesey was one of the few who had seen these horrors at first hand, and had survived, but the question for him remained, what is it about death that makes us so eager to meet it? So eager that we devise newer and better ways of, if not actually hastening the inevitable end, then making life so intolerable? It seemed to Robert that Molesey might have viewed the sight of thousands upon thousands of people willing to cram themselves into airless tin boxes for hours on end as a kind of wilful *surrogate* death, a preparation for the real thing. Vision is bled away from us, our faces are pressed remorselessly into the dirt, until all we have to look forward to is a merciful end to our pain.

What was more natural than that he should have wanted to see for himself what we faced *out there*? From the writings and works of Nicholas Molesey already extant, Robert knew that he had a loathing of the increasing mechanisation of the world, a mechanisation given its ultimate (to that date) expression in the European 'war machine', that production line of corpses, which had taken the lives of so many of his peers and contemporaries.

As the traffic continued to inch its way forward to hardly anywhere at all, Robert felt renewed anticipation for what he eventually would find at the end of his journey. Anticipation, and apprehension.

Once he'd managed to crawl to the correct exit on the motorway, Robert's journey became far smoother. The Molesey house was a former vicarage in an area of 'green belt' land, nestled away in the heart of countryside and only accessible through a rabbit warren of lanes big enough for only one vehicle to pass at a time. After the fourth time he was forced to reverse and find a lay-by, Robert made a mental note to check for a clause in the Highway Code giving automatic right of way on such roads to inbred jerks driving muddy Land Rovers. The house itself seemed to be in dire need of the renovation that was apparently taking place there, judging from the state of the guttering and paintwork. Nevertheless, the crunch of the car's tyres on the gravel drive all too obviously exuded the sound of money, and quite a bit of it too.

He pulled in behind a white van standing sentinel in front of the main entrance. The van's rear doors were open to reveal a pandemonium of paint-pots, grubby sheets and one lone shaven-headed youth in blue overalls, who was at that moment wrapping his sallow, pock-marked face around a sandwich. He registered the BMW's arrival with a look of such vacant vehicular lust that Robert was tempted to drive straight away to the nearest car wash.

In the doorway, an older man in similar overalls was having an apparently heated discussion with a middle-aged woman, and even at this distance Robert could tell that the woman had the edge in this confrontation. The woman's voice and gesticulations were reaching some sort of crescendo as Robert got out of the car and approached.

"... And I'm telling *you*," she was saying, "that if I'd wanted the upstairs bathroom to be Royal Blue, I would most assuredly have *said* Royal Blue, but I didn't, I said *Duck's-egg* Blue, and I'm damned if I'm paying you to completely ignore my instructions! What use is a colour-blind decorator to me? Eh?"

The decorator shifted his weight from foot to foot, his face going a most peculiar shade beneath the splodges of (Royal) Blue that adorned it, and managed to get out a couple of syllable's worth of explanation before the woman, her hands braced firmly on her more-than-adequate hips, launched into the attack once again.

"No, I'll tell *you* what you can do, Mr Gibson. You and that clumsy son of yours – I'll be expecting the value of that vase knocked off your final price, by the way – can get the right paint, from wherever you have to get it, and I don't care if it's only available in Tasmania, and you can come back here *and you can bloody well do the job I'm paying you to do*! Is any of this becoming clear to you yet?"

Mr Gibson, shaking his head, turned and walked away from the woman, passing Robert and hardly even registering his presence, muttering something under his breath that could not possibly be misconstrued as complimentary. With the decorator in retreat, the woman turned her daunting attention to Robert.

"And what can I do for you?"

Not an enquiry, more like a challenge.

"Er ... Mrs Molesey, is it? My name's Pierce, Robert Pierce. From the Webster Gallery?"

Her tone softened somewhat, but she was still a long way from putting out the welcome mat. "I see. We were expecting you earlier."

He apologised, explained about the traffic, but all the woman did was sniff and say, "Well, I'm afraid you've missed Derek. He's gone out, not expecting him back until this evening."

Now there's a shame.

"You might as well come in, then. The stuff is in the spare bedroom if you want to have a look at it. Excuse the mess ..."

She led him into the house, which appeared, for the most part, to be shrouded in dustsheets. The walls were stripped of paper or paint, and the only visible floor was bare board. Mrs Molesey explained that there had been a small fire in one of the rooms earlier in the year, and, although the actual fire damage was limited to that one room, there had been considerable smoke damage throughout the house. The insurance settlement had been generous enough to allow them to completely renovate the place.

"That's when we came across this stuff," she said, ushering him into a small room, the contents of which were an old wardrobe and an even older trunk, which sat in the middle of the floor. The trunk was black, with dull silver edging, and appeared to have some initials in the centre of the lid. As he got closer, Robert could see that they were N.M.

Nicholas Molesey.

"It was up in the attic, along with those paintings." She gave a most peculiar involuntary shudder at the mention of the pictures. "God knows how long they'd been up there, not even Derek knew about them, and he's lived in this house all his life. I think Derek's grandfather must have hidden them away up here after Nicholas died. Didn't want anybody to see them. Can't say I blame him."

Robert opened the trunk with a care verging on reverence. Although he'd been warned by Derek Molesey that there was a considerable amount of stuff, he was still surprised at the quantity of its contents; piles of leather bound notebooks, sheaves of paper bound with string or ribbon, a burlap sack containing (he lifted it experimentally) something hefty and metallic.

"Is it of any use to you?" Mrs Molesey asked.

Robert scratched his chin thoughtfully. "Very possibly. I'd like to take some time over this, if I may. Give it a proper assessment before I come to a decision, and then we can talk about a price."

The woman was uncharacteristically silent for a few moments, looking at the contents of the trunk with an expression that seemed to bear no comparison to the Valkyrie he'd seen a few moments before. It seemed pensive, fearful even.

"Mrs Molesey? Are you all right?"

"Ever since that thing turned up," she said at last, never taking her eyes from the trunk, "I haven't had a decent night's sleep. Do you have any sort of phobias, Mr Pierce?"

"Er ... no. Nothing to speak of."

"I do. I'm terrified of spiders. Absolutely detest the little blighters. Won't go into a room if I know there's one in there. Well, imagine how I'd feel if I knew there was one in the bedroom when I'm trying to go to sleep. I wouldn't dare close my eyes for fear that it would crawl on to the ceiling above the bed and then maybe ..."

She didn't need to complete the description of that particular little nightmare; Pierce had already felt the room begin to sing with suppressed terror. "That's the way I feel now, Mr Pierce, knowing that these ... *items* are in the same house as me."

"You've read them?"

"I don't need to. They don't *feel* right. As soon as I first saw that trunk, those awful pictures ..." She sighed and looked at Pierce for the first time in several minutes, and he could now clearly see the fear in her, unsuppressed, all attempts at rationalisation abandoned. "You won't understand, Mr Pierce. I don't understand it myself. All I know is that I want those things out of my house, and out of here *now.* I don't care about the money. We don't need it that badly, as you can probably tell. If you don't mind, I'd very much like it if you'd take that damn box as far away from here as possible."

Robert closed the trunk. "Won't your husband have something to say about this?"

"Leave him to me," she said. "Derek knows not to push his luck with me – I'll have him for breakfast. No, you just put that trunk in your car and take it away, and don't worry about the money. The way I feel now, I don't think I'd even want to touch any money we made out of the sale of such stuff. It's bad enough with the paintings. The money seems ... well, *tainted*, I suppose I'd have to say."

He lugged the trunk to the car and into the boot himself, despite Mrs Molesey's offer of help; it was plain that she couldn't bear to even touch the box. With the weight of the trunk unbalancing his car's Teutonically-precise suspension, he drove away, offering a cheery wave, smile and beep of the horn in farewell to his new benefactress. She responded only cursorily, eager to put the house's weighty solid oaken front door between herself and the source of her recent unease, leaving Pierce to feel very satisfied with himself.

Somebody up there *definitely* likes me today, he thought.

He didn't take the trunk to the gallery. Instead, he drove back to his flat. He enlisted the help of the porter to transport the box from car to front door, in return for an extremely generous consideration, and situated it in the middle of his living room floor, shifting a large glass coffee table out of the way to make room for it.

So where the hell do I start? The sheer volume of the contents was daunting; he counted twenty-three of the notebooks alone, many of which he discovered by picking through them more or less randomly, and appeared to be written in some sort of cypher.

Typical. If the key to understanding the paintings is in here, then first of all I've got to find a way of decrypting that key.

He turned his attention instead to the loose sheets of paper held together with string. These were more like it; preliminary sketches for some of his better known works, and a lot of stuff that looked like experimental doodles, but executed with the draughtsmanship that characterised Molesey's early work. Here, it was as though he was trying to capture, using techniques that he already half-knew to be inadequate to the task, something that eluded him, something that could not be held into the rigid line and form that his training imposed upon it and which constantly broke free. These sketches would trail off into formless, inchoate abstractions, and would usually culminate in the artist's furious scribbling over the top of what he obviously saw as another failure, but which Robert saw immediately as containing within it the seed of the later work.

He had to give in to the chaos, not fight it. At some point, he recognised this. But when? And how?

He reached into the mass of books again and chose another. This time, he was overjoyed to find that it was written in English, in a spidery script which, though a little difficult to read, was at least comprehensible.

Or at least, the individual *words* were comprehensible. The first passage he chose to read was dated October 15th, 1924:

The Vision in the Flesh I. Yod. By my Hand. The thrusting forth, the patterns radial and extensional, cold, dry, all reddens with the blue-green veined, crosshatched. Enter them. Onwards and upwards, extend the patterns beyond, and the will follows. Take hold of a future event and be present therein, mystery within mystery.

Indeed. Robert put the book down and shook his head. His hand trailed among the volumes, picked up the same book. Opened it to the words, printed large enough to fill the page:

The flesh is in order as it is.
Have faith in the mystery within.

We act our divinity alive
in the ebb and the flow of the flesh.

I am the Passion and the Life,
in my limbs and my lungs and my veins.

The process of reading had never been harder for him; it felt as though these few words had turned his brain to mush, liquidised it. He read the passage through twice more before his mind reformed around the words and squeezed out meaning, suddenly, as though he now saw the faces instead of the candlestick. Now with an even more startling sensation, revelation:

This passage was meant for me. Written seventy-seven years ago with me in mind, like seeing my own thoughts dragged out of a box that was sealed over half a century before I was born.

He slumped back into the leather sofa, mind racing. The book was face down beside him where he set it down, as if concealing the words would stifle their power, and allow him space to think. His hand moved more than once to pick it up again, but some formless, inexpressible fear stayed his hand again and again. The answers – *my* answers – are in there. Do I dare read any more?

Just as his hand finally touched the leather binding of the book, he heard the sound of a key turning in the door, and instead of turning the book face upwards to read, he instinctively snapped it shut and replaced it in the trunk. With the lid down, he felt able to stand up and greet the young woman who'd just entered the room, and who now stood looking at him curiously, a little suspiciously also, perhaps.

"Am I interrupting something?"

"Vicky, hi. No, not really, just some work ..." He was all too aware of how sheepish he sounded.

"Good. I was thinking for a moment you were regretting having given me a key. Just pop in when you're next available, you said, don't bother knocking ... remember?"

Oh, so now she had a key to his flat. He'd forgotten that their relationship had progressed to that stage; it had been so long since they'd seen each other. There was probably a lot more they had (mutually) forgotten.

"Well?" she said, taking off her jacket and shaking loose her reddish-blonde hair. "Don't I even qualify for a welcome back kiss?"

He crossed the room toward her, conscious that he was keeping himself as much as possible between her and the trunk, and she wrapped her arms around his neck, drawing him into a kiss that turned from simple welcoming into one that brought forth from them a deeper longing.

The progression from the living room to the bedroom was an easy one, hindered only slightly by the removal of clothing. The greater hindrance was a Robert's slow response when they reached the bed, initially puzzling Vicky, but spurring her to greater efforts, efforts which paid off more than adequately.

For himself, Robert was likewise puzzled by his initial 'reluctance', and it occupied his thoughts as they lay together afterwards, breathless, clammy and sated. He prided himself on still having the same reaction to such stimuli as he had when he was seventeen (if somewhat greater staying power), so his ego was feeling more than a little bruised at that moment. And yet ... it didn't *feel* like 'a case of the floppies'. There was no denying that Vicky was still, even after some time apart (or perhaps because of it) as good in bed as she'd ever been, and there was no denying his own hunger for her, which had surfaced almost the instant he'd touched her.

But something had distracted him. For a few moments, something had interposed itself between him and Vicky, a shadow that held him briefly back from fully associating into the experience that was unreeling around him.

He had thought Vicky was asleep, but she suddenly raised herself on to one elbow and looked at him with the same amused curiosity she had displayed when she had first seen him an hour or so before.

"So, do you want to tell me what's in that trunk in the living room that's so important you've got to hide it from me as soon as I walk through the door?"

"What makes you think I was trying to hide it?"

"I'm no idiot, Robert, and I'm not blind either. You looked positively furtive when I walked in." She lowered her eyes and said in a mock-conspiratorial tone, "It's not official secrets, is it? Never took you for the James Bond type. Or maybe it's a body, maybe you've done a Crippen and killed a wife I knew nothing about, just to get her out of the way. I think I should just go and look ..."

He grabbed her shoulder as she tried to get up and pulled her back to the bed. She plainly thought that Robert was fooling around, and Robert had no conscious intention of wanting to scare her, but the reaction on her face as she looked up into his was one of playfulness turning to fear. She saw something in his eyes that made her realise that this was no game.

"Christ, Robert ..." she breathed.

"I told you," he heard himself saying, "it's just work. Leave it be."

She was pushing herself up the bed, as far away from him as she could go. His hand was still on her shoulder, and his fingers were pressing painfully into her flesh. Consciousness of this made him release her, and lurch to his feet.

"I'm sorry," he said, avoiding her eyes, "I don't know ... I mean, it's ... oh, fuck ..."

Dimly, he heard her say something that may or may not have been conciliatory, but he wasn't listening. He pulled on his boxer shorts (having found them in the hall) and closed the bedroom door after him. Vicky didn't come after him.

He went to the kitchen, filled a glass with tap water and drank it down in one. Then he filled a second, and, leaning over the sink, poured it over his head, in a desperate attempt to jolt some kind of clarity into his brain. With water pouring down his body from his saturated hair, he turned and looked down the hallway at the trunk, sitting in the middle of the living room like a sleeping serpent. He shook his head like a dog to get rid of the excess water, and approached it once more, cautiously.

Who are you? he asked it. What is it that you're doing?

Settling himself as best he could before it, he opened the lid and reached in. The book which he extracted from its depths was almost identical to the one he had looked at earlier, and he let it fall open at random, letting his eyes come to rest on the first passage that suggested itself. It was this:

Never mind the outlines, the sketches of our biography, the delineation of our boundaries. Explore the fulness of the mystery of our flesh, occupy its volume and be complete, for there is mystery enough herein.

Robert grinned. Tough luck, chum, he thought, you've gotten me too deeply into this to let you off that lightly.

The question was, where next? To decode this material – this *Moleseyana*, as he had come to call it – he needed help. The extent of Molesey's esotericism was far greater than he had suspected, and, despite his success at deciphering the meaning of the earlier passage, he realised that he needed more specialised assistance if he was to complete the work within a reasonable time frame.

Well, where better to go than back to that shop? After all, that Helena did say I'd be in touch again.

He replaced the book, closed the lid, and sat there for a few moments until conscience forced him to his feet and back towards the bedroom. He wasn't too sure how he was going to explain himself to Vicky; he still had no idea how he was going to explain it to himself.

But that, he thought, as Vicky registered his return with a smile (nervous, but a smile nonetheless), can wait till tomorrow.

Helena paused with Sheelagh outside the door of Guiding Spirit as Ken waved goodnight and strode down the damp street, looking every inch the Atlantean High Priest (or something equally alien). Only then did Sheelagh say, "You sure you're all right, love?"

"Yeah. Just flashbacks from the other night. I think embarrassment can be fatal."

Sheelagh turned the key in the lock. "Oh yes. If I were you I'd get well PDQ or suffer *another* dose of the healing power of Flipper."

"God, Sheel, don't start me off again. I had a difficult enough time keeping a straight face earlier. I don't want to mock him, he means well." Helena began to walk, slowly. Sheelagh, she noticed, was keeping pace with her all the way. "I'll be all right, you carry on."

Sheelagh gave her an appraising look. "Right you are,

love." she said, sceptically. Then she stepped between two parked cars, waiting for a line of traffic to pass so that she could cross the road. "Goodnight."

"Night." Helena turned and walked on to the bus stop. Thank Goddess that's over. Worst day I've had since Adam dumped me in Los Angeles. Another day of seeing things, having the jitters, dropping cups, generally acting buggy. And I've got a reading tonight. Oh shit.

It began to rain mistily, and Helena speeded up her pace, arriving at the bus stop at the same time as the bus. Right. Seat by the window; lots of space to gaze into. Twenty-five minutes to sort myself out for whatsername, Joyce Williams. I've heard you're a bit good. The last Tarot reader I tried was rubbish, but my cousin's friend Natalie swears by you. Do you do Saturdays? Yes, Joyce, and at no extra charge (not yet anyway).

It'll be a short reading because I'm buggered and I haven't eaten since lunchtime, so when she's gone it'll be a quick toastie, a bath and an early night. With a bit of luck I'll have a night's sleep this time. No dreams. Please God and Goddess, no dreams. Swirling vortex, the colours of dried blood, hot earth and scorching, roaring sense surround on all six sides, buffeting and bending me until, worn out, I can no longer hold myself up and *it* appears, sweeping down out of a sand storm, pausing, rearing up, filling my vision, and suddenly striking from above and pouncing –

My stop. Where did the time go?

Helena staggered off the lurching bus and back into the rain.

The unmistakable smell of spaghetti bolognese greeted Helena as she opened the door. Hanging her coat up to dry, she went to the kitchen where Debbie was shaking out the spaghetti.

"Hi, Hel. Perfect timing, as always. I made enough for all of us. I want to be out of here sharpish and into town, and Jolie will want to eat quickly when she comes off shift. She's meeting us in Dale's for a few drinks before we hit the clubs. I was going to ask if you wanted to come, but ..." Debbie looked Helena up and down. "I guess you'll be having an early one, yeah?"

"Yeah." Helena took a long, deep breath, smiled. "God, that smells good. And there was me planning on toasties." She took the spaghetti from Debbie and tipped some onto each of the two plates on the table. Debbie followed up with ladlefuls of rich, wine-laden bolognese sauce (vegetarian, naturally) dolloped onto the centre of each plate.

"Too much wine," said Debbie. "Oops," they said in unison, and, sniggering, settled down to eat, Debbie helping herself to a large glass of cheap red, while Helena settled for a glass of water from a bottle in the fridge.

After a few moments' silent munching, Helena caught herself idly twirling her fork in her spaghetti, swirling the reddish-brown sauce, swirling, and looked up to see Debbie watching her. "I'm fine," she managed, taking a small forkful. "How was your shift?"

"Better than your day, I'd say. You want to talk about it?"

"You've been hearing it all week. Bloody picture's still freaking me out." Helena put her fork down and leaned back in her chair. "I had a blackout on the bus home. Barely made it back, I was so wound up. Sheelagh was clucking and fussing over me all day, and Ken –" she started to giggle, "Ken tried to do his Atlantean dolphin healing thing on me. I was freaked out enough without him whistling, clicking and chanting in Dolphin. I kept wanting to balance a ball on his nose." By now they were both laughing. "You know Ken?" Debbie nodded, shaking uncontrollably. "The sight of this lanky guy with a baggy green shirt and turquoise trousers waving a wand like a stick of rock – if laughter's the best therapy, then I'm cured." They laughed, the sound ringing through the cramped kitchen. Helena convulsed with hysteria until the bolognese sauce caught in her throat.

Abruptly, the laughter stopped.

"Deb, I'm really afraid that I'm having another breakdown."

Promptly at seven, the doorbell rang. Debbie made for the door. "I'll let her in," she said. "Now you remember, keep it short, bath and bed. And Jolie will be in by half ten, so don't worry."

The living room was lit only by two small table lamps, and at one end of the room Helena had spread a black silk cloth over a dining table, rarely used otherwise. The box containing her Tarot cards took pride of place in the centre of the cloth, and Helena sat at this table opposite an empty chair. By now, she had managed to compose herself for her client, and with eyes closed she listened to Debbie opening the door and greeting Joyce Williams, before saying goodbye (somewhat forced in its cheeriness, thought Helena), and sweeping out. A moment later Joyce Williams entered the room, dripping rain from her coat and umbrella. Helena barely noticed her client settling down, barely heard her preliminary pleasantries, until she looked up into the eyes of a middle-aged woman, plump with short hair and wearing what appeared to be a pink romper suit. Inwardly, Helena groaned. She took the cards out of the box, removing their purple silk wrapping, and began.

"Joyce, I like my clients to know that what appears in the cards is not the carved-in-stone future, but the greatest likelihood, and that knowing what might lie ahead is a great help to changing it or preparing for it." Joyce was nodding. Good. "You said on the phone, Joyce, that you want a general reading for your life as it seems to have ground to a halt –"

"D'you use the Celtic Cross spread?" Joyce butted in. "Only I like that one. That Tarot reader I saw before, he had a weird spread; I couldn't make head or tail of it, he wasn't making no sense –"

"I use a four elements spread for this sort of thing." And, where necessary, a gag. "We examine the energies at work in your situation using the four elements of Earth, Air, Fire and Water. We explore each of these with the three alchemical principles to get a complete picture of your situation." Joyce was about to say something, so Helena shuffled the pack rapidly and cut it. Shuffle and cut. She handed the pack to Joyce. "Please shuffle and cut the pack."

Joyce began to shuffle awkwardly. "I"m no good at this. My husband says I"m all thumbs."

"Not to worry, Joyce. Just concentrate on what you want to learn tonight."

"I'm busy concentrating on not dropping these cards everywhere. Tarot cards are too damn big, in my opinion. Why can't they make them like playing cards?"

"Some people do, Joyce. Just carry on thinking about what you want to get out of this." Because believe me, you're not the only one who wants to get out of this. I really am *not* in the mood.

Helena retrieved the cards and began to deal them face up, beginning in front of Joyce.

"Three to the East," she intoned, "for the Element of Air and the House of Swords.

"Three to the South, for the Element of Fire and the House of Wands. Three to the West, for the Element of Water and the House of Cups. Three to the North, for the Element of Earth and the House of Coins."

"Aren't you supposed to say a prayer to the Archangels first?"

Um. "Did that before you arrived." Helena resumed dealing. "One in the centre, for Spirit." She dealt this one face down, then held out the pack. "Cut the pack." Joyce did so. "This card," said Helena, "represents you at this time." She took a card.

The Devil.

"He's an ugly scrote, isn't he?" remarked Joyce. "Which Tarot deck are you using?"

"I'll show you later." Helena glanced down at the rest of the spread. Dismay grew in her heart and spread downwards. Even on general lines, this was the most malignant reading she'd ever seen. Most cards reversed to show their worst side, including three trumps. A preponderance of the suit of swords, heralding misfortune. The King of Cups at the volatile position in the South, suggesting the worst qualities in the worst possible place ...

"You all right, love?" asked Joyce.

"I'm ... just collecting impressions of this reading," said Helena. She turned over the Spirit card.

Death.

"Hope it's more cheerful than the one I'm getting," said Joyce.

Helena didn't answer. She was trying to unscramble the meanings screaming at her from the spread. They didn't make sense. This wasn't about grinding to a halt in mid-life. This was obsession, dark and ruthless, the clashing of Fire and Water that eventually explodes; this was hidden terror bubbling below the surface, only to erupt and destroy. This was that painting in Tarot form.

This was someone else's reading. Whose? Helena, shaking with tension, cast around for a likely subject. Someone who's seen the painting. Not me, surely. Someone else at the valuation. Who?

The art gallery guy, whatsisname, Robert. Robert.

Oh God.

The Devil leered up at her, crossed by Death.

Over years I sought the fullness of being, and found clues in the writing and art of ancient Egypt, classical Greece, Arabia, and the Celts.

I sought further, yet never left my drawing room. I filled my mind with primaeval images and words long left unspoken, save by scholars. And throughout this dry, attenuated study I found no mystery within.

Wherefore I went to those who dance the dance of Pan,

when the untamed flesh takes over,

when the skin gleams with sweat,

when the throat cracks parched from the roaring of wild words,

when time holds still while the mystery in our flesh bursts forth like champagne from the bottle, poured out in celebration of our divinity.

Robert shook his head. The intelligible parts of Molesey's journals were full of passages like that one. The rest was a mish-mash of sketches and symbols. He even thought he recognised a few. That one with the two circling apostrophes, that was Pisces, wasn't it?

He poured himself another glass of Sancerre. A Jan Garbarek cd was playing in the background, the saxophone drifting and wailing in harmony with the words in his mind. He toasted the machine, remembering Charlie's bafflement at his musical tastes. "If you think that stuff's weird, sunbeam, you should be reading this." He replaced the glass on his coffee table and picked up the list of contents of Molesey's mildew-scented trunk.

Twenty-three journals, covering the years 1908 to 1929, with a break from 1914 to 1915.

Hunting knife. Decorated with symbols and wrapped in silk.

Wooden wand a foot long. "

Silver goblet. "

Square chunk of slate six inches across. "

Sword with cross hilt and two-foot blade. "

Set of paintbrushes and knives, and a palette.

Box containing Tarot deck.

Two robes, one white, one black.

Nine books. Astrology, Hermeticism, occult texts.

Bag of tubes of oil paint.

Triangular mirror, blacked instead of silvered, a foot along each side.

Two inexpertly crafted medallions, one silver, one steel, painted (luminous?).

Five sketchpads, filled but undated.

Assorted loose papers.

Several tobacco tins containing incense.

Collection of coloured candles, all partly burned.

Quite a list. Start with something I know about. Robert fetched the paintbrushes. They were in poor condition, but each exhibited identical symbolic markings. Some of it looked like Hebrew. Right. Robert took some paper and a pencil from the coffee table and copied the markings on one of the brushes. Then he went back to the box and fished out the articles wrapped in silk, examining each one in turn and copying the markings. At the end he had discovered three things. Firstly, one symbol appeared on every item. Probably some occult name tag. Secondly, the marks on the brushes matched the marks on the wand. Thirdly, Robert didn't have a clue what any of the markings meant. Bollocks. And with nearly forty volumes of stuff to wade through, getting the Rosetta stone to this crap could take a while.

Means learning Hebrew for a start. And Greek, judging from some of the journal entries. And. And. And. He dropped the papers to the floor beside the chair and sighed. No way.

- But this was Molesey, the man whose passion and originality you admire so much.

- The art, yes, but this crap?

- Look at the paint brushes. Decorated with occult symbols. For him the art was one piece with the 'crap.' If you want to understand him, understand his occultism.

- Understand it? One look at it and my brain starts to bleed.

- Afraid of a little work?

- A little?

- You know his life. Didn't you see in his notes a passage about his early life? Where was it? Robert lunged out of his chair and fetched from the box the journal beginning 1921. This one, I think. He flipped through it, searching. Ah.

From my earliest days, I would dare anything.
I would leap any gap, climb any tree, fight any bully.
I would try any skill, break any rule, chase any prize.
I would risk any injury, court any disaster, dare any punishment.

As a boy, I was a rogue, an adventurer.
As a student, I was a Hell-fire rebel.
As a man, I became a soldier, and ah, came my undoing.
Death.

I used to court Death as an intriguing partner in this great game of living. But I grew appalled at His rudeness, blundering into the lives of myself and my comrades-in-arms. I saw Him toss them into the air and drop them broken and twisted. I heard Him tear their flesh and leave them gasping their breath away. In blood-soaked mud I myself wrestled Death as Jacob wrestled the angel, coming away, like Jacob, with a permanent reminder in my gait.

And I have become more cautious of my life. Wherefore I have determined I will not be importuned; I will not be broken in upon. I have wrestled Death on the fields of Mons; I hereby resolve to charm Him in the Temple of the Holy Spirit, which is my body, to enter the mystery of Death and safely pass therein. Amen.

In other words, he was a hell-raiser until his shrapnel wound showed him how mortal he was, and he didn't like it. Going for godhead. Daring, you've got to admit. And to judge from later reports of him, being 'cautious of his life' didn't stop him raising hell. The man had balls. He had ... he had something I want. I need.

He got up and started to wander the room, lost in thought. There was something about Molesey that reminded him of himself, as a boy. He'd been a daredevil too, back then; when you're thirteen years old, mortality is for other people. But like Molesey, that awareness of death – its *rudeness,* its *blundering* – came upon him all at once, and refused to leave.

He opened a drawer in the sideboard, pulled out a photograph of himself, aged about twelve or thirteen. His arm was draped around the shoulders of a younger boy, ten years old or thereabouts. Taken on holiday in Spain, beside an azure-blue swimming pool. Robert's smile was broad, toothy; that of the other boy, more reserved, as he squinted into the sun.

Matthew. His brother.

Matty had always gone along with big brother's games, even when they involved some danger. He hero-worshipped Bobby, would follow him anywhere. One summer's day, Bobby and his friends decided they were going to swim in a deep pool in an old quarry near to their house (very firmly signposted NO SWIMMING- DANGER), and of course, Matty had begged to come along.

He dived in to the pool like all the rest, from the high rocks around the pool. Unlike them, he failed to come up afterwards; his foot caught in the frame of a submerged bicycle, and he drowned.

His parents never said as much, but Robert knew that they blamed him. If there had been some way of making it up to them back then, a way of bringing Matty back, he would have used it. Even if it was only some way of letting them know that, wherever he was, he was all right ...

- Mr Molesey, you have something I *badly* need.

- Then get it.

- I don't know where to start.

- Would not knowing where to start have stopped Molesey? Would it have even slowed him down?

- No. He'd have gone balls-out to find a way.

- What did he do when he needed to find out about occultism?

Wherefore I went to those who dance the dance of Pan.

Find someone who does it already. That place. Guiding Spirit.

Her. The one who had the screaming fit.

Helena.

Only in the light of day, far from the claustrophobia and chaos of his previous visit, could Robert verify that Guiding Spirit was not, indeed, a large establishment. If it were not for the care that Sheelagh and her staff had put into creating a favourable atmosphere for the conduct of business – the smell of sandalwood on the air and New Age music emanating, almost subliminally, from hidden speakers – then it might even be described as pokey. As it was, with only one other customer in the place, Robert felt as if he was doing a very good Sore Thumb impersonation.

As if justifying his self-consciousness, the other customer – a young, shaven-headed man in a tight black t-shirt and baggy, khaki trousers whose multiple facial piercings made him jingle like a christmas tree in a draught when he turned his head, as he did now – looked at him curiously, before returning to his perusal of *The Satanic Bible.*

He couldn't see Helena around. Her colleague with the dreadlocks was at the cash desk, rummaging through a box of books and ticking off items on an invoice, so Robert made a quick recce behind some shelves before approaching him. He had to clear his throat rather ostentatiously to get the assistant's attention.

"Can I help you?"

"Yes, I was wondering if it's possible to see Helena for a moment? If she's not busy, that is?"

The assistant – his name badge displayed the name Ken – looked at him rather suspiciously, and Robert had the feeling that he'd been recognised from the valuation.

"Well, I'll check, but it's her lunch break, she might not even be here right now. Is it important? Is there anything I can help you with?"

They're protecting her. Whatever happened to her last week, it was enough of a trauma to get her friends rallied round, watching out for her.

"No, thanks, I'd rather see Helena, if you don't mind. It's, er ... personal business."

"Is she expecting you?"

Robert thought for a second before saying, "In a manner of speaking, yes."

Grudgingly, Ken retreated to the back of the shop, and Robert was left alone with the Ornamented Man, who had now turned slightly in his direction, as if to 'keep tabs' on him. He's either extremely nosey, thought Robert, or the worst store detective I've ever seen. He was holding the book up a little higher (trying to hide behind it?), and Robert could now see the photo on the back cover of a man who bore a striking resemblance to Ming the Merciless.

Occasionally, the young man's eyes would glance up at him over the top of the book, linger for a second, then resume reading. Robert continued to watch him as the glances became more frequent, and less furtive. The book was lowered slightly; there was the hint of a smile on the young man's face, and every so often his free hand would go up to some of the studs in his lip and toy with them coquettishly.

Ah. Now I get the picture.

He turned and made a great display of studying a large astrological poster on the wall behind him, but couldn't resist glancing back from time to time to see if the young man was still watching. Every time he turned, the man's eyes swung up to meet his.

Oh, Jesus. Why me?

He was on the verge of going up to his 'admirer' and telling him either to desist or get lost, when the sound of the shop doorbell came from behind him. He swung around, just in time to see the young man leaving the shop. As he did so, his admirer turned, grinned, and blew him a kiss.

"It's Robert, isn't it?" said a voice from behind him, and he turned to find himself looking into the eyes of Helena. She seemed more fragile looking than on their last meeting (perhaps understandably) and for an instant he thought that she was going to take fright and back away. He caught a glimpse of himself in a small mirrored 'dream-catcher' above the desk. He was blushing.

"Helena. Hi. Well, er ...you said I'd be back," he said, as flippantly as he could under the circumstances. "So here I am."

"I didn't think it'd be quite this soon. If at all. I mean, I have been known to be wrong about things."

He grinned reassuringly. Despite her fragility, he sensed that she had the sort of strength to claw her way back from situations that might have left others scarred in ways he didn't even like to think about. Moreover, it was a strength of which she seemed to be completely unaware ...

So how come *I'm* aware of it?

"Robert?"

"Hm? Sorry?"

"I was asking if this was a purely social call, or you wanted my help with something. Ken seemed to think that there was a specific reason you needed to speak to me. It's nice to feel wanted, but I'd like to know what for ..."

"Actually, yes, there is ..."

"It's those paintings, isn't it?" She said it with a shudder, eerily similar to the one Mrs Molesey had given when forced on to the subject of the pictures. He nodded.

"I was hoping there might be some other reason."

"Sorry," he said, and meant it. Although he knew that

he had to involve her in this, he felt more than a little guilty about it, and he felt a need to try and ameliorate it in some way. "Look, maybe this isn't the best place to be talking about it. How about a change of scenery? And a drink to make things a little more ... convivial? My shout."

"Well ... I suppose so. I'm still on my lunch break ..."

She turned to check with Ken who was re-stocking shelves a few feet away, but before she could say anything he said, "Don't worry. I'll cover for a while, we're never that busy in the afternoon this early in the week."

Another reason to discuss this off the premises, thought Robert; how much can we actually say with Swampy there leaning over our shoulders?

"OK," said Helena, reaching behind the desk for a thin woollen jacket. "So where are you taking me?"

"I was hoping you could suggest somewhere. I don't know this end of town very well ..."

She pursed her lips in thought for a moment before saying, "All right. I know the very place."

'The very place' was called The King's Head, but to Robert's eyes it was anything but regal. The lunchtime clientele seemed to consist mainly of people in the midst of drinking their Giros as quickly as possible, slumped over lager and brimming ashtrays, what little conversation they attempted having to find a way around the clamor of the jukebox. Not for the first time that day, Robert felt distinctly out of place, but was rather pleased to note that Helena felt no such alienation from her surroundings. Much of the fragility that he associated with her seemed to evaporate in contact with people, and she seemed to know a large number of the pub's patrons that day; many of them even managed a smile when she greeted them by name.

They were served their drinks by a barmaid (another friend of Helena's) who gave them a whole repertoire of knowing looks, without once inquiring as to the identity of Helena's new 'friend'; neither did Helena volunteer any such information.

"Is it just me," said Robert as they seated themselves in a booth as far away from the jukebox as possible, "or are you *deliberately* trying to make yourself the subject of gossip?"

Helena looked at him with barely disguised amusement. "Do you object?"

"Not really."

"Good." She leaned across the table toward him. "It's just that it's been so long since I was talked *about*, I thought I'd have a little fun."

"So glad to have been of help. Is this your local?"

"No, but I used to come in here quite a bit. The landlord's wife used to get me to come in now and again to do readings in the room upstairs for her and her friends."

"Right," said Robert. "What did her husband have to say about this?"

"Not a lot. Not until she ran off with a tall, dark handsome brewery rep, anyway. Well, I'd seen it coming ..." She sighed. "He blamed me for a couple of days, said I'd put it into her head. Thought I was going to get barred. Then he moved his girlfriend in, and everything was fine again. Men, eh?"

"Bastards, the lot of 'em. For someone who spends time in pubs, you don't strike me as a drinker, though." She was sipping at an orange juice, while Robert (conscious that he didn't want to make it too obvious that he was from 'uptown') had a pint of Guinness in front of him.

"I'm not, not really. Well, I occasionally have a few – sometimes a few too many – but I don't particularly like being drunk. I just like pubs because ..." She shrugged, a little embarrassment showing through. "Because they have people in them. I like people. And you see the best, and the worst, of them in a place like this."

As if to illustrate her point, a disagreement erupted at the bar between the landlord (a tattooed Colossus whose entire demeanour seemed to be the phrase DON'T FUCK WITH ME written in the flesh), and a grubby, obviously illiterate little man swathed in faded, ragged denim, who was blearily objecting to his imminent ejection from the premises. From what Robert and Helena could make out, the soon-to-be-ex-customer had made a less than gentlemanly remark to the barmaid, probably the same girlfriend Helena had told him about a few moments before. He had yet to apologise for his mistake, but compromised by leaving as soon as the landlord brought all six-foot-six of himself round the bar and informed him that he could either go home or to the hospital.

"It's certainly entertaining in here," said Robert.

"It's that all right. Anyway ..." Here she heaved rather a long and heartfelt sigh of resignation. "You said you wanted my help with those paintings?"

"Well, not specifically the paintings ..." He explained about the trunk's contents, and his inability to make sense of them. She listened carefully to him, eyes rarely wavering from his face as he described the notebooks and tried (without much accuracy) to quote some of Molesey's words from them. He went so far as to draw some of the symbols he had seen on a beer mat for her.

She sat and looked at the symbols for a few moments, until it became clear to Robert that she didn't have much idea what they meant either. When she looked up, however, it was as though he was looking at someone struggling to extract herself from a trance of some kind.

"Sorry," she said, shaking her head a little too vigorously, sending her wine-coloured hair whiplashing around her face. "I've never seen these before. They're not anything I've ever come across, not runes or pictograms of any kind that I'm aware of." She shrugged. "Wish I could help you, but ..."

"Maybe you still can," said Robert.

"Look, Robert ..." There was an air of tiredness, frustration, in her voice now, as well as something else which Robert didn't want to identify as fear. Don't have another freak-out on me, please, Helena. Your crusty friend would never forgive me.

"Like I said," she went on, "I don't know much about this sort of thing. It's not my field, and quite frankly, I'd rather not get involved in it."

Quickly, without even looking at him, she reached out and put her hand on his arm.

"And if you've got any sense, you wouldn't either."

She knows more than she's telling.

"Too late for that, I'm afraid. This stuff's too important

to let go now." He put his hand over hers. "But if you don't want to be involved, that's ok. All I need from you ..."

She looked up at him.

"You must know somebody who *does* know something about this subject, someone who can help me. Isn't there a name you can give me?"

After some consideration, she extracted her hand from his grip and dug down into her bag, emerging with a rather battered and overstuffed personal organiser. She spent a few moments in silence, poring over its contents, before scribbling something on the back of a slip of paper, and pushing it across the table to him.

"Talk to him," she said. "We've had him in the shop a couple of times, signing books. Sort of an authority on the Occult, apparently. Appears on telly and everything. Funny bloke," She was by now replacing her organiser in her bag and preparing to leave. "Last time he was there he came on to me. Gave me his number, address, e-mail, the works. That's about all he's going to be giving to me, thank you very much."

She got up, and for a moment Robert thought she was going to walk out without saying goodbye, but she stopped beside his chair.

"Robert, this Molesey stuff ... it isn't a good idea. I think you're headed for trouble. Don't ask me how I know that, I just do. And I'm concerned for you."

"Thank you," he said, rising.

"It's not like that." There was more of a brutal edge to that phrase than she probably would have liked, but pressed on. "I just don't like to stand around and watch people sit on railway lines waiting for the train to come along and hit them. But if there's no way I can persuade them to move, then all that's left for me to do is ... stop watching. Good luck, Robert. I'll be thinking of you, but you're on your own from now on."

She left the pub without looking back, leaving him feeling more than a little like a sailor who has just severed his last ties with land. He slumped back into his seat, and scooped up the note from the table, looking at the name with some curiosity, wondering if he'd ever seen it before. *MILES HEARNE.*

Nope, never heard of him. Waiting for the last notes of 'Another Brick in the Wall' to fade away, he pulled out his mobile phone and dialled the number beneath the name.

"... Hi, welcome back. If you've just joined us, our subject today is the paranormal, and we're asking, why the continuous fascination with the bizarre, the inexplicable, the *weird?* Just before the break we were discussing the recent resurgence in crop circle activity in the southwest of England, and all the usual suspects were mentioned as possible culprits – aliens, ball lightning, hoaxers – but at this stage I want to bring in someone that regular viewers of this programme will know well, our resident expert on the occult, our man in the know on the unknowable, Mr Miles Hearne."

Miles Hearne was rather gratified to see that some of the audience started applauding even before the floor manager lifted up his idiot board with the word APPLAUSE on it. He thought he recognised some of them from his previous appearance on this show. Great Mother of Fuck, he asked himself, surely I'm not developing a *following*?

Quick glance at the monitor; OK. Hair's looking pretty good, fly zipped up safely, no spinach on his chin. Pentacle medallion looked quite a nice touch from this angle, too, and there he was thinking that it might look a bit cheesy.

This is daytime TV, Miles, old love. Cheese sells, and the riper the better.

"Miles, welcome back to the show."

"Always a pleasure, Roger." Even more so when you bastards pay me.

"You were listening to our discussions earlier. What's your take on crop circles?"

"Well ..." Pause for effect. "Despite my field of expertise being *sorcery* rather than *saucers*, I'd like to deal with the extra-terrestrial angle first, if I may. Doesn't it strike you as odd that these highly advanced alien races, with the capacity to cross many thousands of light years in the blink of an eye in these remarkable crafts of theirs, haven't found any more effective method of communicating with us than bizarre acts of rural vandalism? Mind you, I could be mistaken, and there could very well be a colony of beings from Alpha Centauri or thereabouts currently resident in Wiltshire, infiltrating the local Young Farmers association, performing strange alien rituals in cornfields, under cover of darkness and cider, and laughing behind their three-fingered hands at what fools these Earthlings are. I'm prepared to be proven wrong."

That got them chuckling; the ones who weren't obviously Space Cadets, anyway.

"So, I take it that you see these circles as more likely the work of hoaxers, then, Miles?"

"I didn't say that, Roger. Looking at the complexity and, dare I say it, *beauty* of some of these circles, I'm quite willing to accept that there is a very serious intention behind their creation. I just happen to think that that intention is very definitely earthbound, that's all."

Audience hands shoot up at this, but Roger, ever the pro, wasn't prepared to pass on the microphone just yet. "Could you elaborate on that?"

"Look at what we're discussing here. *Circles.* Now, if you look at the history of mysticism, both East and West, the circle is a very important, very potent symbol. Jung went into some detail about it; he said it was a symbol of God manifest in the world, an ordering principle, *healing* even. This is a concept common both to Western alchemy, and to Eastern mysticism, where it appears as the *Mandala* of Buddhist art. What seems to me to be the function of these circles appears to have its roots in human, rather than alien, ritual. Eco-mystics trying to 'heal the Earth' by inscribing symbols of Order into the Earth itself, perhaps? Who knows?"

Someone stood up just in front of Roger, who (a little reluctantly) proffered the microphone. The guy – beard, check shirt – was recognised by Miles as one of the 'token skeptics' the researchers have scattered into the audience to provide a bit of 'balance'.

"One of the crop circles we saw recently was a giant smiley face. What possible 'ritual significance' could that have?"

Miles was glad at this point that he was wearing his purple-tinted half-moon specs. He looked at him over the top of them, smiling slightly, and said, "When did I say that these people, or whatever deity they worship, didn't have a sense of humour?"

Another man, down toward the front, had his hand up. Miles had already noticed him out of the corner of his eye, and he'd already piqued his suspicions. There was something about him – his fastidious *tidiness*, there in his neat blue shirt and sober tie, not a (thinning) hair out of place – that screamed *nutball* more clearly than all the howlings of Bedlam could accomplish. Roger descended toward him, microphone extended, and Miles prepared himself for trouble. He wasn't disappointed.

"I'd just like to ask you, Mr Hearne, if you would agree with me that these symbols are, in fact, evidence of something much more sinister than the mere pranksterism we've been discussing."

"Sinister?" He was pretty sure that he knew where this was going now, as it was obvious that this guy hadn't been taking in a single word anyone had been saying. Miles, however, was more than willing to give him as much rope as he needed ...

"Well, it's clear to *me*," (he emphasized the word to indicate that anyone to whom it isn't clear is probably deluded, or worse), "that these so-called crop circles are actually the calling card of Satanic cults who use these fields as sites for their unholy, evil rituals."

Ah-ha. Instincts right on the money again, Miles. Presenting the latest candidate for the Born-Again Fuckwit of the Month prize.

He looked at Roger, who was wearing an expression that was anything but surprised. On past form, it wouldn't be out of the realms of possibility for the producer, or some enterprising researcher, to have dug up one of their more *zealous* Fundamentalist Christian correspondents – the sort who signs his twice-weekly letters of complaint about the moral degradation on display on daytime TV with the words 'Yours In Christ' – and invited him on to spice things up a bit. They wouldn't have given Roger all the details, God forbid; the man may be a pro, but he couldn't play poker to save his life. They'd have warned him to expect something, though. Bastards.

Miles tilted his head back slightly, so his eyes were obscured by the glasses, and closed them for a moment. I know that I really should expect this shit, he told himself, given that I actually chose to follow this path; but for once, just *once,* I'd like to be able to have an intelligent discussion on the subject without the Witchfinder General or one of his lieutenants butting in with this sort of off-the-peg conspiracy theology.

"Well, I'm hardly an expert in Satanism ..." he said, and it's exactly the wrong thing to say at this moment.

"But you are an *Occultist*, aren't you?" Again, the emphasis here designed to equate the chosen word with others such as *Nazi* or *Paedophile*.

"Satanism, sir, is a Christian heresy. I am not, nor have I ever pretended to be, a Christian."

"That much is obvious. May I remind you that the Bible says on this matter..."

Miles was glad that he had some support in the audience at that point, because about then their protests became rather vociferous, and enabled him to disguise the fact that he had pretty much tuned out of the proceedings at the precise instant the guy had started throwing *The Good Book* at him. It's a myth that the Devil, or anyone else for that matter, can be in any way as good at quoting scripture in their cause as these people; their minds are permanently active search engines as regards that *Book*, never experiencing any downtime, always able to come up with the most apt aphorism in any circumstance. Want to know the Lord's position on masturbation, or the International Monetary Fund, or whether it's OK to eat scampi on a Wednesday? They'll tell you, with hardly a pause for breath, or thought. Experience had taught Miles that you just can't argue with these people, and he always listened to experience.

"The occult is a crime against God!" Bible-basher was saying when he chose to tune back into the discussion. "It's indicative of the moral decay in our society that we are sitting here today, discussing this matter, giving valuable airtime to the propagation of Satanic doctrines!"

Large proportions of the audience had given up, as

Miles already had, on trying to argue with the man, and were now content to let their feelings be known by means of laughter. Miles wasn't in a laughing mood, however. His irritation at being 'set up' like this boils through; if they want a show, they're going to fucking well get one.

"Can I just say something here?" he began.

It's at times like this that he was glad of the voice training he had done back in the days when he entertained notions of becoming an actor; the hubbub in the audience settled into attentiveness, and even born-again Fuckwit was silenced, at least temporarily:

"One of the most profoundly depressing aspects of 'the human condition', so called, is its tendency to draw boundaries around the experiences and beliefs of a particular grouping – political, religious, whatever – and define anything outside those boundaries as 'evil'. From the point of view of *primitive* tribal survival ethics," (I can do emphasis too, you see?) "it is, perhaps, understandable, but in modern terms it is an anachronism, and a pernicious one at that. If the spirit of true Evil exists anywhere, it is in the narrowing of human consciousness, the attempt to exclude from experience all those elements, whether ideas or the entire culture, as the source of those ideas, which challenge the prevailing consensus, in order to make 'the tribe' easier to govern. By this definition, one thing becomes apparent; for the past two thousand years, Christianity, in its various forms, has been responsible for more Evil than all the straw men of Satanism or Witchcraft it has managed to produce, right up into the twentieth century. Hitler is often referred to as a 'Satanic' figure, but in truth, he could not have done what he and his cronies did to the Jews of Europe without the precedent of centuries of Christian persecution ..."

"I deeply resent your implication, sir ..." said Fuckwit, huffily.

"Resent all you like, *sir,* but I'm afraid I've had about as much of your malignant imbecility as I'm prepared to stomach. Now why don't you be a good boy and run along, eh? Jesus wants you for a sunbeam, I'm reliably informed."

Body language puts the capper on the insult; Miles turned his face away from him (while his 'opponent' blustered something about the 'infinite forgiveness of Christ'), and crossed his legs pointedly against him. Some of the audience started applauding again, and he couldn't make himself heard. Out of the corner of his eye, Miles could see Roger with his hand pressed to his earpiece, receiving instructions from the producer.

"Er, right ... well, I think at this point we should go to the phone lines, as we have a lot of people waiting to join the discussion, er ..."

That's all I need, thought Miles. A limited audience discussion is one thing, I've done enough of them to be able to cope (most of the time, anyway), but I hate 'phone-ins'. It constantly amazes me that the sort of people who ring these programmes are even allowed near a telephone without supervision; I mean, surely they could hurt themselves ...

"And first up, I believe we have Robert on the line. Robert, are you there?"

"Yes, I'm here, Roger." This guy didn't *sound* to Miles like the usual phone-in material, quite well spoken actually. Still, there's no telling.

"So what's your question for Miles Hearne?"

"Well, actually, I've already tried e-mailing Mr Hearne about this matter, but so far I've received no reply ..."

Hang on; this is starting to ring some bells ...

"I just wanted to ask if you're familiar, Mr Hearne, with the works of an artist of the early part of this century called Nicholas Molesey?"

Ah, right. It's *this* guy. He'd been bombarding Miles with mails for the best part of a fortnight about this Molesey character, about whom he knew absolutely nothing at all.

"Yes, hello, Robert." He was putting as much patience into his voice as he could possibly muster, but this is an ideal opportunity for him to finally fob this fellow off once and for all. "Thanks for mailing me, I'm sorry I haven't had time to reply. I think the Devil has been finding even more work for my idle hands than usual."

Fuckwit gave a very audible snort of disgust at this remark.

"No, I haven't heard of him, and to be honest, I'm

probably not the best person to be asking about this. Art history, particularly that of the 20th century, just isn't my forte at all, I'm ashamed to say."

"Well, that's just it, 20th century art *is* my forte, and I've come into possession of some materials which I really don't understand at all. I think that you might be able to help me interpreting it, as it seems to lean rather too heavily towards the esoteric for me ..."

"What I would suggest you do, Robert," said Miles, heavily, "is post some of this stuff on some of the newsgroups on the net, and see if anyone can come up with anything. I think you might be pleasantly surprised." And you'll be out of my hair, too. Like I've really got the time to be helping some art student complete his thesis on an artist I've never even heard of, just because he happened to name-drop Crowley, or something.

"I might just do that at some stage, Mr Hearne ..."

Oh good. Next caller.

"... But if you don't mind, I might just send a sample on to you beforehand, see what you think. Would that be OK?"

Roger's obviously feeling left out; before Miles can respond firmly in the negative, he butts in and says "I'm sure Miles would be only too pleased to help. Isn't that right, Miles?"

Fuck. "Of course. Send it on to me, Robert, I'll look it over." He wonders if the entire viewing public can hear him grinding his teeth.

"Thank you, Mr Hearne."

"Thank *you.*" A bunch.

"Right," Roger continues smoothly, brightly. "We've got Sandra on line two. Hello, Sandra?"

"Hello? Hello?" The accent screeching out of the studio speakers was Liverpudlian, pitched high enough to alarm dogs. "I was just wanting to ask, like, about this Uri Geller bloke ..."

At that moment, Miles Hearne really, *really* needed a drink.

Pierce had often driven through this area, but until now he'd paid little attention to it. Now, he was somewhat astonished that such environs could be the neighbourhood of something so unorthodox as a magician. This was one of the more 'respectable' areas in the central part of the city, but one which had resisted much of the 'yuppification' which had overtaken so many other sections during the Eighties. There was still a hardcore of 'old' families living here, locals who had been here since before the war, and showed no sign of moving away. True, many of them had to supplement their income by taking in lodgers (mainly students) due to the rising cost of living in the area, but there was still an unwillingness here to give up on the past, a past which had made them what they were.

Phrased like that, mused Pierce, perhaps it isn't such an unusual place for a magician to live.

He inched the car through the narrow, terraced streets, craning his neck every now and then to study a sign or contemplate a parking space. He had located Hearne's address ten minutes ago, but it was in a street set aside as 'Residents Only' parking. Any space which he found would be so far from his destination as to defeat the object of bringing the car in the first place.

At last, he found a parking space, fed coins into the meter, and set out, briefcase in hand, back towards Hearne's address. The weather was on the cusp between stifling heat and imminent thunderstorms, and by the time he ascended the steps to Hearne's front door he was sweating copiously. Peculiarly, he also had that uncomfortable apprehension dragging at his bowels again. He tried to locate the source of his anxiety, without success.

Come on, man, he told himself as he pressed the doorbell; what the hell is there to get nervous about?

As if in answer (he wondered if the door should have creaked, to add to the effect), the door swung aside and a face familiar to Pierce – though until now only in two dimensions – peered out. The trademark purple spectacles were absent, he was barefoot, and he was clad in shorts and a baggy white t-shirt adorned with what looked like Japanese calligraphy, but this was unmistakeably Miles Hearne.

"Robert Pierce, is it?" A brief, firm handshake. "Do come in. Please excuse the attire, but I only got out of bed less than half-an-hour ago."

It was, by then, nearly one p.m.

Robert was led through a hallway hung with some of the most remarkable and disturbingly aggressive examples of African tribal masks that he had ever seen. It was by no means impossible that their placing was designed to discourage unwanted visitors, a kind of anti-'welcome mat'. The living room that he subsequently entered was a whole different matter, however; here too, there was 'ethnic' art, mainly sculpture, either African or Oriental, but it was chosen and arranged to reflect a feeling of serenity, hospitality. To get this far, it seemed, you were most definitely a welcome guest of Miles Hearne. To complete the effect, there were bookcases stuffed with hardback books, many of them obviously first editions (with a most conspicuous absence of esoteric texts; there must be a more complete library elsewhere in the house). There was also Opera – Puccini, if Robert's limited familiarity with the subject was anything to go by – wafting gently from the speakers of a large, expensive hi-fi system in the corner.

A few minutes later, they were sprawled opposite each other on extravagantly comfortable couches that reminded Robert of something from a Sultan's palace (except for the cigarette burns on the arms), nursing Scotches, as Hearne dived straight to the point of Pierce's visit. No prevarication, no idle chitchat; he produced a print-out of the e-mail Pierce had sent to him after the TV show.

"This," he said with face aglow, "is remarkable. Quite remarkable."

"I know," said Robert. "But does it make any sense to you?"

"Isolated from the rest of the material, not very much. There's enough here to hint at the work of a singular mind, though. Did you bring any more for me to look at?"

Robert reached into his case and produced one of the notebooks. "Just this one. It's the one from which the piece I sent to you was extracted, I thought you might like to look at it in context before you choose whether or not to go any further."

Hearne smiled. "Mr Pierce ... do you mind if I call you Robert? I loathe formality ... I think I've already made my mind up on that score."

"Glad to hear it ... Miles."

Carefully at first, but with increasing fervour, Hearne began to flick through the yellowing pages, stopping here and there to read and re-read certain passages. His lips moved as he did so, but Pierce couldn't tell if he was reciting passages to himself or simply providing some sort of *sotto voce* commentary. Every so often he would laugh, apparently in delight rather than disdain, and at last he took to his feet and began pacing the room, book in hand.

After a period of time in which Robert began to wonder if Hearne had forgotten about his presence, he cleared his throat. "What do you...?"

Without looking at him, Hearne raised a hand for silence, then began to read aloud:

We begin with ourselves,
each of us infinite,
without boundaries,
co-extensive with all that is not ourselves;
Infinity;
as below, so above.

We stand at the axis mundi, the fulcrum of Infinity,

(Here Hearne paused, a pained look crossing his face)

from whence we move the world according to our will,
for in Infinity the centre is everywhere and it is Here, Now.

Therefore let us not heed outline, but area;
not surface, but volume;
not there, but Here;
not then, but Now.
Ecce carnem, ecce templum Spiritui Sancti.

Until this moment, Molesey's words had been, to Robert, merely *words*. A puzzle on paper, fascinating for their very obtuseness. But now, spoken in Hearne's beautifully modulated tones (and spoken by someone who seemed to have more idea of the possible meanings behind them than Robert could, as yet, conceive), they acquired life. More, they acquired *power.*

"Do you hear that?" In his enthusiasm, Robert thought he could detect a slip from Received Pronunciation, and an accent – Northern, by the sound of it – peek through. "Do you have any idea what he's *saying* here?"

"That's what I'm here for. Sometimes I feel as if I'm on the verge of understanding, but then ..." He shrugged, helplessly. "Then it just slips away."

Hearne sat opposite him again, and took a gulp of Scotch. He looked down at the book in his hand (looking for guidance from it already?), and seemed to consider for a while before speaking.

"Robert, if Molesey's work is as important as I think it is, on a purely *esoteric* level, then I think we should be working quite closely on this."

Robert narrowed his eyes suspiciously. "Closely? What do you mean?"

"If I'm right, then Molesey can never be understood from the point of view of his art alone. This isn't some sort of bizarre sideline that he got into which took him away from his art; it's central to his world-view. If you want to understand his art, to understand the *man*, then the answers are in here."

"I know."

"I don't think you do. Or at least, you don't appreciate it fully as yet. Fuck knows, I certainly don't, and won't until I've had time to look through the entirety of the notes. You've been looking at Molesey from the perspective of an art critic, but there's more to this man than what you see on gallery walls. I can help you fill in the gaps, sure, but I'll have to work more intensely with you on this, and that means filling in the gaps in your own education."

"Are you talking about writing some sort of study of Molesey? Co-authoring it?"

"Aren't *you*?" There was a note of frustration in Hearne's voice. "Does your ambition only stretch as far as getting Molesey's paintings displayed in that gallery of yours?

Come on, man, think about it. Even if it's a success, Molesey will disappear back into obscurity as soon as the exhibition closes its doors for the last time. There's a whole segment of the public who will take to Molesey on levels far deeper than the merely aesthetic, and I can help you tap into that audience."

For one who aspires 'to walk with the Gods' (as the hyperbolic blurb of one of his books put it), Robert mused, there was more than a little of the huckster about Hearne. It made him wonder whether there was anything beyond the showman, the talk show mainstay. He can talk exceeding well, but (big question) how good is he at actually *walking* the talk?

Probably irrelevant. The simple fact of Hearne's superior knowledge of the subject, and Robert's lack of any alternative avenues of enquiry, was enough to swing the vote in Hearne's favour. And anyway, is wanting something more out of this than an acknowledgement in an exhibition catalogue such a crime?

"OK. So where do we begin?"

"Well, we can start by going back to your place and letting me have a look at the rest of that trunk's contents." He grinned broadly. "Do you have a spare bed, or a couch or something I can sleep on? This might take some time."

"Er ... yeah, sure."

"Good." He got up, and plucked a full bottle of Scotch from the drinks cabinet. "In that case, you can provide the food, and I'll bring along the rest of the necessary sustenance. If you'll excuse me a moment, I think I should get dressed now ..."

With that, Hearne swept out of the room, leaving his bemused soon-to-be-host staring at his receding form like a rabbit looking unblinkingly into the headlights of the car that is about to crush it into the tarmac.

This is incredible. Unbelievable. Unheard of.

How could this Molesey have stayed so forgotten for so long? Not even Miles had any idea of his existence. And yet ... something about him seemed natural, logical, as if he was some sort of missing piece in a puzzle that he had been trying to assemble all his life. Or the first notes of a piece of music that you've never heard before but which instantly takes hold of your soul and won't let go.

Dammit, Miles chuckled to himself, I'm so excited I can't even put on matching socks.

He couldn't let Robert know how excited he was, though; not just yet. He didn't strike Miles as the sort of person who'd break an agreement, but how can you tell? This was the first time he'd met him in the flesh.

I *need* this, he told himself. All these years of farting around with pissy hackwork, being winched out every time some arsehole TV producer needs someone to give a couple of soundbites on the latest hot paranormal topic and they can't get Uri fucking Geller ...

... all these years of waste ...

But now, this. Something that even now, on the basis of one book of scribbles, he could see to be the most momentous thing to have happened in this field since ... what? Crowley? Spare?

No, more than that. Since John Dee, maybe. There were the vague outlines of a whole new system of Magic visible here, something more revolutionary than Miles could ever have dreamed. Someone needed to dig deeper, unearth the whole structure, perhaps discover portions of it that Molesey himself wasn't aware of. And that someone was going to be Miles Hearne.

Oh, and Robert, of course. That was another little bonus of this; with Molesey himself no longer around (oh, how he'd love to have met him, talked with him), it was going to be down to him to transmit the word to the world, and he couldn't do that alone. Robert was smart, enthusiastic, and best of all, completely innocent of any connections with the Magical 'scene'. What he imprinted him with here, now, would be the basis of what could be a whole new school of Magical thought, started by Molesey, and transmitted through little old Guru-Miles.

It wouldn't have been too much of a leap for Miles to start comparing myself to St Paul at this stage, but that might be going a little too far. He had a feeling that the blindness hasn't completely passed. Just wait till his eyes are *really* open.

Scorpion

Now, Miles wondered: where did I put my toothbrush?

It wasn't as if she was turning up uninvited; for God's sake, he'd given her a bloody *key* ...

If she was making a habit of it, just popping up at inconvenient moments and helping herself to the contents of his fridge or something, well, then, perhaps, he might have some reason for behaving towards her in the way he had. But Victoria was no fool; key or no key, she knew that their relationship was still at a fairly tentative stage, the stage where they were still pretty much discovering each other's limitations before seeing how far they could afford to go beyond them. It made sense from her point of view not to force the pace too much just yet.

And despite some odd (no, be honest, downright scary) behaviour on Robert's part, she was still pretty optimistic. Or had been, until tonight.

She'd been in town for the day, her game plan for the attainment of the partnership she sought entailing a certain amount of 'schmooze-time' with the existing clientele, getting her face known. Today, this meant that she had been obliged to attend an awards lunch at one of the city's more prestigious hotels, held to honour some of the leading lights in the nation's purveyors of frozen food. One of the firm's longest standing clients was a company founded in the 1950s by a man still affectionately known in the trade as 'The Fish Finger King'. This man was still held up to the public as the epitome of rugged (yet benign), independent entrepreneurship, the acceptable face of capitalism. All this despite the fact that he had sold out his controlling stake in the company in the mid-1980s to a US-based megacorporation (famous for its shoddy environmental record and use of cheap Far-Eastern labour), and quietly buggered off to a private island in the Bahamas.

So there she was, surrounded by quite possibly the dullest selection of people to be found on God's Earth since Sodom and Gomorrah's neighbours got the message. They all seemed really, really interested in the projected sales revenue for the frozen ready-meals market in the upcoming fiscal year, and were trying very hard to bring Victoria to their level of enthusiasm.

If one of them had put a hand up her skirt, she might have been thankful of the diversion. But no, this was an afternoon of corporate backslapping, cheerleading, and feel-good whooping, and there was a point at which Victoria had to remind herself that this was not, in fact, a meeting of Scientologists, or somesuch.

Behoven as she was to see the whole thing through to its grisly conclusion, she endured, thanks to a judicious supply of Martinis (on the expense account, naturally) and a fixed smile that she was afraid she wouldn't be able to unfix. 'If the wind changes,' she could hear her mother's voice say as Victoria looked upon her own ghastly reflection in the mirror in the ladies, 'you'll stay like that ...'

Then, at seven p.m. she tottered sourly into a taxi outside the hotel, too exhausted to even contemplate going all the way back to her own home. Robert's place was so much nearer, and the welcome so much more pleasant. In theory.

The last time she had used the key, she'd found Robert intent upon the study of a trunkful of mouldy old papers – 'work', he called it – and she wasn't entirely surprised, based on his behaviour that night, to find him once again absorbed in them, whatever they were.

She *was* surprised, however, to find that he wasn't alone. His companion, who rose synchronously with Robert as she entered the room, was a tallish man in (she estimated) in his late forties, with straggly, greying hair and an obvious penchant for dark clothing that immediately set alarm bells ringing in Victoria's brain. She felt his eyes upon her as she crossed the room to Robert, who greeted her with more enthusiasm, and less furtiveness, than on her previous visit.

"Victoria, I'd like you to meet Miles Hearne," he said, once they had broken off their kiss. "He's working with me on this project. Miles, this is Victoria Marchant."

She knew that he was going to kiss her hand as soon as he took it. He gave off that sort of 'vibe', that of the creepy guy with a predilection for olde-worlde courtesy, the sort you wouldn't allow near your grandmother.

"Victoria," he said, with oily relish. "I wish I could say that Robert's told me a lot about you, but I'm afraid he's been discourteous enough not even to mention your existence. Shame on you, Robert."

I'm rather glad he didn't, she thought, as the fixed smile returned by default to her face. The thought of Robert talking about me to this person behind my back ... Jesus.

"It's ... er ... nice to meet you, Mr Hearne. It seems he's kept me just as much in the dark about you. I don't even know what it is that you're working on together."

Hearne opened his mouth to make some sort of reply, but Robert butted in. "It's all a bit complex. As soon as we *can* explain it, we will. Drink?"

"Please."

He fixed her a G&T, then discovered there was no ice in the bucket on the drinks tray. He went off to the kitchen, leaving Victoria and Hearne together on the sofa, alone, with what Victoria suspected might be a rather short supply of small talk.

"So what do you do, Victoria?"

"I'm in Public Relations."

"Interesting. So am I, in a manner of speaking, although I only have the one client."

"Really? Who might that be?"

He leaned in close, uncomfortably close. She could smell the whisky on his breath.

"You might say, Victoria, that I am an Agent of Chaos. In the nicest possible way, of course."

"I'm not sure I follow you."

"We can change that. I could tell you all about it over dinner sometime, perhaps?"

Surprise, surprise, his hand was on her knee. Christ, but he's fast, I'll give him that.

"Look, Mr Hearne ..."

"Please, it's Miles."

"I'm really, ah, flattered by the offer, but you're, well, you're ..."

His eyebrows ascended across the gulf of his forehead as he waited for her to complete the sentence, although the pressure on her knee remained constant.

"... You're a bit *old* for me, I'm afraid."

That did the trick. He released her knee as if stung. When he spoke again, his voice seemed to have acquired the definite hint of a Yorkshire accent.

"Please yourself, love."

With consummate timing, Robert returned at that moment with the refilled ice bucket, and Vicky rose to meet him.

"Robert ..." she hissed at him.

"I know what you're going to say," he whispered back at her. "Miles is staying for a couple of days to help out with the ... project. After that, he'll be gone, and we can spend all the time alone together that you want."

"Days? He's here for *days*?"

"Well, we didn't have anything definite planned, did we?"

"That's not the point ..."

"So what *is* the point?"

Hearne was sitting on the sofa, impassive, apparently oblivious to them, and yet she had the distinct impression that he was hearing every word, and revelling in her discomfiture. Despite all this, she couldn't bring herself to tell Robert about Hearne's 'move' on her just yet; he had set up quite enough barriers between her and Robert in the few minutes since she'd first encountered him, and she therefore had no intention of allowing Hearne the pleasure of seeing her collaborate with him in the endeavour.

"We haven't seen enough of one another lately," she improvised. "I came over here tonight thinking that, well ... it could be like the other night?"

His look told her that he knew which night she meant. He glanced between her and Hearne for a few moments, considering, then said "How about a couple of hours alone? I can't just tell him to push off home after inviting him over here, but I can ..."

"Whatever you can manage." She trailed her fingers across his chest.

He leapt over the back of the sofa to sit beside Hearne, and they spent a few moments in intense consultation (or should that be negotiation?) with Hearne casting the odd lascivious look over his shoulder at her. Eventually, he laughed, got up, and after a quick leer in her direction and a mock-courtly bow, exited the flat.

"He'll be back in a couple of hours," said Robert.

"What did you do? Give him some extra pocket money to go to the pictures for the evening?"

"Something like that."

She started pulling at the buttons of his shirt. "Well, in that case, I hope you gave him enough to see a double feature. With enough left over for sweeties afterwards."

He caught her face in his hands as she moved in to kiss him.

"Do you trust me?"

"Of course. Why ..."

His finger was on her lips. "I want to show you something of the work I've been doing."

She glared at him. "I thought we had other things to do with our time."

He smiled at this. "Don't worry. They're not as unconnected as you might think ..."

Intensity. That was the word. Although Robert had been far from an inadequate lover, he had seemed less *absorbed* in the act in the past; now every touch seemed to Vicky to be charged (at least for him) with meaning, significance. When he undressed her, it had the air of ritual about it, as if he was in the act of revealing something holy not just to himself, but to *her*. He gently, smilingly, rebuffed her attempts to undress him in return, instead urging her (with a minimum of words) to concentrate on the sensations in her own body. This extended to encouraging her to caress herself as his hands wandered from her breasts and pubis to explore other, less obviously erogenous areas: her neck, her hair, the backs of her legs.

He lay her on the bed, still urging her to continue touching herself, as he at last undressed. By now, she was herself absorbed in the act, but as her hands strayed between her legs to try and bring herself to climax, he would move her fingers to another part of her body. Strangely, the pleasure didn't diminish as he did so; it seemed as if he had succeeded in expanding her awareness of her body's capacity for pleasure beyond the realm of mere genital stimulation.

She wasn't ignorant of the body's potential for this sort of altered erotic consciousness; she'd seen articles on it, or similar, in *Cosmo* and other places. But she'd never thought that she would ever actually experience it.

Not that she was detached from herself enough in that moment to think all of this, of course. She was far too busy. So busy, in fact, that she almost didn't notice that Robert was now also naked and lying beside her, his hands upon her.

His mouth was close to her ear. "You've found your body now. All of it. Every sense, every nerve ending, is tingling now, isn't it? No, don't speak. Focus on your body, on the *wholeness*, on the *holiness* of it."

Every part of her body, it was true, seemed flooded with sensation, as if it had all woken up simultaneously and was, for the first time, operating as a single organism instead of isolated patches of consciousness. The only boundary was her skin.

And now, even that was dissolving. Robert had taken her hand and pressed it to his chest, and it was as if he had plunged her straight into his own flesh. She could feel the pulse of his life and hers beginning to merge, synchronise, until it became difficult to tell where *Victoria* ended and where *Robert* began.

So it was that, when Robert eventually penetrated her, lifting her from the bed to lower her gently on to himself, it felt more like the final completion of a circuit; they were now one creature, moving together, breathing together, blended into something greater than the sum total of their simple, mortal flesh.

How long they remained like that, she could not tell, either at the time or afterwards. Their movements slowed, until she felt they might be turning to stone; she would make occasional, almost automatic, attempts to move herself on him and maximise the pleasure, but he would immediately grip her more firmly.

"Don't move your body," she thought she heard him say. "Move your *attention*. Just as it encompasses me now, let it move outwards, around the room, beyond the room, and then ... further still ..."

There was a final moment of purely physical pleasure, as she felt herself tighten around him, somehow discovering the use of muscles that she never knew existed; and then she was one step above that, experiencing his pleasure as well as her own, and upwards again, to feel the joy radiating into the room around them ...

No, the joy that *was* the room around them. And the world around the room. And then ...

There was no difference between the Universe and them, no separation. She heard a word, whispered by the Universe, that sounded like the explosion of galaxies and the touch of a feather combined.

"Ex stasis ..."

No. Something was wrong. The word had severed the connection, had allowed her to find herself again in the void, and she collapsed back into ego like a snake falling back into its basket after the charmer's music ceases. With the fall came confusion, and when she found herself looking into eyes that she thought she knew, but which seemed at that moment impossibly strange, the confusion became full blown terror.

With a cry, she pushed herself up and off him, looking down in revulsion as he slumped backwards, a pained look on his (once more familiar) features, and ejaculated.

"Fucking hell, you bastard!" She wanted to hit him, or hit something, at any rate. "What did you do? What did you do to *me*? Did you drug me? Is that it? I can't believe ..."

She stopped in mid-sentence, realising that she didn't know what she didn't believe.

"This is the second time now, Robert ... it's just getting too fucking freaky for me ..."

Dressing as she spoke, she looked down at him again, sitting there on the bed with a perplexed look on his face and a damp leg, torn between fresh revulsion and pity.

"I can't stay. I'm scared. I don't want any more part of this."

As she left the bedroom, she heard him say her name, almost plaintively, but she didn't stop until she reached the front door, where she found her progress arrested by Hearne, swaying noticeably, and trying to find the door-bell. Obviously, the doorman knew Hearne every bit as well by now as he knew her, and was willing to just wave him past.

Perhaps *Hearne* taught Robert to do that ... that whatever-it-was back there.

She sincerely wished them, as she brushed past Hearne, every happiness together. And dimly, as she stomped on unbuckled shoes towards the lift, she heard a rather slurred Yorkshire accent call after her:

"So, I s'pose a fuck's out of the question, then?"

"Just saw your girlfriend," said Hearne, as he parked himself on the sofa opposite a half-dressed, and singularly concerned looking, Robert Pierce.

"Ex," said Robert.

"What?"

"*Ex*-girlfriend. Very definitely."

Hearne reached behind him and found the whisky, and two glasses, almost without looking. For a moment, Pierce wondered at Hearne's innate freeloader sense for being able to find booze in someone else's house with little or no familiarity with the surroundings. But then, he's a magician, isn't he? Silly of me to forget.

"I take it that the evening didn't turn into an unqualified success."

Robert accepted the offered glass, and swirled it for a few moments before taking a gulp. "You could say that."

Hearne sat back, heaving the long, weary sigh of the professional drinker at the end of an evening when he is confronted with someone else's personal problems. "So what happened?"

"I tried Molesey out."

Hearne spluttered on his scotch. "You did *what*?"

"I tried some Molesey tantra out on her. Just as he says to do it in the book. Just as you said I should."

"Yes, but not *yet,* you gormless twerp! I said wait until you find the right person! And I could tell right off, pal, that she's not the right person. Not for you, and certainly not for this. Besides, I think she might be a lesbian, anyway."

Robert decided there would probably be a better moment than this to ask Hearne what he meant by that.

"Great Goddess, no wonder she bolted. When this sort of thing goes tits-up, all you end up with is a woman who looks at you as if you've just turned up in the bedroom wearing a diving suit. Believe me, I know. With this sort of thing, you have to have somebody who's prepared for it, someone who's willing to go along with you on the journey. As it is, you're now left with a girlfriend – sorry, *ex*-girlfriend – who had no idea what you were doing, consequently got nothing out of it, and probably now thinks that you're one stage away from doing it with livestock."

"She *did* get something out of it."

Hearne sat forward, studying him intently. Robert could almost feel him shedding the alcohol haze, his attention and focus springing to the fore like a jack-in-the-box. "Explain."

"She was there, Miles. She was right with me, all the way, feeling everything I felt, seeing everything I saw. *That's* what freaked her. Not me."

"It can't be ..." He stood up and took to pacing, every so often stopping to turn and look back at Robert and say something like "But that's not how it should work," or "It's supposed to take *years* before ..." Then the silence would reassert itself, a silence that Robert perceived as becoming more and more moody and maudlin.

"It's no good talking about it now," he said, as Hearne flung himself back on to the sofa in a funk. "We'll discuss it in the morning."

"The morning," growled Hearne. "Yeah, fine, the morning." He won't even look at me, thought Robert. As though he's ... jealous?

He didn't feel like pressing the matter. As he turned to go back to the bedroom, a glint of metal on the coffee table caught his eye. He stooped, and picked up the spare key to his flat that he had given to Vicky.

"Here," he said, tossing it to Hearne. "You'll probably need this. We'll have plenty of work to do in the next few weeks, and I don't want it held up because I'm out of town and you're locked out. Try not to lose it. Goodnight."

Strangely enough, Robert slept rather well that night.

Robert dedicated the next weeks to Miles Hearne's notebook. It truly was the Rosetta Stone he'd needed to translate Molesey's symbols and jargon. The Tree of Life of the Kabbalah and tables of correspondences, the four elements, primers of astrology and Tarot, exercises in vizualization and meditation. Robert read these last, but as he told Miles Hearne, he preferred Molesey's own exercises.

By day Robert felt himself marking time in the gallery, fleeing to a cafe to read his precious notebooks during his lunch hours. His evenings he spent researching and, at Miles' insistence, practising a full ceremonial banishing ritual.

"The Banishing Ritual clears the air," said Miles. "Use it before you start anything magical as a way of clearing the decks and focussing on the business in hand. Use it again afterwards to get back to normal life. Auntie Alice," (this was one of Miles' pet names for Aleister Crowley) "used to say 'Banish often, invoke often.' And if you're going to be invoking Mars the god of war, you want to make sure he's not still marching about in your head afterwards. Causes trouble in the pub, that does. Banish, and make it a good one."

Robert was aware that he was causing comment. Charlie had already buttonholed him as he was on his way out of the gallery one lunchtime. "Fancy lunch, Bobby?"

Shit. "I'd love to, but I've got to be off."

"Where do you get to these days? I hardly see you anymore." Pained look.

"Doing some research. Not a sociable activity, I'm afraid."

"Ooh! Anything juicy?"

"I'll – er, I'll show you some time." Strained pause. "I'll see you later." Out!

From behind him, he heard a muttered, "That'll be worth waiting for."

Miles was turning into something of a nuisance, hinting frequently that Robert ought to slow down. "Take a break, for fuck's sake. Have the night off from Molesey, see a movie, get pissed, get laid. Banish with Hollywood."

"According to your notebook, the daily practice of the basic rituals is practically a holy discipline. That's what you did, isn't it?"

"Well, that was a long time ago," Miles replied.

Robert sensed something. "Miles, do you still do these rituals and stuff?" Miles looked uneasy and waffled something about all life being magical for an experienced magician. Bollocks. Robert understood now. He continued practising what he learned from Molesey's notebooks.

Tonight he was reclining with a glass of Moselle and one of Molesey's sketchpads, which contained designs for tarot cards. Evidently Molesey had intended to paint them once he had a full set. How did they compare with the cards in the box? Robert fetched the little wooden box containing Molesey's tarot cards, wrapped in silk. They were greasy with use. There were also two books on the tarot, but Robert found them incomprehensible. A pity, because evidently the tarot was hugely important to Molesey, even more than astrology. He'd written somewhere:

In the Tarot, every magical energy is represented pictorially, to be awakened ritually. To gaze upon a single card is to feel its current stir within. To contemplate a spread of cards is to become awash in the surging interplay of the mighty forces of one's life.

That was that, then. Robert selected a card at random from the deck. The King of Cups. He stared at it, waiting for something to happen. Nothing. He put down his glass and concentrated on the card. His gaze wandered from detail to detail, recognising a symbol, halting in puzzlement, moving on. The King of Cups gazed back slyly, as though conscious of witholding understanding from Robert.

Putting away the cards, Robert sighed and reached for his glass. Tomorrow, back to Guiding Spirit for an idiot's guide to the Tarot. He read from the notebooks until he was tired enough to sleep, then went to bed without performing his nightly banishing ritual.

In practice, it was going to be the weekend before Robert could visit Guiding Spirit. Gregory Webster had gone on holiday, leaving van Lier in charge of setting up a new exhibition. This meant two days of Robert fuming over a quick sandwich before visiting the artist and his works – like Jackson Pollock made from beach flotsam – in a lock-up garage the other side of town. Then, blessedly, came the weekend. Robert had the Saturday off.

It was lunchtime on a fine day and Guiding Spirit was fairly full. Above the murmur of conversation, there was a mix of relaxing music from the cd player and unrelaxing sounds from the kitchen. Presumably, the Atlantean High Priest within was swamped with orders. Helena emerged from the kitchen with a bowl of gruel on a tray, giving a start upon seeing Robert. She deposited the bowl in front of a customer at a nearby table, then got behind the counter.

"Hello, Robert."

"Hello, nice to see you. I need a book on the Tarot. Something written in modern English rather than in nineteenth century esoteric."

"Sure. There's half a shelf of them just there, behind you." Helena pointed, and made to return to the kitchen.

"Hang on, not so fast. I could do with a recommendation, and you're well into Tarot, aren't you? By the way, thanks for the tip about Miles Hearne. He's been a goldmine."

Helena smiled, but seemed uneasy. "That's okay."

He went on. "It seems that Molesey was well into Tarot as well. You two would have got on."

"Really."

"Yeah. He wrote somewhere, "In the Tarot, every magical energy is represented pictorially, to be awakened ritually." I'm just starting to work on this side of his stuff now."

"Your conversation is really beginning to fit in with the shop, you know."

Robert laughed. "Sorry. Even Miles Hearne gets a bit cheesed off with me sometimes. I think he's worried I'll overtake him." He paused. Helena was staring at him. "What?"

"Does he warn you to like, keep your feet on the ground?"

Robert grinned wryly. "He has told me to get a life."

Helena's expression changed to one of concern. "Yes. Has he ever talked to you about the danger of obsession?"

"He goes on about it obsessively." That didn't change the expression on Helena's face. "Are you worried about me?"

"Not really my business." She looked away, then came out from behind the counter. "Now, these books ..."

Helena's day went downhill from there.

She'd sold Robert a book on the Tarot, finding with dismay that she was contemplating sending him off with one of those shallow-end introductions that tell you nothing, for his own sake.

And he was creepy. Your average new agey occultnik wore the witch kitsch and bullshitted about ideas and philosophy, never having walked any of such talk in their lives. They got their spells from recipe books and did neither harm nor good. But Robert talked matter-of-factly about his tantric sex and his invocations of powers that Helena hadn't even heard of.

And he was driven. He was saturated in this Molesey character, waterlogged with an alien mysticism, his own life submerged beneath the overwhelming urge to absorb the essence of a long-dead magician. The author of that painting. The man who painted his dreams and nightmares for me to find.

Helena couldn't wait to get home. A hurried hello to a surprised Jolie, then straight to her own room and out with the Tarot cards. She spread the black silk over her bed, shuffled the cards. Robert. Molesey. Robert. Molesey. Robert. Molesey. That painting.

Dealt the cards. The Moon reversed: entrapment in glamour. Swords, swords. Ruin. Seven of Disks, five of Cups. Eight of Swords for Hearne: intellect with no follow-through. King of Cups reversed for Robert: malignant, secretive and cruelly obsessive. And between them for Molesey, Justice reversed: the balance of the other two, each needing the other to avoid ... what?

One more card. The Tower. The penalty for going too far. Destruction from on high. Helena swept the cards together, reached for her mobile phone. She was too scared to call Robert. She called Miles Hearne.

Strange, but the place felt more crowded than it actually was. Usually, Miles found myself in here on a Friday or Saturday, with the bar chock-full of the sexually desperate and disappointed, spraying the furniture with hormones in some hope of finding companionship, if only for the night.

Much of the time, he was only too happy to count himself among their number. And even if success eluded him, he could find solace in watching the acting-out of the time-honoured rituals of drunken seduction, like some alien anthropologist. He'd been known to lay wagers with himself on the success or otherwise of some stud's endeavours on nearby tables, vowing to leave the establishment at the end of the current drink if his estimate of the guy's technique was in error.

He'd never left this place sober.

Not till now, anyway. Tonight, no matter how much Scotch he poured down his throat, he couldn't seem to feel anything but a kind of grim emptiness that was already with him when he walked in. Foreboding appeared to be holding his brain in a state of unwanted sobriety.

It's all that bloody woman's fault. That Helena. What the hell business is any of this to her? What does *she* know?

He'd never really been comfortable with Tarot. Or any other form of divination. That was *female* magic, in his estimation: passive and smothering. If it were left up to the practitioners of that stuff to guide human destiny, the human race would still be cowering in mud huts, afraid to fart unless the omens were propitious. Oh, he would show it the proper respect in public, of course (a large proportion of his readership was female), but you'd never catch Miles Hearne consulting the cards, or the tea leaves, or the fucking sheep's entrails, before making a decision.

Boldness. Courage is everything. Courage in one's own will. All the truly great figures in magic have known this at heart, no matter how much they may dabble in the 'passive' side of The Work, Dee, Crowley, Spare ...

And Molesey. Don't forget him.

No, thought Hearne, I don't buy it. We create our own destiny, forge it in the shape of our own True Will. All this divination stuff ... well, I suppose it can give you an interesting perspective, but if you start trusting to it too much, as that Helena obviously does, it becomes an encumbrance. It will simply start feeding your own fears back to you.

And am I afraid? Fuck, yes.

He wouldn't be, he knew, if it weren't for Pierce himself. That young man was beginning to disturb him greatly. He shouldn't be doing the things he's doing, not so soon after the beginning of his training.

If it *was* the beginning. Could he be some sort of 'ringer', here just to set him up? If he was, who was behind it? He couldn't be doing it on his own, he's too young. It takes years of experience to develop the kind of loathing of Miles Hearne that could do this sort of thing.

Just ask any of my ex-wives.

That's not it. He was getting paranoid now, thinking that all of this was to do with him. No, he told himself forcefully, I'm not the focus of all this, despite what my ego may try and tell me. I'm just the catalyst for something that was there long before I got anywhere near him ...

Shit, who was he kidding? He wasn't even that. The catalyst is Molesey, and never forget that. Everything he did, every idea he tried to pour into Pierce's head, it's clear that Molesey got there first. Pierce was leaping ahead, faster than he could keep track of him; never mind 'walking the talk', the guy was already *running* and he could barely form a coherent sentence. He possessed some sort of instinctive understanding of the principles of magic that went way, *way* beyond theory, as if he was responding at an intuitive level and bypassing all the theoretical bullshit.

This was a dangerous place. For Miles, if not for Pierce. If he wasn't careful, the little sonofabitch would go so far beyond him, he wouldn't need him any more. To hell with the 'mentor' role in this story, Miles would end up as 'yesterday's man', blinking like an idiot as the new boy went leapfrogging into the distance, with him left behind to seethe and fume.

No way. No way is Miles Hearne going to end up as Salieri to Pierce's Mozart.

That's an idea, he mused. I could always poison him ...

But he reminded himself; this isn't about me, is it? And he certainly couldn't do anything to Robert. He didn't think Pierce knew what he was getting himself into. Whatever innate talents he seemed to have tapped into, he needed someone around him to at least *try* and 'ground' him a bit, stop him flying too close to the sun. Miles had the most horrible feeling that it wasn't just Robert who would get burned if this all went wrong.

But aw, shit, why me?

He was avoiding the one necessary conclusion of all of this: that 'bloody woman' was right. It's all getting out of hand, there are forces acting here, of which Miles couldn't even conceive, let alone control.

But he had to try. There had to be some way of understanding what it was that Molesey was trying to do with his working, some way of getting to it before Pierce did, or at least ameliorating its effects once he got there. And for that, he needed help.

It was curiously quiet in there now, but it still had that feeling of being crowded and noisy. For some reason, sex didn't seem at the forefront of anybody's mind tonight. The more recognisable 'predators', both male and female, that Miles saw there every week were still around, but they appeared only to be going through the motions, wandering from table to bar and back again as if they didn't know what else to do. The rest of the clientele seemed to huddle in clusters, as though they were afraid of being alone tonight, afraid of being without someone, anyone, from whom they could draw reassurance that the world was all right, that *they* were all right. The customary air of desperation was still here, still lingering in the corners like cobwebs, but it had taken on a slightly different form. In the dark of this cellar bar, it was almost as if they were sheltering from something, like animals before a storm.

Maybe he was wrong. Maybe, he said to himself, it's just me reading all of this into the situation. Hell, people still seem to be laughing, getting drunk, just like always. Yeah, that's it. Just my imagination.

I still have to get out of here, though.

Robert squeezed past the leather-jacketed bouncer and paid his money to a greasy youth sat at a table just inside the club. Entering the club, he briefly felt old. This was not a club for dress codes and chart hits. Here you came as you were and the music was postmodern, psychedelic and relentless. The place was packed with young people, with some older ones prowling amongst them.

Like himself.

Young men lined the walls near the dance floor, drinks in hand, watching the dancing crowd. Couples groped in corners. Clusters of people stood and shouted in each other's ears.

Whoever didn't come with friends came with a purpose, usually predatory, but Robert had his own reasons. Checking in his coat to reveal old jeans and t-shirt, Robert edged in amongst the dancers on the pulsating floor, absorbing the heat, the friction of bodies too close together, the dry smoky darkness stabbed by coloured lights and the rhythms that you could feel in the breastbone as the ears took in the white noise beyond the pounding. In the sensory overload, Robert took a deep breath, let it out and began to relax, then to rock, then to sway.

Then he began to chant.

Miles had been on the net for hours, lurking in his favourite chat rooms and having an in-depth conversation with sPyroquin, a name behind which hid ... whom? As far as Miles could tell, there was only one person behind the name, based apparently in New Orleans or somewhere. He (?) and Miles had struck up a fruitful correspondence over a few years, Miles logging on as Frater QSIE, the acronym of his old magical motto, *quid scis, id eris*. He'd used the full version less and less over the years, in some discomfort. *What you might be, you shall become*. And what had he become? Best not to go into that. He'd chosen the motto from the formula of the vision of the Universal Mercury, back in his youth when he'd still harboured dreams of being the herald of the gods, before becoming Miles Hearne the media occultist. Ah well. Ah shit. And sPyroquin, from the beginning of their contact, had offered him ... well, not a sympathetic ear, exactly, but the ear of an intellectual peer and the inspiration of a *successful* magician. Miles couldn't bring himself to describe sPyroquin as a mentor, gods forbid! But with the distant magician Miles could share his most delicate and un-Miles Hearne thoughts.

This evening's sharing of the thoughts had been brought on by an e-mail from sPyroquin, who had earlier sent him:

`>Beloved Frater i sense that something's up. Your last message was weeeeeird, man! That Molesey stuff you sent me, no wonder your apprentice is going freaky on you. Talk to me. In the meantime, i've attached the log of an experiment i did with what you sent me. Laugh about it and remember it happened to me.`

It ended with his personal sign. Miles had responded immediately:

`>You're a nutter. You were supposed to read the damn thing, not try it out. Don't try this at home kids, and all that. You're as big a crash-test dummy as Max.`

This was short for Mad Max, as sPyroquin had christened Robert.

`>Anyway, if you're about, meet me in our usual chat room asap. The boy's got worse.`

He appended his seal and attached a resume of Robert"s latest exploits.

Miles had got a prompt response:

```
   M          D
        M
        A
        R
   M    I   X
        L
        Y
M A N S O N
        !
```

>i read your attachment. Holy fuck. Meet you.

It was now quarter to two in the morning after a long, long session with sPyroquin, and Miles was as exhausted as his bottle of Glenmorangie. He'd just signed off when the doorbell went. Who the bloody hell comes to the door at quarter to two? Miles had an idea. After all, he'd been discussing him half the night.

It was. Robert came reeling in out of the cold, smelling of sweat, sex and cannabis. "Hi, Miles, knew you'd be up. You would not believe what a night I've had."

"If you ask me you're still having it. What have you been taking?"

"Nothing Miles, honest." Entering the living room, he flung himself into a sofa, flushed, Miles thought, from exertion rather than from the cold outside. "What an amazing night!"

"Oh God. All right, let's have it; every sweaty detail." He picked up the empty whiskey bottle and made for the kitchen. "I'm out of Scotch. Red wine do?"

"Yeah, some sort of celebration is in order."

"So you got laid?" Which is more than I do.

"Did I ever! But that wasn't the point."

"Lucky you," said Miles, grabbing the corkscrew and opening the wine. "So what was the point?"

"Molesey's Kabbalistic bodywork."

"Does wonders with a dented wing." Miles poured two glasses, took them back into the living room and handed one to

Robert. "Begin."

"Do you remember that axis mundi stuff Molesey wrote? You know, 'Each of us infinite, without boundaries, co-extensive with all that is' and so on?"

Miles nodded, remembering the tremendous power of the words.

"Well I found an exercise of his which goes something like this:

'Turn your attention to bodily sensations,
then to the whole body sensation.
Be filled with the mystery within,
then turn your attention outwards
and let your sense of fleshly presence
fill the space beyond your flesh.
Thus do away with the nonsense about being a spirit trapped in a body.'"

"I've done something of the sort myself," said Miles. Years ago.

"Well I tried doing it in this night club," said Robert, "and the effect it had – I felt like I was filling the room. And the people there, they all seemed to notice me –"

"I bet. You didn't get your altar out and start performing a ritual invocation, did you?" chuckled Miles, "That's followed by the Banishing by Burly Bouncers."

"Stop taking the piss, Miles," snapped Robert. "Something odd happened. While I was like this, I thought I'd try to communicate non-verbally with the women there –"

"You mean you were on the pull."

"And as time went on they started drawing closer, and one thing led to another in a quiet corner and – "

"Hang on," interrupted Miles. "Women? Plural?"

"Yeah," Robert shrugged helplessly. "And the boyfriend of one of them just let it happen."

"Are you sure you didn't crash out in a corner and dream all this?"

"Positive, Miles. And I swear I'm not making this up. While I was in this state I could do just about anything. Not control people as such," he added with a grimace, "but if there were tablets for charisma and a lucky streak I'd taken the whole bottle. And once it wore off I couldn't get it back again, no matter how hard I tried. It was amazing, it just melted away and I was back to normal."

"You call this normal, then?"

"You weren't there, Miles."

Just my bloody luck, thought Miles. "Well, next time you come across a bottle of this stuff leave some for me." He drained his glass, got up, tottered back to the kitchen, vision swimming. "Still sounds like teenage wank fantasy to me."

Miles awoke gradually and painfully. He was slumped in his armchair, alone in his living room, and sunlight was giving him a headache. And he began to remember.

sPyroquin.

Robert.

Glenmorangie.

Oh shit.

Then he remembered Robert's story.

Teenage wank fantasy? Or what? What has he stumbled on?

Things to do: aspirin,
shower,
email sPyroquin. Either the boy's full of shit or he's completely beyond my control. The wannabe overtaking that never was. That's me. Never was. Didn't even make it to has-been. Great. Like I didn't feel like shit already.

Bugger that: go to step one. Aspirin.

Miles moved gingerly out of his armchair and felt his way to the kitchen.

Strange to think, they were behind that door. After so many years of appearing only in dreams, endlessly spectating on his betrayal, to finally have them in the same house once more ...

He hadn't been able to summon up the courage to go through that door, not since they'd been delivered. And he certainly wouldn't allow anyone else to go near them. There had been some sort of incident at the showing a few weeks back, just as he was leaving; that nice young woman who worked there, the one who spoke to him ... Helena, wasn't it? She'd had some sort of funny turn in front of the paintings. He'd wanted to stay and see if she was all right, but he didn't think there was much he could do even if she wasn't.

That's it. Justify your cowardice to yourself again, just as you did all those years ago.

He had the key in his hand. Turning it over and over again in arthritic fingers, he knew that, sooner or later, he would have to use it, and every postponement made it more likely that what he would eventually confront would be that little bit worse. Guilt is cumulative.

Of course, there was always the possibility that he may not be around long enough to confront it. There was a general consensus of medical opinion that said he shouldn't even be alive *now*; a testament, as his doctor said, to his sheer bloodymindedness.

No, I can't go yet. There's something more I have to do, even if I don't know as yet just what it is. I may get some idea when I go into that room, but sitting out here, looking at a locked door is doing nobody any good whatsoever.

"Sir?"

He looked up, into the eyes of Brenda, his housekeeper. He'd seen the expression on her face too many times over the last few weeks, on too many people; a look of patient, rather bemused concern.

"Are you all right, sir?"

"No better and no worse than ever, Brenda. When you get to my age, that's as much as you can hope for."

She shook her head, sadly. "I'm just off now. It's my half-day. Can I do anything for you before I go?"

"Er ... no, thank you, Brenda, I don't think so. You just run along, I'll be fine. I suppose you're going to the hospital this afternoon?" Brenda's daughter had just given birth to a baby girl, a couple of weeks premature, but giving no major cause for concern.

"Oh, yes," she said, brightly. "I'm almost part of the fixtures and fittings on that maternity ward at the moment."

"Well, you know if you want more time off to be with

Andrea and the baby ..."

"Don't worry, sir. I think she's sick of the sight of me as it is, cooing and fussing ..."

"You don't get to be a grandmother every day, my dear. I'm sure she understands."

"Besides," she went on, rather cautiously, "I'm a bit worried about you at the moment, too. Ever since those things were delivered, you've been a bit, well ... distracted, I think you could say. You spend a lot of time just sitting here, outside this door. What is it with those things? What are they, anyway?"

"It's a long story. I'll tell you about it sometime. In the meantime, you just hurry along. Be sure and give Andrea my love, won't you? And I want to see pictures of the new arrival, too. You've promised them to me for quite long enough."

When she was gone, he eased himself to his feet and shuffled across the corridor to the door. Already, he'd got a lot further in his resolve than he had at any time previously, but still the key lay unused in his hand, the cold weight of it burning a hole through his parchment skin on a direct path to his heart.

A sigh escaped him then, a sigh that transformed into a chest-racking cough which almost persuaded him to retake his seat.

I don't have the strength. I can't face this.

Trust in the flesh. Strength comes from finding the limits of one's own capacity, looking into the wastelands where fear forbids entrance, and taking that step into the unknown. Then, my love ... then we find that those limits, those fears, our shadows, phantoms generated by the mind. And mind is subservient to the flesh ...

Why of all times did he have to remember that now? And why did he remember not just the words, but the look in the speaker's eyes as he said them? A look that, for some reason, made him think of angels; incandescent with love, terrifying as a burning blade.

Shakily, he put the key into the lock and turned. The joints of his arm protested at even this small exertion, but he ignored it, and with the door (at long last) open, he reached for the light switch. The illumination flooded the room, captured and whirled blindingly about by the bare white walls. The room's only contents were five rectangular objects, leaned against the far wall, swathed in blankets like freshly shrouded corpses.

If only they *were* inert ...

While his courage remained, he approached the shapes and, one by one, and tugged away the coverings.

The last time he had seen at close range what lay beneath (many, many years before), his attention had not been fully focussed upon them, and yet they now seemed as familiar and as terrible to him as a scar on the face of a loved one. Three of them, stark in whites and blacks, the colours of bone and the void they contained. One, strange and conspicuous in a frenzied dance of blues and oranges, the joker in the pack.

And the last one. Sitting in the middle of the row, the eye drawn to it with an irresistible sense of conclusion, its very incompleteness adding to its mystery; seen as a whole, there was the feeling that this was the last spoken word in an unfinished sentence.

He so, so much wanted to turn and run. The room began to swim around him, and before he could fall he shuffled to the wall and leant one hand against it to steady himself. The voice of his own panic sounded in his skull, urging him to leave them, shut off the light, lock the door, lose the key, crawl away to safety. Isn't that just the simplest solution? Perhaps, with luck, he could find the strength to die too, and silence the demons that had screamed accusations at him for over seventy years ...

Except. That would be abandonment too, wouldn't it? There was no silence for *him*, was there? He'd seen as much in his companion's eyes as he lay before him on that night, eyes that saw nothing but a kind of private hell of his own creation from which he saw no hope of redemption, and in which he would not be alone.

He saw those eyes now. Whether on the inside or the outside of his own eyelids, he couldn't tell, but he saw them, saw them turn to look up at him, saw the lips in the blanched face begin to form words.

Trust in the flesh. Only through the flesh can the truth be understood.

A pause. A smile.

Howling with terror, he turned and rushed from the room, snapping off the light and slamming the door behind him before slumping into a sitting position on the floor, conscious of the tears on his face and a creeping wetness in his trousers. Now he knew what he had long suspected; that what had been created in 1929 was still in existence, was still desperately searching for egress back into the world of Flesh.

And the man he had loved all those years ago was still in thrall to it.

"Oh, Nicholas ..." he despaired.

Robert came to, sweating, nerves pulling tight, eyes snapping open, panic rising in the gut. He swayed briefly and collapsed from his upright kneeling position onto his side. He lay naked, shivering, his eyes wide, searching the gloom. Panting, disoriented, he struggled to a sitting position, wiping perspiration from his eyes. He took a few deep breaths and looked around properly. The living room, lit by one guttering candle in the window. His silent stereo showing a few telltale lights, video digital clock glowing green.

How long? Seemed like moments, seemed like all night. He was getting used to the fact that he was no longer in that world. The abyssal dark, where the Denizens had come and fastened themselves upon him, where he'd driven them off with a pulse of bright, bright energy, which the Denizens had soaked up greedily, before returning for more, forcing him to throb energy like a demented pulsar until they had nearly exhausted him, when they'd suddenly fled as a darker Shadow than even the abyss fell across him, a black hole in the ocean of dark energy which all but pulled him into its event horizon as he struggled to awake –

"Fuck!" he panted, and finding that it helped, he repeated it until he could breathe normally again. Shaking, he crawled to his feet and tottered to the shower, letting the bright bathroom and the blast of hot water wash away the last clammy kiss of the Denizens.

On his bathrobed return to the living room, he turned up the dimmer switch to banish the dark, put the radio on –

classical, nothing too dramatic – and flopped into the sofa. Then and only then did he let out a tired whoop of relief and satisfaction. Wow. A nightmare, or a really bad astral trip? Where is that world, so I can avoid it next time?

More to the point, what the hell does it have to do with Molesey"s pathworking of Binah, the third Sephirah? Robert had discovered notes on this in one of the later journals, and this is where he went next, finding his place in the journal marked with a Klee postcard. On the card were notes from the lists of correspondences in Miles Hearne"s notebook. "Binah. Great Sea, silver, pearl, black, Saturn, death, dissolution, deep understanding, passive receptivity ..." and so forth. Okay. What was there? Great Sea ... -ish. Black, sense of impending dissolution ... so what were the Denizens? Or that other, darker Shadow? What about the frantic vampirism?

What had Molesey gone there for anyway?

Robert lit a cigarette and hefted the journal again. The bare bones entry of the pathworking which Robert had just attempted to follow, included these notes:

Mar 20, 1925.

Entered Binah to consult (followed a string of symbols and abbreviations, amounting to "Thanatos, God of Death", plus a coded string of attributes) *drawer of limitations, to discover how to erase That without being erased. cf.* (followed a reference to an slightly earlier part of the journal)

Robert hunted around for the passage referred to, and read:

I sought an oracle of Him who guards in silence the boundary of Life and Death. I received this:

Your life, fully formed,
is surrounded by formless void,
as the waters cover the land.
The only way to enter the void
is to become yourself formless and void.

This we call Death. It seems I cannot enter without dissolving.

I therefore resolve to create an Elemental, and to form and equip it such that it can penetrate the formless void and return to me with the mystery thereof. In all its attributes it shall be of one nature with Death Himself, and may thus perhaps escape annihilation.

On a hunch Robert turned to the final entries. Robert had mistaken the terse notes as being simply for a series of paintings, followed by the chronological journal of their composition. Now Robert looked again:

Keyword: Water. Elemental water and the suit of Cups. Queen scale in Briah.

And other Cabbalistic terminology. These were not all mentioned in Miles Hearne's notebook. He would scan this lot and understand it instantly. The first note, interspersed with Greek, Hebrew and symbols, read thus:

Metatron, Archangel of the Presence. Voluminon in brilliant white, phos. etc. VIII to enliven. Seal in black.

It was coming together in Robert's mind. He read the fifth note:

Khamael, the Severity of God. Vol. in scarlet, browns, black. Blood to enliven. Seal in green.

This note reminded Robert of something. He stopped reading to allow his mind to recall. It didn't take long. He sat bolt upright.

"Fuck," he breathed. Finding that it helped, he repeated it.

Helena walked slowly out of the chemist's and took the packet of diazepam out of its bag for the third time already. And if that doesn't work, Dr. Fenton had said, come back and we'll see about that counselling we discussed. She stared at the white packet. Here we go again. Just like in Los Angeles. Only this time, no bastard husband to kick it off. Just some ugly painting. Doesn't even remind me of him. But these things can be triggered off by the most unlikely stimuli, so Dr. Fenton had said, and may simply indicate some unresolved personal issues.

Bullshit. *Ken* could come up with more convincing crap than that one.

She put the packet back in its little bag and stuffed it into her handbag, setting off in no particular direction, coat flapping in the wind as her bus to work roared past. She wouldn"t be going. Not today. Not for at least two weeks, according to the sicknote in her purse. Relax a bit, she could hear the doctor saying, stay off work for a bit, and don't go bringing work home either. In other words, no more appointments for that Tarot rubbish you do, dearie, because it only upsets you. Take your mind off that sort of thing. Watch daytime telly instead.

Bring on the Prozac.

Helena waited for the next bus, and it was only when she told the driver her destination that she realised she was going to the Webster art gallery. Plonking herself down into a seat near the door, she awaited an explanation of events.

On arrival, she timidly asked a smartly dressed woman behind the desk if Robert Pierce was in. He was at lunch and had gone out, and would she care to wait? Helena glanced around the foyer. Occupying much of it was an intriguingly precarious cat's cradle of multicoloured conduit piping and steel cable. It looked as though one well-placed kick would collapse the whole edifice. Besides, she was haunted enough by art as it was. Helena declined and left and no, she wouldn't like to say who called.

To her surprise, she found herself going to work after all. In partial explanation, she handed a bemused Sheelagh the sick note.

"You didn't have to bring it in, love," said Sheelagh, "I could've waited for it."

"I know," said Helena, "I just thought I'd..." She shrugged. Then, "Oh, by the way, Sheelagh, can I borrow the address book a minute?"

"Go ahead, love." Quizzical look.

Helena searched the book for ... what? What did she need from here? She turned the pages aimlessly, attracting more looks from Sheelagh. Then she saw Miles Hearne's name and address.

That's daft! I've got that at home! I am seriously losing it. Nonetheless, she copied it down, waved goodbye to Sheelagh and Ken, and left the shop.

She didn't know the buses to Hearne's part of town, so she walked to the nearest taxi rank and spent money she could ill afford going somewhere she didn't know.

Luckily, the taxi driver knew his streets, and deposited Helena at the bottom of a short flight of steps leading to a varnished wooden front door. She rang the doorbell, composing her speech for the magician. Hello, I thought I'd take you up on your offer.

Blech.

Hello, I'm completely barking mad and I don't know why I'm here.

Helena frowned at this one, and took a moment to realise that nobody had come to answer the doorbell. She rang again, making sure that she could hear its chimes within the house.

Hello. I've come out all this way, so please be gardening or something. I've got to talk to you about these nightmares I'm still having, even when I'm awake, and you and Robert Pierce are in them. Please be in, because something terrible is lurking just below my threshold and it's driving me to a nervous breakdown. Answer the sodding door, because I know you know what's going on and if you don't do something about it I don't know what will happen to me. She rang again, more insistently. It was a big terraced house, without any little path to the rear for her to use. She rang again.

Still no response. "Shit. *Shit.*"

She looked around despairingly at the street, which was empty except for a row of vehicles nestled into the parking spaces reserved for 'residents only'. The space outside Hearne's house was unoccupied, a rectangle of tarmac drier than the surrounding area. Obviously the taxi had pulled into the space only recently vacated by Miles Hearne's car.

She fumbled in her handbag for her mobile phone, found it, then cursed. Got any taxi numbers? She sat down on the top step with a sigh. She remembered Jolie telling her, always keep a few taxi firm numbers on my mobile, just in case some bloke dumps me in the middle of nowhere. Well, you never know, do you? Then she'd erupted into her dirty laugh, the 'ooh us girls' laugh, the laugh that made light of being stranded in a strange area with no friends and no shelter, alone and female, not quite at your best, wondering what the bloody hell you're doing there. Hello, I'm completely lost. I don't know what I'm doing here in the first place but I wish I wasn't. I'm tired, I feel like shit, I think I've made a complete fool of myself and I don't know what to do next. Can you please take me home?

The mobile phone nestled in her hand, taking warmth from her, waiting to be prodded into action.

Helena began to sob.

I take it all back, thought Miles, perhaps the TV industry isn't populated solely by grotesquely unpresentable morons, chancers and con-artists. Some of them are quite attractive.

Take Sophie, for instance. Gorgeous, intelligent, witty and, at that moment, sitting right opposite him. He'd met her at a party thrown by one of the producers of a mid-evening current affairs programme, someone who couldn't actually stand the sight of him – it was mutual – but whose wife was a friend of long-standing (and, on one alcohol-fuelled evening, lying down). The party was held to mourn the demise of said current affairs show, which had been summarily cancelled recently in order to make space in the schedules for more 'ratings-friendly' fodder. This, from Miles' limited exposure to TV on the passive side of the cathode-ray, consisted of game shows in which the public were required to prove just how stupid and meretricious they could be in order to win large quantities of cash. They also included inane soap operas and deeply tedious programmes in which people have their houses redecorated for them while they're out.

Luckily for him, he'd met Sophie while he was still sober enough to hold a reasonable conversation. Nobody had thought to introduce them, and they'd simply fallen into a discussion about the failings of modern television while filling their plates from the buffet. She had been a researcher on the cancelled show, and she was, quite understandably, rather pissed off at her imminent unemployment. He had listened sympathetically to her complaints, nodded in quiet accord, and stole the occasional glance at her breasts. She had no idea who he was, and he was rather glad to be just himself for a change. To his surprise, he had managed to avoid making any unsubtle moves on her, and when he suggested, at the end of the evening, that they meet up again a few days later for dinner at Gotti's, a favourite Italian restaurant of his, she'd accepted happily.

This could be the start of a whole new strategy with the opposite sex, Miles thought. No more Hearne the Hunter. Just plain old Miles Hearne. You learn something new every day. Just don't blow it by a) lunging straight for the tits or b) letting on that you're a professional occultist.

Part (a) of the strategy wasn't easy to keep up, particularly the way she looked in his eyes over the breadsticks, and kept flicking her long auburn hair back over her shoulder. Moreover, her skin gleamed golden in the candlelight and she was wearing a black dress that left her shoulders and most of her legs bare, in a way seemingly calculated to ensure that Miles would not be getting to his feet in a hurry. The conversation was light, flirtatious, and progressing exactly as Miles thought it should, in that Sophie was, as each minute went by, displaying a greater amount of obvious interest in him (utilising the sort of body language that could deafen a social anthropologist at twenty paces) and, correspondingly, a greater amount of obvious cleavage.

Oh, and the way she ate pasta ... well, it verged on the pornographic.

"I really don't think I've met anyone quite like you, you know, Miles," she said, once the main course had been cleared away and the second bottle of Chianti had arrived.

"Is that so? Perhaps you should elaborate before I decide whether to feel flattered or not."

"Well, let's see ... you've told me an awful lot about yourself, but I still get the impression you're holding out on me."

"Hey, this is just the first date. I like to hold something in reserve."

"I bet you do." Her eyebrows waggled comically at him as she sipped at her wine.

"What is it that you think I'm keeping from you?"

"I see. Twenty Questions. If I get the answer right, what's the prize?"

"Personal satisfaction. Nothing more."

"My favourite kind. All right then, guess one; you're in the SAS."

Miles grinned. "With *this* hair?"

"Good point. OK, you're, er, you're the leader of the government-in-exile of some Central American state, awaiting the day of the counter-revolution when you can return in triumph to your oppressed but valiant people."

"I don't even speak Spanish."

"Hm. Are you a famously reclusive novelist, perhaps?"

"A recluse who goes to parties and restaurants? You haven't thought that one through, have you?"

"I know. You're Elvis, aren't you?"

Miles struck his forehead in mock-despair. "Dammit, my secret's out. What do you want me to do? Jump up on the table and start singing 'Jailhouse Rock'? I mean, you deserve it."

She smiled sweetly as she said, "I'd prefer a private show. At my place?"

Suddenly, Miles wasn't so sure that he knew who was doing the seducing here. And he also wasn't sure that he'd be able to negotiate his erection out of the restaurant without serious inconvenience to the other diners.

"That would be –" He got no further when he noticed that Sophie's attention had shifted over his shoulder.

"Is he a friend of yours?" she enquired.

Turning, he saw Gianni, the waiter, in intense

conversation with a rain-sodden young man in a black leather jacket who was gesticulating in the direction of their table. Although there was a heavy growth of stubble framing his jawline, and he appeared to have slept for several days in the clothes he was wearing, there was no mistaking who it was.

Robert. Bloody sodding buggering *Robert*.

Who saw that Miles had registered his presence and started bellowing "Miles! Miles, it's me! I've got to talk to you!" at the top of his voice.

The combination of Robert's behaviour and the glare of the other diners made Miles wish that the mosaic-pattern linoleum beneath his feet would open up and swallow him. He looked up apologetically at the bemused Sophie, and was about to rise in order to deal with Robert at the door when a figure loomed over him.

"Miles, thank fuck I've found you." Without waiting for permission, Robert grabbed an empty chair from a nearby table and sat down between him and Sophie. "That prick of a waiter wasn't going to let me in, but when he saw that you knew me, he let me past."

Thanks, Gianni. You can forget about the tip tonight.

"I've figured out what Molesey was doing." He was leaning on the table in such a way as to dominate Miles' field of vision, turned towards him in order to cut Sophie out of the conversation; whether this was by design or simple ignorance, it was impossible to tell. "I've been working my way through some of the later notebooks, the ones that he completed in the year before he died. He was working on a sequence of *ten* paintings, not just the five we've – I've seen! Isn't that amazing?"

"Robert –" The faces of Robert and Sophie were jostling for attention in his eyeline, Robert's so full of animation (despite the unkempt appearance and the rainwater trickling down his cheeks), and Sophie's frozen into an expression of utter bafflement, which would, Miles surmised, soon turn into scorn if he didn't do something to halt the interloper's flow, and do it quickly.

"Robert, this is all very interesting, and I'd really love to talk about it in some depth with you, but –"

Robert didn't hear the 'but'. "Great. I'll call a taxi, we can get to work on it right away."

"No, Robert, look ... I really can't right now, all right?"

"What are you talking about? For fuck's sake, Miles, this is *it*. His life's work was in this ritual and now that we've got the sequence mapped out, we can get it all. Jeez, it's you who's been going on about how you wished you could be half the magician Molesey was, about how this could be the key to a whole new magical system to replace that tired old Hermetic shit you've been trudging on with for the last twenty years ..."

"Miles?" asked Sophie. "What the hell's going on?"

Miles leaned in close to Robert's ear and hissed "Robert, *this is not a good time.* Now will you just fu –"

"Oh!" said, Robert leaning back suddenly. He looked at Miles with genuine incomprehension in his eyes, then turned back to Sophie. "I'm sorry," he said with a grin, "we haven't met, but my name's Robert Horror and I'm a black magician. Miles here is my High Priest, and he's been teaching me all about sex magic. He told me he had a project on." He eyed her, grinning again. "I was jealous. Hey Miles, perhaps we could try that triangular position."

"That's it." Sophie was on her feet and in her coat before Miles had time to frame a reply. "I'm out of here. I don't know what sort of weird shit you and Merlin here have got cooking, but I'd hate to get in the way. Give me a call if you ever pass by planet Earth again, won't you, Miles?"

"Sophie ..." pleaded Miles, but she was already gone, without even a backward glance.

Miles found Robert looking up at him with the sweetest, most innocent smile on his face that he had ever seen on the front of a human head. It was this that finally triggered the damburst of rage, causing him to grab Robert by the collar, haul him to his feet and bring their faces within kissing distance.

"Robert, you terrible cunt! Do you know what you just did?"

The continued presence of the smile informed Miles very clearly that he did.

"What the fuck – I mean, what right do you have to –

to – *Do you know how long it is since I got off with anyone else besides my right hand?*"

The most deafening sound in all the world is that of a roomful of people simultaneously falling silent. It roared in the ears of Miles Hearne as he and Robert swivelled their heads in unison to look at the gamut of expressions – ranging from quiet shock, through heroically restrained amusement, to simple outrage – that were being directed at them from all corners of the restaurant. In response, Miles released his hold on Robert, who sank back into his seat. Having done this, and straightened his clothing with as much dignity as he could still summon up, he looked back at the diners to find them still gazing in his direction.

"What?" he demanded irritably of the assembly, sending their attention plummeting back to a close perusal of the plates in front of them, like a gathering of food inspectors.

"I am sorely tempted," said Miles, retaking his seat and searching for his lost composure, "much as I frown on necrophilia, to just tell you and Molesey to go fuck yourselves. Except that would mean you'd *still* have a better sex life than me. So I'm going to give you one last chance to engage my interest. Don't waste it."

"I won't," said Robert, helping himself to Sophie's seat. "I worked it out as a result of the Moleseyan bodywork I've been experimenting with.You know, what I did at the club? It's because the whole Tree of Life, the blueprint of the Universe, from mere matter to immortal Godhead, is embedded in my flesh –"

"As above, so below and all that."

"Yes, only Molesey had it the other way round. It's embedded in the flesh of every man, woman and child who's ever lived, like God's DNA. They've just got to ... *activate* it."

He paused, as if gathering his thoughts, absently pouring himself a Chianti into what had been Sophie's glass. "This is difficult for me, Miles, so you'll have to bear with me."

"That's all right," said Miles, sighing inside. "Suddenly I've got time."

"At the top of the Tree is Godhead. Immortal, perfect. At the bottom is our world, our lives, our flesh. The further down the tree you go, the more the blueprint decays. Molesey was after immortality. He was nearly killed in the First World War and he found out how much he didn't want to die. So he created a- a- an explorer, like a satellite mission to Death, by taking an elemental entity and beefing it up into something really heavy-duty to withstand what it might find there. Except –"

"– it killed him. "

"– before he could complete the process."

"Complete it? You mean he hadn't finished?"

"Of course he hadn't finished! Haven't you been listening, Miles? That's what I found in the notes! The planned sequence consisted of ten paintings, not just the five that he actually produced. Each one corresponded to a sephira, a different level of the Tree of Life. And each one was being triggered by a separate ritual. His last journal entry shows he was going to do number five, Geburah. Corresponding to the archangel Khamael, 'The Severity of God', linked to the astrological sign of Scorpio. And the creature he made he gave the survival attributes of Scorpio. He even called it Scorpion."

"Oh, sweet mother of fuck...." Miles put a hand across his mouth in horror.

"You see it now, don't you? Something had obviously happened to it out there. When he brought it back it brought Death with it and delivered it –"

"In the flesh."

"Exactly. It destroyed him. Before he could complete the ritual. And it's probably still out there, Molesey's Death probe, out of radar contact."

Miles saw it all right. "The stupid sod," said Miles, with feeling. "The poor bloody stupid sod."

"So what do think?" asked Robert through his Chianti. "Worth losing a date for?"

"I don't think I'll ever forgive you for that," answered Miles. "But we may have a bigger problem."

"Yeah?"

"This Scorpion, Molesey's Death probe, is still broadcasting out in the god-knows-where, eh?"

"I assume so."

"Those paintings, they're basically homing beacons for the ether, drawing in the essence of their particular sephira."

"Something like that, perhaps, yes."

"That last one, Geburah, Khamael, and so forth –"

"He named them after their archangels, but yeah?"

"That girl Helena saw something from it coming out at her, didn't she?"

"Yeah."

"So that one homing beacon must still be switched on, mustn't it?"

"Oh shit," said Robert, putting down his glass. "Is this a really bad time to tell you Molesey's ultimate aim in all this?"

"Probably, but don't let that stop you. My evening's ruined already."

"He was proceeding downwards through the Tree of Life, from the top with its immortality and perfection, to bring the secret which the Scorpion learned from Death all the way down into our world. Not just for himself. For every man woman and child alive. His stated aim:

'Having drunk deep of the Mystery,
to pour it out upon all flesh.'

"That's in his preliminary notes for the tenth and final painting. Now Khamael – the fifth one – is 'transmitting' from the Scorpion. How?"

"I think I get it." Miles rescued the bottle from Robert and poured himself a very full glass. "Traditionally, these things are created and energised by our attention. Whether you believe in this stuff or not –" (he put a hand up to forestall Robert's protest) "– you recognise that if you put any damn lump of putty or something on your mantelpiece and talk to it every day it becomes more meaningful to you. It's as though your attention gives it a life of its own. Now Molesey had already done this with his paintings, yes?"

Robert nodded. "Any work of art could be said to have a personality of its own."

"And Helena, staring into this thing, picked up on that."

"So where the hell is it now? And what is it doing?"

"Last I heard from Helena, she complained about seeing that damn painting everywhere," said Miles. "She seemed more worried about you at the time, but now I come to think of it..." He pulled a cigarette from the packet on the table, lighting it with the candle. "Like it was on standby, until Helena, who's sensitive to these things, gave it her attention. Now it's like it won't leave her alone. What worries me, lad," and Miles leaned closer to Robert, "is what might happen if this thing goes public and starts fulfilling Molesey's plan."

"You accept this could happen, then?"

"I don't know what to think at the moment," said Miles with a shake of his head, "but I'm enough of a believer to want to do something about it. Just in case, you understand."

"So are we going?"

"Well, first of all," said Miles, eyeing Gianni, who was glowering at him from the bar, "I have to settle up with the restaurant and apologise very nicely for you so that they let me in here again. Then," and here he took a deep breath, "we do something about finishing the work that Molesey started." And under his breath he muttered, "and God help us, every one."

Frater QSIE>It's not just him, Miles typed. This girl Helena - the one who freaked at the sight of one of those paintings - she's still completely bugfuck. Leaves me answerphone messages I don't want to answer. I think she's getting worse.

@sPyroquin>you gotcha hands full there. Watcha gonna do?

Frater QSIE>Not a clue. I admit it, I've lost control of this one. Wish I'd never started with him now. I'm not bloody helping him carry on where Molesey crashed.

@sPyroquin>you bailing out?

>Hello, Magus Helpline calling Frater QSIE. Are you quitting on me as well?

Frater QSIE>Of course I'm not quitting, you cheeky turd, I just don't know what to

do with him. Or with Helena.
@sPyroquin>I hate to lay this Star Wars crap on you Obi-Wan but when you took him on you signed up for the whole deal master-apprentice wise. you don't want him turning into Darth Vader then you'd better fix it now.
Frater QSIE>It's all right for you, you don't get the insufferable git pestering you at all hours with his look what I can do routines.
@sPyroquin>That's right Obi-Wan, and before you take a break for elevenses can I remind you what frickin time it is over here? No offense meant, just that the street lights are still on.
Frater QSIE>sorry sPyroquin. I've been ranting at you I know. All right, I take your point, I've got to sort the boy out. HOOOOOOOOOOOW?
@sPyroquin>I guess you and I, we handhold him through this ten-story ritual thing and get him over that nasty slice in the middle.
Frater QSIE>You mean the bit where the magician dies? Yes, I'm keen to get past that one as well. I have been thinking about simply exorcising the Molesey out of Max.
@sPyroquin>From what you've been saying he may not take too kindly to that. He kinda likes what he's learning.
Frater QSIE>Tell me about it.
@sPyroquin>Heart of hearts, beloved frater: are you up to it?

Pause. Miles was still, his aching back hunched over the keyboard, his last coffee cold by his elbow. Heart of hearts.

Frater QSIE>No.

He pushed himself away from the keyboard, his back exploding with pain. Followed by relief.

@sPyroquin>Good call, Obi-Wan. I say we get a posse of us Jedis to do it together. Run the ritual online, via chatroom, have a few people to support and delete that servitor's ass. With the series completed safely Mad Max may come back down to earth and wear his pointy hat the same way as the rest of us. Whaddaya say?
Frater QSIE>It sounds the most bizarre ill-conceived gambolic escapade since ... well, since the last time Mad Max recounted one of his exploits. Where the hell do you start?
@sPyroquin>Leave the online shit to me. I'll round up the people, design the ritual, lay on a show. Expect details in your mailbox. you concentrate on selling the idea to Max. And send me what you can on the original Scorpion series asap.
Frater QSIE>Oh very well. And thanks.
@sPyroquin>May the Force be with you. One more thing: 'gambolic', is that a word?

"We don't need anybody else," Robert said, gripping his mobile phone so hard the plastic casing complained. "We've got the know-how, we've got the notes, we've got the experience. Over to us."

He was in the coffee shop on his lunchbreak, answering Miles' message. He was sat on a stool at the bar, between a large middle-aged Asian gentleman in pinstripes and a teenage mother struggling with a noisy toddler. They were both giving him the occasional glance. Small wonder.

"No disrespect to you lad," Miles answered, "but you seem to be like blood in the water for what I can only describe as scary shit. That pathworking of Binah you told me about? Not at all how I remember Binah. No astral vampires, no Big Shadow, no *Jaws* theme playing."

"I might not have gone there. For all I can really tell I might just as well have fallen asleep and had a nightmare."

"That's not what you were telling me when you were crowing about it. There are ways to test these things, you know, and if you weren't so, excuse my bluntness, *green*, you'd have used them."

"I managed."

"On that occasion. But if you're going to explore this stuff at least do it carefully. Now I don't know where the bloody hell you went on your pathworking, but if you were expecting Binah you should have been looking out for the Binah signs, which you don't know because you've never taken the trouble to learn."

"Look, Miles," Robert grimaced as he realised he was stubbing his cigarette out in his coffee. The teenage mother stared at him. "All that we need to learn is in the flesh. Not in your notes, not online. The blueprint is in the flesh." The teenage mother hurried her toddler past him, glancing over her shoulder at him as they left for the sunshine outside. She was still staring at him through the glass front of the coffee shop as she went down the street.

"In the flesh, yes. And look what it came out with last time." Miles was getting louder. "All I'm saying lad, is spare my angina: let sPyroquin set up an online ritual. He's pulling together quite a team, apparently. You, me, him, and two others. For mutual support, just in case in the middle of the ritual your scary shit starts up again. We sort it out, we banish with extreme prejudice, we knock off and go down the pub."

"All online?"

"There are bits to do offline, but telling people what's going on is online, yes."

"Webcam?"

"No webcam. One of them wants to remain anonymous. Lots of downloads, though. Each one does it their own way. I would have thought you'd like that."

Robert fished out a cigarette. "And we all get to follow in the footsteps of Molesey."

"I bloody hope not. I don't want to end up the same way he did."

Robert lit his cigarette and pulled a long drag on it. "All right. Let's do it your way."

There was a sigh from Robert's mobile. "Well done. I'll email you the details as I get them."

"I'll be preparing." Robert ended the call. He called for another coffee. Preparing, huh? Preparing for what?

And preparing how?

It was one thing to be full of it with Miles on the phone, but another thing entirely to be alone with . . . with . . .

The Denizens?

The Scorpion?

The Shadow in the Abyss?

To be alone with blood in the water.

Robert made a mental note to go through Molesey's papers. Somewhere in there Molesey *must* have created some sort of protection for himself.

It didn't work for him though, did it?

"Mad Max?" said Robert. "Thanks a bunch."

"It's nothing to what I've been calling you," replied Miles. They were, for a change, in Robert's flat, in honour of the occasion. Never mind that it was two o'clock in the morning and there were neighbours above and below. Miles had prepared a small altar in the middle of the room, using Molesey's old magical weapons and a single candle. Robert had painted a two metre square piece of card in what he assured Miles was citrine, and had hung it in front of the window. He had also done something to one of the light bulbs in the living room, so that it gave off the same sickly orangey-yellow hue. The same colour dominated the screensaver on Robert's computer, which he had decorated with some home-made sigils representing elemental Air. For relief he had used sky-blue for the lines.

All in all, Miles was relieved to be a back-seat driver on this one. Although he and sPyroquin had eventually agreed on the format of the ritual, he had left it to the New Orleans magician to design the details and email instructions to the participants. And while Miles was happy for Robert to take the lead in the Air role, he was glad to be able to observe and direct if necessary. This was one ritual which he felt could go badly wrong.

And I still don't know if I'm the man to put it right.

Robert, though, was still on about his new soubriquet. Like it was a surprise. "And what else was it?" he demanded. " 'Crash-test dummy'?"

"If the pointy hat fits, lad," replied Miles, "wear it."

Robert cut the exchange dead by turning to the computer and logging online, making straight for the chatroom sPyroquin had already prepared. "Bung the music on, Miles, would you?"

Miles got out of the sofa and made for the stereo. "What are we playing?"

"It's in already. Programmed and everything. Just grab the remote and press play."

Miles did so, and Mahler's "Song of the Earth" emerged from the speakers, filling the room, it seemed, from the floor up, like the smell of freshly turned soil.

"Logging-in and entering the temple now," said Robert, his fingers chattering at the keyboard. Miles saw the others' names coming up on the screen in procession.

```
@Russet>sPyroquin here.
Olive>Tohubohu 555 here.
Black>USZAUTZAANP here.
```

How the bloody hell do you pronounce that? Miles thought.

```
Citrine> Mad Max here.
```

Robert turned to Miles. Miles paused, took the keyboard.

```
Citrine>Frater QSIE here.
```

Miles looked at Robert. "Here we go."

```
>I declare this temple open and this gathering complete.  let us banish our surroundings now.
```

In Robert's living room, Miles turns up the music, to drown out what is to follow. The phone is already unplugged and the doorbell disconnected. Miles takes a small dagger from the altar and begins to intone the Lesser Banishing Ritual of the Pentagram to Mahler's Song of the Earth, and Robert joins in, this once.

In New Orleans, it is about 8 p.m. In sPyroquin's apartment block there are no neighbours, only people who live on top of each other. The bric-a-brac which fills his apartment is draped with fox-red backcloths and lit with red lamps. Flames lick out of a small brazier in the centre of the floor. He stands in his rust-brown tunic, his hair freshly henna'd, and pauses for a moment before beginning to tremble. The shaking becomes more violent, sweat breaks out on his flesh, his veins swell until at last a scream breaks forth. The stillness afterward is deathly, and the room becomes an oasis of peace in the noisy building. He returns to his keyboard and his monitor with the russet wallpaper.

Across town from from her occasional lover sPyroquin, Tohubohu 555 has the shared house to herself for the evening. Her room is draped with camouflage netting through which the table lamps pattern the walls and ceiling, and she is dressed in olive-green combat fatigues. Pine incense sharpens the atmosphere and a small electric fountain beneath the computer desk trickles in the background. She briefly raises a goblet of crme de menthe, then places it beside her keyboard. She raises her arms, and with a beatific expression, begins to chant her magical name, cheerleader-style, to stir the magician from within the void of chaos.

"To-hu bo-hu five five five. To-hu bo-hu five five five."

After a short while of liquid repetition, the chant merges into a new current of speaking in tongues, increasing in volume and fluency ...

In Malmo, Sweden, it is about 0300h, cold and dark. USZAUTZAANP stands soberly in his silent, bare black-painted temple, lit only by a solitary black candle and the computer monitor. This room of the house is set aside for his magical practices, and black is a colour he has plenty of. Nobody ever visits or disturbs, least of all at this time, which is his favourite hour. He has little respect for internet occultists, and sPyroquin is a rare exception. For him and for the thrill of transgressing a personal taboo, the magician approaches his computer, the screen of which is black with the lettering in white. Crisply and without pomp, he asks the blessing of Satan and declares himself ready to begin.

His is the first elemental invocation to appear on the screens:

Black>I am Elemental Black in Malkuth, Earth of Earth. With the Coin we redeem.

In Robert"s flat, Miles watches as the others add their parts:

@Russet>I am Elemental Russet in Malkuth, Fire of Earth. With the Wand we create.
Olive>I am Elemental Olive in Malkuth, Water of Earth. With the Cup we preserve.
Citrine>I am Elemental Citrine in Malkuth, Air of Earth. With the Sword we destroy.

Miles takes the keyboard again.

I am the Lamp of Spirit, welcoming you to the Chamber of Malkuth, the realm of the material world. I declare our intention to ascend the Tree of Life, from this the realm of matter to Kether, the Highest, on the way to contact the Scorpion entity and reduce it to its constituent elements, bringing peace to it and to the spirit of Nicholas Molesey. And will this team of off-cuts be up for the job?
Before we ascend the Tree of Life, let us ask the blessing of Sandalphon, the Archangel of Malkuth.

He hands the keyboard to Robert, who accesses the file downloading from sPyroquin, and the sigil of Sandalphon appears on the screen, against a background quartered into black, olive, russet and citrine.

"How did he do that?" asks Robert, who is no slouch himself with online communication.

"I have no idea," replies Miles, "but he did say something about a tame virus he'd trained to do tricks."

Miles intones an evocation of the archangel, typing it rapidly as he does so. The others all answer with various kinds of amen, and Miles and Robert each gaze at the sigil on their screen, waiting to experience the presence of Sandalphon.

After some moments, Robert stirs. "Whoa," he breathes. "Feel this!"

Miles has been trying for some moments to feel something, looking out for all the correct correspondences to appear to mind, but he has all but lost faith in his efforts. Now he begins to notice a subtle change in his mood; sadness, grimness, patience, bleak certainty, as words of Portman come to mind: "Sandalphon is one who sees the birth of a child into the world and his joy is tempered by the full knowledge of the suffering that is to come for the little one." Bleak, bleak pity swells up, encompassing Miles' world, filling his soul and bringing him to the verge of tears. He types:

```
>As the Lamp of Spirit I greet thee Sandalphon, ruler of this vale of tears. be with us and bless our mission.
```

Over the next ten minutes the others acknowledge.

```
Olive>As Water I soak into the realm of matter.  I can sink no further.
Black>As Earth I experience the heaviness of the heart of this world.
@Russet>As Fire I feel smothered, oppressed, and yearn to spring up afresh.
Citrine>As Air I-
```

Miles watches as Robert pauses, wonder in his face, as he tries to put his experience into words:

> I see clearly the greatness and the failings of this world.

Robert rises and goes to the altar. Standing there he seems to Miles momentarily to expand, as though reaching to the corners of the room, and thrusting forth a hand he calls out:

"Receive, Sandalphon, the gift of my response to thee."

He stands, breathing firmly out, hand stretched forth, and when his outbreath is finished and he lowers his hand, it seems to Miles that Robert has been left serene and refreshed. Doubting, but unwilling to be outdone, Miles stands too, and silently stretches forth his arm, but for once, words desert him. Nonetheless, it is as though the bleak, bleak pity drains out of him through his arm and leaving the emptiness within a peaceful silence in the depths of his being. Savouring the feeling, Miles takes the keyboard again, trusting that the others, wherever they are, have done something similar according to their style, taking leave of the presence of the archangel.

>As the Lamp of Spirit I lead us out of the Chamber of Malkuth. let us ascend the Tree of Life to the Chamber of Yesod.

With that, Robert takes over the keyboard and takes them to the next room, receiving from sPyroquin the colour scheme of Yesod and the sigil of its archangel, Gabriel. Miles changes the music.

And so it goes, from chamber to chamber, each playing their elemental role from Yesod through Hod, Netzach and the beautiful Tiphareth, where the experience of the archangel Raphael causes Black to delay for some time, apparently overcome.

So far, so good, thinks Miles, who has been steeling himself for this moment from the very night he and sPyroquin planned the ritual.

Geburah, Strength, whose archangel is Khamael, the Severity of God.

Geburah, where Molesey had intended to meet and

examine his death probe servitor.

Geburah, where Molesey found his greatest fear mutated, amplified, and hurled back at him.

Geburah, where Molesey died.

And since? Miles types:

Citrine>As the Lamp of Spirit, I welcome you to the realm of Geburah, Strength. Let us ask the blessing of Khamael, the Archangel of Geburah.

Again he hands the keyboard to Robert, who summons up the screen wallpaper of Geburah and the sigil of Khamael. The wallpaper is scarlet, the sigil traced in brown. Miles finds it disturbing, and it takes only a moment to figure out why. It reminds him of ...

The painting that caused young Helena to throw a fit.

Miles changes the music again. Holst's "Mars" from the *Planets Suite* begins, threatening, soulless, mechanistic.

Meanwhile, the others are adding their parts:

Olive>As Water, I yield to Strength and meet without resisting.
Black>As Earth, Strength crystallizes in me and becomes firm.
Citrine>As Air, I appreciate the limits of Strength.
@Russet>As Fire, I turn up the heat and give Strength direction and purpose.
>holy shit did any of you feel that?
Olive>I feel kind of strange like Im being occupied.
Citrine>RUOK?
Olive>There's something, I can't describe it, a feeling of I dunno something very big hurtling towards me   my screen's going funny.
Black>Mine also. Same thing.
Citrine>Russet, you ok?
@Russet>shit everybodyout.

Miles goes cold inside. Robert, beside him, is entranced, staring wide-eyed at the screen. The pixels on the monitor are changing colour, deepening to reddish-browns, and the sigil is disintegrating in swirls of ochre and darker reds. Miles acts:

```
Citrine>everybody go to last chamber now.
```

Miles has to nudge Robert out of trance to reaccess the Tiphareth room, then he snatches the keyboard back. sPyroquin is already there.

```
@Russet>It pounced on us as soon as we
started.  And it's infected my graphics.
I feel like I've opened the door on a
raging fire and gotten caught in the
backdraft.
Citrine>How you feel?
@Russet>Hot.  Shitscared.
Black>My screen is breaking up again.
Olive>Guys I've gotto get away from this.
Citrine>Back the way we came, offline and
banish severely.  Now.
```

Miles hands the keyboard back to Robert, whose trembling fingers rattle the keyboard. Nevertheless the swirling brown pattern appears on the screen, obscuring the last text. The screen changes to the emerald green of Netzach with the group's names appearing briefly, but in the time it takes to leave Miles can already see the encroaching swirls of blood-red twisting the images on the screen.

It chases them right back to the Malkuth room, where Robert hurriedly logs offline. From his seat in front of the monitor he looks up at Miles. “Je-sus! What the fuck happened there?”

But Miles doesn't answer. He is staring in horror at the monitor, where Robert's opening screen is dissolving in a maelstrom of reds, browns and black.

In sPyroquin's apartment, the magician yanks the disk out of his computer and disconnects the modem. It's too late, and the virus whorls onto his screen. He pulls the plug and the computer goes dead. sPyroquin swears and stands up in front of his ruined machine.

The flames from his little brazier flare up, casting malignant patterns against the ceiling, by a trick of the light appearing to circle above sPyroquin's head with a deep reddish glow.

Suddenly he feels very unsafe. He tears off his rust-red tunic and makes for the main light switch, but when he turns it on it makes no difference to the circling, spiralling patterns of light from the brazier. SPyroquin's heart begins to pound, for this is beyond even his experience, and he begins to chant the words of a joke he had intended as the final banishing later in the ritual, but the words stick in his throat. The noises of the overpopulated apartment block suddenly roar out of the walls and through the floor and ceiling, and the traffic outside seems to speed up and race to sPyroquin's living room window. There is a roaring in his ears and sPyroquin squeezes his eyes tight shut to blot it out, finding instead that behind his eyelids the darkness is tinged with a living swirling, malevolent red.

In his temple, USZAUTZAANP has also unplugged his stricken computer and stands forlorn in front of his guttering black candle, the only light in the dismal room. He tries to compose himself, but it is as though the sandstorm of pixels on his monitor has cleared to present a desert landscape in his thoughts. He was breathtaken by the sheer beauty of the vision of Tiphareth, like a purity he'd been missing in two decades of magical practice, but now it seemed like just a quick hit of a happy drug, cheap and pointless, meaning nothing but the endless gullibility of the human species. Instead, here he is, alone, still frightened by what nearly overcame him, in a cold dark house which nobody visits, the only light, warmth and companionship being one short-lived candle sputtering its life away on a bare floor. He wonders what he's made of his life.

He kneels with his head in his hands, staying there as the desolation makes itself felt. The nothingness. The emptiness.

He reaches out and snuffs out the candle.

Tohubohu 555 watches helplessly as the virus takes over her monitor, reducing the four colours of Malkuth to variations on red, brown and black, in a cyclone of graphical rage. Then she too disconnects the machine. She cannot, however, disconnect the deep sense of oppression, of being the victim, the prey, of an unimaginable entity. She had felt it as frustration, suppressed ferocity, and had seen in the vision of the circling storm the colours of dried blood, whipping up the hurricane from which there is no escape. Even now she suspects it lurks within, waiting to erupt again, and she dare not look inside to find out. Instead she digs her phone out from behind the camouflage netting, plugs it back in and dials sPyroquin's number.

The phone is dead.

The last strident chord ceases, and in the silence Miles finds the room suddenly stifling. He's alert enough to recognise that whatever happened at the ritual has returned with them. He begins the banishing ritual with adrenaline-fuelled fervour. Robert is still seated, gazing into space, and what he sees there is not to be guessed at.

Miles, dagger in sweating hand, opens his arms wide in the Cabbalistic cross, trying hard to visualise the divine light intersecting in his body as he intones loudly, too loudly for the early hours of the morning, the prayer. He strides the four quarters, drawing pentagrams in the air and fairly shouting the god-names at each quarter, thrusting the dagger forward as though in hopes of spearing the invading entity. He evokes the archangels with the desperation of an emergency call:

"For about me shines the Pentagram, and within me shines the six-rayed star."

He concludes a little less forcefully, as the old familiar ritual imposes its mood. Then Miles glances at Robert.

Robert is sitting unconscious with his eyes wide open. The expression on his face is that of utter terror.

Miles checks him over and can find nothing wrong. But he can get no response from the younger man. He has a choice. Do I call a doctor and let ordinary medicine recover the man's wits? After what we've been through, do I abdicate in favour of the purely rational processes of the local M.D.?

Do I give up?

Or do I sort this out the magician's way?

Am I a magician, or have I been a wanker all these years?

I have been a wanker all these years.

But I am a magician. And he says aloud, "I am Frater Quid Scis Id Eris!" and picking up the dagger again, removes the citrine trappings and banishes and banishes and banishes until at about six in the morning, as dawn first stains the darkness though the now unobstructed window, Robert comes around.

But Miles can tell by looking at Robert that he has not got rid of the demon, only put it out of sight.

For now.

II

Greater Invocation

Scorpion

She was crawling along the ground, head hung so low below her shoulders that her face was almost pressed into the earth. The earth gave off a heat which almost seemed to sear the flesh from her cheeks. But there was no way that she would lift her head, no way. To do that would mean that she would see what was above her.

There were voices behind her. She thought she almost recognised them. They were saying nothing that she understood on a conscious level, simply burbling in tongues that bore no relation to any human language she had ever heard, but the sense of what they were saying was not lost on her.

Look up, they urged her. You know you'll have to, eventually.

She was naked, alone, and tears were pressing at her eyes for release. Damned, I'm damned, this is hell, the hell that's always been with me, *within* me, I've never been able to purge myself of it and now it's consumed me, now that I'm ...

Dead?

No. No, that's not it. It was tempting to give in to the despair. Fuck knows how many times she'd done that in the past, cocooning herself in it, convincing herself that if she did this nothing worse could get at her. But it was something about those incomprehensible voices that made her steel herself against that particular temptation. It was what they seemed to be saying that was so unacceptable, not the voices themselves; if anything, they seemed rather benevolent.

She curtailed her forward motion, and began the slow process of raising her head. As she did so, her eyes widened to extract every last scrap of information, every glimmer of light, from her surroundings. The ground was frozen into convolutions of what appeared to be solidified lava, orangey-red stone that she thought she could hear breathing, though it may have been that the surface was not entirely at rest, and the sound was that of the slow stirring of the rock.

The colouration of the ground may not, however, have been due to the lava itself; there was a heavy redness to the air that she found that, on turning her face heavenward at last, was emanating from a sky that seemed to be on the verge of boiling. The dark clouds were marbled through with streaks of sanguine red in perpetual, frenetic motion. She found herself, almost against her volition, following the path of these 'veins' as they moved above and behind her, spiralling inward toward a hub situated directly above a great sceptre of rock. At first, she could not identify if the rock was either natural (if such a word was truly applicable here) or artificial. A glow of even deeper red was beginning to emanate from this central point, clearing up the mystery of the structure's origin by illuminating windows, masonry, and, at its very apex, something that bore a peculiar resemblance to a crown or coronet.

What's more, it was beginning to look familiar to her.

As she looked, she could see a figure standing at one of the windows, and she was gripped by a terrible fear. She shouted out, and saw him (she knew the figure to be male) look down at her.

But even as he did so, she saw in the sky the exact likeness of something terrible which had already infected her consciousness, something which she was only now seeing in its full terrible glory. A jagged blade of light cut down from the axis of the storm into the crown at the top of the tower.

Flames instantly leapt from all of the windows, and through her screams she watched as a lone figure was propelled from the window, falling directly toward her, his familiar face transforming into another as he approached, linked only by mutual terror.

His scream reached her. Merged with hers.

"Robert!"

"Helena?"

There was a face close to hers, but it had changed, become female. It was a few moments before Helena managed to attach a name to it.

"Debbie ... er, hi ..."

"You having that dream again?"

Helena shook her head as she sat upright, while Debbie's nursing instincts clicked into place and had her puffing up the pillows.

"No, this one was different. Well, sort of ... a lot of the same elements, but a lot of new stuff as well."

"Like Robert, you mean?"

Helena looked at her friend with a mixture of surprise and embarrassment. "Did I actually call his name out?"

"Christ, yeah." Debbie grinned. "In fact, my first thought was that you'd gotten lucky tonight. But then ..."

"Then what?"

Debbie shrugged. "Then I realised you sounded more *concerned* than anything else. Like ... like you're watching somebody you care about going through some terrible experience and there's not a bloody thing you can do about it."

You don't know the half of it, Helena thought. And it's more than just concern for Robert himself; something was telling her – perhaps it was part of what those incomprehensible voices in the dream were trying to say – that this whole business, whatever it was, could have wider, more terrible repercussions.

Something's changed. It's all jumped up to a new level, tonight ...

She looked at her bedside clock. 4:02. She remembered someone referring to the period between 3 and 4 a.m. as *the hour of the wolf*, the time when you're most vulnerable to the 'night terrors', when nightmares bite just that little bit deeper. It was tempting for Helena to try and rationalise all of this in similar fashion, as simply the product of her natural sleep patterns and her current rather, ahem, *unsettled* state of mind.

Tempting, but not convincing. She disconcerted Debbie by suddenly throwing back the bedclothes and springing to her feet.

"Going somewhere?"

"Well, not back to sleep, that's for sure," said Helena. "I have a feeling today's going to be quite busy for me, so I wouldn't mind making an early start."

Debbie yawned, shaking her head in bafflement. "Have it your way. You won't mind if I go back to bed, though, will you? It's only that I've got this thing called *work* at nine o'clock this morning, and ..."

"Go on, then. Sod off." Helena hugged her friend, at first with requisite casualness, but then more tightly. The realisation that more was at stake than the mind of Robert Pierce had taken hold, and was colouring her life with terror for all those around her.

As Debbie stood, Helena heard her friend's slipper scuff on something on the floor, just on the other side of the bed. Debbie reached down and picked up a rectangle of blue-backed card.

"I thought you'd take more care of these things, seeing as how they're a big part of your livelihood."

"Funny," said Helena as Debbie handed her the errant Tarot card, "I don't remember bringing any of my cards up here recently."

It was one of her standard Waite deck, her favourite one for readings because of its relative simplicity and its visual familiarity to even the Tarot novice. She turned it over in her hand, and froze, the breath held fast in her chest.

"Helena? Are you OK?"

There was a pause while Helena recovered her composure, and a further one while she considered what to say. Eventually, she settled on obfuscation.

"Nothing. It's nothing. Just felt a bit weird for a second

there, probably shouldn't have stood up so fast. I'll be all right, really."

Debbie 'hmm'-ed sceptically, tightened her dressing gown about herself, and with one last reassuring smile, left the room. Helena was left to stand and stare in wonder at the card in her hand.

XVI. The Tower. A tall, crown-capped edifice being struck by lightning and bursting into flames, as figures fall from the windows to their deaths on the rocks below.

Ever get the feeling that someone, somewhere, is trying to tell you something ...?

"... Look, all I need is some sort of contact number for him. Yes, I'm quite aware what time it is over there, and I've already apologised," (about fifteen bloody times) "but this is something of an emergency. Didn't I make that clear?"

The voice on the other end of the phone continued to yammer on about being dragged out of bed, but this time, at least, Miles could hear the sound of pages being turned in the background as she searched for a number, any number that might get this crazy Brit out of her hair. He'd been on the phone for over an hour now, trawling through all of his stateside contacts in the hope of finding one who might be able to put him in touch with sPyroquin. He was rather surprised to find that even people who'd been in contact with the man for a considerably greater length of time than he had – years, in some cases – knew only slightly more about him than Miles had been able to glean.

Eventually, he'd managed to get hold of the soon-to-be ex-wife of someone who'd been quite close to sPyroquin, and he was lucky enough to find that the guy hadn't taken his address book with him when he left. Careless, but for Miles, at least, fortunate. Potentially.

While the half-conscious murmurings and paper rustlings continued to pour into Miles' ear all the way from New Orleans, he was keeping one eye on the figure that was, at the moment, sitting immobile on the couch, staring into space. The periods of silence between the 'lectures' were getting shorter, that much was sure. Any second now, Robert would, in all likelihood, get to his feet and begin pacing the room, and the words would follow a minute or so later.

What he was talking about, Miles had no idea. Robert hadn't yet figured out a way to reduce his flow of speech to a rate at which it could be understood (apart from the odd word or phrase – *flesh* seemed to figure quite heavily), and he was still too busy trying to find out what had happened to the other participants in the ritual to devote much energy to this task.

The woman on the other end of the phone came back on, to inform Miles that there didn't seem to be any entry for sPyroquin in the phone book ...

"Oh, terrific, bloody *terrific*. Look, are you sure ..."

However, if he'd let her finish, she'd tell him that there was a number in the book that appeared to have a New Orleans area code, next to ...

And here she read out a surname, which he realised, in light of his e-mail exchanges with sPyroquin, must be the 'real' moniker of TohuBohu 555. He scribbled the details on a piece of paper by the side of the phone, tore it off, fended off the drawled complaints of his unwilling communicant with a hopefully sincere-sounding 'thank you', and hung up.

Before he could dial this new number, however, Pierce's voice began to ring out in garbled declamations from the living room, like some Speaker's Corner loonytoon on fast-forward. Miles got up and stood in the doorway, fascinated and infuriated in equal measure by what was issuing from Pierce's mouth.

Concerned too, of course. Don't forget 'concerned'.

He found now that he could make more sense of Pierce's ramblings (he had, as yet, no better way of describing them) if he only paid closer attention. The reason why the word 'flesh' appeared so many times was that the same phrases, the same *passages*, kept re-occurring, as if on some sort of tape-loop. What's more, with each cycle, they had more 'flesh' (so to speak) on their bones; Miles was getting the distinct impression now of something emerging from the gobbledygook, a more defined form, a *structure*.

And buggered if it doesn't sound familiar.

"... *formless and void* ... everything that we are is

simply an instant of stillness in the eye of the Mother of Storms ... to understand what is beyond we must dare to leave the safety of *the self* and surrender ourselves to the chaos ... we must *become* that chaos, bind it into every cell of our being ...

"*Explore the fullness of the mystery of our flesh* ... for all the apparent order that we see in ourselves, we are nothing but turmoil, flux ... the eternal sloughing of the skin of the ancient reptile within ... from decay, comes renewal, and this is so in every instant of time ... at every moment, the flesh is in constant change, but we maintain an appearance of permanence, of *order*. Can there be any greater proof that the flesh *is in order as it is*, that no matter what we may do to it? We cannot alter its essential sanctity; we mutilate it, paint it, disguise it in a thousand ways from our own disgusted gaze, our religions denigrate it as an obscene prison for the 'spirit', but all of this is merely a refusal to face the reality of our own slow, eternal mutability ... the spirit is *in* that mutability, that chaos!"

"*Ecce carnem! Ecce templum Spiritui Sancti!*"

And so on, and so forth, et cetera. It took Miles more than half an hour of intense attention to fashion some sort of coherency out of Robert's 'whirling words', and even then he had to restructure a lot of it in his own mind even for it to make *that* much sense. But there was no mistaking the style that Robert was, whether consciously or not, attempting to emulate. Miles had seen it – right down to a large proportion of the phrasing – in the notebooks of Nicholas Molesey.

Then Miles watched as Robert, apparently exhausted by the effort of releasing these words, would slump back into the couch and, after a moment's disorientation (during which he would occasionally look in Miles' direction, almost pathetically, as if begging for some kind of explanation), revert to his previous state of lethargy.

I have to know what's going on here, thought Miles. Something happened during that ritual, something far more catastrophic than I've ever seen before. I can't raise sPyroquin, and something tells me that, whatever it is, it's worse by far than anything I'm looking at now.

He returned to the phone, and dialled the number that the woman had given him. After a few rings, there was the distinctive click and hiss of an answering machine ...

Oh, shite, I hate these fucking things ...

And then an unfamiliar voice broke in, a woman with an extremely sexy Deep South lilt and a timbre that made Miles instantly think of cigarettes, bourbon and sex:

"Hi there, this is Janice –"

(*Janice?* Her name is *Janice?*)

"– and as the smarter ones amongst you will already have figured out, I'm not home right now, so if it's important, leave a message after the tone. Some advice though? *Make sure it's important.* I get really pissed at time wasters. This means you, Mr Cold-calling-insurance-salesman-type-guy. OK? Bye."

Miles had only the briefest of intervals between the end of the message and the promised tone to make a mental note to get to know this woman better one day, but he made it good. Then he began speaking.

"Janice, hello, this is Miles Hearne ... er, you'd probably know me better as Frater QSIE. I'm just ringing to find out what's going on over there. I haven't been able to get a response to e-mails from either you or sPyroquin, so I'm trying the direct approach. Get back to me as soon as possible, I need to know what's going on. There's some weird stuff going on at this end too. And have either of you heard anything more from, er, whatsisname, USZAP- UZUPU- that guy in Malmo?" He intoned the number at Robert's flat into the mouthpiece. "Keep me informed. Bye."

He tried to think of anything more that he could be doing here, but his brain appeared to be on the verge of complete shutdown. He couldn't recollect feeling this tired in, well, ever. Sorcerers weren't supposed to lose vitality with age; it was one of the attractions of the job. You get old, you grow a beard down to your knees, you become a venerated and powerful mage.

Not only that, you get a bigger staff. With a knob on the end.

With this thought in his mind, he flopped down into the armchair opposite the still moribund figure of Robert, and almost instantly began laughing. Where the strength came from to maintain this mirth, he didn't know, and didn't care; he wasn't even particularly sure what he was laughing *at*. But tides of hilarity engulfed him, and while he made some initial effort to keep the noise down (out of some misplaced desire not to wake Robert up, as if that were even possible), he was soon roaring and shrieking, the sound of which inspired him to even greater amusement. He slid off the chair.

Banish with laughter. Way to go, Miles, matey.

The laughter subsided, leaving him feeling drained but slightly euphoric. He was looking up at the ceiling of Robert's flat, absorbing himself in its whiteness, the whiteness of a blank page. A few minutes before, he would have been tempted to fill the emptiness with words, explanations, stories to fill in the gulf between his experience and his theories. But right now, he didn't care to try.

His head tilted downward, and he found himself staring into the eyes of Robert Pierce. The very awake, very *alive* eyes of Robert Pierce. And beneath those eyes ... a smile. Sort of. It clung to the lower half of Pierce's face as though it had been recently transplanted from somewhere else, and was still unsure of the territory.

"Miles ..."

Slow, sibilant. His name hissed away into silence, a silence Miles didn't feel like breaking just yet.

"Miles Hearne?"

He nodded. So did Pierce, as if a suspicion had been confirmed. Then the younger man looked down at his hands, flexing the fingers.

"Robert ... are you all right?"

At first, he didn't react, and Miles had a moment of unease as he wondered if he'd even recognised his own name. Then, without looking up, Pierce spoke.

"I'm fine. In fact, Miles, I think it's safe to say that I've never been better."

"But you were ..." Bloody hell, how do you tell someone that he's been behaving like a complete balmpot for about four hours? "You were behaving a bit oddly."

"Was I?" He glanced at Miles, all innocence. "Sorry. Must have been overdoing it, had a bit of a funny turn. You know how it is."

No, not really. "I'm still trying to find out what happened to sPyroquin and the others."

"Oh yes?" Robert did not even attempt to feign concern. "Well, I'm sure everything will be all right."

"I wish I had your confidence."

"Miles ..." He smiled, this time more confidently, mouth tilted at a strange angle. "Look at me, Miles. *I'm* all right, aren't I?"

"Are you? I'd like some independent verification of that."

"You worry too much."

The phone rang, cutting off any reply that Miles might have made. Pierce watched him curiously as he got up to answer. Their eyes were still locked together as a tremulous voice, after a rather uncertain pause, whispered from the earpiece.

"F–Frater?"

"Yes?" It had taken Miles a few moments to realise that he was being addressed by his magical name. "Janice? Is that you?"

"He's dead."

Miles closed his eyes tight. This was it, all his worst fears of the last few hours given form. Dear, sweet Goddess, what have we done?

"How? How did it happen?"

"They don't know ... not yet. His apartment, it, it was gutted, his body was burned so badly they don't know if he was killed in the fire or he was dead before that ... oh shit ..."

He could hear her restrained sobs, the sound of fingers passed through hair in agitation, the occasional sniffle. He waited for her to speak again.

"I saw it too."

"Saw what?" Silence. "Janice, what did you see?"

"The thing that killed him. It was here too, with me, in this room. I think it's still here ..."

"Janice ..." He tried to maintain the composure in his voice, for her sake, but he wasn't sure how well it was working. "Janice, are you still there?"

"Yes. I'm here."

"Can you describe it?"

"No. I mean, I can ... I *could* ... but I don't want to."

"Please, Janice ..."

Deep breaths on the other end of the line. Damn me for doing this, but I have to *know* ...

"Something took over the monitor. It was ... red. And alive. It was like it was coming out of the screen at me, straight into my head. At first, it looked like a sandstorm, swirling and blowing, and I had this feeling that if I looked at it for too long it would just take my eyes out ... but it wasn't sand, it was the colour of blood, like a blood storm ..."

She paused, and Miles thought that she might not begin again, but then she continued:

"I couldn't take my eyes off it, though, that's the weird thing. Had me completely fucking tranced. I don't even remember switching off the computer. What did I do, Frater? Is it my fault?"

"No, Janice, no –"

"But it's still *here!* I don't think I could sleep right now anyway, but even if I could, I wouldn't, you know? 'Cause, 'cause, if I did, it would come and get me in my dreams. Wouldn't it? It would. Wouldn't it?"

Yes. Yes, Janice, I think it probably would.

"What do I do now, Frater? I keep wanting to ring Lee," (by this, she probably meant sPyroquin) "and ask him. But he's dead. He's *dead.* What do I do?"

Miles was still considering what to say when there was a soft click and the line went dead. Maybe it was accidental, maybe the question had been rhetorical, maybe she'd just given up on receiving an answer.

sPyroquin was dead, and the woman he had just spoken to was, quite obviously, now a quite different person to the funny, confident, even *brash* young woman he had heard on the answering machine. Of the remaining participant, the Swedish guy, there was not a trace. Perhaps he was dead too. Miles didn't really want to know just yet.

And Robert? He was still sitting on the couch, looking around him, smiling like an imbecile, apparently at ease with the world. A moment's rage. Miles wanted to go over there and wipe that stupid grin off his face. At least one person was dead because of his fixation on Molesey, and all he could do was sit there and fucking well *smirk?* Miles clenched his fists.

No. Banish that. He closed his eyes and tried to visualise the anger, and instantly he was looking at a vortex of crimson energy, spiralling towards him ...

He leapt to his feet, eyes wide. Panic surged, quickening his pulse, bringing heat to his face and pain to his chest. He huddled into himself and lurched toward the bathroom. There, with the door safely locked behind him (he didn't want Robert seeing him like this, not now), he sat on the toilet and cupped handfuls of cold, cold water from the basin to his forehead and mouth. Robbed of his ability to banish in his usual fashion, he took (for no readily apparent reason) to singing the chorus of 'Yellow Submarine' to himself, over and over. Slowly, the crisis passed, and his pulse resumed its usual serene rhythm.

So, he said to himself as he composed himself in the bathroom mirror, it looks like I got a dose of whatever-it-was as well. What now?

He emerged and re-entered the living room. Robert hadn't moved. Miles was beginning to wonder if he'd lost the ability.

"Do you know, Miles," Robert said, " I don't think I've seen a sunrise in ages." Miles followed his gaze; he was looking across the room, watching the dawn through a gap in the curtains.

"All these things that I've been missing. The simple things. The things that make life, well, worth living, I suppose. I dare say I'm not alone in that – this is, after all, the 'modern world' – but it's only at moments like this that you realise how much we live inside our minds, how much we avoid the purely physical. It really is an epiphany, Miles. A bloody revelation."

"sPyroquin's dead."

Robert looked at him curiously. "I'm – sorry," he said at last, as if he had been trying to recall the right etiquette for this situation. "Were you very close?"

"Never met him. Aside from that, yes, I suppose you could say we were."

Robert nodded with a look on his face that could have been interpreted as a parody of sympathy. Then, with a briskness that surprised Miles, considering Robert's recent torpor, he stood up.

"Well, you'll be wanting to get along then. Thanks for everything, Miles. A pity it turned out this way."

"Yes," said Miles. "Isn't it."

Robert strolled toward him to usher him to the front door, and Miles noticed, for the first time, that there was something different in the way he moved. In the enclosed space of the living room, it was difficult to be sure, but Robert appeared to be limping. And not with the awkward hobble of a man who's just pulled a calf muscle or sprained an ankle; this was the assured and practiced, almost *fluid*, motion of a man who has lived with an infirmity for a long time and has compensated his balance accordingly.

At the front door, with Robert holding it open for him, Miles turned and said, "So, you're sure you're all right then?"

"Quite sure, thank you, Miles. No need to worry about me. You just look after yourself, all right?"

With this, Robert reached up and touched Miles on the cheek, lingeringly. For one moment, he thought that Robert was going to kiss him; then the younger man, seemingly remembering that this was not, in fact, someone else, pulled his hand away, smiled sheepishly and said:

"And, er ... I'm, um, sorry again about your friend."

Miles felt the door close against his back, and the stirrings of panic began once more in his belly. He made it to the lift, out of the building and out to his car before the tears of anger and frustration and fear spilled from him.

Oh, dear sweet Goddess, what the fuck have I done?

Somewhere around her third cup of coffee, Helena finally had to admit to herself that she had absolutely no idea what she was doing. The day had started – once that dream was out of the way – so full of promise and portent, but had now dragged itself to a weary halt in a town centre cafe, grotty of decor and greasy of spoon, where she now peered out at the rain-slimed street and tried to make sense of her jangled feelings.

To assist in this process, she fumbled with the packet of tranquilisers from her bag, popped one from its protective bubble, and downed it with a gulp of luke-warm coffee. It did occur to her that it may, perhaps, be as a result of her intake of tranx that her momentum had slipped away from her. But this was balanced against the certainty that if she hadn't popped the pills, then the panic that still lurked in the background of her mind would by now have brought her low.

Trouble is, she mused, there's so much stuff out there that reminds me of, of that thing. Right now, for instance, she was looking at the reflection of a red traffic light in a puddle disturbed by the impact of large raindrops.

She pulled her mobile phone from her bag as she replaced the pills, and considered trying Robert's number once more, or Hearne's as a last resort. Most of the day had been spent in futile attempts to contact either of them, and this persistent failure had intensified her conviction that something very, very serious indeed had happened. Moreover, there was still the nagging feeling that, if anyone was in any sort of position to help him (all right, *them*) out of this situation, it was her.

It was *me* he was falling towards, remember. I'm the only one who can break his fall.

Fuck. How many tranx have I got left?

With the caffeine and valium still struggling for supremacy in her brain, she paid up and slouched out of the cafe, away from the pervasive stink of nicotine and bacon and into the pervasive stink of petrol and hot tarmac. Earlier in the day her umbrella had chosen to turn itself inside out in a gust of wind, and so, with no other protection against the elements, she turned the collar of her coat up and tried to hide herself inside it. Even with her face turned toward the pavement, however, the wind and passing traffic conspired to spray water across her cheeks and into her eyes.

She looked up periodically to get her bearings – even though she had not, as yet, settled on a destination – and each time she did so she saw the rear lights of cars through a lens of rain, turning and twisting them into bizarre patterns. Patterns that Helena knew to exist more behind her eyes than in front of them.

At length, still having no clear idea where she was going, she ducked into a shop doorway and rested her face against the cool glass, and she tried to calm herself without once more diving for the chemical assistance in her bag.

Am I going crazy? The thought had returned to her more than once in the course of the day, but so far the intensity of the dream – and her other experiences of late – had bolstered her shaky faith in her own sanity. The thing with the card this morning had further served to give her the sense of being on some sort of Divine Mission; but what if it had been merely another coincidence? What if the episode at the gallery had been simply the re-occurrence of her long-suppressed psychosis, an episode which had managed to imprint Molesey's painting on a weakened and susceptible mind? What if...?

What if I could stop thinking like my fucking therapist for a minute, and get some sort of a grip?

She was aware of the eyes of the people on her in an adjacent bus queue as she turned around, glancing surreptitiously for the most part, but one small boy was staring at her as if she had grown another head while he watched. Perhaps he wasn't far wrong. Helena stuck her tongue out at him, and he turned hastily to bury his face in his mother's side. The rest of the queue shifted uneasily, to further conceal their previous interest.

Strangely cheered by this, she took out her phone once more, and – this time without dialling Robert's number first – keyed in the number for Miles Hearne. Initially, the answer machine started up, and since Helena was in no particular mood to leave a message for anyone, she moved to break the connection. She was halted by a faint, almost hesitant "Hello?" from the phone.

"Mr Hearne?" She still couldn't bring herself to call him Miles.

"Who's that?" Suspicious. Almost – fearful?

"It's Helena. Helena McCallum."

"Oh." A pause. "Look, is it important? Only I'm busy –"

No you're not. Unless you count shitting yourself as

'busy'. "It is, rather. I've been trying to get in touch with you all day."

"Like I said, I've been busy."

"Has Robert been busy too?"

Pause again, just for a beat this time, then "I haven't spoken to him today."

Liar.

"What do you want with us? I'm presuming you want to talk to us about the same matter."

"Well, I suppose you could say that I'm just inquiring after the health of the two of you. I had this funny feeling that you might be ... a little under the weather."

"Really. And why would you say that?"

I've got him, thought Helena; he wants to say something, but he wants to find out first what *I* know. "Look, I think this would be a whole lot easier if I came round and saw you –"

"No. No, no. Not yet, anyway."

"All right. We'll cut the bullshit here and now, if you prefer.Call it an exchange of information. *Quid pro quo, Clarice,* and all that. I'll tell you what I know, you reciprocate. OK?"

He hesitated. "I'm not –"

"I've been having dreams. Scary dreams. Ever since I saw that painting by Molesey, I haven't been able to get it out of my mind. Literally. I'm seeing it everywhere I look when I'm awake, and it's managed to become part of the landscape of every fucking dream I've had since that day. And that's not all. I'm seeing Robert Pierce in these dreams as well, and it's not in a nice way, either. In every one of them, he's in some sort of terrible danger, like he's at the heart of it all, and he needs my help to get him out. But I don't know how. I wish somebody would explain to me what the hell's going on here, because I'm beginning to think I'm going insane, and believe me, I know what that's like, because *I've been there* –"

"Helena –"

"Am I going buggy again? That's what my ex-husband used to call it. Going buggy. 'Oh, don't worry, everyone, it's just Helena going buggy again'. In the end, he couldn't take it any more. This time, I'm not sure *I* can take it for much longer. I'm on my own now, there's no-one to tell me I'm going buggy."

"Helena?"

Most of the fear, the wall he had built around himself, had gone from his voice. He had heard, obviously, what he needed to hear, just as she had said what she needed to say.

"I'll contact you soon, we'll meet. I can't do it just yet. It's too soon. But ... but I can tell you right now some things that I think you should know. First of all, you're right. Something bad is happening. I'm not sure exactly what it is, or what we can do about it. That's why I need time to work things out."

"How much time do we have?"

"That I don't know either. But if we go into this unprepared, it could be just as bad as if we did nothing at all. Look ..."

He sounded as if he was trying to work out how to say this next bit, which accounted for his hesitancy when he eventually said it.

"The only thing I'm sure of is that you're not mad, you're not 'buggy'. Not one bit of it. And you're certainly not alone. I'll be in touch."

There was the softest of clicks on the other end of the line, and he was gone.

The feeling which swept over Helena was a curious mix of relief *(I'm not mad!)* and unease *(oh shit I'm not mad)*. She stepped out of the shop doorway, and was confronted by the gaze of the small boy she had poked her tongue at a few minutes before. The rest of the queue, by now more irritated by the continued non-arrival of their bus, paid her no heed.

She smiled at him this time. He once more hid his face in his mother at the sight of the 'scary woman', who fervently hoped, as she walked away down the street in search of a taxi to take her home, that she was the scariest thing he'd have to deal with.

Nicholas Molesey. Nicholas Molesey. The name throbbed in Robert's brain all the way home from Miles Hearne's house.

Memories tinged with sepia, rose and fell, an infinity of voices swelled and dropped in a dull roar, punctuated always by the name. Nicholas Molesey. Nicholas Molesey. Nicholas Molesey.

He walked in one one direction for a while before noticing that it wouldn't take him to the flat. His hip was aching, so he made his way to a bus stop. Waiting in the early-to-work queue, it dawned on him that he could call a taxi on his mobile. Why hadn't I thought of that? What's the matter with me?

He sat in the taxi, dazed and disoriented, and struggled to remember the address of the flat. The taxi fare was an outrage, and the coins seemed to swim in his hand. Once back in the familiar confines of the flat, though, he became a little more at ease. He fell onto the bed and was instantly asleep.

Not that he was at peace. Visions of mud and fire alternated with collages of artworks and faces. And the Abyss. The thick, tangible dark and its Denizens, swirling around him, fastening themselves on him, dropping away in apparent confusion and fear. The Shadow falling across him, as its origin rushed upon him from the black like a goods train, zeroing in on and hounding him as he thrashed to escape, the pressure wave of its onrush driving him headlong as it suddenly appeared –

He awoke, sweating. The Shadow had a voice, and it was saying, in a swelling roar, *Nicholas Molesey. Nicholas Molesey.* And it had a name of its own.

Scorpion.

Everything seemed foreign, from the shower to the coffee machine. And it made him more determined to make sense of the overlapping, contradictory impressions the world was giving him. He found some notes written many months earlier. He found an address and some directions. He didn't trust himself to drive the car, so he called another taxi, and in due course found himself marching through an out-of-town cemetery in the late afternoon sun, searching for the Molesey family crypt. It was a rare edifice even for the older part of the cemetery, and he had little difficulty finding it, a squat square Gothic building fit to inspire the horrors. The lock was large but in poor condition. He searched around for a moment, settling on a length of railing from a nearby grave, and dug out the lock from the frame. He levered the door towards him and it slowly gave way.

He'd brought a torch. He didn't remember having put it in his coat pocket. He switched it on and advanced into the tiny chamber, noting the stone slabs behind which were housed the remains of the Moleseys since the late 1800s. He wiped some of the stones over in order to read the names thereon, until finally he found:

Nicholas Edward Molesey
born 20th Nov 1889
died 6th Nov 1929
beloved son of Edward James Molesey
and Elizabeth Hannah Molesey

O grave, where is thy victory?
O death, where is thy sting? (1Co. 15:55)

Where indeed? The answer came unbidden.

Scorpion.

The voice calling, *Nicholas Molesey. Nicholas Molesey.*

The death probe, returning to unload its findings for its creator.

The simple elemental, enhanced to enter the dread bourne and return, and return it did, warped beyond all imagination by its sojourn in the Abyss of Death.

The entity, created like its namesake, tough and fierce, given the cold hard survival characteristics that would enable it pass through Death, returning with those same characteristics amplified to the point where they were unbearable even to its master.

The Scorpion, even now loose in the world, unleashing its lethal wisdom in ever-increasing circles. Seeking once more its missing master, ravenous with hunger to fulfil its mission, to deliver the truth about Death.

The Scorpion, manifesting in a world unfitted to receive it.

A world in danger from the gaping tear in the veil of

Death, through which at first we glimpse –

Scorpion.

O Death, here is thy sting. That there are worse things than death.

Scorpion. You have to be stopped.

He touched the words cut into the stone of Nicholas Molesey. They said nothing. They were cold and still.

Naturally. There's nobody home.

He is not here. He has arisen.

He pulled a penknife from his jacket pocket. He didn't remember bringing that either, but unquestioningly he opens out the smaller of the blades and scratches carefully at the soft stone of Nicholas Molesey's tomb. It carves easily, and he painstakingly adds to the epitaph, in thin angular lettering, the words:

He is not here. He has arisen.

He steps back, right arm aching from the effort, and views his work. Then he places the torch on the floor in front of him, butt down, shining up onto the low vaulted ceiling as he gazes at the words, exhausted and entranced. Then he speaks, and his voice sounds different, no longer his familiar voice, speaking words which arise unbidden:

"We begin with ourselves,
each of us infinite,
without boundaries,
co-extensive with all that is;
as below, so above
to Infinity."

He raises his arms out from his sides, and the words continue:

"We stand at the axis mundi,
the fulcrum of Infinity,
from whence we move the world according to our will,

for in Infinity the centre is everywhere
and it is Here, Now.
Ecce carnem, ecce templum Spiritui Sancti."

As he speaks, the torchlight in the tiny crypt seems to soften and diffuse, and the atmosphere thickens around him. He feels a warmth in his abdomen, a heat and pressure which first increases, then spreads throughout his body, rising up his back until his hackles rise, his scalp and forehead break out in sweat and his hair stands on end. Face flushing, he is impelled to speak:

"The flesh is in order as it is.
Have faith in the mystery within.

"We act our divinity alive
in the ebb and the flow of the flesh.

"I am the Passion and the Life
in my limbs and my lungs and my veins."

He sways as the sensation rushes through him again, then again, until the ebb and flow of the flesh pulses with his breathing and he can barely stand for the continual wringing out of his body. The blood vessels of his hands and forearms are engorged with blood, and he realises that he still holds the penknife. Still throbbing with energy, blood roaring in his head, he opens out the larger blade and slashes across his left palm, barely feeling the drag of the blade through his flesh. As the blood emerges he steps forward and rubs his reddened palm into the words newly carved into the stone. Then, dropping the knife, he rubs away the blood from around the lettering until they stand out against the pale stone, glowing like an after-image seared into his vision. The rushing sensation overpowers him once more as he stands, unsteady, gazing at the words which gaze back at him, and the wave of heat and pressure seems to reach out beyond his skin. It fills the tiny chamber as well, and with a scream which is thrown back and forth by the stones of the dead and leaves his ears ringing, he falls to his hands and knees, shattered, gasping for breath, the sweat running down his arms and dripping off his face onto the stone.

He stayed like that for some time, vacant, exhausted. When he felt able to stand he noticed the sweat marks on the stone floor, left by his knees and hands, one palm print darker than the other. The torchlight had returned to normal, and the blood-anointed lettering on Nicholas Molesey's stone no longer glowed back at him.

Until he closed his eyes.

He picked up his knife and torch and left the crypt. The confusion of earlier had passed, and everything was falling into place now. He saw everything with new eyes, inspecting his hands as though they were not his own, energised with a new sense of purpose.

And triumph. Pulling the door of the crypt until it was very nearly closed, he took a deep breath and exhaled, savouring the movement of the air in his lungs. He had a purpose, a mission to fulfil urgently, and his very existence was at stake, but for the moment it was good to be alive. He smiled to himself and made his way out of the cemetery and into the approaching night.

He is not here. He has arisen.

>the shape just appears out of nowhere, at first i thought it was some freaky fucking screensaver that had got onto my hard drive, but it wont go away even when u move the mouse, and then it only stays for a minute or so and then its gone.whats more its started doing something to my head like im seeing the bastard everywhere.scary shit.ne1 else come across it?

Oh yes, said Miles to the screen, I'm quite familiar with it. In fact, you might even say I was midwife at its birth.

He'd been monitoring the chatrooms almost constantly since the day of the ritual, and the first confirmations of his fears had started trickling in about 12 hours later. Naturally, those first reports had been on the occult boards-- sPyroquin's 'tame virus' appeared to have been designed to raid the address books of every recipient and mail itself to everyone therein before the recipient had even opened the offending message himself, and of course, the address books of those taking part in the online ritual had been full of people with similar interests.

Within 24 hours, however, the infection had spread into the general online community,and now the Net was alive with pleas for assistance from those whose systems had been invaded by something that, although it appeared to cause no harm (as yet) to software, hardware or data, was having some rather peculiar after-effects on the user. One person had said that it was like having

`>the image burned onto my retinas`

like he'd been staring too long at the sun.

Right now, he was watching the first report hitting a newsgroup devoted to the study, breeding and care of computer viruses. Reading some of the previous postings, Miles had been rather taken aback-- relatively innocent as he was of the ways of the 'hacker'-- at how much delight these people seemed to take at spreading mischief and disorder. There was no political or ideological agenda that he could make out, just the simple joy which a child takes in pissing from a high window, or pulling the wings off a fly.

These people might just be worth talking to if they ever grow up, thought Miles at one point.

Almost instantly, the replies to the guy who had asked for confirmation of what he'd seen were coming in. It had, it seemed, spread now as far as Japan and Australia, judging from the poor English of the responses; and the effect was much the same. Everyone who saw this thing was apparently doomed to keep seeing it, whether they were in front of the computer, walking down the street or asleep in bed.

And that's the curious thing, Miles realised fairly quickly. The visions were uniform, and the effect just as disturbing, whether the one afflicted was in Kyoto or Cardiff. This wasn't simply some sort of culturally based phenomena, it was working on a far deeper, more *universal* level. Miles was left wondering whether it would have the same effect on some

Amazonian native as it was having on his more supposedly 'sophisticated' cousins.

Must remember to ask next time I bump into one in the post office queue.

He went back to the occult chatrooms to see what shape the latest discussions on the problem were taking. Curiously, he found that discussion on this phenomena had, if not exactly dried up completely, then certainly reverted to its original trickle. Other concerns had taken the place of theorisation on the nature of the thing which had invaded the consciousness of all those who had encountered it; a whole barrage of 'flaming' was underway when Miles logged on, apparently triggered by the most trivial of disagreements between two of the regular participants. From the sketchy details that Miles managed to glean from the abuse, it looked very much as if some minor (in his eyes, anyway) point of procedure surrounding the proper invocation of some god-form or other had magnified a personality clash between these two persons into a full-on battle. No-one was yet at the stage where it could be called a magickal 'duel'-- Miles very much doubted whether these two clowns were capable of doing much more than was already going on-- but the potential for a much more serious conflict, in whatever form, was there. Moreover, the conflict was spreading outwards from the original combatants to various other individuals who, in taking sides, were becoming every bit as heated and immoderate in their language. This, for example:-

>how you've got the nerve to call yourself a sorcerer I don't know, far as I can see you couldn't even summon up a hard-on in a whorehouse, let alone a demon

-or this:-

>you're nothing but a fucking fraud, a posturing little wanker with all the charisma of a week-old dogturd, you only got into magick cause even the dungeons & dragons crowd threw you out for being too

```
much of a nerd
```

-though occasionally the abuse became *really* personal:-

```
>why dont u go fuck yourself u
motherfucking piece of donkey shite & then
go and fucking well DIE so we can all
laugh ha ha and then i can come and piss
on your grave u childmolesting diseased
bastard cunt
```

My, my. The spirit of Oscar Wilde lives on.

After a few hours of reading this sort of thing, a peculiar impression occurred to Miles. This type of aggressive, inflammatory (not to say illiterate) rhetoric was not unusual on the Net, but he couldn't recall seeing it in quite such quantity, and with such relentless duration. On clicking over to some of the other chatrooms that he frequented, he was rather amazed to discover that similar arguments were in progress there also, ranging from the nascent to the fully-fledged abusefest. And nowhere was there anything more than the most fleeting mention of the computer virus which, only a day or so before, had been exercising a considerable portion of their attention and energies.

Something has happened here. It's as though... as though those who saw the shape on their computer screen have been changed in some way.

No, wait. I'm jumping ahead of myself. I've got no evidence to support that, just an intuition. I don't even have any idea whether the people who are at each other's (virtual) throats today even saw the thingy yesterday. All I know is...

Absolutely nothing. What's there to know? I've found myself on the shakiest of ground here, and I'm not sure where to tread next. If there are any 'rational' explanations for all of this - and if anyone so much as mentions 'mass hysteria', I'll rip their throat out - I'd like to hear them. I could do with some sand to stick my head into right about now. And as for the 'irrational' explanations, well, I'm running about half a dozen of them simultaneously in my brain right now, and none of them make for pleasant viewing. One person dead, one missing, one in the middle of a psychotic episode, and that's not counting Pierce. If I had even the faintest idea what had happened to *him*, I'm sure I'd have a better picture of what's going on. And probably be even more scared.

Air. Miles had a sudden and irresistible urge to get out of this house for a while, get some fresh air, reassure himself that the world wasn't disappearing down a black hole with the maniacal cackle of demons sending it on its way. He didn't even bother to switch his computer off, simply got his coat and walked out of the door.

The persistent rain of the last few days had diminished to a morose, clinging drizzle, stirred by a chill northerly breeze. He was rather glad of it; it gave him something more tangible to focus upon than the events of the last few days and his own burgeoning sense of helplessness. It was mid-afternoon, before the day's homeward rush began, and there were still some patches of clear asphalt visible between the cars.

Miles had no clear idea where he was going; movement was all that mattered. He considered finding a pub where he might swamp some of his anxieties with Scotch, and actually got as far as pausing at the entrance to one or two before deciding that, just this once, he might give sobriety a chance. Besides, he had a suspicion that he might be needing to call on as many brain-cells as possible in the near future.

He turned the corner on to the High Street, and found himself marvelling at its wondrous drabness, its almost supernatural *normality*. If there was such a thing as the Platonic 'ideal' of the High Street, then this was surely closer to it than any other town in Britain could muster. Newsagent, launderette, Indian and Chinese takeaways (next door to one another, as though huddled together for mutual protection), fish-and-chip shop, bookmaker, estate agent, off-licence, supermarket; if it weren't for the monolithic presence of transatlantic invaders - Starbucks, McDonalds, Blockbuster - it would be almost quaint. Now, all of the smaller businesses picked up their trade from the dregs left behind by the 'occupying force' of the Big Three. And if these three should decide to relocate, and the focus shifted to the edge-of-town 'enterprise parks' as it had elsewhere, then the shutters would come down on this street once and for all.

Nostalgia. Miles usually railed against it, but right now it was a comforting friend. Things were changing too fast for him at the moment. Too fast, and in directions he didn't care for very much. He had an uncharacteristic longing for stability and predictability, for the kind of security that the child demands of its environment.

For a while, he sat on a bench outside the library (itself an edifice of stability, as pompous and grey and quintessentially Victorian as it ever had been), watching traffic and people come and go. He received a few curious glances from passers-by, the kind of look reserved for those who insist on sitting bare-headed in the rain and- judging from the way he smiled- enjoying the experience. Many of them would no doubt tell their loved ones of the strange drunk/junkie/pervert (delete as applicable) who had smiled at them in such an unnerving manner that afternoon. Miles was glad for them, that he could be the source of the reaffirmation of their own normality. It made his smile all the broader.

He got up at length to go into a nearby newsagent to buy a chocolate bar, which he munched thoughtfully as he wandered back down the street. His route took him past the mouth of an alleyway between two shops, and as he happened to look down into the shaded recesses of the alley, past the prone figures of upended wheelie-bins with their spilled innards of now-soggy cardboard and plastic, he saw movement. Human movement.

He wanted to see what they were doing there. That was the only way he could justify his actions afterward, in going down the alleyway toward the furtive activity-- simple curiosity. There may well have been more to it than that, but nothing that Miles wanted to consciously explore.

As he got closer, he could see that there were two of them, teenage boys, no more than seventeen years old, one of them white, the other black. They were standing a few yards apart, facing one wall of the alley, engaged in some act that consumed their attention so completely that they didn't notice Miles until he was almost standing directly behind them.

It was the white boy who noticed him first. He reached

over and nudged his friend, pointing at Miles as the newcomer squinted into the shadows to make out what it was they had been doing.

"Fuck off, grandad," said the white boy.

"What's that you're doing?" Miles had by now seen the spray-cans in their hands, but his question carried-- at least to his own ears - no challenge, no condemnation, just simple interest.

"You deaf?" said the black kid, reaching into his pocket for something else that Miles couldn't see. "We told you to fuck off."

The light was so poor in the alley that Miles had, at first, wondered how anyone, even the most devoted graffiti-artist, could work with any accuracy, but as his eyes acclimatised to the gloom, he realised that they had obviously been at work here for some time; he had disturbed them just as they were putting the final touches to their masterpiece.

The boys said something else to him, their tone of anxious menace intensifying with every word, but Miles didn't hear them clearly. He had just begun to make sense of the image they had been spraying on the wall...

They were upon him before he had a chance to say anything more to them, slamming him back into the opposite wall with a force that expelled the air from his lungs in one painful burst. His legs gave way beneath him, and he slumped, gulping for breath, as they closed in around him, pummelling him with fists and Nike-clad feet. There was no point in trying to fight back; Miles concentrated on protecting his head from the worst of the blows. This meant that the rest of his body was relatively vulnerable - a kick to the kidneys, which Miles feared would leave him pissing blood for a month, emphasised this - but he had no intention of surviving this as a brain-damaged husk in an intensive care ward, ventilated and catheterised and vegetative for the rest of his natural.

One of his attackers, however, wasn't standing for any of this behaviour. Miles found his hair grasped, and his head pulled from the shelter of his arms. He was looking into the eyes of the black kid, but between them was the silver glitter of something else, waving to and fro before his nose as if the boy was trying to mesmerise him.

oh fuck he's got a knife

The point of the blade was pressed up against his chin, forcing his head back against the wall. Meanwhile, he felt the hands of the white kid rummaging inside his coat, finding his wallet. Just as this was removed from his pocket, there was a shout from somewhere behind and to the left of him, a shout which caused his attackers to look up, startled. The white boy, still clutching Miles' wallet, was up and away immediately, bellowing for his comrade to follow him as he did so.

The boy with the knife, however, hesitated, and in that instant Miles saw exactly what was coming. He never knew quite what it was that tipped him off - the merest glint in the boy's eye, perhaps, or the way he half-turned away from Miles to allow him more room to move - but Miles instinctively brought his arm up in a defensive block that stopped the downward sweep of the boy's arm slightly more than halfway through its intended arc. He felt a cold pain in his forearm, saw the boy lurch backward off-balance and then stumble after his friend.

He heard the sound of more running feet, then, coming from the other end of the alley. Three sets, to be precise; two of them pounded past him while a third stopped. A face loomed in his field of vision, the face of an elderly Asian man.

"It's all right, they're gone. You're safe now."

As the old man helped Miles up to a sitting position, his two other rescuers, a burly, long-haired man in motorcycle leathers and a smaller man wearing what appeared to be mechanic's overalls, returned.

"They got away," said the biker.

"I'll know them again, though, little bastards," the mechanic added.

"I know them, too," the old man said, sadly. "They come into my shop regularly. I think I know their parents, as well. They're little tearaways, but..."

"But what?" The mechanic stooped to help the old man lift Miles to his feet.

"Well... I never thought they were capable of this sort of thing. I mean, stabbing someone..."

"You all right, mate?" The biker had a mobile phone in his hand. "I've rung for an ambulance and the police, they'll be here in a minute."

"My arm..." Miles looked down at his forearm where the blade had cut him. It had torn through his coat and the shirt underneath, but fortunately-- and Miles still had enough of his wits about him to see this-- the wound underneath didn't appear to be too deep.

"Just relax, you'll be OK soon. Was there much in your wallet?" The old Asian man had a voice as soothing as a balm to Mile's jangled nerves.

"Few quid. Some credit cards, all of them maxed out. Not much of a haul..."

He managed a weak smile.

"That's the spirit. Come on, let's get you to the end of the alley. The ambulance will be here soon."

He resisted the old man's attempt to steer him out of the alley at first, though. He wanted to see more clearly exactly what it was the boys had been so intent on painting on to the wall. For a few moments, he stood in silence and looked, then allowed himself to be escorted away.

"Bloody vandals," said the old man.

Miles didn't pay him any more attention. The nausea he was suddenly experiencing was not shock from the attack; it was a recurrence of the terror he'd been feeling all week. The ground was further away from his feet than he had realised.

By the time Miles Hearne was released from hospital, the following morning, the graffiti had been washed from the wall by a diligent council anti-vandalism squad, who would be most alarmed to find a similar hand at work in several locations across the city. They also found the significance of the strange red 'spiral' effect the artist repeatedly used mystifying, to say the least.

Maybe I should ring him now. It's been two days. He might need help.

The urge to contact Hearne had tugged at her for most of the intervening time since their last conversation, but for most of *that* time Helena had been able to rationalise it as concern for the man; he had, after all, sounded fairly shaken up on the phone. But she was clear enough in her mind (for now, at least) to be able to see that it was her own anxiety that made her want to ring him, the craving for further reassurance that she wasn't on the brink of another breakdown.

It was a reassurance that, by this time, she craved desperately. The days had been punctuated by the recurrence of the visions, waking dreams that not even the diazepam could prevent. By now, these visions had started to invade her perceptions so completely that she could barely leave the house for fear of seeing the crimson cyclone-effect somewhere in the pattern on an advertising hoarding, in the play of light on the stained glass of a church, on the cover of a magazine.

So she stayed in the house, behind drawn curtains, with the TV off (no telling what I'd see if I put that thing on), huddled into an armchair trying to put some order into the pandemonium in her head. Various teas were tried, and they distracted her for a while, but when she found herself considering having her first cup of fully-caffeinated coffee in several years, she realised that she was simply aiming at distraction rather than alleviation.

May as well hit the booze, if that's all I'm after. And considering the amount of tranx I've taken over the last few days, that would be relieving the problem a bit too permanently ...

The despair that washed over her at this realisation almost made her think that, perhaps, that was precisely where all of this was leading. This ... *thing*, whatever it is, seemed to be pressing her to go in one particular direction, the only direction that may offer some kind of release from its constant presence. If you want to get away from me, it seemed to be saying, you'll have to take the biggest leap of all.

Wouldn't that be better than all of this ... this ... oh, shit, I don't even know what to call what I'm going through. If I don't know what it is, how can I fight it? And there's nobody to help me, no-one to guide me through it all. The one person who could help has barricaded himself against the world (sensible, in many respects) and won't let anyone near him. Despite what he said, I *am* alone. Maybe not crazy, but alone.

She found her handbag in the corner where she'd discarded it, and rummaged in it for the pills. There were still about twenty left; would that be enough?

Probably. If I take enough booze with them, it'll do the trick. Now where does Debbie keep her vodka?

In the sideboard, of course. She always kept a regular supply in, for those impromptu vodka and orange fuelled girls'nights-in that happened with increasing frequency around then (between straying boyfriends and work problems, there was always some excuse for the 'mutual support group' to convene a session). The bottle was three-quarters full, Helena noted – hey, maybe there's a little remnant of optimism in me, after all – and she pulled it from its hiding place to stand beside the diazepam on the coffee table. Then she sat for a while, contemplating the decision represented by the conjunction of those two items.

Acting as if on autopilot, she removed a pill from the packet and unscrewed the top of the bottle. Maybe if I just do one, she thought, it'll give me the impetus to do the rest, and with this in mind she threw the pill into her mouth and swallowed it with a gulp of vodka.

The coughing fit subsided eventually, leaving behind a recollection of just why she didn't drink spirits that much anymore. It also left her with a feeling of vague guilt, not for the act itself, but for her lack of consideration in not leaving a note. They deserve, she reasoned, at least *some* kind of explanation.

A note. Pen and paper, why the hell can't you find pen and paper when you really need them?

At last, she found a yellow block of Post-It notes and a biro beside the phone, and settled herself into the armchair, under the baleful, impatient glare of the vodka and diazepam. Only when she had done this did the realisation strike home:

What do I write? How can I explain this to anyone else when I can't even explain it to *myself*?

After a few minutes of attempting to apply words to her predicament, and failing each time to do anything more than touch the nib to the empty paper and draw it back again, she hurled the pad and pen across the room with an inarticulate wail of fury. The pen left a black comet streak across the white wall, a mark that their fastidious landlord would notice as surely as a pile of horseshit in the middle of the carpet. Still swearing to herself, Helena fetched a damp cloth from the kitchen and squatted in front of the offending blemish, rubbing energetically at it as if trying to wear her way through to the other side of the wall.

Even as the ink stain began to disappear from the wall, however, so another shape began to insinuate itself into its place. The cloth Helena had been using had apparently last been used as a dishcloth, and was now leaving behind soap smears, which followed the circular motion of Helena's hand. As she watched, the smears began to fill up with colour, the colour of blood, and seemed to be trying to reach out of its two dimensions into a third, to reach out to *her* ...

She leapt backward, convinced that it would at any moment pounce at her face. Falling on to her back, she rolled over into a foetal position with her arms around her head. For minutes, the only sound was that of her own quickened respiration.

Courage returned to her slowly, allowing her only gradually to raise herself from the supine state and turn her attention once more to the wall. There was nothing there; even the soap smears had dried and disappeared.

She sat looking at the bare wall for the best part of half-an-hour, waiting for the thing to come back, but it never did. Quite what she would have done if it had decided to return, she had no idea, but her absorption in this vigil kept her from pondering again that other act, upon which she had embarked earlier. It was only the sound of a car pulling up in front of the house that jolted Helena back into activity. Through the window, she saw Debbie getting out of the passenger side of a blue Mondeo, waving goodbye to her work colleague in the driving seat, approaching the front door.

In a frenzied blur of activity, she replaced the vodka in the sideboard, the pills in her handbag, and was curled up once more in the armchair with a book in her hand, the picture of domestic comfort, before Debbie entered.

"You don't want to know what a fucker of a day *I've*

just had," said Debbie, flopping on to the sofa.

"Try me," said Helena.

"If you insist. But before I start –"

"Cuppa?"

"Christ, no. I need something a lot stronger than that. There's some vodka in the sideboard. Have one yourself, if you want."

"Er ... no thanks. Not right now."

Resisting all attempts by Helena to steer her in the direction of ice, or orange juice, or anything that might have slowed down consumption, Debbie poured a couple of fingers of clear liquid into the glass and downed most of it in one go. She slumped back, ignoring the fact that she was still wearing her coat, and swilled the vodka around in the glass a few times before deciding that she was ready to speak.

"Well, it didn't get off to a good start. One of the patients went into renal failure five minutes after we started the shift, and had to be shunted off to intensive care. She was OK, but the consultant decided to chew *us* out because the previous shift hadn't updated the records after her last dose of medication the night before. Like it was our fault. But then, he's always been a bastard, that one.

"Then Mrs Ashe went and died. You know, the old dear who's been with us for a month? Complications after she had a hip replacement? I'm sure I told you about her. Anyway, one minute she's fine, next minute, gone. Well, not quite next minute; she had about half-an-hour of babbling first, which we didn't really take much notice of, she's been on some new stronger painkillers recently and they've been giving her some strange hallucinations. Maybe we should have paid more attention – these were positively weird, from the way she described them, not the sort of 'oh, there's my mum come to call me in for tea' thing that we were used to.

"She was sitting up in bed, crying, howling like a baby. Terrified of something. Sister tried to calm her down, but she kept saying that she could see something in the corner of the room, up toward the ceiling. When we asked her what it was, all she could say, over and over again, was 'red, red, red', like that. Oh, except once she did say something about a merry-go-round.

"And then she went quiet, and we thought she'd gone to sleep. But she didn't wake up. She was such a lovely old thing, too, everybody liked her ... Helena, are you all right?"

Helena had been staring into space for over a minute before she finally shook herself free of the host of decidedly unpleasant ideas that had been vying for her full attention. "Have you heard anything else like this recently?"

"No, I don't think so," said Debbie. "Why? What do you think...?"

An expression of dismay crossed Debbie's face, and she sat bolt upright, slamming the glass down on to the table perhaps a little too hard. "For God's sake, Hel, we're not back to that bloody painting, are we?"

"Is there any way you can find out if anyone's come across anything similar?"

"Helena –"

"*Is there?*" The vehemence of the demand, and her own persistence in asking it, surprised even Helena; for Debbie, it was like a physical blow, and she reeled slightly in her seat before recovering.

"Well, I could ask around, I suppose ... I'll do it in the morning."

"Thanks." Helena's weak smile went some way towards apology, but she wasn't yet prepared to try and justify her behaviour. That could come later, when she had found out for sure that she was wrong. She picked up her handbag and went to the bathroom, leaving a chastened Debbie to sit and look at the bare walls, as she had done for most of the day.

When she had finished flushing the remainder of her diazepam down the toilet, she then retired to her room, to consider her next move. She had a feeling she was going to be busy for a few days yet.

It's only the promise of sex that keeps us coming, thought Mark as he surveyed the interior of Rebel's. And everybody believes that gay clubs are the best. Hah.

It was 'Taboo Night' in the only place for miles with the nerve to hold one, and the dark sweaty club was heaving with fetish costumes. What the bloody hell are these people dong here? Even if all gays did dress like the Village People – which we don't – that's no excuse for foisting frogman clothes on our club. Where is taste? Where is style? For fuck's sake! Mark himself was dressed just a little less wildly for the evening in tight black trousers accentuating his lithe frame, and a baggy metallic blue shirt that showed off his short bleach-blond hair. On reflection, he probably looked like an out-of-work flamenco dancer.

Mark was having a bad night. For one, Keith from the office had had a real go at him for going to Rebel's, repeating the phrase 'nancy dress party' until the whole office had heard it umpteen times. For another, Mark had been single for too long now. Yes, that was partly his fault for being so choosy after Damien. The club-music clones he found attracted to him seemed no more than shallow water shagarounds, which he remembered ruefully, having been himself. But not these days.

A large duck had struck up a shouting conversation with an even larger dominatrix in front of Mark, obscuring his view of the dance floor. Suppose that's just as well. There's nothing there I like. A few ex-lovers, one guy who keeps trying to catch my eye, but I'm sure he's the one Tony said likes to give it rough.

The duck and dominatrix moved away and suddenly Mark saw him. The one for me, half-decent-looking, similar age to me, talking and laughing with Kieran's crowd by the bar. I'm sure he wasn't with them a few minutes ago. Looking a little odd amongst them, dressed a tad formally, a bit goth, straight dark hair down to his shoulders, the only one in the group with no piercings and no silver jewellery. New to the scene. So how does he know Kieran's crowd?

Mark picked up his bottled beer and made his way through the club, avoiding the dance floor and the rough trader, who pursued him with his eyes, to the bar. Start with Kieran.

"Hi Mark," said Kieran, noticing him and giving him a quick appraising glance. "Funny night for you to be in."

"I must be desperate," Mark answered. He gave a sideways look at the dance floor. "I'd have to be fucking desperate for this lot."

"Don't knock what you haven't tried, lover," said

Kieran with a grin, and made to turn back to the others.

"Who's your new friend?" cut in Mark.

Kieran said, "I'll introduce you," in a voice which said geroffim he's mine. "Nick," he shouted to the stranger, "this is Mark. Mark, Nick."

Nick turned to face him fully, raised a hand and smiled in what would have been a merely welcoming manner if the pupils of his eyes hadn't flashed open wide into two bottomless wells of desire. Mark went numb. Oh my god I want him I want him. His cock gave a thump of awakening. He stuttered a greeting while he recovered his composure. Kieran looked grumpy for a moment, then said to Nick, "Shall I let you two get acquainted, then?"

Nick said something quietly in Kieran's ear, and Kieran's face lit up. He gave Nick a quick hug and turned, put one hand across Mark's neck and pulled him close. "You've pulled, you bastard. Enjoy. Tell me how it went." He released Mark, winked and left them to it.

"Uh – how do you know Kieran?" asked Mark, to kick-start the conversation.

"I just went to the bar and here he was."

"You mean you've only just met?" said Mark in amazement. "You looked like you've known each other for years."

"He's very sociable. I think he fancies me."

They swapped cigarettes and talked a little, not moving from the bar, smoking and sipping their bottled beers.

"I haven't seen you around here before," said Mark, fishing.

"I haven't been here before."

Why not? "Are you from round here?"

"That's right. But this is a bit of a new scene for me."

Mark had an intuition. "You've only just come out?"

"That's one way of putting it," said Nick with an enigmatic smile. God he's good-looking. Mark's cock thumped again. He changed the subject. "What happened there?" he asked, indicating a light dressing around Nick's left hand.

"Cut myself on a knife. Nothing terrible," he added as Mark was about to sympathize. He gave that smile, the pupils dilated, and Mark's cock thumped some more. So did his bladder. He didn't want to leave Nick to his own devices with Kieran and others obviously circling, but he had to go. "I'll be back in a minute," he said, killed his cigarette, and made for the toilets. The route was clogged with people, and there was nothing for it but to squeeze past the rough trader, who gave him a calculating stare and made it hard for him to get past.

Mark hated club toilets. Not because of some of the things that went on in them, but simply the smell of them. How anyone could have sex in these he didn't know. He pulled his engorged cock out at the urinal and peed, feeling himself deflate slightly as the pressure on his bladder went down. He zipped and turned to the sink. Standing there was the rough trader.

"He's a wimp," the man said through pierced lips. "You need a real man. A man who'll give it to you the way you like it." He advanced on Mark, pressing him close against the wall. This close, he was a good foot taller than Mark and more heavily muscled. Two others in the toilet hurried past, glancing uneasily at Mark. "Come out with me and I'll show you what a real man can do." He gripped Mark's wrist, then his crotch.

"Get off," said Mark unconvincingly. He didn't feel able to tackle this one, this sort of thing happened rarely in the club.

"Don't you get it?" the other man said, with that calculating stare again. "You're leaving here with me and I'm going to give you what only a real man can give you." He pulled Mark away from the wall and forced him towards the door. "Open it."

Mark thought of resisting, thought better of it, and pulled the toilet door open. Standing just outside of it was Nick. "Pulled again?" he drawled. Mark gave him an imploring look.

The other man shoved him through the door and faced Nick. "You can't have him. You'll have to go and fuck yourself."

"I don't think so," said Nick coolly. "Would you like to dance instead?"

"What?" The rough trader's face screwed up in amazement.

"Come on. You and me, on the dance floor, now.

What's the matter?" Nick asked, grinning wickedly, "Feeling a little faint?" He gestured mockingly towards the dance floor.

The other man strode towards the retreating Nick, brushing roughly past Mark, who watched open-mouthed as the two men made themselves space in the middle of the floor. The music pounded on.

"I know a dance that's just right for tonight," called Nick above the din. "It's called 'Punish Me.' He stripped the dressing off his hand and Mark could see a recent-looking gash across the palm. Nick held the hand up, fingers pointed at the ceiling. He swayed along to the music, and for Mark time seemed to slow down to the rhythm of Nick's movements, as the other man begins to sway with them also. The clubbers surrounding them seem transfixed, unable to act or get away as Nick raises his wounded hand higher, as though signalling to the rough trader who stretches erect, following the hand, eyes fastened upon it. Nick is saying something to him but Mark can't hear what it is, but the other man's face is going slack and the violence seems to drain out of him and into Nick, whose face takes on that hard, calculating stare. Then Nick closes his hand into a fist and the other man contracts as if in the grip of a huge claw. As Nick twists his forearm the other man groans loudly, swaying as though he would fall to the floor if he could. Mark sees drops of blood falling from Nick's tightly clenched fist and hears him speak in the most commanding voice he's ever heard:

"Say 'Punish me.'"

The other man is beetroot red, even under the multicoloured flashing lights, but shakes his head tightly, grimacing.

"Say 'Punish me.'"

The rough trader's jaw works, but Mark can't hear if anything's coming out. A dominant-submissive couple, she in black PVC with her partner in a leotard, on a silken leash, huddle together in the face of this display. The game isn't played like this. Mark glances around to see if the bouncers have noticed, but the two standing by the exit don't seem to have realised what's going on.

Nick is smiling coldly, keeping his left hand upraised

while he bends to dabble the fingers of his other hand in the few drops of blood on the floor. Then he steps up to the other man and anoints his forehead with the blood. He says something else that Mark can't catch, and the other man's eyes fill with fear. Nick retreats a step, then flicks his arm down like a whip, spattering the other's face with blood and the man drops to the floor, writhing feebly in the foetal position, clutching at his heart.

Finaly the bouncers take notice and move in on the dance floor. Time returns to normal for Mark.

One bouncer took hold of Nick, the other grabbed the rough trader by the armpits and dragged him off the dance floor. Mark followed them to the exit and out into the street.

"It's all right," Nick said gaily to the bouncers who stood silent and closed-ranked in the doorway. "I didn't bring a coat." He stepped over the body of the other man and said to Mark, "Yes that was creepy for you, yes I'm all right, no he's not all right, no I barely touched him, yes I'm going home and yes you can come with me if you still want to." He waited, head on one side, one eyebrow cocked.

This is so fucking freaky. What the fuck just happened? Why am I even thinking about going home with this weirdo? All right, he saved me from whatever, but this is too fucking freaky and I've got the shakes now and I must look like a complete fucking teenager and oh my god my cock is trying to batter its way out of my pants and I'm scared shitless and I want him I want him I want him.

Nick's flat was a twenty minute drive away in a wine-red BMW parked a few streets from Rebel's. Mark sat silently throughout the journey and Nick didn't press him, although he did chuckle and say it had been a long time since he had last been thrown out of an establishment.

The flat itself was neat and tastefully, if eclectically, furnished. Nick was evidently into art in a big way. Mark fingered an ebony mask, which hung by the living room door.

"Masks are amazing," Nick commented, ushering Mark into the living room. "That one belonged to a witch doctor in Senegal. It was said that whoever wore the mask took on the personality of the witch doctor. Then again," he said with a chuckle, "that might be a pile of nonsense concocted by the trader who sold it. There might be hundreds of copies of the thing in drawing rooms all over Europe. But somehow," he added, stroking the mask's cheek, "I think not."

"What happened at the club?" Mark blurted out.

"Call it instant karma. Or an application of Newton's law of equal and opposite reaction. Or call it an exchange of energies. Although calling it that is a bit like calling sex an exchange of fluids."

"Do you do subtitles? You know, English translations?"

"Sorry." Nick disappeared into the kitchen, re-emerged with a bottle of gin and a bottle of Bacardi. "Which?"

"Bacardi."

Nick disappeared again. His voice floated out. "The chap thought he was domineering by nature. But domineering people are deep down saying 'Punish me.' So I did."

"Why that though?"

"I needed the energy he was giving off. For what I have to do I need that energy of violence and destruction, and he's going to supply me with that energy until I've finished what I have to do." Nick entered the living room, a glass in each hand, and handed one to Mark, standing over him.

Mark glanced suspiciously into his glass. "And me? Have you got plans for me too?"

Nick smiled, took Mark's glass off him and drank deeply from it before handing it back. "Right now I need the opposite energy, that of life, creation, generation. It's all right," he added as Mark, remembering the dance floor, began to panic. "Taking that chap's energy by violence was suited to the violent energy it was. The energy I need from you cannot be taken by violence. It can only be mingled and shared."

"And what does that involve?" Cautiously sipping the Bacardi, as though you could taste a Mickey Finn.

"You might call it an exchange of fluids. I call it the ecstasy of two becoming one flesh." Smiling, Nick held out his wounded hand and Mark, heart thumping, paused, then finally took Nick's hand and allowed him to lead him to the bedroom.

They unclothed each other slowly, the tension building as Nick had them both sitting cross-legged on the double bed, erections pointing at each other. "Sit up, take my hands," said Nick, "and feel the balance point behind your belly button." Mark adjusted his balance until he thought he had it just right, then with some pushing and pulling with his hands Nick adjusted him some more, and suddenly his posture became easy and his mind clear. They held each other's gaze, looking deeply into each other's eyes as Nick intoned:

"We begin with ourselves,
each of us infinite,
without boundaries,
co-extensive with all that is;
as below, so above
to Infinity.

"We stand at the axis mundi,
the fulcrum of Infinity,
from whence we move the world according to our will,
for in Infinity the centre is everywhere
and it is Here, Now.
Ecce carnem, ecce templum Spiritui Sancti."

Mark notices a warmth in the bedroom, and a difference in the quality of the light; it is as though diffused, bathing the room in a gentle glow. Was my drink spiked after all? He wonders, as he begins to feel himself enlarging, like Alice in Wonderland. Drink Me. Or was that to shrink. Nick's hands feel warm and electric. Mark feels as though he could encompass the room, the building, more. A tingling begins from his asshole, whooshing up and filling his whole body. It's dizzying and he's tempted to let go of Nick, but the other man continues,

"The flesh is in order as it is.
Have faith in the mystery within.

"We act our divinity alive

in the ebb and the flow of the flesh.

"I am the Passion and the Life
in my limbs and my lungs and my veins.

"Trust in the flesh,
not in the fear.
With your flesh enter the unknown,
and then, my love,
the fear will be your servant,
and will bow down to the mystery of the flesh."

Mark begins to discover a level of lovemaking he's never suspected could be reached. Commencing with his hands, every part of his skin that Nick touches becomes erotically sensitive as never before. Every stroke, ever tap, every pressure creates an erogenous zone and then, as the touch and pressure becomes more urgent, the erotic sensations seem to seep through his skin and enliven Mark's very flesh, as though engorging his entire body with charged lust.

Mark follows Nick's lead in slow, slow touching, stroking, licking, kissing in slow motion, and wherever Nick's skin contacts his, he experiences a spread of arousal, one delicious nerve ending at a time. Then, when Nick pushes him onto his back and kneels between his legs, Mark is ready ready ready now now now, but Nick even more slowly takes him by the legs and pulls him to the edge of the bed and, feet on the floor, spits into his hand, anoints his huge bobbing cock and pushes it into Mark's desperate anus. Mark gasps as he feels it slide into him, filling him with pulsing warmth. He's ready to come but Nick, smiling, says "Not yet," and presses a finger into the place between Mark's balls and his asshole. To Mark's amazement, the urgency to spurt eases off, although the orgiastic sensations swell up as before. And Nick, instead of pumping him, remains stock-still, throbbing inside Mark, his expression relaxed and trance-like as he murmurs to himself things which Mark cannot catch. The connection between them seems to broaden until Mark begins to feel that Nick is completely inside him and he inside Nick. He can no longer really tell where the one lover ends and the other begins, as though there is only one orgiastic sensation, only one flesh to feel it.

Mark sees in his mind's eye the two of them in the centre of a kind of yin-yang symbol, only the two colours are black and red, revolving around each other and around the two lovers, a merry-go-round, a spiral galaxy, slowly at first, then increasingly quickly; and, as the colours merge, Nick takes hold of Mark's cock with that sensual electric touch and slowly, so slowly wanks him until he comes for what seems like forever, his body so overwhelmed by orgasm he can only notice dimly that Nick is pumping his load into him and the vision fades.

Mark lies spent, legs dropping down over the edge of the bed, and Nick kneels before him, momentarily engulfing Mark's cock with his mouth, then pushing Mark's cock and balls aside, licks his asshole out. Nick pushes his left middle finger into Mark, who moans, not knowing what's happening next, but Nick removes his finger and lays it to Mark's lips saying, "Taste us." Mark lifts his head to lick the extended finger, then drops back onto the bed, exhausted.

Nick stands upright, his cock still enlarged from his recent erection, his body flushed and gleaming in the soft light. Arms raised from his sides, he takes a deep breath and intones:

"And so it begins."

"You know, Philip, you really should be somewhere we can keep a closer eye on you. At your age ..."

"At my age," said Philip Burgess, patiently, "it hardly makes any difference one way or the other where I am, does it? Whether I'm at home or *in* a home, it'll happen when it happens, and that's all there is to it."

Dr Tyler sighed. She'd had this sort of conversation with him more times than she could count, and it always ended the same way.

"Of all my patients, I think you're the stubbornest old sod of the lot. Why I continue to put up with you, I don't know."

"I make you feel young again," he replied with a grin.

"I *am* young. I'm only thirty-seven."

"Well, there you are, then."

She finished taking his blood pressure, and removed the strap from his arm with a hiss of velcro. "Blood pressure slightly up again. Are you still taking the medication?"

"Every day, as ordered." He raised three gnarly fingers in a boy-scout salute.

"I might have to request that you go into hospital for a few checks, just to be on the safe side. The anti-inflammatories seem to be keeping the arthritis on hold, for now anyway, but you're still having problems with the old hypertension. That worries me, to be frank."

Philip shook his head. "Jennifer, my dear, you know as well as I do what my response to that will be."

"Oh, yes. You'll refuse. You always do. Sometimes I think you could be lying under a bus and you'd refuse to go in the ambulance." She sat down beside him on the sofa. "You can't go on like this indefinitely, Philip. Something's happened to you recently, hasn't it? Something you're not telling me about?"

"What makes you think that?"

"Woman's intuition," she said. Actually, it was the intuition of his housekeeper, Brenda, who had confided her worries about her employer to Jennifer a few days before.

"I won't confirm or deny anything, not for now. I'll tell you this, though – there are certain matters that I have to attend to at the moment which require that I stay active and alert. When they're taken care of, I'll consider doing as you ask and submitting to all the pokings and proddings that your old quack of a consultant at the hospital might care to inflict upon me. How does that sound, eh?"

"Do you –"

"I have no idea how long they'll take to sort out, no. But if you're worried that I might 'peg out' before then, you can rest assured that I have no intention of allowing anything of the kind to happen to me before I'm good and ready. Now, do we have a deal?"

"All right, all right." I am probably going to regret this. Most likely before he does.

"Excellent. Well, if that's all ..."

Her mobile phone trilled at that moment, giving her the excuse to turn away from the intensely slappable, self-satisfied face that Philip had chosen to put on.

"Hello, Jenny Tyler ..."

She soon found another good reason to be glad she wasn't facing him right then. The voice of her receptionist was low, and heavy with emotion. It was a small community, everybody knew everybody else.

But there would be one person they would not now get the chance to know.

"I'll get right over there." She turned, dreading the prospect of looking Philip in the face, knowing that he would see the pain there instantly. She was right.

"What's happened?"

"I've ... I've got to get over to Andrea's house, right away."

"Andrea? *Brenda's* Andrea? What's wrong, is she –" He halted, in mid-sentence, staring at her. "It's the baby, isn't it? Oh God ..."

"A cot death, by the looks of it. They've already taken the baby away for ... anyway, they need me to go to Andrea's house, give her some sort of sedative, she's very ... you know ... oh, Christ."

His housekeeper's family was probably the nearest thing Philip had to a family of his own these days, and she could tell that one more cord in his heart had snapped at that moment. She sat beside him again, and embraced him, as much for her own good as his.

"Philip, I'm sorry ... I'll come back as soon as I can."

"No, don't worry about me. It's Andrea and Brenda and the rest you should be concerned about now, not me. You go. I'll be fine."

She insisted that he not escort her to the door, as he was still wont to do, and he didn't argue this time. The last sight she caught of him before she left was of an old face, on the verge of tears, turned upwards as if looking at something in the upper part of the house, whispering something. Perhaps he was cursing God. Perhaps he was justified.

I just spoke to her on the phone. Brenda, that is. She seems all right, but we both know she's putting on a brave face. We've all been doing that, over the last few days. But I don't feel brave, not any more.

It still bothers me, coming up here to talk to you like this, but I don't think there's anyone else I can talk to. I'm so afraid, Nicholas. So very afraid.

Something terrible is happening, and I don't know what it is ... but *you* do, don't you? In some way that I don't understand, you're at the heart of it.

But how can that be? You're *dead.* I saw your body, I saw your coffin go into the ground – if only from a distance. But all of this has happened since these paintings of yours appeared. I don't think it can be a coincidence.

I should burn them, all of them. Perhaps that would stop it. But I can't. They're all I've got to remind me of you. That's terrible, isn't it? All of this horror ... that poor baby ... it's because I'm too much of a 'fond, foolish old man' to part with the past, the only part of it that means anything to me. That's why I'm here now, talking to the damn things; there's part of you in them, the only part I'm ever likely to see again.

You saw something before you died, didn't you, Nicholas? Was it the same thing that Andrea saw over the crib of her child, in the small hours of the morning? Something that seemed to breathe fear, so terrifying that not even a mother would brave it to save her own baby? Did the baby see it, too? I hope not. I hope not.

Help me, Nicholas. I don't want to see it too. I want to die peaceful and full of love, the kind of love I had for you. The kind of love I haven't known since then.

I can't stay here any longer. My heart's pounding like a kettledrum as it is. But I'll be back. Just on the off chance that one day, one day I'll get an answer from you, a sign.

I'll know your voice when I hear it.

Emma was just making herself a coffee when there was a knock on the door.

She didn't like to answer the door. She was alone in

the house and nobody was expected. Whoever was on the doorstep was not welcome. But then neither was she, in this area, and it paid to be careful.

Two years ago she had dropped out of her media studies degree in disgust at what she'd found, and had drifted from bedsit to friends' floors to this rather nice squat on Bethlehem Street. She and her boyfriend Robin had been introduced last year to the two couples who shared this large old house which stood detached among the semis of the street. They had been doing it up and were looking for a few more stable people to fill the space reclaimed from dereliction. Robin's best friend Julian joined them when the attic became available, and they lived quietly and communally, attracting as little attention as they could. They had made some furtive enquiries into who owned the property, but had got nowhere, and having put so much into the old house, they lived uneasily with the prospect of a knock on the door from the owners.

The knock on the door was repeated more forcefully.

Emma thought about not answering, but after the third knock she answered loudly and irritably and went first to the front window to check out the stranger. He was average height, fairly slim, dark hair, thirties. Neatly dressed, but not an obvious bailiff, salesman or religious nut. Reluctantly, she went to the door and opened it.

"Yes?"

"Hello," said the man in a friendly enough way. "My name's Nicholas and I've come back to my house."

Oh god, she thought. It's finally happened. She had a wild impulse to slam the door on him.

"At least," he said, "it used to be my house. I lived here, many years ago."

"Oh." Okay. But not back down from red alert yet.

"And you are?"

"Emma. I – we – live here now."

"Of course you do. Do you mind if I come in, Emma?"

And before she knew where she was he in he was past her and into the hallway, gazing around like a tourist.

"Excuse my nosiness," he said with an embarrassed smile, "I was hoping to recognise it. It all looks ... unfamiliar."

"We've done a lot to it," Emma said. "It was derelict for years before we came along to look after it."

The stranger looked more closely at her, taking in her old clothes, her dreadlocks, her nose piercing, and he smiled gently. "You've done well. You've turned it into a home."

Emma couldn't restrain a burst of pride, but told herself, remember he's a stranger. What's his game?

"You said 'we' live here now," he continued, making for the living room. He had a slight limp, she noticed. And a surgical dressing on his hand. "Are they in?"

"Uh – not just yet," she answered, hating to part with the information. Hating to admit to the stranger that she was alone with him.

The stranger turned sharply to face her. "I need to talk to them. All of them. Will they be here soon?"

"Yes, quite soon." Not soon enough.

"Good. I'd like to wait for them." The stranger glanced around, then went past her again towards the back of the house. "Please don't mind me being curious about the house. Kitchen through here?"

"Yes –" Emma was still running to catch up with events. "Do you want a coffee?"

"Tea if you've got it," he called from the kitchen. She went in after him and bumped into him coming the other way. "Sorry, Emma. Do you mind if I have a little look around?" And without waiting for her answer he was going up the stairs.

She caught up with him at the second landing, blocking him from the passageway. "These are all bedrooms."

He nodded. "I won't intrude." Then he was up the stairs to the attic.

"That's a bedroom too," she said sharply.

He stopped, turned, and came back down. "That's something we have to talk about," he said.

"Why?"

"Because that's the room I'm moving into."

He sat and drank his tea and made small talk. Emma answered guardedly, berating herself for having let him in. Alone with a nosey stranger. And what do I know about him? Nothing. And that bullshit about having lived here "many years ago"? What is he, thirty-five? How could I be so stupid?

After the longest hour of Emma's life, the others began arriving. First Steve and Heather, a thin couple approaching middle age, quiet and a little frightened at the turn of events. Then Sue, quickly followed by her partner Ryan, tall, rangy and ready to throw out the intruder at once. However the others agreed to wait for everyone to be present before taking any action.

"So you're back," said Ryan, sneering, rolling a cigarette. "Let the place go a bit, didn't you?"

"It's a long story," replied Nicholas with a faint smile.

"Then you'd better shorten it because you won't be here that long," Ryan snapped back. He lit his roll-up and grinned. "And you reckon you're moving in to the attic, eh?"

"That's right."

"Julian's room."

"So I'm told."

"I can't wait for him to come home. You haven't met Julian." And Ryan snickered to himself.

"I'm sure he'll be fine," said the stranger. The others stared at him. Oh no, he hadn't met Julian.

A little later there was a commotion outside. Voices, heavy footsteps and a booming laugh. "Hear that?" said Ryan to the intruder. "That's Julian."

Emma joined in the general sitting up in anticipation. The living room door swung open and in came Robin alone, a lean twenty-five year-old, hardened and suntanned from outdoor work. He took in the tableau of the living room. "Who's this?" he asked.

"This is Nicholas," answered Ryan. "He's come to kick Julian out of his room."

"Oh really?" Robin's tanned face lit up. "Can I watch?" He turned and shouted towards the kitchen. "Ju! Someone to see you!" and he moved out of the doorway.

Julian came in, head and shoulders above the others, big and bearish and black from the sun, with dreadlocks down his back and his beard foaming down over the open front of his lumberjack shirt. Emma had been waiting for this moment, and turned to face the stranger.

He rose and offered his hand to Julian. "Hello. My name's Nicholas, and I've come back to my house. I have something very important to do here, and I want your room in order to do it."

Julian ignored the hand, folding his forearms across his barrel chest and looking down on the stranger in amusement. "I didn't hear you say please."

The stranger lowered his hand, apparently not at all put out. "Do you mind if I explain it to you?"

"Go on then."

"Upstairs?" the stranger motioned upwards.

"Here is fine. Anything you've got to say, we can all hear it. Away you go."

"Perhaps upstairs – or outside – would be good," Ryan cut in. "I'm quite happy to follow the argument blow by blow," and he gave Nicholas a nasty grin, "but I don't reckon Steve and Heather fancy the sight of blood."

And indeed, Emma noticed, both of them were looking more anxious than before.

"All right," said Julian, showing his teeth. He motioned to the stranger. "Come into my parlour," and they both went upstairs. Ryan and Robin sent them up with roars of laughter, and the others began to look a little better.

It was almost an hour before they returned, by which time the household had become bored with waiting and had begun to make dinner and fill the waiting with small tasks. A very sober Julian called everyone into the living room and announced, "I know this sounds really fuckin' weird, but I think Nicholas should be allowed to join us. I've seen, and he's right, you know. Something big and bad is going down and I'm going to help him in every way I can. I hope you'll do the same. But it's up to you."

Emma looked on in disbelief as they all digested this. Steve and Heather had dismayed looks, Robin was baffled, Sue, always the deep one, seemed to withdraw into herself. Only Ryan objected violently, but he was eclipsed by Julian.

Through it all Nicholas stood silently, not speaking in his own defence.

At last Ryan said, "I still have the veto, unless I can see for myself. You –" he thrust a finger at Nicholas, "what's so important that even Julian believes you? Come on."

"Don't go there man," Julian answered for him. "He showed me and that was too much."

"I want to know," Ryan insisted. "Really speaking we should all know. No secrets."

"Do you really want to see?" said Nicholas, speaking for the first time. "Even after what Julian told you?"

"Yes I fucking do. You're not staying in my house – *my* house – until I know why."

"Very well. Come with me."

Nicholas led them all upstairs to the attic, where they all gathered inside the door except for Nicholas and Julian, who stood in the center of the room. It was sparsely furnished; just a mattress and duvet on the floor, a cane chair, a calor gas heater, a wardrobe at the far end, a remnant of blue carpet in the middle of the boards. Dusk was deepening through the skylight and the attic was already getting cold. "This," said Nicholas, "is where it all began."

And he paced in a circle around the patch of blue carpet as he told them a story, a story of a sorceror, of Death and its Angel, of tragedy and of danger, and Emma and the others become more and more still, transfixed by the storyteller as he goes round and round, and at last he gestures Ryan to come forward, and Ryan does so as though in a dream, and the sorceror's tale comes round to the Scorpion's frantic search for its erstwhile master and its desperate urge to unburden itself of its deadly wisdom, and its circling like a shark when there's blood in the water and it could be anywhere and nowhere, and he holds up his bandaged hand and tears off the dressing and shows a gash in his palm which he reopens with a penknife and he lays his hand or Ryan's forehead, leaving a mark, saying "It's the blood that it senses; it was born with blood and will go on until it is sealed with blood, and it is the blood that will call it, like a homing beacon, if that's what you dare to be," and suddenly Ryan gives a scream which nearly empties his lungs and he falls to the floor.

Emma and Sue both rushed to him but he screamed

again and again and again, loud and long and inexhaustible. Where he found the energy to scream continuously like that Emma didn't know.

Ryan was still screaming when the ambulance arrived.

"Well, something's going on, that's for sure. We haven't been this busy in here since the Millennium. Come to think of it, the sort of things that people are buying right now are quite similar, too."

Sheelagh took another sip of tea – some new noxious infusion that Helena couldn't identify, and didn't care to try – and looked once more around the shop. Although the familiar, soothing music was playing, and all was, at that particular moment, calm, there was a sense of repressed tension in the place that occasionally tried to put its head above the covers; couples having whispered, self-conscious disagreements that would, in all likelihood, spill over into a full-blown 'domestic' as soon as they left; an elderly woman dropping her books and giving vent to a stream of incongruent obscenities; customer complaints about the non-arrival of ordered items that were even more ill-tempered than was customary.

Even the usually mild-mannered Ken wasn't immune. A few minutes before, Helena had been treated to the sight of him losing his temper with the till, an item of technology with which he'd never had a particularly close relationship, and bashing it several times until she'd had to go over and talk him through the procedure.

"What are they buying, exactly?" Helena asked.

"At the moment, we're having a run on Nostradamus. Now you know as well as I do that the old bugger doesn't shift most of the time half as well as he does when there's some sort of crisis that's got people rattled. Remember the panic buying we had after the September 11th thing? It's like that all over again. But this time, I have no idea what's triggered this off, none at all. Not just Nostradamus, either. Here, have a look ..."

She pulled a print out from under the counter and placed it in front of Helena for her inspection. It was a breakdown of the recent 'best-sellers' and, sure enough, there was Nostradamus right at the top. But crowding on his heels were other volumes of prophecy, none of which could be said to make for optimistic reading. Biblical prophecy, Mayan prophecy, *The Mothman Prophecies*, right the way down to little books of homilies garnered from the UFO 'greys' which told us to get our collective arses in gear and build that bloody space ark before the asteroid hits.

Helena wondered what message Ken was getting from the dolphins, and hoped it wasn't 'So long, and thanks for all the fish'.

"How are you feeling, Sheelagh? Noticed anything...?" She searched for the right phrase which could describe what had been going on without causing unnecessary alarm. Gave up. Shrugged helplessly.

"Anything out of the ordinary, you mean? No, not really."

"Oh." Good.

"Mind you ..."

Uh-oh.

"My migraines have been getting a bit out of hand recently. And you know the way I see all sorts of strange lights and things when it starts coming on? Well, they've gotten a bit different, all sort of –"

"Swirly?"

Sheelagh looked at her curiously. "Yes, that's it, exactly. Swirly. How did you know?"

"I'll tell you sometime. Ken, hi."

Resplendent in tie-dyed t-shirt and faded yellow jeans, Ken had ambled over to join them, having found a brief respite in the dispensation of prophecy and his continuing struggle with the demon masquerading as a till.

"Couldn't help overhearing the pair of you," he said. Underneath the greying dreads, his hearing was as acute as ever. "I've been noticing some pretty strange stuff going on, as well."

"You haven't mentioned anything to me," said Sheelagh, huffily. "I *am* still the proprietor, you know."

"Oh, it's nothing to do with the shop. What's going on in here is just part of what's happening generally. Haven't you picked up on any of it yet?"

"That's just it," Sheelagh replied. "We were just

saying that something seems to be occurring, but we've got no idea what it could be."

"Neither have I. But you don't have to go very far to see that there's an aggression out there that wasn't there before. Fuses are shorter, is what I'm getting at. If you ask anybody what the problem is, though, and I've tried, then they'll deny that there *is* a problem. With themselves, anyway. A few of the more sensitive types may have noticed that *other people* are acting a bit weird, but they're not seeing it in themselves yet." It was apparently true that Ken certainly wasn't.

What Helena said next would, at any other time, have been said with a certain amount of tongue wedged in cheek.

"Has Unnas got any theories about what this all might be?"

The mention of Ken's Atlantean 'contact' made Sheelagh look up in surprise, while Ken himself took a deep breath, glanced around him to check no-one else was 'tuning in', and leaned in close.

"Between you and me, he seems worried. *Very* worried. But like everything else at the moment, he's not making much sense. Keeps talking about 'whirlpools' all the time ..."

Oh, fuck, not him too.

Suddenly, Ken gave a cry and slapped a hand on the counter, causing both women to leap back in shock. "*Now* I remember! There was one thing above everything else lately that seems to have got people all worked up, just came back to me what it is. You know I've got friends in that squat out on the other side of town? Place called Bethlehem Street?"

"Yeah, I remember you mentioning it," said Helena.

"Something really strange has been going on there lately –"

"Ken," said Sheelagh with a sigh of sorely tried patience, "from what you've told me about that place before now, strange is par for the course. Wasn't this where that guy used to live, the one who kept a snake that he said was the reincarnation of his mother?"

"It was an iguana," said Ken, matching Sheelagh in the irritation stakes, "and it was also his grandmother. No, it's even weirder than normal. Apparently some new guy has moved in there, freaked the whole place out. Some of the guys who've been there for years have upped stumps and left."

"Can't they just get rid of him?" said Helena. "I mean, if he's causing that much disruption –"

"Not as easy as that. I said he was freaking the place out, I didn't say that a lot of the people there weren't happy to go along with it. If you ask me – and I'm assuming that you would have, at some point – I think there's some sort of spooky cultish vibe going down there."

Sheelagh grunted in agreement. "Wouldn't surprise me. That road has had a history of weirdness, even before your pals moved in there, Ken. I seem to remember something about that artist bloke, the one you liked so much, Hel, the one we exhibited, something about him in connection with that area."

Cold fingers linked together in Helena's mind and spine. "Molesey?"

"That's him. I remember my friend Maggie, the one who was selling those bloody paintings, saying at one point that he'd actually lived there for a while. Maybe even died there, I can't recall."

Helena preferred to think later that she did, actually, remember to say goodbye to them both before she rushed out of the shop.

The Webster Gallery didn't fit in with any sort of picture Helena carried in her mind of what a gallery should look like. Partially, this was because she had spent many a dull afternoon as a child having whatever natural interest in Art (with a very pronounced capital 'A') she possessed, battered out of her by a series of school trips to galleries in London, under the tutelage of a string of teachers who would obviously have much rather been in the nearest boozer.

It may have had something to do, also, with the design of the Webster itself. Its flat black-glass exterior and lack of any real advertisement that this was, in fact, an art gallery (until you got up close), put Helena more in mind of an office building. This was probably deliberate; the Webster brothers were not creating a cultural edifice here, for the general betterment of their fellow human beings, but rather an investment business with art as its chief commodity. They sniffed out which artists were, at that time, 'hot', or likely to be so in the near future, staged large exhibitions of their work and took hefty commissions of whatever sales were made. The artists, and their existing agents (who were also on a commission) were more than happy at this arrangement, even if it cut into their pockets, since for the Webster to take an interest in you meant that you were, as they say, 'on the up and up'.

But it was an odd place for someone like Robert Pierce to work, Helena mused. She hadn't met him that many times, but she had come away with the impression of a man dedicated to art as a spiritual and sensual – almost *holy* – pursuit. To be chained to Mammon in this way, particularly in regard to something that he loved with such a passion, must be especially painful for him.

She assumed that he still worked here, anyway. She hoped this was the case; there was another alternative shuffling around the fringes of her consciousness that she didn't want to consider just yet.

If she'd been possessed of the kind of *front* or *chutzpah* that someone like Debbie or Hearne (most of the time) wielded with such thoughtless grace, then she would have gone straight around to that squat and investigated for herself. But for Helena, that was something she didn't want to consider until all other possible sources of information had been exhausted. And even then, from what Ken had told her in a phone conversation a couple of nights earlier (the evening of the day she'd worried them all by rushing out of the shop like an arachnophobe from an exotic pet store), this mysterious new 'guru' wasn't exactly big on keeping up good public relations.

The receptionist in the lobby had obviously been chosen more for her decorative qualities than for any long-term experience in customer services, judging from the way she hesitated upon first being confronted with Helena.

(And there was I, thinking that I was 'dressing down' for just this eventuality. Perhaps the red boots were a mistake. I might have thought a little longer before deciding on the purple lipstick, too.)

The receptionist glanced briefly – but all too noticeably – in the direction of the uniformed security goon sitting on the other side of the lobby, who was dividing his attention between perusal of the new arrival and his well-thumbed copy of *Bravo Two-Zero.* As Helena looked at him, he twitched his hairless head in a kind of paternal 'Don't worry, I'm here' gesture.

Helena looked back at the receptionist. The girl had coaxed her face into a smile that must have been her dentist's *magnum opus*, and through this she emitted noises that Helena could only construe as a greeting.

"HimynamesKirstywelcometotheWebstergalleryhowcanIhelpyou." She celebrated this triumph of communication by resuming breathing, much to Helena's relief.

"Yes, I was just wondering if it's possible to speak to Robert Pierce?"

The smile that was (if Helena had disentangled the greeting correctly) called Kirsty just looked at her. Helena considered repeating the question, but this time deliberately misplacing the gaps between the words, just in case this was her sole mode of communication.

"Er ... if he's not too busy, that is?"

Kirsty's eyes wavered. "Robert ...?"

"Pierce, yes. Robert Pierce." Helena said, then went on, in an attempt to fill the wordless void, "He works here as a buyer."

"Buyer. Right." The girl turned to her computer, and began – using just her index fingers and a typing method that involved withdrawing her hands from the keyboard every few seconds in apparent mortal terror of being attacked by the rats that lived beneath the vowel keys – to call up information.

"I'm very sorry," she said at last, "but I can't seem to find his name on my list. Are you sure he works at this gallery?"

"Positive. Look, are you sure that you've spelt his name right? P-I-E-R-C-E."

"Yes, that's –"

"R-O-B-E-R-T?"

The Smile was a little annoyed now. Helena could tell

by the way her jaw clenched, as if to brace the rebelling facial muscles. "Yes. Robert Pierce. No-one here by that name. AnythingelseIcanhelpyouwith?"

This last utterance was banishment, not a query. Not being in the mood to be banished so summarily, a stream of vivid imprecations queued up behind Helena's teeth ready to be launched smile-wards. A voice from behind her prevented her, at the last possible moment, from releasing them.

"Sorry, Kirsty, did I hear you say something about Robert Pierce?"

A young woman in a dark-blue trouser suit was standing beside Helena, eyes moving from her to the receptionist and back again from beneath a rather troublesome fringe of blond hair, which she was constantly – and probably unconsciously – pushing back from her face.

"Oh, er, yes, Miss Keating," said Kirsty, "do you know the gentleman?"

"I know him quite well, actually. He does actually work here, he's just on ... er ... extended leave at the moment. Would you like me to take it from here?"

"Would you?" Kirsty repeated, with such obvious relief that Helena wouldn't have been surprised if she'd leapt across the desk and kissed the newcomer. "That'd be marvellous. Thank you."

Guiding Helena away by the arm, the woman leaned in close and said, conspiratorially, "It's her first day, would you believe. Not that I think she's going to be up to much as a receptionist, anyway. She was hired by one of Bobby's favourite people in this world, a guy called Tim van Lier, and I think he was paying more attention to the reaction she was getting from inside his pants than any other qualifications she may or may not have." (Thought as much) "My name's Charlotte Keating, by the way. Charlie to my friends. Bobby's one of those friends, much good as it's done me. I take it from the fact that you're here that you haven't seen him for a while either?"

"No, that's right. Mine's Helena, Helena McCallum. I was hoping he'd be in work, or at least you might know something of his whereabouts." Good Goddess, I'm starting to sound like 'McCallum P.I.'. "Looks like I'm wasting my time."

"Well, since you're here, why don't we waste some of it together? I'm just getting off for lunch. There's a restaurant around the corner that does some great vegetarian food ..."

"How did you know I'm a vegetarian?"

Charlie smiled. "You don't look like any sort of carnivore to me. Am I wrong?"

"No." Helena smiled back. "You're not wrong."

"It's funny, though," said Charlie thoughtfully as they exited the building, "Bobby never mentioned that you were a vegetarian."

"He spoke about me?"

"Once or twice. I had to mine him for details though." She saw the puzzled look on Helena's face and apparently took it for affront. "Oh, don't worry. I didn't get much out of him. He's good at keeping secrets, that one."

"Evidently."

The restaurant was called *L'Avventura*, which gave Helena some extremely mixed feelings regarding the culinary experience upon which she was about to embark. Vegetarian she might be, but *nouvelle cuisine* (if such a thing still existed, and had not been supplanted by something even more pretentious) had never been to her taste. She preferred her 'leaves and bark' (Debbie's phrase) in substantial portions, a sorry fact which accounted for her continuing sensitivity about her size.

Surprisingly, the food was not in any way pretentious, and served in satisfactory quantities; she had opted for the vegetable moussaka, a conservative choice but one which would give her a good idea of the quality of the whole menu. Charlie (not wanting, she said, to look like a cannibal in her company) had chosen a goat's cheese salad. They both ate while indulging in what was, to Helena's mind, some conspicuously innocuous chitchat, none of which veered even close to the subject of 'Bobby' Pierce. Helena had, at first, been drinking wine, but on seeing that Charlie was on mineral water, had switched to the same thereafter.

Charlie's choice of beverage was a calculated one,

Helena guessed. There was some major grilling to take place between the coffee and the arrival of the bill, and it was plain that she wanted to be in a correct frame of mind to pursue it. Damned if I'm going to fall for that one, thought Helena.

"So," said Charlie, right on cue as the coffee arrived, "how did you meet Bobby?"

"At the Molesey showing. I work at the *Guiding Spirit* bookshop."

A look of suspicion crossed Charlie's face. "Really? I thought you'd known each other long before that."

"No. I'd remember."

"And I was sure he'd said something about you being in PR, or similar."

"Wrong again, I'm afraid." Helena looked at her suspiciously. "What exactly did he say was our relationship?"

"Well, apart from saying that he'd had a girlfriend for a couple of months –"

"Wait, wait, wait," said Helena. "Girlfriend? He told you that *I* was his girlfriend?"

"Yes. Of course, he didn't mention your name, but ..."

It is a strange experience, and a comic one, to see the penny visibly drop behind someone else's eyes. Charlie's expression was one which Helena could imagine on the face of a cat suddenly discovering that the rodent it had been stalking was, in fact, a Rottweiler.

"Oh shit. You're not his girlfriend, are you? I've gotten it completely wrong again, haven't I?"

"Er ... 'fraid so, yes."

Charlie slumped backwards in her seat, casting her eyes to heaven. "If there is a God, do you think he'd have a word with the bloke Down Below and arrange some serious Ground-Swallowing type action on my behalf? Do you? 'Cause I could really do with it about now."

She straightened up again. "Helena, I'm so, so, *so* –"

"It's OK, really." She finally gave vent to the laughter she'd been suppressing. "With someone like Robert Pierce, I'm not surprised people jump to wrong conclusions. He doesn't leave you with much else, does he?"

"You're telling me. In all the time I've known him, I

don't think I've gotten more than a few hints from him about the existence of a private life. He told me that a girlfriend was on the scene, but that could have been a front for all I know. It's just as likely that he gets his jollies from fiddling about with the penguins down at the zoo. Now, as regards art, he'll talk on the subject constantly. Which is fine, it shows that the Webster have hired someone who cares about the subject, but sometimes ... well, I really wonder if there's room for a woman in his life."

Did Helena pick up a little more than casual conjecture in that last remark? Something like regret?

"To be honest, that's part of the reason I'm here," said Helena. "How ... well, I suppose the word would be *immersed* ... does he get when he's got the scent of something? An artist that he likes, that is?"

Above the rim of her coffee cup, Charlie's lips pursed in thought for a moment. "Up till now, I would have said that he could get enthusiastic, but not obsessive. But recently ... he's been worrying a lot of people."

"Recently being, since he discovered Molesey?"

"Well, since those paintings showed up, anyway. And more so since he found those notes."

"Notes. You mean the ones that turned up in that trunk."

"Right. I think he's also been hanging out with some occultnik, trying to make sense of what's in them. Since he started hanging out in this guy's company, we've seen less and less of him at work, which suits that bastard van Lier no end. Helena? Are you all right?"

This is my fault. It all started when I put him in touch with Miles Hearne. Probably not Hearne's fault, judging from that last conversation I had with him, he's as scared as I am, maybe more so. But it dates from that moment. I should have told him to leave it be, just fuck off back to his nice safe job and not even think about Molesey again.

Who am I kidding? He'd have found his way to where he is now with my help, or without it.

"Charlie, do you think that he's obsessed enough to do something like ... oh, let's say, move into Molesey's old house?"

"I haven't seen much of him lately, remember, like you, but ..." She hesitated for a second, considered, then said with great sureness, "Yes. He was halfway to doing something a bit fruitcakey like that when I last saw him. God knows what stage he's at by now."

She looked at her watch, shaking herself back into the moment.

"Whoops, time I was back at the art-mills. Tim will be whispering my name with poison barbs attached into Greg Webster's ears any minute now." She summoned a waiter and asked for the bill. When it arrived – and Helena wasn't totally shocked to discover that the cost of their 'light lunch' would cover two thirds of her weekly wages from *Guiding Spirit* – Charlie insisted on picking up the whole tab.

"Charlie," said Helena, "I don't usually even let blokes do that." The protest was prompted by real embarrassment, but she was secretly relieved.

"Forget about it. This was my idea, remember? Besides, I'm not just paying for the meal."

They were almost at the door of the restaurant before Helena asked her what she meant by that.

"Helena, you are the first inroad I've had into Bobby's activities in six weeks. It was worth it just to compare notes with you. Admittedly, there was more than a little prurient nosiness in there as well, but girlfriend or no, I'm glad I met you. Bobby will be, too."

"If he remembers me, when next we meet."

Charlie looked at her, and her demeanour was suddenly very serious indeed.

"I'm worried about him, Helena. But what he's gotten into, I don't like at all, and at heart I'm a coward. You're not. You wouldn't be here chasing after him if you were." She embraced Helena, and said into her ear:

"Find him, Helena. Find him and save him from whatever mess he's gotten himself into. Somehow, I don't think there's anyone else who can."

She pressed a card with her contact details on it into Helena's hand, and rushed off into the early afternoon throng, still flicking away at that stubborn hair which fell across her eyes. Helena stood outside the restaurant for a long time, looking at the card in her hand, thinking about the weight of expectation that was falling upon her shoulders.

Bugger. I suppose this means I can't put off visiting that house any longer.

The occupants of the Bethlehem Street squat were having a house meeting. There were two items on the agenda. Firstly, what to do about Ryan. Secondly, what to do about Nicholas.

Heather made tea and coffee for them all – nearly all – Nicholas wasn't invited and remained upstairs doing something doubtless unspeakable with that guy Mark who had helped him carry his belongings upstairs a few nights ago. They smoked and drank and argued. Emma sympathised with Sue, who still hadn't stopped crying and who placed the blame for her troubles squarely on their new tenant, but she remembered all too well what she had seen – whatever had happened to Ryan, Nicholas hadn't laid a finger on him, and Ryan was tough and strong-minded.

Or had been. He was still in hospital, catatonic, unable to do anything for himself. He could be moved; whatever pose they put him into he would keep, immobile, until he was moved again. But he could neither feed nor toilet himself, and rarely surfaced from his catatonic state. When he did it was to stand bolt upright, shriek, and collapse once more. Which brought Emma and the others to Item One. With the involvement of the hospital had come the interest of a mental health worker, and the anonymity of their squat was under threat. They argued about the degree of threat, considering that they actually had some rights as long-term squatters, and no landowner had yet turned up. Still, questions would be asked.

And Item Two. The lurker in the attic. Sue made no secret of the fact that she wanted him out. Steve and Heather tended to side with Sue. They had begun this squat together and had nurtured their lifestyle for several years, no bother to anyone and nobody bothering them, and now it was all coming apart thanks to the stranger upstairs. But they couldn't quite bring themselves to dismiss Julian's contribution.

Julian admitted that he didn't like having the bloke

here either, but he was adamant that what he had seen and, he believed, what Ryan had seen, justified the stranger's presence. For now, Robin would have sided with the others, but he and Julian were fast friends, and while Emma knew how puzzled he was at Julian's faith in the stranger, he wasn't prepared to attack it.

And Emma herself? She didn't know what to think, but she couldn't shake the overwhelming impression that despite the stranger's story not adding up, he meant what he said. It was just that that implied that some turbo-charged demon was running amok in the world, spreading death and madness, and it had to be stopped *in their house.*

The argument had run late into the evening, and while tempers had run high earlier, everybody was just plain burned out now. Emma could tell that they were all mellowing, and some sort of consensus was just around the corner.

There was a hammering on the front door.

They all stopped talking. Nobody called this late in the evening.

More hammering on the front door, then laughter. The sound of glass smashing.

Julian got up. "I'll see." He went and opened the door, the others trailing behind him. Outside were half-a-dozen young men, the city's finest, pissed. The closest one said, "We're squatters. We"ve come to move in."

"Help the homeless!" called one of the others, and they laughed.

"Big Issue!"

"Let us in, mate, we've got nowhere to go."

"You're not coming in," said Julian. "This is our house."

"No it isn"t." The ringleader looked up at Julian, smirking.

"Go away."

The drunk at the back threw a lager bottle through the living room window. As it smashed Heather and Sue yelped, Emma flinched, and the drunks cheered. Robin pushed past Julian. "You cut that out right now!" he snapped.

"Or what?"

"Or I"ll batter you. Now fuck off."

Suddenly Robin and the ringleader were wrestling on the doorstep, falling to the ground and writhing. Julian bent down over the ringleader when one of the other drunks went for him. Steve, older and gentler, dithered as Emma and the others pitched in to separate the men. And the rest of the gang closed in. One of them stooped to pick up a bottleneck.

"WILL YOU STOP WHAT YOU ARE DOING!" roared a voice, and Emma glanced over her shoulder to see Nicholas descending the stairs with his slightly uneven gait, his sidekick Mark in tow. His eyes were fixed on the centre of the melee. Robin and the ringleader were back on their feet but still entangled, and Nicholas waved the rest aside to approach these two. "Apart. Now."

To Emma's amazement, the two men promptly disengaged themselves. Nicholas stepped between them and said, "Robin, stay here with the others," then striding past the ringleader, said, "You come with me," and he went out onto Steve"s nicely kept front lawn, the other man trailing behind.

Heather, Steve and Sue retired to the living room, where they watched through the broken front window. Emma stayed in the doorway with the remaining three men. The rest of the gang had retreated some way down the path, leaving the lawn to their leader and to Nicholas.

"He has got something about him, hasn't he?" remarked Julian. Mark nodded. Robin said nothing, but looked like he'd just found something to think about.

The ringleader squared up to Nicholas, ready to fight, but Nicholas shook his head ever so slightly and reach out slowly with his left hand. He touched the man gently on the upper lip. "Got a bit of a nosebleed there, son," he said, showing the blood on his middle finger. Then he dabbed it on his own forehead, leaving a red spot. He began walking in a circle, the other man wheeling to remain facing him, Nicholas extending his left arm towards him, keeping his gaze on him and saying to him, "because we bleed, we know we live. The blood is the life. And when we play blood games we play with our lives. I have a blood game I know you"ll want to play. It"s called 'Come and Get Me'."

At this the ringleader starts forward but Nicholas shakes his head again. "Not yet. It's your turn first." and he pulls out a penknife, opens it with his teeth. One of the gang reaches into his own pocket, but Nicholas gestures him to stillness, and cuts across his own left palm with the blade, baring his teeth, still walking the circle. The blood wells up and he clenches his fist. When he opens it again the whole palm is dark and glistening in the light from the living room.

He discards the knife, and advances, palm forward, on the ringleader. He places his palm on the other man's forehead and says:

"Say 'Come and Get Me'."

The other man is silent. Emma is wondering why he's allowing this liberty to be taken with him. But she isn't really surprised. Mark beside her is shaking his head, looking horrified. What does he know about what is about to happen?

Nicholas halts in front of the other man. "Say, 'Come and Get Me'."

"Come and get me," the man croaks, and falls to his knees. Mark gives a little moan. Emma glances quickly through to the living room. The others are enrapt in the scene outside.

The gang on the path stand silently. They look like they've been drugged. Nicholas approaches them, walking up and down the path as though inspecting troops. "Your friend has begun to play the game of 'Come and Get Me'. You should take him home and look after him. He will need you. You two," he gestures to two at the far end, "take him away. When he's finished playing the game, you will all play it in his place."

The one who had gone for his knife comes to life. "In your dreams," he says.

"No," says Nicholas, with a terrible smile. "In yours." He reaches his arms out as though to embrace them all. They flinch. "You will know when it's time to come to me. You will need me as much as I need you. And I look after my own. Now go."

Nicholas turned on his heel and came back to the house. Those by the door let him past and Julian closed the door. Emma caught a last glimpse of the gang outside taking away their stricken leader. Nicholas went through to the living room. “Is everybody all right?” he asked. All of them, even Sue, grudgingly, nodded to him. “Good. In future,” he added, making for the stairs with Mark, “call me first. As I said, I look after my own.” And he went up the stairs, with his slightly uneven gait.

Mark, looking sick, went up behind him, and, after a moment, so did Julian.

With a glance at Robin, Emma joined them.

OK, so the address is right: 144 Bethlehem Street. It took a while to prise the full details out of Ken – he's still in his over-protective mode at the moment – but in the end he couldn't think of any good reason for holding back on me. Good. Now I have no excuse not to get myself over there and find out *directly* what's going on, and if a certain person is as involved as I think he is ...

And it was at this point in Helena's train of thought that the anxiety crept back in once more; she had successfully managed to delay this moment by finding one good reason after another to exercise caution. Now there was nothing between her and confronting whatever was currently living – and stirring up havoc *(fuck why did I have to use that metaphor)* – in Bethlehem Street.

Still, it wouldn't be wise to simply walk up to the door and ask if Robert Pierce was there. It might be more prudent to just stake out the place for a while, see who was coming and going, and if there were any familiar faces amongst them. But staking someone out (here the word ‘stalking’ entered her mind uninvited) requires planning. She wouldn't simply be able to stand on the other side of the road and gawk like a tourist outside Buckingham Palace; the ideal thing would be to be able to park up opposite the house and watch from the safety of the car. Not half as conspicuous.

One small problem; Helena didn't own a car. Didn't even drive.

Debbie did, however. It had been off the road for a while, due to the kind auspices of the MOT inspectors and a garage which seemed to be run by Pancho Villa. But she had taken back ownership just this morning, and so ...

Scorpion

Helena looked at her watch. 12.45. Debbie's lunch hour, and she always switched her phone on in her lunch hour. She propelled herself to the other end of the living room sofa, snatched up the receiver, and dialled the number.

"Hello?" Her voice was muffled.

"Don't talk with your mouth full."

"As the bishop said to the actress, yeah, I know. Hang on a second." There was the faint sound of someone slurping a drink, followed by a couple of seconds of coughing, and then Debbie's voice came back on the line. "This had better be good. After the morning I've had, I was looking forward to an hour or so of peace and quiet."

"Why? What's been happening?"

"Oh, it's been chaos. We had this guy admitted a few days ago, just spends all his time either completely catatonic, or, when he is conscious, just screams the place down. Today he decided to spend most of the morning conscious. Do you know what it does to your nerves having somebody shrieking their lungs out for hours on end? Not to mention what it does to the other patients? What's more, his girlfriend was with him all the time, and she didn't want him sedated because she was afraid he wouldn't wake up again."

"God. So what did you do?"

"Well, we eventually got hold of his parents – we've been trying for a couple of days, but his personal details are a bit sketchy, he's a squatter, you see – and got their permission to knock him out. Girlfriend wasn't happy about it, but he seems OK now. Sleeping like a baby ..."

"Deb ..." Helena was not at all eager to hear the answer to her next question. "What part of town was this guy's squat?"

"Can't recall at the moment – but there is something strange I do know. I've heard from some friends on other wards that there's been a few people admitted from the same area as this guy recently. Just yesterday for instance –"

"Was it Bethlehem Street?"

"Yeah, that's it." A pause. "How did you know?"

"Long story, Deb. Listen, it's your day off tomorrow, isn't it? I need to ask you for a favour ..."

Let's go to town, Nicholas had said, and Emma had simply agreed. Robin would have been furious. But then he'd been furious for the last couple of days. The night she'd first gone up to the attic with the others, Robin had been waiting up for her when she returned four hours later. So jealous, even though Nicholas was obviously fucking Mark. She and Robin had had a big row, for which he claimed moral victory because she couldn't explain to him what they had done in the attic. It took a certain mind-set – 'gullible', Robin called it – to experience what they had experienced in that upper room. The things Nicholas began to teach them about expanding your awareness beyond your body, about feeling the elemental energies moving within her flesh. And beyond ... and about Protection.

"Imagine," he said, "these which you experience are all around and throughout us. And the more we interact with them, the easier it becomes to do so. They seem attracted to us because we pay them attention. They thrive on our contact.

"But not all that is out there is good to us. Therefore we protect ourselves. We do what we have to, then we hide ourselves away from their sight." And he taught them the Protection: "It's like finding oneself in a pit of poisonous snakes," he told them. "You must withdraw into yourself, be perfectly still, avoid rousing them and drawing their attention." This he called putting out the house lights of the Temple. To Emma it was much like pretending to be out when unwelcome visitors come sniffing round.

Especially the Scorpion.

The Scorpion was an entity they definitely did *not* want knocking on their door. The Scorpion, whose touch was death or madness, whose passing caused havoc. The Scorpion, about whom Nicholas warned them not to think about too much, as that would be enough to attract it.

Talk about a Catch 22. If you think of it too much it'll come and get you. So don't think of the Scorpion. Don't think of the Scorpion. Don't think of the Scorp – shut up. Stop thinking about it.

That, Nicholas told them, is how to play 'Come and Get Me.' But how that related to what went on with that drunk the other night Emma couldn't work out. And Mark wouldn't talk about it, save to say that he hoped the guy lasted longer than the last one.

And Emma could explain none of this to Robin. He said it sounded like raving, and after one more bitter quip about Emma having taken the bullshit pills, she stormed out and slept in the living room, never mind the cold breeze through the broken window.

It wasn't as though she was even a great believer in the occult. She'd been on the fringes of the New Age in her time, but had never taken such stuff seriously.

And now it was circling her life like a great white shark. She had become aware that below the surface of her existence was an abyss from which god only knows what could rise and snap her up at any time.

Surely Robin could understand. But no. He remained like more and more people they knew, bewildered and frightened by the upsurge of events. The whole district seemed to be in the grip of madness. The neighbours were giving them furtive looks and no longer speaking. The drunks – when had that ever happened before? The strange atmosphere in the local shops, like a riot was expected any time. And nobody knowing what's going on.

Except us. The squat on Ground Zero. We will keep up the Protection, we will help Nicholas to do what he has to do. Whatever that is.

Last night they had been joined by someone Nicholas had met in the newsagent's. Her name was Sonya, she was in her mid-forties, and she seemed to know a lot about the occult. As she talked to Nicholas, it left Emma and the others asking what the conversation was about. Nicholas had replied, "Having mastered Death, how do I master Its angel, the Scorpion?'

Emma and Julian had glanced at each other, none the wiser.

Then, this morning, with Julian and Robin in work, Sue and Heather at the hospital, and Steve glazing the boarded-over living room window, Nicholas announced a trip into town. Mark and Sonya weren't around, so it was Emma who accompanied him.

He made straight for a New Age-type shop called

Guiding Spirit, which had a cafe on the premises. He installed himself at a table, armed himself with fags and coffee, and scrutinised everyone in the shop, beginning with the staff, from whom he was getting strange looks.

"What are we doing here?" asked Emma.

"We need more people," Nicholas replied. "I'm sure there is someone here who could be useful, like Sonya." He noticed Emma's face. "You're great because you're picking it up quickly, but I need some people who have a head start, who are in touch with these things, and there's one person in particular who would be good. But she doesn't seem to be here." He sipped his coffee.

"Why is that woman staring at you?"

"We've met, in another life. She runs this place. She's probably trying to figure out where she knows me from." He smiled at her and waved. She nodded back. "Is Helena in today?" he asked across the shop.

"She's off sick. It's Robert, isn't it?"

"Nicholas," he corrected with a smile.

"Oh, sorry." The woman glanced at Emma. "Hello, love. I'm Sheelagh."

"Oh, hi," said Emma, off-balance, and Sheelagh gave her a quizzical look before offering them a menu.

They ate and talked. Well, actually, it was mostly Nicholas talking, teaching Emma more things about the elements, the energies in the flesh, the entities. Other cafe users were obviously tuning in, one or two of them to snigger at what they heard, others to frown soberly. Nicholas was noticing each reaction, including when the tall weirdo popped his head around the kitchen door to gawk at them. Emma was getting embarrassed, but Nicholas smiled at her reassuringly.

"I don't do this everywhere I go. It's deliberate. It's a bit like scattering fishbait on the water. I'm hoping somebody will rise to it. Somebody who could be useful to us."

Emma carried on being embarrassed for another hour, by which time Nicholas had struck up a conversation with a man in his twenties who fancied Nicholas, judging by his demeanour. His name was Paul and he remembered Nicholas from Rebel's nightclub and wasn't it spooky about that guy who died? And Nicholas replied.

When they left, Paul came with them and drove them to the squat. He fitted in well, recognising Sonya from Guiding Spirit and Mark from Rebel's.

That evening, Nicholas taught his group to focus as one unit. "We are going to call someone to us," he announced, producing a sheet of paper. It was painted in watercolours, with a background of blues and greens, darkening towards the centre, from which seemed to emanate a jagged spiral in orange. At the very centre was a silver painted 'H'. "Her name's Helena," Nicholas informed them, "and I want you to stare at this voluminon and think of her being here." And he described her appearance, encouraging them to focus together on the paper, feeling their joint concentration, staring, staring until the silver painted 'H' leaves an after-image on Emma's vision at every blink, until Emma loses track of time.

Nicholas speaks, reading from his notes:

The Vision in the Flesh Two. Heh. The Face of the Queen.

See in yourself a chalice in your heart,
brimming over with the purest water.
Look deeply into it,
allowing the eyes of your spirit to scry the waters,
until her face becomes visible,
until she comes closer and closer,
until she joins us here ...

And Emma begins to see a woman just as Nicholas describes, a short woman in her late twenties, with straight dark hair, fair skin and large brown eyes, which right now are tight with stress. She seems distraught, lost, and Emma tries to speak to her, but cannot, and nearly weeps with frustration. And after a moment the image fades like the after-image 'H', and Nicholas calls Emma back to herself. Coming round, she sees the others looking pensive. Sonya has tears in her eyes.

Nicholas leads them in the Protection and they break for tea and coffee. Downstairs, Emma then found her housemates silent and grim. Ryan had taken a turn for the worse, and had had to be heavily sedated. Emma could say nothing and gazed uneasily through the new glass of the living room window. And then she saw one of the gang of drunks from the other night approach the front door. She opened it to him.

His name was Jeff. His friend, the leader of the gang, had gone psychotic, driving everyone out of his shared house and barricading himself in one room. Jeff was scared. He was looking for the man who cut his own hand the other night. He'd said they'd know when to come to him, and he looked after his own.

So Jeff joined them, much to everyone's disgust.

Except for Nicholas. He asked Jeff about the rest of the gang, learning that they were all spooked and lying low, for whatever reason they did not know. But Nicholas nodded in understanding.

"Blood in the water."

"Remind me again," said Debbie, "why I'm spending my day off sitting in my car, in the pissing-down rain, on a street I don't know, watching you watching a house that looks about as derelict as your sex life?"

"Because you've got a car," said Helena, distantly. Her eyes hadn't strayed from the house on the opposite side of the road in all the – Debbie glanced at her watch – hour that they'd been there. No-one had entered, no-one had left. The only thing connected with the place that appeared to be moving was the mass of discarded fast-food packaging, newspapers and carrier bags in the small, enclosed front yard; occasional zephyrs would stir this detritus into a desperate, frantic *ronde* that would subside as suddenly as it had begun.

"Well, naturally, that explains everything. Thanks."

Helena didn't respond.

"Do you mind if I put the radio on, then?"

"I'd rather you didn't. I need to concentrate."

So, thought Debbie (and nearly voiced the thought out loud), I'm supposed to go mad along with you, am I? They stayed silent for a few minutes, then Debbie said:

"Are you sure you've even got the right place? Maybe

this Ken of yours got the address from his dolphin friends. They're not renowned for their sense of direction on land. They're not so hot in the water, either, from what I can make out. If they were, Greenpeace wouldn't have to push them back out to sea so often ..."

With a 'tsk' of irritation, Helena reached over and switched on the radio. The local commercial station; thirty seconds of Britney asking to be hit one more time, followed by three minutes of commercials so inane and amateurish that Debbie at first thought she was listening to some sort of parody, or post-modernist 'jape', until she realised that they simply weren't funny enough.

And now, the news. Top story: the continuing furore about the pedestrianisation of the town centre. Then, the latest on the dead body found outside a local gay bar a couple of nights before (the police had established, after intensive investigation, that the body in question had been gay; this was seen as a major triumph on their part). Way down the list, the customary name-checking of the current global sites of war, famine and death, which would only rise up the running order if someone with a tenuous local connection happened to be involved.

Thank God for the British small-town mindset, Debbie told herself. Such faultless feeling for the *real* priorities.

She changed station a few times – prompting more displays of tried patience from Helena – before switching the radio off again. "So, what do we do now then? I've never done a stakeout before. Isn't somebody supposed to go for doughnuts, or something?"

"Not hungry."

Oh, you are *so* full of the joys of spring today, Helena.Your gratitude is quite overwhelming, too. I get my car back yesterday after three weeks of intensive jiggery-pokery at the garage, and what do I end up doing with it? Sitting in it and asking for permission to use my own bloody radio. And do I once hear a single word that sounds like 'thanks'?

Debbie's temper started to surge to the surface. "Helena, I ..."

Helena 'shush'ed her, and pointed down the street. A

strangely attired little harlequinade of punks, crusties and unclassifiables – about five in all – had turned the corner and were walking towards them. They crossed the road just before they got to the car, and approached the house they'd been watching.

"Recognise any of them?"

Helena shook her head. "If one of them was Robert, he's changed more than I thought."

"Wait a minute ... I think *I* recognise one of them," said Debbie.

"Which one?"

"The girl just going through the gate. Dark hair."

"I see her. Who is she?"

"The girlfriend of that bloke on my ward, the one who does all the screaming. She's the one who wouldn't let us sedate him until his mum and dad overruled her, remember? I think her name's Sue something-or-other."

The squatters had all entered the house by this point, and their vigil appeared to be back to square one. Debbie's heart sank. She'd thought for a wonderful moment that the end of this torment was in sight. "I know I'm asking this a lot, but ... what now?"

"We'll give it another half-hour. If we haven't seen anything conclusive by then, we'll call it a day."

"And if we *do* see anything?"

"Dunno. Hadn't really thought about it."

"Hel, be realistic. If this Robert bloke is in that house, there's no way you're going to be able to connect him with what's been going on around here. From what I can make out, all those people who've ended up in hospital recently – aside from the Bethlehem Street connection, which, I grant you, is a bit odd – haven't got any sort of link whatsoever."

"It was you who pointed out all the weird things that have been going on in this street, Deb."

"And, Christ, am I regretting it. Please, Hel, for me, let's go home."

Helena smiled, wistfully. "I suppose I have been a bit ... well, shitty, haven't I? This isn't your problem, and here I am, dragging you along with me 'cause I can't face the prospect of getting wet while I'm chasing my wild geese."

They hadn't noticed the girl approaching. She was simply there, at the driver's side window, tapping on the glass. Her sudden appearance startled both of them, but Debbie in particular had cause for alarm, as the face just inches away from her own was not the sort to inspire good feelings at close quarters. It was thin, sallow (a junkie, perhaps?) with evidence of recently removed piercings in nose, ears and one eyebrow, the whole face surrounded by lank mousey hair. Debbie rolled down the window.

"Hi," said the girl. She paused, waiting for acknowledgment, and when this was received, went on:

"I live in that house over the road? The one you've been watching?" This was said without rancour. "My name's Emma. Nicholas sent me out here."

"Oh?" said Helena. "And who's Nicholas?"

Emma seemed to struggle for an adequate reply to this. "He's ... just one of the guys."

"So why's he sending you out here to talk to us, Emma? Why doesn't he come himself?"

Debbie wasn't sure of the wisdom of baiting the girl like this, but she kept her peace. An assumption that Helena knew what she was doing was probably the best bet at the moment. If Helena's intention was to disorient the girl, then the tactic was certainly working; she looked back and forward between the two of them for a moment, then apparently decided to press on regardless.

"I've just come with a message. Nicholas is asking if you'd like to come in for a minute, have a chat. That's all."

"I see," Helena said, thoughtfully. "That's very nice of him."

The rain was starting to drip from Emma's head into the car, and Debbie started wishing that her friend would come to some sort of decision on this. She had no great desire to go into that house, but she was damned if she was going to let Helena go in alone.

"Well, I'm not sure. I mean, no disrespect to you, Emma, but Debbie and I aren't in the habit of going into houses to have 'chats' with complete strangers, are we, Deb?"

"No. Right. Absolutely not."

Emma looked puzzled. "Don't you know Nicholas? He says he knows you. You *are* Helena, aren't you?"

Helena nodded dumbly. Emma, now even more confused, turned and looked up at the house. They both followed her gaze; someone was standing at the attic window, looking down at them. From this distance, they couldn't make out the face.

Without warning, Helena was out of the car. Debbie had time to only register the most incoherent of protests, but she still wasn't going to be left behind. She fought herself clear of the seat belt and past the by now utterly baffled Emma to get to Helena's side.

Thankfully, Helena was making no attempt to approach the house. All she did was find a vantage point on the pavement from where she could, apparently, get a better view of their spectator, and even then she had to squint and edge into the road slightly before ...

She straightened up, and Debbie had the feeling that a connection of some kind had been made. Although she couldn't make out the shadowy figure in the upper window as well as Helena could, she could sense his eyes upon them, no, upon *Helena*. There was an almost palpable energy in the air between them; for a few moments, everything else ... the rain, the sound of the traffic moving past them ... seemed to fade. All Debbie could sense was the figure at the window, a figure who seemed to be moving his hands in some sort of pattern in front of his body.

Then she felt her shoulders seized, and she was once more looking into Helena's eyes.

"Come on. We're going."

Suddenly alert, but still not wanting to look up at that window, she climbed into the car and turned the ignition. Over this, she heard Helena say to Emma:

"Give our apologies to Nicholas, tell him we're much obliged for the invitation, but we're rather busy."

"Some other time, then?" said Emma.

"Oh, definitely."

Debbie's attention was so focussed on the dashboard

that she didn't look up until Helena got back into the car; she didn't even see Emma going back into the house. In fact, she didn't want to look at that house ever again.

"What the hell happened there?" she asked, once she had taken the car, screeching, down the road and away from *that place*.

"Nothing. Nothing at all."

Debbie looked at her sceptically.

"Except that I found what I was looking for, of course."

"I thought so! That Nicholas bloke ... he's this Robert of yours, isn't he?"

"No. Not any more." Helena paused, sighed, a sound full of anxiety. "To find Robert, I'm going to have to get a lot closer. And I'm going to have to get past Nicholas."

She didn't say any more. Debbie approved.

On the face of it, the auspices weren't good. All the street-facing windows had their curtains resolutely drawn, and there was no glimmer of light to be discerned escaping through them. To add to this, Helena had now been pressing the doorbell more or less constantly for ten minutes, and she hadn't been able to hear even the most furtive movements from within. If Hearne was in there, he was keeping the lowest of profiles.

It was dark, it was cold, and the rain was, if anything, getting worse. She hadn't asked for Debbie's company, or taxi service, this time; drawing her into this any further would be irresponsible in the extreme. She'd been only too aware of her friend's reaction to the encounter with Robert/Nicholas at the Bethlehem Street squat, and this had awoken her to the scale of the problem that she was confronting (if not, as yet, its precise nature). More and more, it was becoming clear that she had to deal with this alone.

She only wished Hearne would speak to her. She didn't want to be quite *that* alone, just yet.

Time for one last, desperate gambit. She pushed back the letterbox and leaned in close to it. "Miles? Miles Hearne? Are you in there?"

Silence.

"If you're in there, answer me! I need your help, Miles ... this thing's getting out of hand, I don't think we have very much time before ..."

She fumbled for words; in truth, she had no idea what the outcome of all this would be if left unchecked.

"Tell me what to do, Miles. I know that I'm the one who has to stop all of this, though fuck knows why it had to be me, but I need somebody to help me!"

More silence. Thick, heavy, oppressive, like her voice was being absorbed and digested.

"Hearne, you bastard, I know you're there! You said you'd be in touch to tell me what to do, well we don't have any more time to wait for you!"

From within the house, there was a scurrying, scuffling sound, like unshod feet on carpet. It seemed to be coming from up the stairs. She put her eye to the letterbox, but could make out only darkness.

"Miles? Is that you?"

A voice. Soft, and measured. "I'm not ready yet."

"Ready or not, it's coming. We have to face up to it, and it's not going to hang about until we're prepared. I've seen it, Miles. I've seen *him*."

More scurrying; he had approached to halfway down the stairs. "Molesey?"

"Or Pierce. I'm not sure who it was. It looked like Robert, but ... Jesus, Miles, do we have to discuss it like this? Open the fucking door, will you? *Please?*"

A moment or two of hesitation, and she heard him approach. It took a disconcerting amount of time for him to unlock the door; she counted at least four different kinds of lock. These may be absolutely no use against the whatever it was that they were facing, but she couldn't fault his caution.

He'd looked better. *Smelled* better, too; whatever his current priorities were, bathing wasn't one of them. Even in the gloom, she could see that he'd lost a good deal of weight, so he obviously wasn't eating properly, either. He had a beard. Under other circumstances, it might have suited him, but here it just contributed to the overall 'unkempt loony' effect.

And one more thing; just below the sleeve of his grimy

t-shirt, on his left arm, there was a scar. Fairly recent, apparently. She decided not to mention any of these personal deficiencies, and most especially the scar. If it were relevant, he'd volunteer the information. Best not to push things just yet.

Silently, he ushered her in and (once he'd meticulously relocked the front door behind her) gestured her towards a back bedroom where she could see a faint glow. On approaching, she saw the flicker of candles, and was surprised to find that the room was festooned with the things; every available surface had one situated upon it, so much so that the room was dotted with archipelagos of congealed wax. The furniture had been moved aside (a single bed stood on its side beneath the curtained window) or, in the case of the wardrobe she had squeezed past on her way in, out of the room entirely. The carpet had been rolled back to make space for more candles, but there was a clear area in the centre of the room, which was occupied by a few cushions, a blanket, and a pile of books. Towards one corner, she spied a hoard of baked bean tins, both used and unopened.

Well, that accounts for at least *part* of the smell ...

"Miles, what have you been up to in here?"

"Preparation."

"Oh. Is that what the candles are for?"

He looked genuinely puzzled. "No. I needed light. To read by. I turned off the electricity."

"Right. Yes. I'm sure that's wise ..."

Hearne sighed, realising that he would have to explain further. "I can't afford *any* connection to the outside world, none at all. That's how it's finding its way around, you see. The world is so ... so ... *interconnected* today. In many ways, that's not a bad thing, I suppose, but it could also be our downfall."

"And you think it's going to get at you via the light socket? Or come at you out of the washing machine?"

"Don't be a smart-arse. I'm taking no chances, that's all. I can't afford to. None of us can." He stepped into the cleared 'circle' and rummaged around in his books for a moment before producing a scrap of paper. "And I particularly couldn't afford to while I was working on this."

It appeared to be written in some form of personal

shorthand, interspersed with what looked like runes, and some menacing looking sigils. She spent a few minutes studying it, desperately trying to mine some sort of meaning from it all, before giving up and looking at Hearne in exasperation.

"What does it ... er ... do?"

"It's a spell of protection," he said, with an implicit 'isn't it obvious?' in his voice.

"For who?"

Here he looked decidedly sheepish. "Well ... I suppose that you ... that is, anybody ... *could* use it. With a few modifications."

Helena's jaw dropped. "For fuck's sake, Miles, is this *all* you've been doing? The world's being forced into the blender out there and all you can do is barricade yourself in your bedroom and work on some way of keeping *yourself* out of it? I was prepared to cut you some slack because I thought you were genuinely working on a way of striking back against this, this, *thing*, but now I find you've just been concerned to cover your own arse. Well, thanks. Thanks a bunch." She scrunched up the paper and threw it back at him. "Go fuck yourself, you selfish bastard."

She turned on her heel to march out of the room, the house and the life of Miles Hearne, but he was upon her before she could get more than a couple of steps. She found herself swung around to look into a face more full of real despair and terror than any she had seen in the last few weeks. Including her own.

"Do you know what you're facing?"

"What? Of course I don't, that's why –"

"Well, *I do.* I've worked it out. It's way out of my league, Helena, it's way out of *everyone's* league. I don't think there *is* a way of stopping it. It's taken me this long to put all the pieces together, and now I'm wishing I hadn't bothered. I'd be happier not knowing."

"Not knowing *what?*"

"For a start, it's too late. It's too embedded in the mass psyche for us to even begin to think of a way of getting it out. You've presumably been seeing the news reports, am I right?"

She nodded. There was no way of avoiding them these

days. Well, maybe by barricading yourself in your house and turning off all the power ...

"So, if we're talking about blocking the influence of this thing, we really are talking about shutting the stable door after the horse has bolted. It's in every one of us already, simultaneously, and it won't go until it gets what it wants."

"Which is?"

Hearne raised an eyebrow. "Well, Molesey, of course."

"But he's ..." No, he isn't. "Shit."

"Couldn't have put it better. And if I'm right, then Molesey – or Robert Pierce, if you prefer – has already put up some pretty heavy defences against the entity. The sort of comprehensive magickal 'fortress' that makes my efforts look like boy scout stuff."

"Oh, you're bang on the money with that one." And she told him all about Bethlehem Street, at the end of which he sat on the floor cross-legged, deep in thought.

"He's setting up a whole series of decoys and blind alleys," Hearne said eventually. "That's why the thing is out there causing its havoc. Since it can't find him – Molesey – it's trying to download its information into everybody it meets. Which is everybody who sees it."

Helena sat beside him. "What information?"

"It was a magickal entity sent out to bring back information about death, and what lies beyond it – a probe, if you like. But from all I can gather, what it discovered sent it insane, and its 'programming' demanded that it imparted this information to its creator."

"And that's what killed Molesey."

He nodded. "But Molesey died before he could banish the entity – there were more paintings in the sequence that would have discharged the Scorpion. So it's still out there, and because the process was interrupted, it's still trying to find its creator in order to complete the task for which it was created.

"And because of my stupidity, and my vanity, I managed to unleash it upon the whole bloody world."

"How? Miles, I don't understand ..."

"That online ritual I set up. sPyroquin, the magician who helped me set it up, created a computer virus that replicated the effects – as near as we could make out – of Molesey's last finished painting. It escaped from the confines of an obscure painting, where it would have been seen by very few, and got on to the Net. Now everybody's seeing it, even if only subliminally, and recreating it in many cases. It's become a 'meme', and a particularly malign one at that."

"Right," said Helena. "So this virus, this 'meme', is providing a conduit into this world for this Scorpion thing. Question is, how do we stop it?"

Hearne barked a short, harsh laugh. "Helena, haven't you been listening? It's *already out there.* It's currently curled up in the base of the brain of every single, man, woman and child on the planet, thanks to the miracle of technology. There's nothing we can do."

His head sank onto his chest in an attitude of despair and acquiescence, but it raised again pretty sharply when Helena smacked him hard on the shoulder.

"I'm not accepting that!" she snarled at him. "If it's a virus, then there must be some sort of cure. It's just waiting for us to find it."

"Look, I'm sorry, Pollyanna, but don't you think I've run every possible solution to this business through my brain a dozen times each already? None of them work. The sheer logistics of coming up with a 'cure' as you put it that would reach into the heads of the entire world's population and yank this thing out again ... it's just not feasible."

She fell silent, considered for a few moments, then said:

"Maybe we can't drag the Scorpion out – but maybe we can starve it out."

"What do you mean?"

"You said that Molesey, if he'd lived, would have found a way of discharging the Scorpion, right?"

"If you're suggesting that we complete the sequence, I can't even paint a skirting board ..."

"Nothing of the kind. By the looks of it, Robert/Nicholas will have to get hold of the paintings and figure out some way of getting rid of the entity without allowing it to download the info it's accumulated."

"Well, yeah – the paintings are like a pentacle, or Solomonic Seal, in classical magic; they're the connection behind the astral plane and the mortal. In this case, they're the connecting point between Molesey and the Scorpion. If he can destroy them, then the poor bloody thing is stuck out there like a dog eternally looking for a lamppost. We've already seen the first effects of what it does when this happens ..."

"So," continued Helena, "what we have to do is get to the paintings first and perform the banishment for him. If that happens, then presumably the Molesey personality will lose its reason for existence, and we might be able to get Robert back."

Hearne looked sceptical. "It won't get rid of the thing from the minds of the people who've already seen it. For them, like I said, it's too late."

"Maybe. But we'll have cut off its main source of nourishment – if the thing itself is gone, then the 'meme' will soon run out of steam. We'll have to keep our heads down for a while, hope that we don't get wiped out by the thing's sheer momentum ... but it's worth a try, isn't it, Miles?"

He didn't answer her. Turning to the window, he took hold of the thick curtains and threw them aside. From the uniformity of the darkness outside, devoid even of the most distant streetlights, she guessed that his house backed on to another. The view, she thought, must be truly, er ... *memorable* in daylight.

"Helena, come here."

Obediently, she moved to his side.

"You have to know what you're facing. You have to *see* it."

"I *have* seen it. I try not to, but –"

"Actually, you haven't. All you've seen of it is its reflection, in dreams, or those representations which your brain constructs for you out of the raw material of everyday experience." He turned to look at her, his face more serious and determined than she had seen before. "If you're going to confront it, you have to know what you're seeing. So I'm going to have to show it to you. I'm going to take you behind your own eyes and introduce you to the Scorpion."

"Now you're being *really* scary," she said.

He took her shoulders and turned her towards the black mirror of the window. In the light of a dozen candles, her face looked paler than was comfortable. The flickering on her skin looked as if there were already beasts just below the surface, jostling to get out.

"Look at yourself, Helena. Look into your own eyes, and listen to the sound of my voice. See nothing else, and hear nothing else. The eyes are windows on the soul, or so the poet says, and I want you to look through those windows and see what's on the inside. I want you to see what's in there, Helena. Look into your own eyes, and then look *beyond* your eyes. All the time, keep listening to my voice, keep it there with you, remember that I'm here all the time for you.

"Feel your breath, Helena. Feel the air going into your lungs, leaving them, entering, leaving, *in*spiration, *re*spiration, and remember that that breath is not just yours, it is the breath of the Scorpion, the creature that lies at the centre of your brain, that looks out on the world through your eyes.

"You can feel it now, can't you, Helena? Feel it stirring inside you?"

Yes.

"It wants to emerge, Helena. It wants you to see it, so it can speak to you, tell you what it knows. Let it come forward, let it swim upwards into your eyes. It has so much it wants to say ...

"Relax into yourself, its passage through you will be so much easier, keep your breathing steady and slow, steady and slow, feel it rising to meet you. There is no fear, no pain.

"Now, Helena. Let yourself see it."

No.

"You must. Don't fear. It cannot hurt you, you are its mistress, it comes only at your bidding. See it, Helena. See it now."

Pain. Pain, and confusion, and fear. Not mine; it comes from somewhere else, somewhere inconceivably distant and yet so close that I feel as if I stand on its threshold. The domain of paradox, of opposites united, flowing into one another seamlessly, fluidly ...

Fear, and Serenity. Joy, and Despair.

Life, and Death.

It sees that I await it, and rushes blindly towards me. It is the face of all terrors: the Demon Lord on his three-headed mount, breathing fire, with sword aloft; the voice of the storm; the child lost in darkness and silence.

It is the messenger of Death.

It is the Scorpion.

It wants to embrace me, unaware, in its imbecile passion, that its embrace will destroy me. My breath ... I can't contain the fear ... fear outweighing all else ... the scream forming in my chest ...

Its sting swirls over and towards my eyes ...

There is a barrier. It cannot reach her, something has interposed itself between her eyes and the beast. Its shape confounds her senses, as if it exists in many dimensions at once, but as the entity retreats howling into the darkness from whence it came, the shape begins to peel away those extra dimensions until it exists in only two, and is revealed as a simple design upon a piece of card ... held in the hand of Miles Hearne.

He is whispering intently into her ear. "By your command, and by this sign, it is repelled. Do you hear me, Helena? It is *gone.*"

His arm is around her shoulders, but this cannot prevent her from slumping to her knees. Her eyes dart around the room, finding mundane things ... the curtain rod, a cobweb in the corner, an empty tin of beans ... with which to banish the nightmare.

"I saw it," she said eventually. "I can't describe it ... I don't want to ... but I saw it."

"You know it now," said Hearne. "You'll know it when you see it again."

She let herself fall forward until her forehead touched the floor. "Why me? Why does it have to be *me*?"

He sat beside her, and his hand trailed through her hair, trying to comfort her.

"Just chance, I suppose. Right place, at the right time, and all that. But there's more ... you're a Wiccan, aren't you?"

She sat up. "So?"

"A follower of the 'Female' magical tradition. A

daughter of Isis."

"Like I said ... so?"

He rummaged through the books on the floor again and produced one, holding it up for her to see the title.

The Golden Bough. "Have you read this?"

"Well, sort of ... I've given it a thorough skimming, put it that way."

He placed it, open, in front of her. A passage had been highlighted with blue marker.

"Read that bit. While you're doing that, I'll go and make some tea. We've got things to discuss."

She was left with the book, alone, and it took her a few minutes to pick it up and read as instructed. The passage told how Isis, after the death of her husband/brother Osiris (in the month of Athyr, when the sun was 'in the sign of the Scorpion') fled down the Nile attended by seven scorpions, raising from the dead those who were harmed by the scorpions, in pursuit of Osiris' coffin; when she found him, he, too, was resurrected by Isis.

Isis. Mistress of Scorpions, Queen of Magic, Conqueror of Death.

Do I have to *become* Isis? All because I was 'in the right place, at the right time'?

She stood once more and, with no little trepidation, looked again at her reflection in the window. Perhaps it was the light playing tricks once more, but she looked different; something in her face seemed more stable, more serene. Like an image in marble.

Maybe I don't have to *become* anything. Maybe it's already there.

Naren Patel examined the front page of the newspaper with great care. He wasn't, ordinarily, a man given to needless worry, but there were things going on in the world around him that he didn't understand, and didn't like. His intense perusal of the local paper was making this unease deeper, as it concerned the plague of apparently motiveless violence that was creeping across the city.

He was used to violence, of course, and he was very

used to uncertainty; they had been constants in his life – and the life of his family – since they had come to Britain from Uganda in the seventies, due to the kind auspices of Idi Amin. But this was different, this was *scary.* He'd been not much more than a boy when Amin had expelled the Ugandan Asians, and he remembered it as something of an adventure; but now, the look that his father had worn during the last months in Africa made sense to Naren.

He'd already managed to read between the lines of the article and tease out one of the facts of the matter which the media had neglected to clarify. This was most definitely not the racially motivated type of violence that everybody seemed to think; sure, there were incidents of violence directed against Asians, against blacks, against those whose accent marked them out as 'different'; but these were simply the most visible edge of the problem. It ran far wider, and far deeper.

That incident the other week, for instance; his father (who still insisted on coming into the shop to 'help out' on a regular basis, despite retiring and handing the business over to Naren a year before) had, with a couple of other men, chased off two youths who'd mugged and stabbed a man in a nearby alleyway. The boys who had carried out the act had been known to them, local lads who, while having something of a reputation as petty lawbreakers, had previously shown no inclination towards violence.

Naren sighed, replaced the local paper on the top of the pile, and picked up one of the nationals, the *Guardian.* His eyes flicked over the front page for a moment, scanning the headlines, and he found to his dismay that what was happening locally appeared to be taking place also on both a national and international level. Wars that had been thought to be long dormant had suddenly, for no readily apparent reason, flared up once more. 'Race riots' were occurring in places as diverse as Los Angeles and Calais (where a 'holding camp' for asylum seekers had been attacked by locals spurred on by right-wing extremists). More suicide bombings in the Middle East. More sectarian violence in Belfast. More mutual sabre-rattling between the USA and Iraq.

This stuff had been commonplace before now, of

course; but now the participants in each conflict appeared to have no conception of why they were behaving with such belligerence. Even the soundbites from the various press spokesmen betrayed only a kind of aggrieved confusion. As for the columnists and pundits who filled the Comment pages ... well, they made about as much sense as they ever did.

There was more besides; something about a 'computer virus' that was causing much consternation worldwide, something that turned your screen into a red swirl, infected all data held in the computer memory, and which was becoming so virulent that it was being widely forecast that the Web itself might just implode. Due to his limited interest in computers – to Naren they were tools, nothing more – this was registered only dimly on his mind, but it became one more piece of evidence for the prosecution.

The world, Naren Patel concluded solemnly, was going insane.

The bell rang to announce the arrival of another customer, and without looking up, Naren folded the paper and put it back on the newsstand. When he turned, he saw only the leader of the group who had just walked in. Tall, shaven-headed, resplendent with tattoos. Neither he nor any of his comrades said anything, but Naren Patel knew instantly that the world's insanity was paying him a visit.

"Hello, Paki," said the tattooed man.

They didn't kill him. They ransacked the shop, emptied the till (having forced him to open it), and left laden with as much alcohol as they could carry. They had beaten him, kicked him, verbally abused him and urinated on him. But they hadn't killed him.

His wife and daughter, who had been away visiting his father when all this happened, thank God (he didn't like to think what would have happened to them if they'd been with him) told him how lucky he was. So had the hospital staff, repeatedly, between the time when he'd been admitted and his discharge the following morning.

He didn't feel lucky. They had shown him how vulnerable he was, how unable he was to defend both himself and those around him. In a world gone mad, he was powerless against that madness. Everything which constituted his own personal world – his very identity – had been ripped out of him and trampled, before his eyes.

He sent his wife and daughter to stay with her sister, where they would be safe – as much as anyone could be. Her sister had a large family, many strong and able sons around to look after them. His father insisted on coming round to help with the clear-up, but after a day in which, although the visible damage to the shop was largely put to rights, the *stain* remained, Naren insisted that he go home.

Alone in the silence of his home, and the ruin of his livelihood, Naren wandered for a while, looking at the world as though it had lost all colour, and dimension, and life. He went into the small bathroom, just behind the shop; one of his assailants had been in here too, had defecated into the sink and smashed the mirror above it. The shit was gone, but the bathroom mirror still hung there, transformed into a web of glass that reflected a thousand bruised Narens back at himself, each one of them as pathetic and contemptible as the last, all spiralling inward toward nothingness.

He nodded, understanding what was required of him. Then he stooped, picked up a stray shard of glass that still lay on the floor beside him, and rolled up his sleeve.

Finding the location of the paintings turned out to be a lot less difficult than discovering the name of their current owner. For a start, Sheelagh and Ken had subjected Helena to what amounted to the third degree about her motivations in finding the owner, her current mental state and (in what resembled a family inquisition, much to Helena's amusement) Miles Hearne's intentions toward her. The latter she evaded with a politely worded, but nonetheless firm, request that they mind their own business; and their concerns about her state of mind were assuaged with equal forthrightness (for now, anyway).

The question of her reasons for contacting the old man who had bought the paintings was not so easily answered. Helena had no intention of telling them exactly why it was so imperative that they find him, but, since there was no way that

Sheelagh would release the details without some sort of explanation, she had to come up with something, and quickly.

"I'm not after the paintings," she said after some thought, adding a little shudder of unease, which would help to convince them that the thought of seeing them again was the very *last* thing on her mind. "The old guy was interested in a Tarot reading, but he didn't give me his name or address. Considering the amount of money he shelled out on the paintings, it could be very lucrative. Just the sort of thing to help me get myself sorted out again."

Torn between their sympathies (which Helena had played upon rather skillfully) and their surrogate-parental duties, Sheelagh and Ken went into a huddle and, at long last, produced the information.

His name was Philip Burgess. A little preparatory detective work by Hearne and herself soon sketched in a basic biographical outline; born 1912, into a middle-class family (his father was a ledgers clerk for a textile company); early life up till 1933, when he graduated from Oxford with a degree in Classics, a blank; was for a few years a journalist until the outbreak of the second world war, when he served in the army with some distinction, notably in North Africa, where he rose to the rank of Major in a combat infantry regiment and was – as a photograph from an old newspaper testified – personally decorated by Montgomery after El Alamein.

After the war, he went into publishing, became the managing editor of a major company which specialised in academic textbooks, retired in 1977 to a house on the outskirts of his home town, where he still lives. Never married; but there were hints of 'close friendships' with a number of men during his life, one of whom was a moderately famous Shakespearean actor. No scandal had ever attached itself to his name, however.

"Doesn't explain the interest in Molesey, though, does it?" said Hearne, as they drove to the address which Sheelagh had supplied. "Far as I can see, it's the standard English life. Apart from the war record, he could be any old Home Counties closet queer."

Helena tutted at his decidedly non-PC terminology. "There's a lot of room between the lines, though. He seems to have guarded his privacy rather well for someone who's been living the 'standard English life'."

"Comes of having to keep his shagging preferences quiet for all those years, doesn't it?"

"No, it's more than that. I met the man, remember – seeing those paintings was having quite an effect on him, and I don't mean in the same way as they had on me."

Hearne was quiet for a while, apparently in thought. He didn't even react when someone cut him up at the motorway exit, a baseball-capped twerp who had the audacity to give him the finger in the rear-view mirror. Helena simply shrugged; there was an awful lot of that sort of stuff going on at the moment, three murders in the last week directly attributable to 'road rage', according to the news.

Of course, they had a shrewd idea what was *in*directly responsible ...

"He'd be the right age, you know."

She looked at him sidelong. "Right age for what?"

"To have known The Man Himself. Molesey."

"He'd have had to be pretty young."

"Well, from what we know of Nick, that's just the way he liked them. Young, and pretty. What do you think?"

"It would explain a lot, I suppose." The image of his eyes, apparently lustrous with tears, on that day at Guiding Spirit came back to her. If there had been something between them, it was fairly obvious that it had been more (for Burgess, at least) than a casual fling. "But there's only one sure way to find out."

Burgess' house was an old farmhouse – 18th century, Helena guessed – standing alone in a few modest acres of land north of the city. Once upon a time, the acreage must have been considerably greater, but now the land was hemmed in on one side by an industrial estate (otherwise known as an 'Enterprise Park'), on another two by a modern housing development, and on the fourth by the motorway. Fortunately, from the house itself, very little of these modern accretions to the landscape could be seen, for which Helena was grateful. One day, this land too would probably be overwhelmed by that ghastliness, become part of 'the Waste Land', and she considered how horrible it would be for Burgess to see them creeping nearer, nearer, every day, the slow, patient jackals of modernity waiting to pick him off.

There was a car already in front of the house when they pulled up, a sleek black Mercedes, its engine idling. A driver sat in the front seat, reading a newspaper. The front door of the house was open, and there was movement within.

They parked to one side of the drive, and strolled toward the house. The driver of the Mercedes looked up at them as they approached, all too obviously taking in their somewhat unorthodox appearance. Helena was in her long red coat, buckled at the waist, her purple boots showing underneath; Hearne was in blazer, jeans and a threadbare Adidas t-shirt that looked as if he'd owned it since his student days, and smelled as if he hadn't washed it in as long. He folded up his paper and stepped from the car.

"Hello," he said with quiet concern, and a flicker of a smile. "Are you here for the funeral?"

Helena gulped. "Funeral?"

"Ah. I see you're not."

"Excuse us," said Hearne, "but Mr Burgess is ..."

"He's in the house. You're lucky to catch him, we were just about to leave. His doctor wanted a quick word with him before we all left, just to be sure he's up to it. Personally, I think she worries too much. Tough old bird, that one."

They had both drawn a long sigh of relief. Excusing themselves from the driver, they approached the front door. A woman in a black coat was talking into a mobile phone.

"Look, I told you, Sharon, I'm *not on duty* this morning, I'm going to the funeral ... Well, Tony's just going to have to cope, isn't he? It's not my fault that they couldn't arrange a locum. Tell him to do what he always does, prescribe some antibiotics and get them to call back when their head's actually dropped off. Bye."

She thumbed the 'off' switch, still mumbling curses, and only then did she realise that she had an audience.

"Oh. Sorry. Didn't see you there."

They smiled, trying to make out that they were every

bit as embarrassed as she was.

"We ... er, well ..." said Helena. "We were wondering if Mr Burgess was free to have a quick word."

"He ... that is, we ... were off to the funeral. Was he expecting you?"

"Not exactly. But it is sort of urgent."

She approached them, and, after checking behind her to ensure that she wasn't overheard, spoke in low tones. "I'd advise against talking to him at the moment. This whole business is a bit upsetting for him, you see. Maybe you could call again? Tomorrow, perhaps?"

Helena was about to reply when Miles touched her on the shoulder, and insinuated himself past her. When he spoke, it was in the tone he usually reserved for his television appearances, or when he was in full-on seduction mode; a smooth, accentless drawl that made the listener think that they were the only person in the world worth speaking to, ever.

"We're really sorry to be such an inconvenience to you both at such a terrible time, Doctor, er ..."

"Tyler. Jenny Tyler." Tentatively, she proffered a hand, which he took with the utmost solicitation and gallantry (so much so, that Helena thought for one moment he was going to kiss it).

"May we introduce ourselves first and foremost. My name is Miles Hearne, and this is my friend Miss Helena McCallum."

Helena nodded and smiled at the doctor, but the woman hardly noticed, so caught up was she in whatever Miles was doing.

"We have some business of a rather delicate, and *personal* nature to discuss with Mr Burgess, and I'm afraid that we've driven rather a long way to see him." Not strictly true, but worth throwing in. "And since we have to begin our journey back quite soon, you would be doing us the most *enormous* favour if you could just persuade Mr Burgess to part with a few moments of his time. I'm sure you understand."

"I'm not sure about Jenny," said a voice from behind her at that moment, "but I think *I* understand. Hello, Helena."

In his black suit, Burgess looked even more sombre,

and quite a bit frailer, than on their last meeting, but Helena was still impressed by the dignity with which he carried himself. She had noticed a selection of walking sticks arranged neatly in a rack beside the door, including the one he had been carrying when he was at the shop that day, but she knew that if she was to inspect them more closely, she would find little evidence of use.

He approached her, moving past Miles (who looked somewhat less than happy at this interruption; obviously he had his own secondary agenda regarding Dr Tyler) and the still-stupefied doctor, took her hand, and kissed it with just that display of old-fashioned gallantry which Miles had missed; coming from Burgess, however, it seemed *correct.*

"I had the strangest feeling that our paths would cross again. Don't ask me why."

"Oh, I think I understand," said Helena.

He asked Dr Tyler to give them a few moments alone, and if she had been in any mood to argue, her dazed mind overrode all such objections. He ushered them into the living room, having been introduced to Miles (and given a rather peculiar, if not suspicious, look by him), and sat them opposite him on the other side of a large, ornate fireplace.

"I'm afraid I can't spare you very long," he said, " as I have a prior engagement, as you can see..."

"Yes," said Helena. "Family? A close friend?"

"In a way. Although I never actually met the deceased."

Miles snorted. "It happens."

Puzzled by Miles' interruption, he briefly explained about the baby.

"We're really sorry. We wouldn't intrude if it weren't so very important."

"So what can I do for you?"

There was the tiniest of pauses, and Helena said, "I think you know, Mr Burgess."

It was interesting to see how he automatically looked upward, presumably to the room where the paintings were stored. "Yes. I think I knew the moment I saw you."

Helena made to speak, but Burgess held up one curled

hand.

"I also knew exactly the reason for your visit. And I have to tell you now – my answer is no."

Hearne sat forward in his chair and spoke for the first time. "Mr Burgess, I'm sorry to press you on this, but those paintings are far more than mere paintings ..."

"I'm well aware of that, Mr Hearne. They mean far more to me also than their mere aesthetic or financial value. You see, I knew Nicholas Molesey."

They exchanged a glance. Hearne's face wore an almost annoying 'I-told-you-so' expression.

"You are the first people I have spoken to of this in ... well, ever, I suppose. Times have changed, in this way, at least, for the better. We were lovers."

"We'd guessed as much," said Helena. "But it was more than that, wasn't it?"

Burgess nodded, sadly. "You'll have doubtless heard of his proclivities before now. His sexual liaisons were more than mere dalliances, though; every act was designed to heighten his consciousness as part of an ongoing ritual to ... to ..."

He stopped, chuckled. "Even after all this time, I'm still not entirely sure what his intentions were. We never discussed the matter."

"Surely though," said Hearne, "if you were involved ..."

"Does a pen understand the words which it is used to write? Can a match understand the concept of 'fire'? His 'conquests' were simply a means to an end for Nicholas."

"All of them," said Helena softly, "except you."

"Even myself, at the beginning. Quite what it was that led us to something more lasting, of that also I'm rather unsure. Perhaps initially he saw in me a potential, as a disciple perhaps. I was bright back then, quick-witted, eager to learn. But I quickly came to realise that these pursuits of Nicholas were beyond my understanding. They frightened me no little bit, too, I can tell you. So, bit by bit, I became detached from that aspect of Nicholas' life."

"But you didn't abandon him, or he you," said Hearne.

"I find that curious."

"Did the 'sex magick' continue?" asked Helena.

"Yes, but not with me. I had no illusions about Nicholas being my 'exclusive property' – these experiments of his were too important to him for me to even broach the subject of discontinuing them, even for so trivial a reason as my jealousy. So he found his 'catamites' elsewhere. What did I care? It was my bed he came back to, again and again. And there was no 'magick' to be found there, unless it was the kind that lovers have made every night, for all time."

Helena leant in closer. "Mr Burgess –"

"Please, my dear. Philip."

"Philip. I have to know – were you there when he died?"

His eyes closed, and she knew that an image was forming on the inside of his eyelids, one that had been tormenting him for over seventy years. He nodded.

"And those paintings were with him too, weren't they?"

He took a deep breath. "Yes. He was working on one of them – that damnable one with all the red swirls – when he died. I think it killed him. Is that silly of me?"

Helena took his hand again. "No. In fact, I think it may be responsible for more than just Nicholas Molesey's death. That's why –"

"Don't ask me to give to you, Helena. Anything but that. I couldn't risk –"

"What?" Hearne barked. Helena looked at him sharply, but he pressed on. "What couldn't you risk?"

"If that painting killed Nicholas, then isn't it vital that I keep it from the world? I should have destroyed it when I first bought it, but, stupid sentimental old fool that I am, I refrained. Now my mind's made up – I'll do it when I get back, later today."

"No!" Hearne almost shouted. "Don't you see, that's what –"

He stopped as Helena clutched his arm, painfully.

"Please, Philip – if you do that, you may just make things worse."

"You have a better idea?"

"Yes!" said Hearne before Helena could stop him. "This thing has to be banished properly –"

"More magic, eh?" There was a new, bitter edge to Burgess' voice. "No. No, I won't allow it. It was the magic that destroyed Nicholas, and that magic is held, embodied, in those paintings. You're quite right, Helena, the forces in that picture *are* responsible for more than one death. I have reason to believe that the reason I am wearing black today is because of that picture – somehow, it has been resurrected. Well, no more. I'm going to stop it."

Helena and Hearne looked at each other, in quiet despair. The old man had turned his face against them, determination set into each line of his face, tautening his loose muscles until they could almost hear them vibrate. He would not be debated on this issue. After a moment, however, he turned back, smiled ruefully and said:

"Please, Helena, Miles, don't think too harshly of me. I do this because I know it to be for the best. It will pain me to do it, because it will be severing the last physical tie I have to Nicholas, but nevertheless, now that I know what it is, I *will* do it. If there is any redemption possible for me, for Nicholas, then it is in this act. I failed him once. I won't do it again."

Dr Tyler appeared in the door, to inform them that they had to go now as the funeral would soon begin. The 'they' she referred to was not just herself and Burgess; it was a subtle hint also to the visitors.

Quickly, Helena scribbled her telephone number on the back of an envelope she found in her bag, and passed it to Burgess. "If you change your mind – or if you just want to talk ..."

"Thank you, my dear," he said. "I think I may be needing all the sympathetic ears I can get in the near future."

They walked him to the door and helped him into the waiting Mercedes; as Helena made to let go of his arm, he turned suddenly to her, and, with confusion and hurt still reigning in his voice, even after all these years, said to her:

"They wouldn't let me go to his funeral, you know that? Nicholas' family. I never saw his body go into the ground.

I never said goodbye." His voice began to break. "It won't happen again."

He patted her arm in farewell, before the door was shut on him and the car moved away.

"That's it, then." Hearne trudged back to his own car looking, almost comically, like a sulking schoolboy. "We are most definitely fucked. Might as well go home and kiss our arses goodbye."

"No," said Helena with a certainty and ferocity inverse to Hearne's passive acceptance of doom. "It's not over yet."

"So what else is there left for us to do?"

"We might not have to do anything," she replied. "Remember, we're not the only ones playing this game. And since the other players don't know what sort of a bad hand we just got dealt ..."

She looked back at the house. She could almost hear the house groaning from the burden it carried, the tumour within.

"We have to be ready to move. Soon."

Old men should be used to attending funerals. To live so long is to spend one's time, when not contemplating one's own demise, watching one's contemporaries going one by one into the ground. By and large, Philip had accepted this fact; but this ...

This was different. A lone pallbearer, a small white coffin, a man and a woman standing together, clinging to one another desperately and occasionally looking into each other's drawn and dazed faces, apparently searching for something. Philip had a fair idea of what they were looking for; they were groping around for some clue as to how they should mourn someone they had barely known. Their child.

Her name, for a few weeks, had been Francesca. She had not been baptised. The face of the old priest as he led the service had been admirably calm and composed, but behind it there was, in all likelihood, the questioning of a God who would take the life of one so young, and – if doctrine was to be strictly followed – send the child's soul spinning down to hell.

And if that's not what he's thinking, mused Philip, then he bloody well ought to be.

There was not much said. He had, with Jenny's assistance, paid the grieving parents his deepest condolences, and been rewarded with a weak smile and handshake from the baby's father. Andrea nodded acknowledgment, but still didn't appear to be present in more than body. Philip wondered if she was still sedated.

Brenda invited him back to her house for a 'small get-together' afterwards, but on this occasion he declined. The healing process traditionally starts with the ritual tea and ham sandwiches, over which memories of the deceased can be traded; this time, however, it didn't look as if there would be much conversation.

So he sat on a bench in the graveyard, sheltering under an umbrella from the persistent, irritating drizzle (will it *ever* stop raining?), and waited for Jenny to return with the car.

It was here that he realised he was being watched, and had been for some time. He couldn't explain how he knew this; all he knew was that his nerve-endings felt a sudden tingling, the hair on the nape of his neck standing to attention. He turned his head slowly, and saw the young man, standing a few yards away. The stranger wore a long black coat, and the rain had plastered his dark hair in strands across his forehead. The corners of his lips were curled upward slightly, in an almost-smile.

He looked familiar, too, but for the moment Philip couldn't place him.

"Can I help you?"

The stranger's smile broadened. "I would say that you probably could, Philip."

Do I know him? I hope not. I hope this is just some sort of elaborate and tasteless joke. Something within me so much does *not* want to know who this person is.

"You're going to say that I have you at a disadvantage. Well, that's not strictly true, Philip. It's *me* who's at the disadvantage. That's why I'm here."

He sauntered over and sat beside him on the bench. Instinctively, Philip edged a little further away.

"What do you want? Is this a robbery?"

"You take me for a mugger. That's priceless. Quite

priceless." The amusement, if it could be said to be such a thing, was cold and superficial. "No, Philip, I'm not out to rob you of anything that you are not in a position to give to me freely."

The man stopped, considered for a moment, then went on.

"Actually, I'm not sure if robbery would be the right word, even if I were to take them without your consent. *Redemption* might be better. After all, the paintings were mine, to begin with ..."

Philip looked him fully in the face for the first time. There was something about the eyes, a confidence in the gaze that suggested they had once shared a greater intimacy. Although he was aware that his memory was beginning to fade in some respects, Philip knew that, had he shared anything more than a casual acquaintance with this man, he surely would have remembered it.

"I'm afraid, sir, that I don't even know your name."

At this, the stranger looked thoroughly bemused. "You mean that you still haven't worked it out?"

He edged closer still, put a hand on Philip's shoulder. "Philip, it's me. Nicholas. I'm *back*."

The old man stood as though an electric charge had passed through him. "You're insane. Whoever you are, you're –"

"I know it's hard to believe, but it's true. I'm here again. I harrowed hell, and emerged on the other side. You can't imagine what it was like – pursued through the netherworld by something so terrible that I didn't dare look into its face. Something that was trying to tell me what it had seen in those depths of death to which I was resisting being consigned. Something *I* had created."

He stood, and approached. Philip turned his back on him.

"It's still pursuing me, Philip. When I found myself summoned back, it followed me even then. It won't ever give up. So far, I've managed to elude it, set up false trails and blind alleys to throw it off the scent, but I can't carry on like this indefinitely. I need those paintings back in order to put myself beyond it, forever."

"Are you working with those people who called this morning? Hm? Is that it? Have you moved on to Plan B now, since asking me for them directly didn't work? Trying to scare me into giving you – them – the paintings. Well, it won't work. I'm not that gullible, or that easily scared."

Even as he said it, he wasn't so sure about the truth of that last statement.

"So, you can go back to Helena and tell her that I'm –"

"Ah. Helena. So she's been to see you already." 'Nicholas smiled, turned his face towards the grey sky. "Then there's an added urgency to all of this."

"What are you talking about?"

"I'm afraid you wouldn't understand. But then, you never did, did you? I could never make you see that what I was doing was more than the esoteric dabblings of some spoiled, bored little rich boy."

"That's not true! I never thought of you –"

What am I saying? He's drawn me into his game, making me think of him as Nicholas. No. No, I won't play.

"It doesn't really matter, of course," said 'Nicholas', pressing the advantage. "Your understanding isn't necessary, merely your compliance. Willing, or otherwise."

"Whoever you are, I'm going to tell you this once, and once only. Those paintings are now mine, to do with as I please. And it pleases me *very much* to go home right now and destroy them. I should think that this would please you very much, too, since they seem to be the source of so much anxiety to you."

"It would not," said the stranger, simply. "Certainly, their destruction – at the right time – would not be of any great consequence, but if they are destroyed prematurely, it would leave my pursuer out there with nowhere to go but me. No, it must be summoned back into the painting – back into the portal between this world and the next – and then banished with the proper ritual. Only then can the paintings be destroyed, and with my blessing."

"Gibberish. Utter gibberish ..."

'Nicholas' came closer, and this time, for some reason, Philip found himself unable to back away. "You won't be able to destroy those paintings, Philip. I'm in every one of them, part of my soul is embedded in each brush stroke, and the more you try and damage them, the more you will realise that you are causing me harm. Me, Philip. The man you love. The man who loves you. Not even death could eradicate that love. And the more you try and harm them, Philip, you will understand that you are harming not just *me,* but you are harming *yourself* also. Just as you harmed yourself all those years ago when you left me in that house, left me with nothing but the cold darkness for company ...

"We are joined, Philip, you and I. What causes me pain causes you pain also. I want you to understand that. I want you to understand it *now* ..."

He reached out and took Philip's hand, squeezed it hard. A wave of terrible anguish swept through him, followed by nausea.

"When you raise your hand against them, Philip, you will feel nothing but pain, and fear. The thought of damaging them will thereafter be abhorrent to you. You will be harming me, the living breathing being whose hand you now hold. You can understand that now, can't you? You can't do that to me again, you won't be able to let yourself do that, will you?"

Later, he couldn't be sure if he had provided him with any sort of answer; his attention was so wholly occupied with the eyes which seemed to be burning holes in his soul, the voice which swept away the rest of the universe and consumed him utterly. His next memory was of a car pulling up beside him, and the dark shape of his 'lover' retreating into the distance like a vampire at dawn.

Jenny was at his side. "Sorry we took so long, somebody had parked a van right up close to our car, couldn't get out until they chose to move it. Bunch of hippies, by the looks of it. Who was that man you were talking to?"

"Just ..." He shook his head, trying to clear the fog in his brain. "Nobody. It was nobody."

"Didn't look like nobody to me. He was holding your hand ..."

"Jenny, I don't mean to sound brusque, but can you just forget about this and get me home. I'm very, very tired ..."

Put like that, she didn't have much choice. She and the chauffeur helped him into the car and they pulled away, past the church, their speed far too respectably slow for Philip's liking.

At the gates of the churchyard, his attention was seized by movement among the gravestones along one of the boundary walls. A group of unkempt young people, probably the 'hippies' Jenny had mentioned, were milling around, and one of them – a girl, by the looks of it – was crouched in front of an old and partially toppled headstone. When they got closer, he could see that she was drawing something on the stone with either a felt pen or a lipstick.

A red spiral.

This casual desecration would have been enough to disturb him, but the sight of a tall, dark-haired man in a long black coat, looking upon the endeavour with an air of amused paternalism, sent further shivers through him. As the car pulled alongside, this man turned his head and smiled directly at him briefly, before he was obscured from sight.

Philip was exceptionally glad when they turned on to the main road, and their speed increased; though he wasn't sure if it would ever be fast, or far, enough from that smile.

He insisted on being left alone. That much was essential; he was only too aware of how his ensuing actions would appear to an outsider. By overplaying his tiredness, it was a simple matter to send Jenny on her way, fuss and hover at the door as she did on the way out.

From the kitchen he fetched a carving knife. There was an axe in the shed, he knew, but it was considerably heavier and would require more effort to use. He hadn't exaggerated his tiredness *that* much. The effort of climbing the stairs put emphasis on this point. He had to stop on each landing as he ascended, huffing for breath and hissing angry imprecations at his body before continuing.

The first qualms appeared as he reached the door of the disused bedroom where the paintings were stowed. These were not too difficult to dismiss, as they seemed to centre merely on the mundane financial loss that the act entailed. *Might as well have just burned that fifteen thousand straight away, and cut out the middle man.*

But once his natural inclinations against such a wastrel display had been conquered, he found other, deeper reservations setting in as he swung open the door. The red spiral painting was leaning against the far wall as he entered, and just for a moment he saw it as he had for the first time, on that night in 1929 when he saw, sprawled beneath it with the candlelight moving on his pale skin like maggots, the body of Nicholas Molesey...

Philip, it's me. It's Nicholas. I'm back.

No it wasn't! It couldn't have been him. I said that I'd know your voice when I heard it, Nicholas, telling me what to do, but that wasn't you speaking. That was somebody I don't know, trying to ape you, trying to *be* you, using the words you may have used but twisting them against me.

In a fury now, he lifted the knife and lumbered forward. His legs seemed to tie themselves in knots of agony before he could reach his target, and he found himself plummeting toward the floor, but still his right arm – more in reflex than in rage – struck out as he fell. The point of the blade embedded itself in something, and the knife was torn from his grip.

The sound was instantly in his ears, his mind, his whole body, and he rolled onto his side, hands over ears, to try and blot it out. He looked up at the painting of the red spiral, which loomed above him now. The knife jutted from the upper part of the canvas, just below the frame, and although the image itself had not been affected, it seemed as if the painting itself had been wounded and was bellowing out its pain.

But this sound was not unfamiliar to Philip. He had heard it, on that same night in 1929, from behind a locked door. The picture was screaming with Nicholas' voice. The agony, and the fear, were tangible ... and apparently contagious, for Philip's every nerve ending felt aflame, and his mind boiled with anxiety.

I'm here, Nicholas.

Fearing that his heart would give in at any moment, he struggled to his knees and reached out one wavering hand to clutch the hilt of the knife. With difficulty, his fingers closed around it, and the momentum of his movement in falling forward again pulled it from the painting. It clattered and span into a corner. Philip lay still, his breath laboured, his chest as heavy as stone.

The scream diminished, and faded away.

You won't be able to destroy those paintings, Philip.

God damn you ...

You are harming not just me, but you are harming yourself also ...

... and God help us all.

Difficult though it was, she had managed to stop herself from remembering her dreams. All those years of patiently noting down each one as soon as she had awoken, in the hope of extracting some sort of meaning from them (from her unconscious, or perhaps elsewhere?) had to be rigorously unlearned. For the time being, they had nothing to tell Helena that she didn't already know, that wasn't already out on the streets and shrieking from the rooftops. Now, although she still had them, there were very effective shutters that came down as she woke and prevented her from carrying the horrors into her waking state.

One of the horrors had a voice just like her mobile phone's ringtone. This fact stayed with her as she surfaced from sleep, and disconcerted her considerably. It was a peculiar demon indeed who could sing the theme from *Scooby-Doo*.

Before she had time to process the information telling her that it was, in fact, her phone making this noise, somewhere close by, it had stopped, to be replaced by the gruff voice of someone who, by the sound of it, was most definitely *not* a morning person, saying "Hello?"

She sat up, and recalled where she was; the sofa in Miles Hearne's living room. She must have fallen asleep here last night, fully dressed, after a day of debating their next move, but she didn't have the faintest idea where the quilt covering her had come from.

Miles? Miles Hearne, are you in danger of becoming a gentleman in your old age?

"Can you speak up please? I can't quite hear you ..."

He was talking into her phone. What was he doing talking into her phone? She looked at a nearby clock – 7.03 a.m. What was he doing talking into her phone at 7.03 in the morning?

"Hang on a second. I'll just get her."

He held the phone out to her.

"Helena – it's the hospital. Something about Philip Burgess ..."

"You were well away in dreamland last night," said Miles.

Helena thought about asking him not to phrase it quite like that, but decided against it. "Was I?"

"That phone of yours rang about four times before I came downstairs and answered it for you. I find the music from *The Flintstones* irritating at the best of times."

"It's not *The Flintstones.* It's *Scooby-Doo.*"

"Whatever." He was silent for a moment, looking out through the windscreen at the early rush hour traffic, distorted through the smeared rain and the pulsating, hypnotic rhythm of the wiper blades. "Did they tell you what had happened to him?"

"Some sort of accident, they said. They didn't seem too sure themselves."

Miles sighed. "Well, at least he's alive. Like that chauffeur said yesterday, he's a tough old bird."

Helena chose not to answer. In some strange, inexplicable way she felt almost responsible for what had happened to him; she kept thinking that she should have stayed close to him, to the paintings, not allowed either out of her sight.

I've failed him. That's what it amounts to; I failed him.

Strangely, as soon as she heard these words in her head, another stronger voice cut in.

– *You couldn't have prevented this.*

– Oh, couldn't I?

– *No. This was inevitable. Everything is happening as it should.*

– Really.

– *You are Isis. This is as it must be.*

– Right. I'm a Goddess. Pretty feeble Goddess who can't even protect an old man ...

– Not even Isis could protect Osiris. All will be well.

– Fuck Isis.

"What?" Hearne's eyes left the road for a split second, enough time for a motorcycle dispatch rider to appear out of nowhere and nearly end up on the bonnet. Having performed the time-honoured ritual of winding the window down and shouting the word *"Cunt!"* at the biker's diminishing form, Miles turned back to her.

"What did you say that for?"

"Say what?"

"Don't mess me around. You said the words 'Fuck Isis', didn't you?"

"I may have done." Shit. I didn't say it out loud, did I?

"So – explain."

"Miles, I'm tired. There's a lot of stuff going on at the moment – I don't know if you've noticed – and it's wearing me down. So if I start talking to myself now and again, then you'll just have to forgive me ..."

"It's *what* you said that bothers me, Helena. I think you're still fighting yourself, you're still in two minds. You need to be *focused.*"

"Easier said than done."

With a smooth and signal-free movement – drawing justified disapprobation from the cars behind him – Miles swung the car off the road and pulled into the forecourt of a petrol station. He turned off the engine.

"You were the one dragged me back into this before I was ready. You wanted to know what it was that you had to do. Well, I told you. I *showed* you. I thought you were prepared for what's to come. It's been you that's been telling me that it's not over, it's not over, all the time, and now you tell me that you *can't do it?"*

"I didn't say that –"

"As good as. Listen, Helena, you saw me as I was when you came to find me. I didn't think we had much of a chance of beating this thing, I was more concerned with protecting myself. It was only you that convinced me to get back into the fray. Now, now that I know what we're facing, I still think we're facing the sort of odds that would get you laughed out of any bookie's on the face of the Earth. But I know we have to at least try. And I can't do that without you there. You're more important than me in all of this, Helena. You're the balancing force that's needed to integrate him – Pierce, Molesey, whoever he is.

"If Pierce manages to banish the Scorpion *his* way, it'll be out there causing havoc for all time. Same if the old man destroys the pictures. In fact, that might be worse, because then it would probably go back to Pierce and destroy *him* the same way it destroyed Molesey, and then there would be no chance *ever* of integrating him with the Scorpion. That's the key – integration. And you're the only one who can carry that out."

"Yes, but why me?" wailed Helena.

"Why *not* you? The Isis force, if you can call it that, it doesn't read your CV before it picks you, you're just there, at the right place, at the right time. All you have to do is, well, go with the flow, I suppose."

"And what's the alternative?"

"The alternative –" His eyes lighted upon something outside the car. "*There's* the alternative."

An argument had erupted between two men on the forecourt a few yards in front of them. From the few coherent syllables that Helena could make out, it appeared to be about nothing more than the fact that one driver had pulled into the pump in front of the other, blocking him in, just as the latter was about to pull away. It was fairly obvious that this was very shortly about to tip over the edge into outright unpleasantness. In the car of the 'blocked in' driver, a woman leaned over from the passenger seat to shout to her male companion. At first, Helena assumed that she was trying to defuse the situation, but closer attention revealed that she was encouraging him to 'flatten the fucker'.

"In a little while, those two are going to be at each other's throats, quite literally," said Miles. "And they won't be the only ones. The violence will steadily get worse, until –"

"Until it's not just minor punch-ups in the street we have to worry about. Christ, and I thought the world situation was bad enough as it is." She smiled, ruefully. "Sorry, Miles. The doubts – they're more persistent than I thought."

"Just don't give up, that's all. That's what we're here for – cheering for each other. Don't worry, I'm not going to get all mushy on you ..."

"Wish I could say the same of them," she said, indicating the combatants outside, who were now nose to nose, screaming. "There's going to be some mushy faces in a minute, and I'd rather not be a witness to it. Can we go now?"

Miles started up the car and (carefully) eased his way past the battle zone. As they pulled back on to the road, Helena noticed that there were people on the pavement, standing, watching, waiting for the fight to reach its natural conclusion. There was a look on their collective face that disturbingly resembled rapture.

The A&E department at the local hospital was well versed in the procedure for dealing with major emergencies, as a large and very messy train crash the year before had testified; but it had little experience in dealing with large-scale eruptions of insanity.

That was what this amounted to. What was usually reserved for a Saturday night – and then only after the pubs had shut – was now happening twenty-four/seven. It was currently just after nine a.m., and the cubicles were full of people nursing wounds from having broken bottles pushed into their faces, drivers who'd managed somehow to upset their fellow road-users, and wives whose weekend bouts of 'falling down the stairs' (again, usually after their spouses had returned from the pub) had started to spread to the rest of the week. The waiting room was similarly full of people – blacks and Asians figuring rather prominently – who appeared to have encountered violence in one form or another.

"Looks like a field hospital on the Russian front in here," said Miles. "I know I shouldn't be surprised, but ..." He shrugged and shook his head hopelessly.

"Stay focused, Miles." Helena smiled inwardly at her use of Hearne's phrase back at him. "We have to find Philip."

The receptionist seemed to be having problems

focusing, also. At the same time as she was having to deal with some rather irate people on the telephone, she was fending off the complaints of prospective patients who had been, apparently, kept waiting this last hour. At one point, she ignored all of the above to call after a suited, agitated looking man (obviously an administrator of some kind) hurrying past:

"Mr Muir! Mr Muir! Have you managed to lay on some help for me here yet?"

The man turned slightly, as if to answer, but then simply shook his head and hurried on.

"Bastard," mouthed the receptionist, and returned to her 'client-juggling' act.

"Hello, I –" said Helena, once the man in front of her had wandered off, still unsatisfied.

"One moment, *please,*" the receptionist huffed back at her. She began fumbling through a stack of files in front of her, and it quickly became apparent that she wasn't actually doing anything, merely attempting to give the *illusion* of activity, probably just to give herself a few moments breathing space. Much as Helena sympathised with her predicament, she had other priorities.

After a suitably polite interlude of a minute or so, she tried again. "Look, I wonder if I could just ask –"

"I'm busy, can't you see that? If you'd just –"

"I really don't have time to wait, so if you could just tell me where Mr Philip Burgess is at the moment, we won't be bothering you any more."

The look on the receptionist's face took Helena aback for a moment, but then she noticed that the rest of the reception area had fallen silent too. She turned, and saw every face in sight gaping in her direction. Miles Hearne was also, it seemed, rather surprised, but in his case this was mingled with amusement. Still perplexed, she turned back to the receptionist.

"Are ... are you a, um ..."

"Relative?" She could have told the truth, but instead simply said what she thought the woman would want to hear, the words that would assist her in getting them away from her. "Yes, that's right."

A hurried consultation of her notes. "He's through

there. Cubicle 5."

Miles was at her side as they passed through the double doors into the corridor that the receptionist had indicated. "Amazing. Bloody amazing."

"What did I do?"

"Didn't you hear it? Fuck, no, maybe you wouldn't. That voice that came out of your mouth ... if you'd told the entire room to drop their pants and fart the Hallelujah chorus, they'd have only stopped to ask you what key it should be in."

"But, Miles ... I didn't *do* anything."

"Maybe not. But you did it anyway. Ah, here we are."

They pulled the curtain aside and peeked through, cautiously. The figure on the bed looked shrunken, still, and clad in the regulation hospital gown, even more frail, if such a thing were possible. But it was unmistakeably Burgess, and as they pulled the curtain behind them, his eyes opened, and his head raised slightly. His face was bruised, and seemed a little swollen.

"Ah. You're here. Splendid. I was wondering whether they'd have time to ring you and pass my message on. They're a bit snowed under, poor things."

"Philip ... easy." He was trying to sit upright, and the effort was too obviously causing him discomfort. Helena sat on the bed beside him, trying initially to prevent him from moving too much, then, realising that such a thing was unfeasible, settled for trying to make his movements as comfortable as possible by adjusting his pillow. As she did so, she also saw that there were bruises on his body, around the neck, chest and back. Furthermore, she saw, almost lost in the angry swelling around his right eye, a wound, dressed with a small transparent sticking plaster.

"What the hell happened to you?" she gasped, but the answer came almost simultaneously. "Robert Pierce. He paid you a call, didn't he?"

"Is that what his real name is?" said Philip. "He calls himself Nicholas when he calls on me."

"You've seen him before then?" Hearne asked.

"Not before yesterday. He introduced himself at the funeral. At first, I thought he was allied with you in some way, but I know now that you would never, never ..."

He gripped her hand, tightly. "Helena, that man ... he took the paintings."

"I guessed. I'm sorry, Philip, I know I should perhaps have warned you about him ..."

"Would it have made any difference? Between that man, whoever he is, and myself, there was little room for compromise. Something had to give, and that something was me. If you'd been there, you'd have just been injured, too, and for you he wouldn't have held back."

Hearne leant in closer. "You mean because of what you were to Molesey?"

"Yes, and more," said Philip.

"Tell us what happened," said Helena. "Don't leave anything out. It might be important."

He sighed deeply, closed his eyes, and told them. First he told them about the meeting in the cemetery, and the subsequent, abortive attempt to destroy the picture; and he told them how he afterwards managed to drag himself downstairs, away from the baleful, mocking glare of that great, red, spiral eye.

"I considered ringing you then, Helena, but I was still unsure as to whether this was some sort of game in which you were involved. In my terror, I began to suspect that everyone was involved with this 'Nicholas'person; the two of you, Jenny Tyler, Brenda and her family. I even had a horrible vision of the child being 'sacrificed' as part of some plan to ensnare me.

"Fortunately, this paranoia didn't last. You may not agree with me on this one, Helena, but sometimes reason can be the most potent magic of all, and it's something that I've always been rather good at. It took me a few hours of silence, of meditation, but I managed to extinguish all the 'demons' that had been gnawing at me. I felt quite elated, to tell you the truth; whatever hold that man had put upon me – some form of hypnosis, no doubt, though of a subtle and elegant kind – I was confident that I had broken it. I even began making plans for another try at cutting the heart out of that monstrous painting, when I was rested.

"I must have fallen asleep late in the evening, slumped

in my chair beside the fire as I sometimes do, but the instant I woke up I knew something was wrong. There was a coldness to the air I realised was the result of either a downstairs window or door being open to the elements, and I'm most careful about ensuring such things are firmly closed.

"I listened for a few moments, but could hear nothing. So I got up and crossed the living room to the window, pulled aside the curtain, and saw a face. It was briefly illuminated for a moment by the light from the living room, but then it was gone. There was the sound of a shout from outside, and from the dining room, on the other side of the hall, a response.

"Startled as I was, I instinctively darted for the nearest available object which could be used as a weapon, and came up with a heavy ornamental poker from beside the gas fire. Even as I lifted it, the first of them appeared in the doorway, a young man wearing a hooded sweatshirt, the hood up, and a baseball cap pulled low across his forehead. I had no time to warn him off, he simply rushed at me.

"Young and strong as he was, I managed to duck under his rather ill-conceived attempt at laying hands on me, and dealt him quite a hefty blow in the side with the poker. Went down like a sack of potatoes, wheezing and whining for assistance.

"It was with him so quickly I barely had time to register it was even in the room. This one had learned from his comrade's error; he grabbed the arm in which I held the poker and tried to pull it from my fingers. I wasn't going to give up that easily, however, so I let go of the poker with my left hand and struck him with as much power as I could. It wasn't much – I can barely make a fist, let alone punch someone with it – but it took him by surprise and while he was struggling to work out what was going on, I tucked my leg behind his and let his own backward momentum send him sprawling."

As Philip described the combat, Helena noticed a little of the life come back to his face; obviously having something tangible to fight against at last was rather a relief after all this abstraction and hocus-pocus. For the first time, as he continued to recollect the fight, she could see the war hero side of him in action.

"Unfortunately, he decided not to relinquish his grip on

me as he fell, so I went tumbling along with him. I think that's when I got this cut on my eye; hit it against the fireplace. I managed to hang on to the poker, however, and to his arm. I wasn't letting go of either of them, I knew all too well what would happen if I did.

"Then I felt someone else join in. I think it was the chap who I'd laid out a few moments before. He was punching and kicking at me, punctuating each blow with a rather uncreative use of the English language, as if this was all now, for him, most definitely a personal matter. I don't know how long I lay there; keeping track of time is quite rightly, in these circumstances, not a priority. But I could feel consciousness slipping away from me a little more with each blow that landed, and I was desperately trying to hang on to awareness for as long as I could. You see, if I blacked out, I didn't think that I would ever wake up again.

"All of a sudden, I felt another presence in the room, one that I recognised. The attack ceased, abruptly. I think words were spoken by the newcomer, angry words, but I'm not sure I can remember what was said. My next recollection is of the same hands that had been hitting at me only moments before lifting me up and placing me gently back in my chair. That, of course, is when the pain truly began.

"A face appeared not a matter of inches away from my own. It was 'Nicholas' or whatever his name truly is.

" 'I'm sorry,' he said. 'This could all have been avoided if you'd listened to my advice, Philip. They won't hurt you again, though; I won't let them.'

"Behind him, through the living room door, I could see some of his comrades, followers, call them what you will, taking the paintings out of the house. The one carrying what I think was the red spiral picture – they'd covered them in sheets – stopped briefly at the door, and I felt as if the damn thing was mocking me again.

" 'It's all over now' he said to me. His voice, strangely enough, didn't sound unkind. 'We won't bother you anymore.' He touched my cheek briefly, and for a moment – silly as this may sound – I had the distinct impression that this was, actually, 'my' Nicholas in front of me. Something about the voice, I think. Or the touch. Or ... I don't know.

"He and his friends left then, but not before I heard him, in the hall, making a call to the emergency services. He told them I'd had an accident, fallen down the stairs, or somesuch. When the ambulance arrived, I don't know why, but ... I told them exactly the same thing. Why did I do that, do you think?"

Helena shook her head. "Perhaps ... perhaps he *is* Nicholas Molesey. There certainly doesn't seem to be much left of the Robert Pierce that we knew."

Philip sighed deeply. "Yesterday, I would have argued with you about that, but now ... now, I don't know what to think. You may be right."

"Whoever he is," said Hearne, impatiently, "it's largely irrelevant. He has the paintings, and without them, we have no chance of discharging the Scorpion entity."

"The what?" said Philip. Then he seemed to realise what was being discussed. "Oh. That. Yes."

"We have to stop him, before it's too late," said Hearne.

"We may already *be* too late," Helena replied, pushing strands of limp, unwashed hair back from her face. "He's had the paintings for a few hours now as it is."

"No ... no, we have some time yet. Another day, I think."

They looked at one another, brows furrowed in perplexity, then at Philip.

"What's the date today?" he asked.

Hearne pressed a button on his digital watch. "Er ... the fifth. November the fifth."

Burgess nodded. "Then it will take place tomorrow."

"Why tomorrow?" asked Hearne. "Why not today?"

"I thought you had done your research, Mr Hearne. It was on November the 6th 1929 that Nicholas Molesey died."

Hearne looked blank for a moment, then closed his eyes and slapped his forehead.

"Of course! How could I have forgotten? He chose this day very carefully, didn't he? And if Pierce is to carry on from where Molesey left off, he has to start the Working again from *exactly* the same time as Molesey. Thank you, Philip."

"You can thank me, Miles, by assisting me in getting out of this bed and this hospital. You too, Helena."

"Philip," began Helena, "do you really think ..."

"No, it's probably not wise, but nevertheless I have to do it. So you can either help me, or I can do it all by myself. And there's every chance that, *if* I do it all by myself, being so old and frail and decrepit, I may do myself some serious harm. You wouldn't want that, now, would you?"

"Decrepit, my arse," said Hearne with a chuckle. "There's more iron in your soul than in an entire Panzer division."

"Oh, well." Helena picked up the bag containing Philip's clothes at the side of the bed, and passed it to him. "I suppose I'd better wait outside. Miles will help you get dressed, won't you, Miles?"

She exited before Hearne could register his protest.

Since it would obviously take some time before Philip was dressed and ready to go, she decided that she needed some fresh air. She strolled back through reception – getting a most peculiar look from the receptionist - and stood just outside the main doors of the A&E department. In the company of about half-a-dozen other people (most of whom were puffing away furiously on cigarettes) she watched the ambulances rolling in, steadily, one by one, and discharging their passengers. Most of these people were nursing obvious marks of violence, bloodied noses and so on, and these were just the *walking* wounded.

Even her unpractised eye could tell that those who came off the ambulance on a gurney were in a far more serious state. None of them seemed conscious. One of the unconscious ones was a child, a boy of about ten or eleven. His head was bandaged, held firmly in place, and he had a tube in his throat. His face was a mask of blood.

Please, somebody (thought Helena), tell me he did that while skateboarding, or something.

The doors behind her opened, and a young white man – limping quite visibly – hurried past her. She'd seen this one in reception earlier, trying to avoid the gaze of a group of Asian youths who were sitting opposite him. She'd thought then that there was most definitely some sort of issue between this one and the Asian boys, who, aside from having no visible reason for being in the casualty department themselves, were palpably in the mood for blood. One of them had been going periodically up to reception, apparently to ask if there was any news of a friend undergoing treatment.

As if to confirm her suspicions, the Asian boys passed by Helena a few moments later, in pursuit of the white boy. They followed him quietly out of the gates of the hospital, their eyes never wavering from him. She was rather glad at first that she wouldn't see how this particular story ended, then realised that, standing where she was, she would in all likelihood be seeing that young man returning to the hospital. Returning in a considerably worse state than on his previous visit.

Answer; don't stand here any more.

She was about to turn around and walk back into the building when the sight of a woman crossing the hospital car park caught her attention. It took a few moments for her to work out just why the woman was so familiar to her.

Helena had last seen her entering the house in Bethlehem Street. There, the woman had stood out from the rest because she kept her head down, in contrast to the others who seemed to be oblivious to the attentions of the world. It marked her as someone who was out of step with the others.

Now, although she was alone, she still kept her head angled toward the ground slightly, the fluorescent pink strands in her dark hair tumbling across her face. Her hands were deep in the pockets of the old raincoat she wore, and she appeared to be walking in the general direction of the intensive care units where Debbie worked.

That settled it. An idea, up till now only nascent and embryonic in Helena's mind, now took on very definite form and potential. She set off across the car park in pursuit of the woman.

Taking care not to get too close, she trailed the woman through what seemed like miles of cold, lime-green corridors; she was following the signs to what Helena knew was one of the male wards. When she eventually turned into the ward she knew to be the one on which Debbie worked, Helena stopped, to consider her options.

Do I dare confront her? There's no guarantee that she's as 'out of step' as I think she is, that could just be wishful thinking on my part. All this could do is further alert Nicholas (can't think of him as Robert Pierce any more) to how close we are to him, prompt him to put up more defences.

But at this stage, do I have any other choice? We have (if Philip's right) just about thirty-six hours in which to find a way into that house and do whatever it is we have to do. No, I have to do this, and do it quickly.

Unchallenged, she prowled the ward, peering into each room leading off from the main section of the ward, but seeing no sign of the woman. The door of the last room on the left, at the end of the corridor, was half-closed, and she had to put her head virtually all the way around before she could ascertain that the figure standing beside the bed – looking down at a man who lay staring, barely blinking, at the ceiling above – was the person she sought.

"Helena?"

She couldn't have said her name any louder if she'd used a megaphone. Helena spun around to see Debbie standing at the other end of the corridor, looking at her disapprovingly.

"What the hell are you doing here?"

Helena set off towards her at a trot, intending to quiet her down by whatever means necessary, but had covered only about two-thirds of the distance when the sound of a door squeaking behind her made her turn. The woman stood in the doorway of the room, recognition dawning on her face.

Before Helena could say anything, she bolted in the opposite direction, away towards the other end of the ward.

"Helena, what –"

Without pausing to answer Debbie, Helena set off in pursuit again, this time at a run. She hit the swinging double doors at the end of the corridor only seconds after the woman, yelling for her to wait. There was a further set of doors about twenty yards ahead, but at that precise moment a tall trolley loaded high with dishes and the remnants of patients' breakfasts was negotiating its way through them. Helena's 'target' turned and darted down the corridor leading off at ninety degrees to that one; only by a sudden burst of speed did Helena manage to duck into that same corridor between the trolley and the wall, still yelling, if by now a little hoarsely from lack of breath.

It was a dead end. The room at the end of the corridor was locked, and the woman, after a pause to consider her rapidly diminishing options, turned and ducked into the first open door she could find. Helena followed her, into an empty office, currently dormant due to some renovation work in progress; roof panels were missing, and an open toolbox lay in the middle of the floor. When she entered, the woman was trying to open the door to the adjoining room, which was also locked. She screamed "Fuck!" at the door, a vulgar 'Open Sesame', but this also failed.

"Please," said Helena, "I only want to ..."

The woman swung around, and Helena had a brief glimpse of the naked panic in her eyes before, with a speed that surprised her pursuer, the woman lunged for the open toolbox and snatched up a screwdriver. She held it, trembling slightly, on a level with Helena's face.

"Leave me alone! Just fuck off and leave me alone!" There was a hint of Irish to the accent.

"I only want to talk to you."

"I've got nothing to say."

"How do you know until you try?"

This threw her. Her eyes, which had been agitatedly assessing the chances of getting past Helena to the door, fixed on Helena's own. When she next spoke, her tone was more conciliatory, more pleading.

"All I want to do," she said, "is see Ryan. Why can't you just let us be?"

"No-one's stopping you, er ... what's your name?"

A pause, then quietly; "Sue."

Helena smiled. "Sue. Hi. I'm Helena."

"I know who you are. That's why I want you to leave us alone."

"I didn't want to get between you and Ryan. In fact," and here she thought that a judicious untruth was called for, "I wanted to see him myself."

"Why?"

"I wanted to see how he is. I wanted ... to see what Nicholas did to him."

In the silence which followed, as Sue thought about Helena's response, Helena could hear noises at the far end of the corridor outside, and realised that their little game of 'tag' would shortly be bringing them some unrequired attention from the hospital security. She thought she heard Debbie calling her name also, panic just under the surface of her voice.

"I think we should go back to Ryan. They're looking for us."

After a few moments, Sue lowered the screwdriver, and tossed it back into the toolbox.

"Come on then." It was a challenge, as much as an invitation.

They walked out of the office side by side, staring straight ahead, just as Debbie emerged from one of the other rooms in the corridor. She seemed on the brink of some comment, but one look at Helena's face – and at Sue's – restrained her. Instead, she dropped into step beside them, appearing with them in the ward much to the consternation of the sister, and the security guard with whom she was having an intense conversation. Helena caught a glimpse of their reflection in a window as they passed; for a moment, they looked like some bizarre trio of feminist gunfighters on their way to a showdown. Which, in a sense, was not far away from the truth.

"What the hell is going on?" the sister demanded. "Debbie, do you know this person?"

"I can explain," said Helena pre-empting Debbie, who could only dig herself deeper with a reply. Her own attempts at clarification were themselves cut short, however.

"No, it's all right," said Sue. "She's with me. I'm sorry, this is ... all my fault."

Interspersing her words with more contrite apologies, she explained to the glowering 'authorities' – and to an *ad hoc* audience of patients, who had gathered around them despite the best efforts of staff to move them on – that Helena was an old friend, but there had been a misunderstanding between them some years before, and she (Sue) had panicked. It was all sorted out now, though; more apologies at the end.

The sister glared at them some more, gave them a stern talking-to on the subject of the dire consequences of disrupting 'her' ward in the future, and stomped off. Sue turned and walked into Ryan's room. Helena made to follow her, but was stopped by Debbie's hand.

"Can *I* at least have some sort of *believable* explanation?"

"No time. Have to talk later." She smiled placatingly at her. "Didn't mean to get you in trouble, though."

"You never do," Debbie mumbled and stalked off.

In the room, Sue was sitting by the side of the bed, looking down once more at the recumbent, staring form of her boyfriend.

"I don't know what to do now. Ever since Nicholas did this to him, I've hated him so much, but ... I've been so afraid of him too. It's like he's holding Ryan's soul hostage, and if I do anything out of turn, all he has to do is just close his fist, and ..."

She looked up, tears in her eyes.

"He's killed people, you know."

"I know." Including Robert Pierce?

"He's bound to find out I've been speaking to you. He's got eyes everywhere, has Nicholas. And when he does ..." She held up her hand, closed her fist. "But I keep asking myself, is death any worse than this? Maybe Ryan should die. Maybe I should too."

"No, don't say that." She sat down opposite her. "There's a way out of all this."

"I knew you'd say that," said Sue. "That's why I did what I did out there. I figured, I've got nothing left to lose. Someone's got to stop him."

"I'll need your help," said Helena.

"I figured that too. I can't promise I won't get scared again, though, like I did out there."

"That's OK. I'm pretty scared too." Understatement of the Millennium.

Sue looked at Ryan's gaunt, immobile face for a while, pondering. Then she simply leant over, kissed him on the forehead (lingering a little; this could be the last time, after all) and stood.

"Right," she said. "I suppose you want my help to get you into that house, first of all."

On the evening of November 5th, two Asian youths, walking down a street in a predominantly white district of town, found themselves being 'shadowed' by a group of young white men of roughly similar age. The white boys began shouting abuse, mainly of a racial nature, at the Asians, who declined to respond, choosing instead to make a run for it as the crowd behind them began to swell.

In the torrential rain, they took a wrong turning and were stranded in a cul-de-sac on the edges of a large, and notorious, housing estate. The Asian boys tried to make their escape through the garden of one of the houses, but were caught, dragged back into the street and beaten to the verge of unconsciousness with fists, bricks, anything that came to hand. Fireworks – bought earlier that day, ironically, at a shop owned by the uncle of one of the boys under attack – were stuffed into their pockets (according to one witness, they were also inserted into the mouths and anuses of the boys), petrol was poured over them, a match was struck.

The resultant 'bonfire' was visible for some distance around. Muffled explosions were audible amidst the whoops and shrieks of the participants. By the time the emergency services were called (and arrived, under a hail of bricks and bottles), the boys' incinerated remains had been doused by the rain. It appeared also, as was confirmed by post-mortem, that parts of the bodies had been removed, possibly as 'trophies'.

For those who were first on the scene, however, two abiding images remained: the residents of the Close, who stood on their doorsteps, or in their windows, watching the proceedings with a kind of detached, transfixed fascination, and the small girl who, dressed in a red plastic anorak, sat in the street and, with her finger, stirred the blood in the puddles into a constantly rotating spiral.

"Look what I can do," she said.

Scorpion

The constant howl of sirens was difficult to ignore, for the four people who gathered for an impromptu 'council of war' in Miles Hearne's living room that evening; but although it added a kind of urgent soundtrack to their discussions, none of them commented on it.

"Why can't we just go around there now, and get them back?" asked Helena. She was getting somewhat fidgety at their lack of action; there was something within that was aching to be brought out into the open.

"I don't think it will be that easy," said Philip, fatigue dragging at every syllable. "Nicholas appears to have a fairly good idea of what we're doing by now. He'll have taken precautions to ensure that the paintings are safe, until he needs them."

Sue nodded. "Right. I think I heard him say that he's going to stow the paintings somewhere else for now, bring them round to the house late tomorrow afternoon. I've got no idea where, though."

"OK," said Hearne, "so it doesn't look as if we'll get the chance to do anything until the shit's on the verge of hitting the fan. Any suggestions as to what we can do until then?"

An awkward silence. They looked at each other for any glimmer of inspiration, but found little to put into words.

Helena ran her hands through her hair in exasperation. "There must be *something* we can do ..."

Philip made his suggestion: "Keep our heads down. And stay away from that house until it's absolutely necessary for us to be there."

"That may be an option for some of you," said Sue, "but not for me."

"You're not telling me that you're actually going back there tonight?" Helena was aghast at the very suggestion. "You'll just be putting yourself at risk again –"

"Every second I'm here is even more risky for me. Nicholas – and the rest – will be wanting to know where I've been. For all I know, he might already have some idea that I'm with you, but it's pretty unlikely. I'm hoping he'll be too wrapped up in what he's doing to question me too hard, but it's best not to push it."

"She's right," said Hearne. "And besides, we need her on the inside to get us access for tomorrow."

Sue barely said goodbye to the others as she left the room; perhaps, Helena thought, she might see it as too final. She insisted on walking her to the door, however.

"I don't need to tell you to take care," she said.

Sue smiled. "Not really. But ..."

She left the sentence dangling until Helena prompted her to finish it.

"It's just that, now that I know I'm not alone, I don't feel so bad. Someone's watching over me."

"Us?" The idea of the three of them as her guardians – as *anyone's* guardians – seemed preposterous to Helena.

"Yeah. Me and Ryan, we used to look out for each other. It used to get us into shit with the others in the house. We were such a tight little unit all on our own. With him in that hospital, I've felt all alone. Vulnerable. Nicholas and the others, I think they've been capitalising on that. But now I feel stronger again."

She put her hand on Helena's shoulder. "And it's you in particular makes me feel strong. You're at the heart of all of this, Helena. It doesn't take Einstein to work it out." Unexpectedly, she threw her arms around Helena and hugged her tight. "I promise I won't let you down," she said. Then she turned, and hurried out into the night before Helena could say anything else.

The evening settled down. Philip stayed at Miles' house overnight, phoning to reassure Brenda that he was all right. Helena went home once she was happy that Philip was looked after.

And Miles retired to his study, and made notes. And Banished. And collected his magical implements, long unused. And Banished. And, with desperation in his voice, called upon the Goddess Isis to bless their undertaking.

The following day Helena turned up on his doorstep again, and she began to learn what it means to be a Goddess.

Meanwhile, Sue, in the house on Bethlehem Street, was trying to avoid the attention of Nicholas. However, he seemed to want to check in with everyone today.

As if he knew.

He seemed calmer today, yet he made a point of speaking to each member of the group in turn, a smile here, a touch there, his penetrating gaze searching out the inner thoughts of each. And one by one the group would be called upstairs to see him alone.

Sue was dreading her turn. She watched, as first Mark, the favoured one, then Emma, floated downstairs from their meeting with beatific smiles, politely refusing to divulge what had transpired and saying simply, "Wait and see." Oh, she was waiting all right. Paralysed with the fear that Nicholas could divine her role in tonight's ritual, and had prepared something awful for her, just as he had for Ryan –

Stop that. She put on her coat, to leave the Wicker Man festival atmosphere for a few hours, and stepping out of her room, walked straight into Nicholas, who was leaning against the wall, head cocked to one side. "Leaving us?"

"I'm off to visit Ryan."

"He's not going anywhere, Sue." Nicholas laid his hand on her arm. Sue resisted the urge to shake him off. "Tomorrow we'll all visit him together. He'll like that. And things will be very different. Especially for you."

"Uh – right." Get out get out get out.

"When you come back, I'll see you upstairs. Wouldn't want you to be left out, would we?" The eyes, searching, searching. Go blank.

"Tell you what, Nicholas, let's do it now, shall we? Then it's done."

"All right Sue," and he led her upstairs. "And then it's done."

She passed several of the others on the way, and they smiled and whispered to each other. Sue tried to show nothing of her mounting apprehension, but images of Ryan kept intruding. Go blank. Go blank.

The attic room was even more bare than usual. Nicholas' mattress had been pushed to the far end, and the centre was dominated by the trunk, on top of which was a solitary candle. Nicholas indicated that Sue sit on the floor facing him across the trunk. While watery sunshine from the skylight interfered with her vision, the candle lit Nicholas' face from below as he knelt facing her, the flickering flame throwing shadows across his face.

"Place your hands on the trunk," he said, and Sue obediently laid them flat either side of the candle. He reached over and covered them with his own hands, and she flinched.

"Look at the flame," he intoned, "and gaze at the elemental life within. See the spirit of the flame leaping, writhing, stretching and falling back, and feel its presence." Sue, fighting to remain still and not run screaming down the stairs to sanity, now tries to give the impression of complying. His words pour over her, insinuating from her imagination the fleeting glimpse of the spirit trapped in the candle flame, the ephemeral presence dancing in the semi-darkness, vibrant with pulsing vitality as she begins to notice her own feelings gradually matching its movements, as the figure in the flame becomes larger and larger, always elusive, flickering in and out of awareness, as the words of Nicholas continue to call it forth, as the dance of the flame becomes the dance of her own thoughts, burning torchlike, heating her skin and bringing beads of perspiration to her forehead, and when Nicholas' hands finally withdraw from her own she feels herself flaming within, with a bright clear purpose.

To master the Scorpion.

Mark let himself in, carrying one of the paintings. Jeff and the others followed, unloading the wrapped paintings from the van which Jeff had stolen some nights before. Nicholas had been most insistent that he alone handled the paintings until he had covered them over, and neither Mark nor Jeff had succumbed to curiosity. Thoughts of Ryan discouraged them. Through the living room doorway he glimpsed Sue sitting in a sofa, glazed over and still. It would wear off shortly, as he could testify. He hoisted the painting to the attic room, and Jeff and his two mates followed.

The others in the house moved with quiet purposefulness, preparing for the ritual to come. Nicholas had retired upstairs, getting himself ready, and Mark and the others waited at the attic room door until Nicholas opened it for them, silently gesturing them inside.

There was one painting still in the van. Mark went down for it, and sliding it out of the van pulled away some of the wrapping. Beneath it was a patch of ugly reddish-brown oil paint, like a bloodstain on a sheet. Mark stared at it for a moment, then felt himself being pushed aside. It was Nicholas, taking the painting from him and hurriedly covering it over again. "Don't," he said. "Not a good idea at the moment." And he took it upstairs.

Mark closed up the van, taking a look up and down Bethlehem Street. The air was oppressive and still, thunderstorm weather. But that didn't fully account for the unease he felt as he surveyed the all but empty street. Where was everyone? Were they all watching this place, waiting, as he was, for the climax of events tonight? Was the world full of innocent bystanders?

Innocent? Mark shook his head and went indoors, his mind full of pictures of bloodstained sheets.

Philip refused to let Miles talk him into going back to hospital. He was wise enough in his years to know that whatever was happening, he should be present to the end.

This time.

He would be there at the finish of what began in 1929. And there was no time to delay. The hour was approaching, his body was failing – his head throbbed continually and he had even more difficulty getting about than usual – and he had a growing sense that time was running out.

For them all.

He had rested throughout the day, seeing Miles coaching Helena in her part this evening. Much of it made no sense to Philip, but it revived memories of some of the things that Nicholas – *his* Nicholas – used to come out with. And in the course of the day a certain quiet had descended upon Helena. There was a gravity about her, something which Philip couldn't rightly describe but the frail young woman seemed more ... imposing.

Miles, on the other hand, seemed more intense, barely able to contain himself in the run-up to the evening's events. He reminded Philip most of the ward sister who had attended him the night before, directing, moving things about, issuing reminders, with the businesslike crispness of those who are truly under pressure. And the supply of profanity from Miles' lips had, for the moment, run dry.

At last the time came. Miles packed his paraphernalia into the car and went to help Philip. The old man gratefully took the proffered arm, and had just got to his feet when Helena entered.

"Is your Tarot deck handy?" she asked Miles. Still, holding up Philip, he gestured towards a bureau drawer and Helena fetched out a deck of cards wrapped in black silk. She closed her eyes briefly, then cut the pack. "This one's for us," she said, and looked at the exposed card. Her lips pursed, and she showed it to Miles, who grunted.

"Seven of Wands," she said, putting the pack back together. "Valour. When all else has failed, and all resources are exhausted, the only hope of success is the few who nobody could expect to fight on."

"Less than inspiring," added Miles grimly.

Helena cut the pack again. "And our one hope is ..." She didn't look at the card, but showed it to the two men.

Miles nodded slowly. "The High Priestess."

Philip looked on curiously as Helena slipped the card into her coat.

"Let's go," she said.

The group was gathered in the attic room. The dull orange glow of streetlights reflected off low clouds down through the skylight. Ten wide candles lit the frankincense-smoked temple from inside, arranged in a circle around the group who themselves encircled Nicholas and the trunk. Each of them supported a painting, facing inward. Five of them were the paintings they'd taken from the old man's house, the other five had been prepared by Nicholas in private, and Sue couldn't tell which was which.

Sue and all the others had been unsure what to make of

the paintings. They were little more than canvasses of colour, striking colours it had to be said, but they seemed to convey a mood rather than an idea. Mark, right opposite Sue, was supporting an ugly reddish-brown swirling piece that gave her the horrors. Next but one to him, Heather was holding an equivalent painting, but in greens, all rendered dark by the faint orange light from above. She looked frightened. Sue herself was holding the painting with the most colours, a patchwork affair of green, black, reddish and orange. Nicholas had told her that its name was Sandalphon and that from it they would "pour out the mystery on the world."

Sue wasn't sure about that last part. Now that the initial daze of her ritual with Nicholas had worn off, she found herself questioning her part in all this. Somehow she had to get away and let Helena and the others into the house, but she didn't see how that would be possible.

And, strangely, she almost wanted this ritual to succeed. It would be done, finished, and maybe Ryan would be all right after all.

Maybe.

They now all join in on the Protection, even Sue wholeheartedly pitching in for that. Then Nicholas burns some more frankincense, sending grey smoke billowing to the ceiling. It is quite warm in the temple now, heavy and close, Nicholas walking a circle, sweeping past each of them in turn, holding in one hand a short wooden wand, painted red. As he does so, he says, "First, we unlock the portals of the Sephiroth, so that when the time comes, the Archangels will come to us. And then we shall deliver the world."

He walks the circle again, this time stopping at each one and pointing the wand at them, beginning with the brilliant white painting held steady by Robin.

"Metatron, Archangel of the Presence. We call upon you to draw to us all the powers to take part in this, the opening and closing of the doors of Death." And they all repeat, as he traces over the black glyph at the head of the painting. And as they all gaze at the painting, the brilliance of it seems to spread, to move, to open itself to more brilliance still. It is as though a spotlight shines through the fabric of the painting, and its image stays on Sue's vision until Nicholas traces the glyph once more, and the brilliance seems to fade. Sue, looking furtively around, sees what appears to be a reflection of that brilliance lighting up the faces of the others, and she feels separate from them, wrapped in darkness in comparison.

And so forth, from one to the other, with mounting ecstasy, until Nicholas stands at last in front of Sue, points the wand at the painting she holds, and announces, "Sandalphon, Anointed One, we call upon you to draw to us the forces of this world, to raise them to us so that we may pour out the mystery upon all the world."

Sue feels an electric connection to the painting in her hands, and although she cannot see it, she glances at the faces of the others and sees what she can only describe as enormity. The faces looking her way seem to behold some great and terrible reality, and Nicholas himself is enraptured, eyes closed, swaying slightly, and she finds herself swaying ever so slightly in time to him. The atmosphere becomes more and more oppressive as the others repeat after Nicholas the words of evocation, and Sue finds panic clawing its way up her chest at the thought of what they might be letting loose on the world. She trembles violently, trying at first to control herself but finally dropping the painting and lunging for the door.

As she escapes, she hears Nicholas intoning, "And when you return, it will be done."

Philip sat in the back of the car, intently watching the back of Helena's head. Quite what he hoped to see, he didn't know, but he watched anyway. She had been silent so far as they drove through the town towards Bethlehem Street, staring ahead of them as though hypnotised by the lights of the cars in front. So quiet, so seemingly passive.

And yet, he knew that she was anything but. She was radiating an energy that filled the interior of the car, made the enclosed space seem oppressive and full of peril. But the real danger was not for himself and Miles; the focus of her attention was still some way distant. He felt as if he were riding in a tank, sitting close to the source of something with a terrible potential for destruction, but secretly glad that he was not on the other end of the gun.

Up ahead, beyond the pointless thrashing of the windscreen wipers, he could make out flashing lights, fluorescent jackets, urgent movement. Miles slowed the car.

"What's going on?"

"The road's blocked off. Police." Miles thumped the steering wheel. "Damn."

One of the yellow-jacketed figures hurried towards them, halting at each stationary vehicle to offer a few hasty words to the stranded drivers. Miles lowered the window as the officer splashed to his side and leaned in, water cascading from the top of his cap as he did so.

"Afraid this road's closed for the time being, sir."

"So I see," said Miles huffily, "but why?"

"There's a disturbance going on just ahead. It's being dealt with."

"Disturbance?" said Philip. "You mean riot, don't you?"

The young officer glared into the back seat. "I mean *disturbance,* sir."

"How long before –" began Miles.

"No idea, sir, but we'll try and ensure that you're moving again soon."

"So what do we do till then?"

"I suggest you sit tight, sir," said the policeman, then added, glumly, "And thank your lucky stars that you're in a nice, warm car."

Miles rolled the window up and turned to Helena. "We could have done with the Isis voice about then."

"No point," she replied. "Unless you seriously think that I can levitate the car over the hold-up."

She rubbed condensation away from the inside of the passenger side window, and peered out. After a few moments, she tapped at the glass with her index finger.

"Pull in over there."

Miles leaned over to see where she was pointing. "That's someone's drive. It's private property –"

"Just do it."

With some difficulty (and some muttering), Miles

managed to extricate the car from the queue and pull it into the indicated driveway. He brought it to rest behind a maroon Jaguar.

"Now what do we do?"

"We walk. What else?" She turned to Philip. "Will you be all right?"

"A little rain is the least of my problems. We walk."

The rain was heavier than Philip had expected. It descended on to his bare scalp with the impact of tiny hailstones. He pulled his raincoat over his head, and with Miles' help, followed after Helena, who was striding away from them, bareheaded, her hair twisting in the wind like serpents trying to escape.

Someone shouted after them. Judging from the tone, it was the owner of the driveway which they had just commandeered. They ignored it.

They caught up with Helena just in time to see her path intersect that of a rain-drenched policeman, older and considerably larger than the young constable to whom they had just spoken. He loomed over Helena, and when he spoke, it was in a tone which in ordinary circumstances would have sent even the most foolhardy challengers on their way. Exactly what the man said, Philip couldn't afterwards remember. Neither could he recall Helena's reply.

The important thing is that five seconds later that same officer was standing looking at them with a foolish, vacant and extremely scared look on his face as they strolled past him in the direction in which he was, presumably, intending to prevent them going.

And this, thought Philip as he and Hearne trudged in Helena's wake, was the same girl who had seemed, to him, so fragile and vulnerable on their first encounter. There was a momentary surge of fear in him for her; he wondered if she had fallen prey to a similar force which had consumed her friend Pierce and transformed him into the creature who now called himself Nicholas Molesey.

Up ahead, they could see the first signs of 'disturbance'; a car on its side, burned out, the last embers of flame being doused by the rain. It blocked traffic access to a main shopping area of the district, and even before they turned into the road, Philip had guessed what they would see. An orchestra of alarm bells pealed for assistance, and went unheeded. Helena drew to a sudden halt to survey the carnage, Philip and Hearne close in behind her.

The focus of trouble had, fortunately, moved to the other end of the thoroughfare, and they could see the crowd in the street lost in some form of collective ecstasy as the windows of shops were caved in and the contents hauled out into the air. Electrical equipment – TVs & sound systems, computers, even microwave ovens – was of course the most highly visible booty, and they could see these items being carried in triumph away from the scene, but they had a shrewd idea that a fair amount of 'liberated' alcohol was by now fuelling the flames, both actually and metaphorically. People rushed past Philip and his companions, clutching tightly to their chests whatever material goods they had been able to snatch out of the chaos, while the crowd enthusiastically fought over what was left.

"Do we have to go through that?" asked Philip.

Helena nodded.

"Why?"

Hearne answered for her. "This is the most direct route to Bethlehem Street. We don't have time to waste. Besides, the side roads are likely to be just as dangerous, if not more so – less option for escape."

Without waiting for further discussion, Helena strode on. They faced no challenge from the individuals who fled past them; these were the jackals who lurked on the fringes of the battle, picking off what gain they could before they made their escape. No, thought Philip, the real danger will come when they approach the centre of the riot, when they find themselves face to face with those who instigated all of this.

As if in response to Philip's fears, there was a flash of light, and an exultant roar. Someone had pitched a Molotov into the window of one of the decimated shopfronts, an off-licence, now apparently emptied of anything useful. In quick succession, there was a chorus of screams, and the eruption through the flames of a trio of figures, themselves engulfed and burning. Perhaps they were looters who had not got out in time. Perhaps they were staff.

Either way, they fell, writhing and shrieking to the pavement, desperately trying to extinguish the flames, as the onlookers began to howl with laughter at their predicament, making no attempt to assist. The hilarity ended only when the three figures ceased all movement.

When Helena moved towards the conflagration, Philip resisted Hearne as he tried to follow. It was not conscious cowardice; simply that the horror of what he had just seen had frozen him to the spot. Almost instantly, she seemed to sense what was happening, stopped, and turned towards him.

Her hair, her face, her eyes, haloed in fire, she appeared to be some vengeful angel, ready to cast them all into Hell. He feared for a moment that she was about to loose her fury upon him, and had never felt quite so close to damnation as at that moment.

But she smiled at him. Reached out her hand. Touched his arm.

Said, "Don't fear. You'll be safe."

Courage leapt from her and into his heart like an electric charge. He looked to Hearne, who was also smiling. *His* faith in her hadn't wavered. This time, when Hearne ushered him on after Helena, there was no resistance.

Instead of walking along the pavement, and skirting the crowd that was now once again looking for a focus upon which it could pour its fury, she strode into the centre of the road and headed straight for it. As they got closer, Philip could see that several fights had broken out in the very heart of the crowd, each of which had accumulated its own 'audience', circling around the antagonists and encouraging them to greater acts of violence. On the outskirts, lone 'scouts' prowled, Molotovs primed and ready in hands, looking for the next target. It was one of these who first saw Helena and, having whistled to his mates for assistance, sauntered toward her. He was naked to the waist, glistening with rain and sweat, his upper arms adorned with tattoos of dragons, his head shaved.

"Hello, darlin'. Come to see the show?" He leered at her, making it quite clear what kind of show he had in mind for her. His friends, all male, were quickly at his side, arranged around Helena, Philip and Hearne in a rough semi-circle.

Helena said nothing.

"Well, don't worry. You stick with us, you'll be safe enough. We'll look after you, won't we?"

"Fuckin' right we will," somebody said, to much laughter.

"Get out of our way," said Hearne. Their assailants looked at him and Philip as if truly seeing them for the first time.

"Looks like someone else is in need of looking after, eh?" the leader said. "Sure we can find someone to take care of you too."

He moved toward the two men, but at that instant Helena's hand shot out and rested, gently, on his bare chest. Taken by surprise, the gang leader stopped in his tracks and looked at her, expressionlessly at first, then with a widening grin.

He turned to face her, full-on, and her hand began to wander his chest, lightly drawing complex patterns there that Philip at first thought merely to be random 'doodlings'; but as he watched he began to realise that there was a definite purpose behind them.

"What?" the leader said, and only then did Philip realise that she was also speaking – or rather mumbling – as she traced these patterns. She was looking the man straight in the eyes, but the words were obviously not intended for him. Not directly, anyway.

A curious expression passed over the man's face as Philip watched. It went from arrogant, cocksure hostility to bewilderment, and finally – as Helena leaned in close to whisper something directly into his ear – outright terror. He took a step backward, and his comrades looked at him in amazement. One of them touched him on the shoulder.

"Gaz? You OK?"

He rounded on them with sudden violence. "Let them through! Any one of you bastards so much as touches them, he'll have me to deal with!"

It was apparent from their reaction to this that Gaz was not someone you wanted to cross, not even in numbers. Without so much as a murmur, their ranks parted, allowing Helena and the others to pass through. Philip kept his eye on Gaz until they were a safe distance past them; however, the man was watching Helena with that look of terror frozen into his features.

No, not terror, it was *awe.*

At his side, Hearne chuckled. "That's my girl," he said.

"Something you taught her?"

"Not really. I just took the blinkers from her eyes, made her see the *real* Helena. And it's not over yet, oh no. Wait until the full invocation takes place ..."

Unsure whether he would enjoy seeing such a thing, Philip followed them through the downpour, aware now that the rain had soaked him through to the skin, as the crowd parted before them to give them a wide berth. Some sort of unspoken 'grapevine' was in operation here; they were still coasting on the waves set up by their belittling of Gaz.

This bubble of safety followed them all the way through the streets, allowing them a clear view of the carnage in all its monstrous glory. Cars burning and overturned; shops looted; blood swirling in the gutters. A number of bodies lay in the street, some moving, others not, all unattended. Some of the fallen were police officers, in full riot gear, torn apart by the mob before their fellows realised the scale of the ignominy they faced here and withdrew, at least for the moment.

This was the nightmare that had sprung from Nicholas' mind, the nightmare he had seen in his sleep every night since Mons. And now he was imposing it on the world, trying to exorcise it, seal himself away from it.

If Philip had any doubts that they were dealing with his former lover, these were finally eliminated by the scene around them. Burgess clung to Hearne's arm a little tighter, his eyes never moving from the form of the embryonic Goddess before them, sweeping the chaos aside like so much smoke and dust.

And together, they moved onwards, ever onwards. Towards Bethlehem Street.

Nobody had come downstairs after Sue, but she kept glancing at the staircase from where she sat hugging her knees in the dark, under the living room window. Outside, despite the heavy rain, people were gathered in crowds, shouting, running, and there was a building burning at the end of the street. Possibly the shop. Damn. From upstairs the smell of frankincense and the sounds of music and chanting clawed at her nerves still further, and she hoped and prayed that her three guardians would come soon. Where was Helena?

More music from above. 'Saturn, Bringer of Old Age' from Holst's *Planets Suite*. Until Nicholas' arrival, she'd been quite fond of Holst. She couldn't remember which of the paintings was linked to this music, but it meant they were 'opening the portals of the Sephiroth'.

Whatever that meant, it was bad news. Sue hugged her knees tighter in the darkened room. And suddenly, as both the rioting outside was momentarily hushed and the music upstairs hit a quiet patch, Sue heard a furtive tapping at the window. Carefully, she peeped over the windowsill. Three white faces peered back at her through the rain-distorted glass. The central face, closer, seemed to glow in the dark.

Helena.

Sue ran to the door and let them in, dripping wet, silent. She showed them into the living room. Miles, carrying a large black holdall, glanced upstairs and gave a nod. "Saturn. If they're going through the Sephiroth from one to ten, they're on number three." Sue shrugged, Philip grunted, Helena said nothing, but her face was set in an expression of – Sue couldn't put a name to it, but there was calm, there was power, there was a sense of...

Infinity.

Sue stood back and let them prepare. Miles had the coffee table in the middle of the room and the rest of the furniture pushed back. Philip helped himself to an armchair, sinking deeply into it with a sigh of relief.

Helena too, once she'd put on a flowing white robe over her clothes, stood back, still and recollected, while Miles donned a white hooded robe. The coffee table now bore a black cloth, on which burned a single white candle illuminating a metal chalice, a dagger, a wooden plate and a short wand, all highly decorated with symbols Sue didn't understand. But as Miles picked up the wand, she recognised it as a brother to the one being used by Nicholas upstairs.

Then upstairs, silence. And as by now the rioting had resumed, the dimly lit living room was filled with the noise of violence from outside. And in bizarre contrast, pleasant music from upstairs. Miles' face briefly showed dismay, then he addressed the others. "Mozart's *Jupiter* symphony," he explained. "They're moving on. We'd better get a move on ourselves. We'll start with a Banishing."

Sue had no idea what a Banishing was, but it reminded her of Nicholas' Protection; the drawing of boundaries, the powerful words spoken forcefully in the four cardinal directions ...

... and the feeling in the air, the change in atmosphere, a hush, an expectancy, as though the world is scrubbed clean, ready for what is to come. From out in the street the sound of breaking glass adds to the general noise, but the four figures in the living room remain still and silent, breathing in the light scent of a small incense stick with which Miles is anointing the room.

Picking up the dagger, he begins to chant, with no notes, the words seeming to arrange themselves. He glances at Helena, who provides the words to Miles' gestures, having produced a purple scarf and put it on like a priest's stole. "I call upon Gabriel, Archangel of the Sephirah of Yesod, to bless our efforts and to give us the power of Yesod to complete this work of transformation."

Sue recognises the Gabriel reference but that is all, but as she watches Helena, she notices the younger woman's eyes begin to focus a short distance ahead of her.

Miles waves his dagger in the air, murmuring more incomprehensible phrases, and for Sue the air seems to thicken. It coils like the incense smoke, yet instead of dissipating there is a sense that it is forming something there in the room with them, a presence almost tangible, and Helena speaks again:

"In the name of God, Shaddai el Chai
I invoke Thee, Isis
Thou who art clothed with the Sun
Thou Queen of Heaven

Thou Soul of Nature
Thou Mother of all things.
Come to me Queen Isis
who restored to life Osiris as Lord of the Underworld
who commands scorpions
come to me
and dwell in me
now."

And Helena's face, glowing in the candlelight, gazing just ahead of her, seems to focus closer and closer, and at a signal from Miles, she steps forward into whatever radiant mystery she sees.

Upstairs, the music changes again. "Mars, Bringer of War".

In the temple upstairs, Mark holds aloft the voluminon of Khamael, while the others stand like Roman legionaries in the circle, each one's painting grounded like a shield while the right hand is clenched in a fist held over the heart chakra. Nick – Nicholas, he corrects himself – at the centre of the circle, holds his wand towards Khamael as he intones, his words gathering passion as the music builds, the pounding rhythms of Holst matched by the stamping feet of the group. Mark cannot see his lover's face, but the words of invocation are shouted out, spat, roared above the gathering din and the faces of those he can see glisten with sweat as they shout the name of Mars in counterpoint to the stamping of their feet.

At the quiet centre of the music, as though by a signal, they all become still. Nicholas continues his ecstatic calling forth of the power, though less loudly than before. Mark lowers the voluminon to see Nicholas and the others down on one knee, eyes fixed on the red vortex in the young man's hands. But there is something wrong. Their expressions do not bear the stamp of martial fervour, nor the ecstasy of the presence of an archangel or god. Each face is frozen in utter horror, with the exception of Nicholas, who seems to have been waiting for this moment for a long time. He stands, exchanging his wand for the dagger on the lid of the trunk, and squares up to the voluminon. Pointing the dagger at it, he yells above the resurgent music:

"In the name of the archangel Khamael,
In the power of Mars, the god of war,
In the virtue of Geburah
And in the name of Pluto, Lord of the Underworld,
I bind you, Scorpion, to this ...

(he outlines the voluminon with his dagger)

... and I command you to remain within it.

The others remain still a moment, then Emma screams, dropping her painting, and scrambles backwards into the wall. Ranks broken, they all back away from the confrontation, and Mark, fearing but he knows not what, drops Khamael to the floor and backs away from it as it falls backwards as though chasing him. He sees Nicholas looking more terrified than any of them, and he tries not to catch the gaze of whatever looks up from the spiralling horror at his feet. Although Nicholas tries to get the group back into circle, Mark doesn't dare approach and knows that the others don't either. The air is hot and dry, and although they thrash their heads from side to side and scream, their eyes are irresistably drawn to Khamael, from whence it seems a maelstrom sucks them in, and they sway, they stumble, they crawl towards the vortex.

Nicholas alone stands his ground, shrieking magical words in languages long dead, but whatever has taken over the temple has him in its grip as well.

Holst's invocation of Mars reaches its blasting, nerve-shattering crescendo, and the CD player jams on the final bars, blaring them out insistently, over and over into the thickening atmosphere. Some of the group are prone on the bare boards, Mark is backed up against the door, Nicholas sways, gesturing defiantly with his dagger. Then he winces, his face twists in agony and he drops to the floor, clutching his heart.

And Mark gets shoved out of the way as the door is

opened roughly behind him, sending him sprawling towards the abomination in the centre of the room. He rolls to avoid it and finds himself looking up at ...

At a Goddess. Robed in white, with a silver coronet on her head and a scroll in her hand. The vision in the flesh, the face of the Queen. She strides into the room, with a white-robed man with purple stole, priestlike, behind her. She glances down at Mark and lays her hand on his head. At once he feels calmer, and when she gestures him out of the open door he goes gladly, greeted there by Sue and an elderly man. He makes for the stairs and safety, but the old man restrains him, saying, "Stay, or regret it for the rest of your life."

Miles treads in the Goddess' footsteps, tracing figures in the air with the wand and intoning invocations to Isis, partly to ensure that the Goddess remains with them, and partly to fight off his own crippling doubts. The acid test of his occult belief, which he has avoided since his neophyte days, has come upon him and he knows too well how ill-prepared he is. Goddess, I am not worthy ... and have I actually *done* anything here? Is this just an impressionable young woman in a trance, or has an awesome power really descended on us to help us overcome another awesome power? And if it has, am I in any state to do it justice?

The atmosphere in the attic room is supercharged, hot, as though terror is condensed into the air. On the floor the red painting glares balefully up at them, and the repetitive crashing sound from the CD player pounds panic into the wide-eyed hosts of the power they summoned. Miles feels a surge of dismay at the force into which he has just intruded, and briefly thinks of fleeing, until Isis turns her radiant face to him and touches him once on the forehead. He immediately feels the panic ebb, and he takes control once more.

Stepping over bodies, striding to the CD player, he yanks the plug from the wall, and in the sudden silence, Isis speaks:

I am Isis
who am clothed with the Sun
Queen of Heaven

Soul of Nature
Mother of all things.
Who restored to life Osiris as Lord of the Underworld
I am the Queen who commands scorpions
and I come to restore that which has been sundered.

And stooping, she grips the painting on the floor and holds it to her in an embrace. She raises it aloft, gazing into its depths, and she begins to tremble, first gently, then with increasing violence. Miles moves forward to help her, but seeing him, she shakes her head and gestures to Robert.

Robert is curled on the floor in the foetal position, face twisted in pain, mouthing something Miles can't make out. The priest of Isis helps the other man up, but Robert can make it only to his knees, and his eyes are fixed on the mandala of the Scorpion, glaring down from above the Goddess.

She lowers the painting, supporting it against Molesey's trunk with one hand, and lays her other hand on Robert's head. This breaks his gaze, and he looks up, blinking, into her eyes. Smiling, she says:

Nicholas. Nicholas.
For too long you have run from Death.
You cannot escape your Death
for your Death belongs to you
and is restless without you.
Receive Death to your bosom
and trust in me
for I am here to tell you
that from your Death you shall be restored
and like Osiris before you, made whole.

Then she addresses the painting:

Scorpion. Creature of the Great Waste.
You have been lost for too long,
and your wanderings have brought only

suffering.

It is time to cease
for the purpose for which you were born
has been fulfilled.
Be still in the presence of your maker.

As she remains frozen, one hand on the painting and the other on Robert, it seems to Miles that a current is passing through her from one to the other. But as she begins to tremble once more, it becomes clear that there is a struggle going on, and she can barely maintain her position. The air thickens and coils once more, and Miles becomes aware of the others in the room moaning with fear, and of the growing noise of riot outside.

Like being jolted from sleep, disoriented, shaken, Robert blinks into the eyes of ...

Helena?

Robed in white, shining, pulling him forth with her eyes, willing him on. Yet at the same time, Molesey, shrieking in his head, howling incantations of protection as another – something amorphous, dark, maddened – circles, penetrating ever closer. The voice of Molesey goading the other and the robed Goddess exerting all her will to draw them safely together.

Robert finds himself, kneeling on a wooden floor, suddenly aware that only *he*
can break the deadlock.

It's done, as always, with blood.

He picks up the fallen dagger by the blade, rises to his feet, swaying, and takes the Goddess' hand in his own free hand. Then he squeezes the blade tightly, feeling the blade burst through the skin and slice the flesh. It is answered by a squeeze of his other hand by the Goddess. Dropping the dagger, he advances on the painting, stumbling and falling to his knees. But now he looks squarely into the face of Khamael, and the voice of Molesey within ceases its gibbering and assumes a new dignity:

I am the Passion and the Life
in my limbs and my lungs and my veins.
Behold the Scorpion.
Sent forth, return to me.
Returning, be scrutinised.
Scrutinised, be still.
Before your maker, be at peace
and be sealed in the blood
and the mystery within.

Reaching to the painting, he anoints it with his blooded hand.

"It is finished," whispered Robert, and collapsed.

Like a wave breaking, all that has been pent up within, rushes forth in a release of radiant power, and as it diminishes, as the wave washes back, it leaves behind a young woman, exhausted but glowing from within, awestruck at the power that has been hers. She looks around the room, seeing with new eyes, and realizes that something of the power remains.

Helena sighed, a deep one, and gave Miles a quizzical look. "Wow," was all she could say.

Miles would have agreed wholeheartedly if he'd had any power of speech at all. Then he recovered himself enough to see to Robert. The young man was unconscious but breathing regularly, Miles noted with relief.

Sue's first action was to check out how the others were. Emma and Robin were in each other's arms, and Sue didn't know which was sobbing more. Likewise Steve and Heather. Sonya, Jeff and the others sat on the floor looking dazed. Looking once more at her housemates, she remembered Ryan, and quietly, she wept.

Mark felt the old man sag against him, and dutifully held him up while searching Nick's face for signs of life. He caught the eye of the priest, who was positioning Nick carefully on the floor. "It's all right," said the older man, "Robert's alive."

And indeed, the face that used to be that of his lover now seemed to be that of a stranger, even in unconsciousness.

Then Mark followed the priest's gaze. He was now looking, not at Mark, but at the old man, who hung limply in the young man's arms.

"Somebody call an ambulance," said the priest. "Now."

Epilogue;

Licence To Depart

There was no way that they were going to get him to go to bed. If he'd wanted 'bed rest'– and Jenny was most insistent that he did – then he would have stayed in hospital. But Philip wanted to come home, to spend what little time he had remaining to him in familiar surroundings. And not just his bedroom.

He'd had to make some compromises, though. The December weather was far too cold for him to be able to sit in the garden as he'd wanted, so he had to make do with the conservatory. Brenda was still there to fuss over him, of course, tucking blankets around his legs, making him endless cups of tea (until he told her, politely but firmly, that he'd prefer a Scotch), trying to engage him in idle conversation. She meant well, naturally, but at the moment he wanted to be left alone, to enjoy the peace and serenity while he still could.

Not long to go now. Not long at all.

But there was so much left undone, and unsaid. He wanted to speak to Miles Hearne, and thank him properly for what he'd done for him, and check on the progress of Robert Pierce (still in the psychiatric unit) to find out if any of the personality of 'Molesey' still remained. But most of all, he wanted to see Helena, the woman-child who'd become a

Goddess in front of his eyes.

Unlikely that any of this would happen now. These people were still following their own paths, seeking some sort of understanding from the fire through which they had just passed. If only he had more time ...

But for Philip, the journey was over. The ghosts that had been raised in 1929 were now put to rest. Nicholas was at peace. Best if I just slip away unnoticed.

No, he thought. *Something* has to be said. He called out to Brenda, asked her to bring him the pile of papers on his desk in the study.

Sorting through what Brenda had brought to him, he found a copy of the will which he had drawn up months before, leaving the house and everything in it to Brenda and her family. He also found three or four rough drafts of a letter he had tried writing to Nicholas on several occasions down the years. He thought that perhaps if he could express his feelings about what happened, talk to Nicholas as if he were still here, he might be able to overcome the guilt, and the grief which never diminished.

But he couldn't do it. Too much English reserve, he supposed, coupled with the feeling of silliness inherent in writing a letter to someone who will never read it.

Now, however, he had a new idea; he would write to Helena. He would be able to express himself better without the eyes of the Goddess upon him. To this end, he took up his pen and began to write.

> My Dearest Helena,
>
> Please forgive me, but I had to speak to you just one last time. I realise that in all of this matter, I have been little more than a bystander, and that I may even have slowed you down. But for me, it was essential that I was there to witness all of this, the final resolution of something that began in 1929.

For over seventy years, I have been wracked with guilt over leaving Nicholas there, in that house, alone. Although I know that he was already dead, I felt that if I had stayed with him, just for a little while, I might have been able to do something to put him at rest there and then. Quite what that 'something' would have been, I don't know, but I know that my lack of courage in staying with him has been a pain in my heart for longer than you can know, or dream.

But now, thanks to you, and Mr Hearne, that pain is gone. My Nicholas is safe, safe from the unfortunate beast which he unleashed, and which turned against him. A beast which was a part of himself.

I wish I could express my gratitude more fully in some way, but I am left with these mere words to try and communicate something of what these events have meant to me. When we first met, you were a small, vulnerable young woman, buffeted by life's storms, looking to find something upon which to build a life. It was my privilege to see you find that 'something', and to see you transformed into ... well, perhaps I should leave it to you to decide into what you were transformed.

Once again, my dear Helena, my profoundest thanks. I

> do not think that we shall meet again, face to face. But I want you to know that you have been responsible in these last days for the salvation of more than one soul. Bless you, and give my fondest thanks and regards to Mr Hearne also.
>
> Your Loving Friend,
> Philip.

It took him nearly half an hour to write this; his hand ached and he had to stop periodically to let the pain subside. Once it was done, however, a profound sense of satisfaction overtook him, which triumphed over even the most insistent pain. He placed the letter in its envelope, addressed it to 'Helena McCallum, c/o Guiding Spirit Bookshop', sealed it, and lay it aside.

There was no more to do. He watched the December sun fading through the trees, astonished and delighted at the display of light and beauty that was for him, and him alone.

Oh, Nicholas. You should be here with me to see this.

When the light faded, Philip Burgess closed his eyes.

Philip's funeral was a small affair. Helena, Miles, Sue and Mark found themselves trying not to draw the attention of a couple of middle-aged relatives who evidently barely knew Philip, a few elderly gentleman friends of his, his doctor, and Brenda, his cleaner and her family. Some of these had been at the inquest.

Helena was mortified in their presence. The faces of all the Bethlehem Street people had been plastered over the front of the local paper under the headline "Scorpion Cult Night of Terror." The investigation was still going on, and despite the verdict of the inquest Helena was certain that all present at the funeral were blaming her and the others for Philip's death.

And who was to say there was no truth in that? There was a reporter at the cemetery, clicking away with his camera as Helena and the others laid their friend to rest. They could look forward to further coverage in the rag.

Afterwards, Mark and Miles went their separate ways, and Helena and Sue went back to the Bethlehem Street squat. The area was almost back to normal now, the burned-out cars and other debris cleared away, broken windows and other damage to houses and shops patched up, with the exception of the one shop in the next street, which had been demolished. It left a gap in the street like a missing tooth.

Sonya, Paul, Jeff and his mates hadn't been seen since the inquest. The squatters were preparing to move out. They had lost their incognito, and the neighbours gave them accusing looks but wouldn't speak to them. Emma was packing upstairs. She and Robin would be leaving soon. The rest, minus Robin and Julian, were in the living room, smoking, planning their futures.

One bit of good news: Ryan had come out of his catatonic state on the night of the ritual and stayed out of it. He was nearly well enough to come home.

Wherever that would be.

So much suffering. So many lives ruined. So many deaths. And while the world picks up the pieces, Helena wondered, do I really know what happened?

Robin and Julian returned from work. They were carrying a can of petrol and they looked purposeful. "Those paintings upstairs," said Julian, "can go."

"Some of those belonged to Philip," Helena pointed out. "They're not yours to get rid of."

"No disrespect, love," said Julian, "but he doesn't need them now, does he? And the heirs to the estate are not gonna miss the Scorpion paintings, are they? No, so we get rid of them. Somebody asks, there was an accident. With everything that's been wrecked or burned down round here lately, who's gonna care? So we're just making sure." And they brought the paintings downstairs and out onto the back lawn.

Helena helped carry the paintings down, and had a moment of alarm when she realised she was carrying the reddish-brown one that had caused her the fit all those months ago. It was still a disturbing picture, an ugly picture, but now it was inert. Whatever had lurked in there once was gone.

Nevertheless, it went on the bonfire with the others.

Just to put everyone's minds at rest.

They cleared all the paraphernalia out of the attic room and chucked it into the trunk. Julian and Robin looked at the trunk, then at each other.

"Bonfire?"

"Bonfire."

Helena began to remind them that the trunk belonged to Robert, but then thought better of it. Half the paintings had been his as well. Here I am, she thought, making decisions on other people's behalf like this. Whatever next? And she helped empty the contents of the trunk onto the bonfire in the back of the house, both of which had once belonged to Nicholas Molesey.

She said her sad goodbyes and went home. Debbie was in, making paella.

"Hi Debs. Busy day?"

"Getting quieter now," answered Debbie, steaming up the tiny kitchen. "I think it's safe to say the madness is over." She emptied the paella onto two plates. "Good timing, as usual."

Helena produced a bottle of red and two glasses. "The madness is over," she said. "I'll drink to that."

They ate, they drank, they talked, they giggled. They got thoroughly plastered.

The following morning, a rather fragile Helena turned up at Guiding Spirit. "You still don't look at all well," said Sheelagh anxiously, "are you sure you're ready to come back?"

"I feel like shit," said Helena, and Sheelagh's eyes widened. "A vast improvement. Four cups of coffee and I'll be fine. How's business?"

"Fine," said Sheelagh, making for the kitchen and the kettle. "Since all that trouble came and went we've had loads in here searching for the meaning of it all." Filling the kettle, she grinned at Helena. "It's an ill wind, and all that. By the way," she added, putting the kettle on, "that big pagan crowd you used to be with were asking for you yesterday. Seems you're in demand as the goddess Isis."

"Oh for goodness' sake."

"True, love. And we've had a lot of enquiries for Tarot readings and so forth, asking for you by name. Seems you're famous, love."

"Oh yeah, you're looking at the next Miles Hearne." And for the first time, Helena began to understand the man. Whether she had been touched by the presence of a Goddess, or was merely touched, she didn't know or care. But something she had never felt before was welling up within her now. There was an awful lot of people out there who were lost, frightened, a mystery to themselves, and the season of the Scorpion had brought them face to face with their poverty and ignorance. What they really needed to know was that within each of them was a God, a Goddess. She could vouch for that. She could help them reach that. That was what Miles had wanted to give to people before he sold his soul to the media.

"By the way, love," added Sheelagh, "did you get the letter we passed on?"

"Yes thanks." It had been from Philip. He had died the same day.

Helena drank her coffee, head throbbing, mind racing. Today, she vowed, she would think it through, she would draw up plans, she would begin to live like a Goddess. So much suffering. So many lives ruined. So let's get started.

She finished off her coffee and muttered, "And so it begins."

"And from the shockwaves across the world," that bastard Roger was saying, "to the man at the centre of occult controversy, media magician and e-mail exorcist, Miles Hearne."

Smile for the cameras, thought Miles. Thanks a bunch for the crap intro Roger you bastard.

"Miles, you just saw our special report on these terrible events. The rioting and violent crime recorded around the world, the panic in the financial markets, the extraordinary crash of the world wide web – is there really a paranormal explanation for it all?"

Here goes. "I have *no* explanation for it, Roger.

Somebody just mentioned sunspot activity, and indeed there apparently has been a lot. It could be that for all I know, or any global environmental anomaly causing something like the midsummer madness that afflicts some regions every year."

"It's said, isn't it, Miles, that this madness was initially spread on the Internet. What could do that?"

If you only knew. "Well that might help explain the worldwide spread of the phenomenon, but as for what, your guess is as good as mine."

"Oh, come on, Miles, I realise the enquiry into Bethlehem Street is still in progress, but surely you can shed some light on what happened that night."

Back off, shitface. "As far as I'm concerned, that story was just one of many, many dramas, as we saw on your report."

Shitface wouldn't let it go. "But isn't it true, Miles, that the leader of the so-called Scorpion cult claimed to be controlling these events worldwide?"

"That sounds a bit far-fetched, wouldn't you say, Roger?"

That bastard Roger was now trying for the throat. "What *were* you doing there, Miles?"

I don't believe I'm going to say this. "No comment."

That grinning bastard Roger was now leaning forward conspiratorially. "Come on now, Miles, it's unlike you to be shy about your otherworldy exploits. Surely there's something you can tell us."

He asked for it.

"This is embarrasing. I feel a complete tit."

Miles, ceremonially bathed and robed, bustled about in his study. His white hooded robe felt ridiculous on him as he tidied the room, switched off the phone ringer, drew the curtains (should've done this first – what a sight for the neighbours), and prepared the altar on his living room coffee table. Six big white candles, purchased this afternoon, illuminated the room, and he stoked the incense in a burner on the mantlepiece, sending off clouds of grey sandalwood smoke. Bugger the kabbalistic correspondences. He liked sandalwood.

Today was the day to find out if he really could find

his way again. Over recent months, his failure to control Robert, the death of sPyroquin, hiding from the Scorpion, having to pass the crucial invocation onto Helena, all whispered failure in his ear. All because of his greed, wanting shares in the Molesey current.

Or was that a bit harsh? He had recognised something missing in himself, and thought he'd found something which could supply it. He had been alert to the dangers, but despite his standing by first Robert, then Helena, he had always felt unequal to the challenge.

At least he'd stood by them.

And so, like a returning prodigal, he had sought out the teachings of his youth. The rituals that he had learned from Portman and the others, with the spirituality, and the humility, that went with them. All these he had left behind to follow a career as a media mage. A career probably ended by that last TV interview.

"Listen, you wanker," he'd roared, getting to his feet, "what we've just been through wasn't put on for your entertainment. Or yours," he'd added to the studio audience. "People are dead. The survivors are wondering what the fuck hit them. Nobody who was closely involved will ever be the same again. A major shitstorm has swept through our lives and we don't need tossers like you picking through it for soundbites. Fuck you."

T. B. Roger, to give him credit, had stayed cool under fire. "If that's how you feel Miles, why did you agree to come on the programme?"

Then he'd really lost it. He'd blasted Roger, he'd blasted the producer, he'd paced the studio blasting the audience. And the silence that followed was only broken when the director or someone finally said, "I reckon we'll have to cut that last five minutes."

Pity.

Now to see if he'd thrown it all away for nothing. Feeling self-conscious, Miles raises the appropriate dagger and performs a traditional Banishing Ritual. This at least is familiar through recent practice, and he takes the time to calmly, firmly enunciate the words of power, to appreciate the energy flow in the Kabbalistic Cross and to greet the Archangels. He stands alone in the space, lit only by soft candelight, pauses, then disdaining to consult the book nearby, continues the ritual. Words long left to gather dust in the corners of his mind spring forth fresh and bright. Actions long ago abandoned with excuses that all one's life is magical now regain the full expressiveness of when they were first mastered. He feels just as in those times many years ago, the calming, the charging, the sense of being at the pivot of the universe, in the presence of holy ones. Finally he stands with his arms, throbbing and warm, stretched out to either side, and tilts his face heavenwards, simply saying:

"Let
"the divine light
"descend."

And to tears of joy come the cleansing and the peace.

Leaving the flat wasn't easy, not at *all* easy. For all of a fortnight now, since they'd seen fit to let him out of the hospital (nuthatch, loony bin, call it what you will), he'd stayed resolutely within the walls of Home Sweet Home. Reacquainting himself with the life and memories of Robert Pierce, only straying out to buy groceries and alcohol from the nearby 24-hour supermarket, and then only in the wee small hours when he could be assured that there would be few people about.

But now he'd had the summons that he'd been dreading. Greg Webster wanted an 'informal chat' with him to discuss his future with the gallery.

He attired himself in the same grimy t-shirt and jeans that he'd worn for the last couple of days. If he was going to be thrown to the lions, he was damned if he was going to dress for the occasion. He dithered somewhat over whether to have a shave or not, however; he had a week's growth of beard, and wasn't sure whether it would confirm their opinion of him as a nutcase. In the end, he spent so long debating the issue that he didn't have time to shave.

One thing which Robert didn't feel ready to do at this stage in his 'recovery' was drive, so he did something he hadn't done in many years; he took the bus. This, he soon discovered, carried with it a whole bag of anxieties all its own. For one thing, he couldn't get rid of the terrible feeling that everyone on the bus knew who he was, and was looking at him, whispering about him. Sometimes, he would whirl around in his seat to try and catch the 'whisperers' in the act, as it were; but of course no-one was paying him the least attention, or they were at least giving a good impression of paying him no attention.

He tried to take his mind off it by looking out of the window at the cityscape passing by him. This was equally disturbing. The city was still in the process of recovering from the riots, which had carried on under their own momentum for another thirty-six hours or so after the Bethlehem Street ritual, before fizzling out. The city centre streets were punctuated with the boarded-up windows of small shops whose owners had not, apparently, been able as yet to complete repairs and reopen, if they ever would.

Every so often, he would see on a wall the faint traces of a red swirl, which only time would obliterate.

And all the time, Robert Pierce would hear in his head a voice – his own, thankfully – repeating over and over: *You're responsible.*

All this carnage, all those deaths (eighteen, at the last count), all that madness; and at the heart of it, me. Simply on account of one person's desperate need to validate his own existence, so many other existences were snuffed out, so many other lives were ruined.

- But I didn't kill them.

- *Not directly, no. But you loaded the gun.*

- It wasn't me. It was Nicholas –

The voice in his head didn't even dignify that one with a reply.

He got off two stops earlier than he needed to for the gallery, but this was deliberate. He needed time, both to clear his head of the gnawing guilt, even if only for the moment, and to prepare himself for his encounter with Webster. Somehow, though, somewhere along the way, the two things merged in his mind until the voice of his own conscience became that of Greg Webster.

"I'm sorry, Robert, I've decided that we can do without a mass killer in the Webster's employ. Not good for business, you know? Close the door on the way out, there's a good fella ..."

The crowds on the pavement seemed to be deliberately jostling him; he was a lone swimmer moving against an implacable tide, one that was intent on sweeping him away. They knew what he was, what he had done. Each one of them had suffered and lost because of him.

He lowered his head and hunched his shoulders up defensively around his neck, trying to offer as small a target as possible. He still occasionally rebounded off passers-by, like some dishevelled pinball, drawing the odd aggrieved comment, but in this fashion he managed to make it to the entrance of the gallery and haul himself through the doors into the air-conditioned reception area.

And what's the first thing he sees on passing through those portals?

"Well, well. If it isn't our erstwhile colleague, Mr ... er, I'm sorry, I've quite forgotten your name."

Van Lier was lounging against the reception desk, the smirk on his face mirrored by the one on the face of the receptionist, a girl Robert had never seen before but towards whom he conceived an instant dislike. He said nothing, merely sauntered towards the two of them and tried to affect a businesslike air.

"I'm here to see Greg," he said. "I have an appointment."

"Of course you do. And I think we all know what for, don't we?"

"Name, please?" said the ghastly receptionist. He told her.

"Oh, yes, that's it. Robert. Bobby." Van Lier was quietly beside himself with joy at all of this, Robert could tell. His entire career could be said to have been a lead-up to this moment, this orgy of *schadenfreude*. "How've you been keeping, then? I heard something about you being in ... hospital, was it?"

"That's right. Hospital."

"Oh, dear. Nothing too serious, I hope?'

"Not any more. I'm fine, thanks for asking." He thought about encouraging the receptionist to get a fucking move on, but kept his peace.

"Well, it explains the, ahem, *unkempt* appearance. I was going to say how much your standards have slipped since you were with us last, but since you've not been well ..."

The receptionist put the phone down, gave him the falsest smile he'd ever seen, and said he could go straight up. He turned to go.

"Well, best of luck, *Bobby*. Still, if things don't go right for you, you could always try a change of career direction.'

Robert stopped dead still, fists clenching and unclenching, waiting for the punchline.

"I mean, you could always take up *basket weaving*.'

The self-control required to resist turning around at that moment and punching Van Lier was considerable. As he got into the lift, Robert rated it as his biggest triumph of the day so far.

"Robert, hi, come on in. Take a seat. I'll be right with you."

The office hadn't changed much in the weeks – months, as much as that? – since he was here to receive his 'commission' to look into the possibility of acquiring the works of one Nicholas Molesey. The desk was more cluttered, and the omnipresent muted TV was now showing a 'Carry On' film. Aside from that, no difference.

Webster was leaning back in his chair, examining with great interest the contents of a file in his lap. Every so often, he would grunt and make a note on the sheet he was reading, before pushing it back into place. He was in no hurry to start the meeting, that much was obvious.

Unless, thought Robert, the inquisition has already started. That's probably my employment record he's reading.

At last, Webster put aside the file and turned his attention to Robert. "Sorry about that, Robert. Some stuff that needed my attention rather urgently, you know how it is."

"Sure. No problem."

"Look, Robert," he said, paused, and sighed deeply. "I'll cut to the chase. You've been off work now for, what, three, maybe four months?"

"Something like that."

"I know something of what's been happening, what you've been going through ..."

Oh do you? Really?

"You're recovering well, I hope?"

Robert shrugged. "Well enough."

"Good. Good." Webster wasn't enjoying this either, that much was quite plain.

"The thing is, we've had a hole at the centre of our operations for some time now, because of your absence, and we've had to delay some major plans which I'd been hoping to implement. I really can't delay them any more, not if I want this gallery to move on, grow, expand ..."

"I see."

"And, let's be honest, Robert, you haven't recovered enough as yet to be able to return to work ..."

He looked down at himself, at the tattered jeans he wore, and scratched his beard.

"I think it's best we ... go our separate ways."

Robert nodded. "Yes. Yes, you're probably right."

"You'll get a very generous deal from us, I'll see to that. And should you want a reference at any time, I'll provide you with one so glowing you could read by it in the dark."

Robert smiled. "Thanks. But at the moment ... I have other plans."

Webster didn't ask what they were. Robert didn't offer the information. Instead, he asked a question of his own.

"Just what are these plans you have for the gallery?"

"Well, funnily enough," said Webster, leaning back in his chair once more, the tension and uncertainty gone from his voice, "it all goes back to that conversation we had in here a while back. The one where I said I'm looking to take a more hands-on approach to running this place?"

"I remember."

"Well, one of the things I'm going to do is create a new Director of Acquisitions post here. Up till now, it's been left to individual buyers to try and drum up interest in particular painters or projects. Most of the time they don't have the clout to make any impression on the board, particularly with the likes of Tim Van Lier doing his best to kybosh everyone else and align himself with the latest 'big thing'. He's a good pen-pusher, but when it comes to art, the security guard has better taste than him."

"So – how's he clung in here so long?"

"Like I said, he's a manipulator. He has friends on the board. My brother thinks quite highly of him, but then my beloved brother thinks highly of anyone who's prepared to kiss his ring on a regular basis. And the artists he promotes – like that tosser Justin Maxwell – do bring money into this place, oh yes. But I'd rather that we made money on our own terms, with our own voice, rather than just jump blindly on to the bandwagon. You follow?"

"Better than you think."

"That's why I'm creating this new post. The director of acquisitions will be someone with the requisite artistic nous to sniff out new, exciting stuff – stuff with a bit of vision to it – before anyone else does. The buyers will have someone on the board to put their case, a case based not solely on what artists are currently most commercial. And I'll be working very closely with this person." He paused, smiled ruefully. "You know, a while back, I *was* going to offer the job to you."

"That ... might have been interesting. So who's getting it now?"

"This doesn't leave this room, right?"

"Right."

Webster leant forward, conspiratorially. "Charlotte Keating."

Robert grinned, genuinely pleased. "Good choice. You won't regret it."

A more wicked smile crossed Webster's face. "Promise me one thing, though, Robert, would you?"

"Sure"

"Be sure not to mention this to Tim on the way out. He thinks he's a shoo-in for the job. I want that pleasure myself..."

Tim was still in the lobby when Robert emerged from the lift, obviously eager to see Robert on his way with a few more well-aimed sneers. He straightened up visibly as Robert approached, prepared for battle.

He plainly *wasn't* prepared for the bizarre experience of his bitterest enemy extending a hand towards him. Tentatively, he took it, the smirk now desperately trying to conceal the confusion below the surface.

"Well, 'bye, Tim. It's been fun."

"Er ... yes. Bye."

Robert turned, walked a few paces, then stopped and turned back to look at Van Lier. For a few seconds, that was all he did; just look. Then something else took hold, something that began in the gut and within moments had seized control of his entire body.

He was laughing. Hooting and holding his sides. Van Lier's discomfiture made the hilarity all the greater, and pretty soon he was pointing also, at that lugubrious face as it sought to settle on the proper reaction to this behaviour.

Robert left before he was thrown out. But the mirth followed him home, and the city seemed a different place for it.

By the time that Robert received his visitor – his first in many, many weeks – a change had overtaken him. *Consumed* him, in fact.

The laughter had acted as a kind of purgative; all of the doubts and guilts which had stricken him only hours before were washed away, perhaps not permanently, but for long enough for him to see what depth of shit he now wallowed in, both literally and metaphorically.

First of all, he tidied the flat. Beneath the strata of dirt and kipple, he found that there was something of himself – the Robert Pierce which he had only recently rediscovered – lurking in the shadows of the place that filled in a few of the gaps in his memory. Books found hibernating down the backs of sofas, menus for restaurants he'd forgotten about, a telephone number scrawled on the back of a cinema ticket stub ...

The photograph of a brother, long, long dead.

There was a man here, hidden in these disparate

elements, waiting to be reconstituted. A man whose life amounted to a hell of a lot more than he had suspected (more than he had allowed himself to suspect), and which was too complex and fascinating to be thrown away on guilt and pointless self-recrimination.

What I have done, is done. What I will do ...

He pondered his options as he showered, shaved, changed. There was, in truth, only one *real* option, the one which had been at the heart of everything he'd been doing over the last few months, and further back, *years* back. From the cupboard in the bedroom he produced his sketchpad and his charcoals, and settled into the living room sofa.

Rubbish. Absolute fucking shit.

The first three sheets were discarded with the same rage, the same litany of dismissal. It took him that long to work out exactly what it was that he was attempting to capture. If (at some later date) pressed to express it in words, he could only say that here was an attempt to capture, in two-dimensional form, the struggle to reconcile and unite something that has become sundered; not merely in three- or even four-dimensional space, but in an *infinity* of dimensions, beyond those which are amenable to our everyday senses.

We are blind to these other dimensions, wilfully blind. Terrified. We refuse to even consider that they exist. And yet ... they wait for us. Without them, without our understanding of them, we cannot be whole. So we pretend to ourselves that we confront them, by weaving them into our dreams, but only on our terms, in our image. And those who do try to see them as they are ...

They run from the reality of it all. Don't they, Nicholas?

What he drew in those hours, the precise shape and form of it, is not important; at least, that's what Robert told himself, much later. They were a key, and the door was, at long last, beginning to open.

Somewhere during the evening, the bell on another door rang, jolting Robert rudely from his labours. Swearing profusely – of all the fucking times to get a caller, why *now*? – he got up to answer it. His mood altered suddenly, drastically, when he saw who the caller was.

"Charlie?" he stammered. "What the hell are you –"

At the sight of her quizzical expression, his tone softened. "I mean – hi. Good to see you. *Great* to see you."

"Good recovery, there, Bobby. Can I come in?"

He hustled her into the living room, where his sketchpad lay face-down on the coffee table.

"Been busy, have you?"

"Er – just a few doodles. Want anything? Coffee? Tea? I've got some of that Belgian lager in the fridge that you like ..."

"No, no thanks. I can't stop long. Greg's taking me out to dinner to discuss my new job. You heard about that, I gather."

"Yeah. Congratulations, Madam Director. You deserve it, really you do."

She looked at him reprovingly. "You should have come to see me earlier. I was quite hurt when I heard that you'd been at the gallery and not moved heaven and earth to find me."

"Well, Tim sidetracked me. You know how it is. How is my favourite denizen of Planet Tosser, by the way?"

"Not the happiest bunny in the warren. But that shouldn't surprise you."

Robert almost started laughing again, but choked it back when he realised he'd probably be asked to explain himself, and wouldn't have the faintest idea how to begin.

They sat opposite each other in the living room, and looked at one another awkwardly for a while before Charlie leaned forward, suddenly serious.

"Robert, I just want to –"

"Look, Charlie, if you're about to try and kickstart a conversation about my recent attack of the loonytoons, I'd rather you didn't. I don't know how to talk about it myself. One day, maybe, but not now."

She nodded. "Have you spoken to Helena?"

Hesitantly, "No."

"I think you should. If there's one person who understands better than anyone what you went through, it's her."

"I will. But not yet. I know I have to speak to her – I owe her quite a lot of thanks – but there's some stuff I have to do first."

She turned her face away from him slightly, and he at first thought that there was a more serious reproof in her expression. But her eyes had fallen upon the sketchpad; she seemed to be assessing the risk quotient in asking him about it.

"I've been doing some sketching," he said, pre-empting her gallantly.

"Really? Can I see?"

"Sure. Don't know what you'll make of them, though ..."

She picked up the book and flicked through, her face inscrutable.

"Well?" said Robert at last.

She looked up, but not at him. "I've never seen anything like this."

"Hm. Not sure I like the sound of that."

Now she looked him in the eye. "No, Bobby ... this is ... it's ... Christ, it's *amazing.* Unique."

"So you're saying they're good."

"Bobby, this is better than good. This is ... amazing."

"You used that one already."

"Give me time, I'll think of some more. This, *this,*" she slapped the pad for emphasis, "is what you should have been doing all along."

"Maybe. Bit difficult before now, though. I'll explain one day."

"At your first exhibition at the Webster, I hope. Shall we say a year from now?"

"Deal." They shook on it, laughing. Their hands stayed clasped for perhaps a little longer than was necessary.

"Shit, I have to be going. I'm meeting Greg in fifteen minutes." She got up.

"Look, Charlie, you, er ... you won't be a stranger, now, will you?"

"Course I won't. I have to keep the talent happy, don't I?"

She moved to hug him, thought better of it for a second, said, "This dinner with Greg ... it's strictly business, you understand."

He did. He said so, happier on the inside than the smile on his face, warm as it was, let on. They hugged, said goodbye, parted.

There was a glow to the night that he hadn't noticed before. Standing at his window, he saw the city more radiant than he'd seen it in some time. Perhaps ever. The year was slightly more than a month old, but the sense of renewal still hung in the air.

With sleep not even a consideration, Robert Pierce went to the hall cupboard and took out several bundles, wrapped in sheets; easel, canvas, oils. He brushed the dust off them, and set them up in the living room. For a while, entranced by the possibilities inherent in this set-up, he just sat and looked. Then, he propped up the sketchpad, open at one of his more intriguing 'doodles', on a chair.

And he began to paint.

Brian Willis & Chris Poote

Edited by Brian Willis
ISBN: 09531468 63 £6.99

Heart
Simon Morden
ISBN 09542267 £4.99

Cuckoo
Richard Wright
ISBN 095422 £4.99

Coming Soon:
December 2002
The Percolated Stars
Rhys Hughes
ISBN 0-9542267 47 £4.99

For more information on RazorBlade visit:
www.razorbladepress.com

Printed in the United Kingdom
by Lightning Source UK Ltd.
93272